National Bestselling Author
CAIT LOGAN

With her sizzling debut novel,
Cait Logan captured the hearts
of readers everywhere . . .

"A very special new talent . . . The fire and spark between the protagonists is really exceptional, generating and maintaining the best sensual and romantic tension seen in a long time . . . Ms. Logan is destined for great things!"

—*Romantic Times*

Her reputation grew with her heartfelt novels of love
and desire, RUGGED GLORY and GAMBLER'S
LADY. Then, her wildly passionate sagas of the
untamed West made Cait Logan a
national bestselling author . . .

TAME THE FURY

"Definitely a book for readers who adore sizzling verbal sparring and a relationship between hot-tempered lovers!"

—*Romantic Times*

WILD DAWN

"An exciting, stunning, and intense book that will touch readers' hearts and souls."

—*Romantic Times*

And now, Cait Logan presents her newest,
most thrilling Western romance . . .

NIGHT FIRE

Diamond Books by Cait Logan

TAME THE FURY

WILD DAWN

RUGGED GLORY

GAMBLER'S LADY

NIGHT FIRE

NIGHT FIRE

CAIT LOGAN

DIAMOND BOOKS, NEW YORK

This book is a Diamond original edition,
and has never been previously published.

NIGHT FIRE

A Diamond Book/published by arrangement with
the author

PRINTING HISTORY
Diamond edition/March 1994

ISBN: 1-55773-986-2

Diamond Books are published by The Berkley Publishing Group,
200 Madison Avenue, New York, NY 10016.
DIAMOND and the "D" design
are trademarks belonging to Charter Communications, Inc.

PRINTED IN THE UNITED STATES OF AMERICA

10 9 8 7 6 5 4 3 2 1

To the women who endured the hardships of the Oregon Trail and to the men and women who preserve this great heritage

Prologue

....

Baton Rouge, August 1845

Jean Gaspard, a powerfully built man, ran through the sultry night. His heart throbbed with fear, which seemed to flood his lungs, and forced his bowed legs to run past their endurance. He stopped to rest against the thick trunk of a tree heavily laced with hanging moss. Sweat born of running and fear chilled his forehead. His eyes bulged as they sought the shadows.

Lucien Navaronne D'Arcy had pledged to kill him.

D'Arcy's younger sisters had been taken north of Fort St. Vrain by Gaspard and his men. The girls were used as prostitutes until they had taken their lives two nights ago. D'Arcy had challenged and killed each of their captors—Gaspard's aides—methodically. Now he wanted Gaspard's blood. Known now as the Dark Avenger, D'Arcy was ruthless, calculating, deadly.

"Bastard!" Gaspard cursed, his breath swaying the moss in the still night. Insects and frogs stopped their chorus, and Gaspard was left with only the sound of the heavy drumming of his own heart.

1

In the hot night, D'Arcy's menacing presence chilled Gaspard.

Gaspard's eyes wildly searched the shadowy trees. The D'Arcy sisters had stuffed the slaver's coffers from last November until now. He closed his eyes, pushing away the fear. Lucien D'Arcy's hard, arrogant face filled Gaspard's mind.

"Prepare to die well, Gaspard," D'Arcy had murmured smoothly when Gaspard had tried to buy his life before the sisters' elegant funeral. The softly accented, deep tones had chilled Gaspard, who recognized the sound of death. . . .

A blade hissed, cutting through air and ending in a hard crack, as it sank deep into the wood a half inch away from Gaspard's throat. "D'Arcy . . ." the frightened man whispered and realized with shame that he had relieved himself.

His predator stepped from the shadows, jerked the blade from the tree, and lifted Gaspard's heavy jowls with the sharp tip. The tip of D'Arcy's blade drew a drop of blood, and Gaspard realized it would not be the last. D'Arcy was tall and lean, a hunter with a deadly purpose. Gaspard recognized the darkly handsome, arrogant features D'Arcy shared with his sisters. D'Arcy's light eyes strolled over Gaspard's face coolly. Gaspard shivered, recognizing the cold steel deep within the other man.

Only a man whose soul had been forged in the fires of hell would have eyes that cold, a mouth that hard—

"In March I returned to Fort St. Vrain to take my mother and sisters to Oregon country. They were not with our trusted friends." D'Arcy spoke too softly. He slid the blade around Gaspard's throat, leaving a slight scratch. "Last year I traveled from Oregon country to Sante Fe. Sante Fe had become too dangerous for my family." Gaspard held his breath as D'Arcy continued. "With my father dead, I was responsible. I was taking my mother and sisters to Oregon country, to a homestead my father had wanted. My mother became ill near the trader's fort. . . ."

D'Arcy's light-colored eyes burned into Gaspard's fearful ones. "When my mother recovered, she begged me to make our home ready in the Willamette. Against my better judgment, I left her and my sisters with trusted friends and the servants." The pressure of the blade increased slightly against the captive's throat. "Winter was savage, allowing only one or two passersby to carry messages between us. Then nothing. When I returned in March, the servants and my mother were dead. My sisters—"

The blade moved down Gaspard's throat, burning the flesh. "My sisters were gone. The trail was difficult to find. You took them in November. It's August now, a year since I saw them . . . your dying time."

"They poisoned themselves! Their death was not my doing!" Gaspard protested, pressing back against the rough tree trunk.

"Really?" D'Arcy smiled coldly. "Why would they want to die? You sold them for prostitutes. Yvonne lost a baby along the way. They suffered no discomfort, their pride remained intact? I remind you, Gaspard, that my sisters were raised gently. They were always protected against the *filth* of the world."

"D'Arcy! Have mercy!" Gaspard cried out.

The moss swayed near D'Arcy's broad shoulder, and a Canadian woodsman suddenly stepped forward and whispered urgently, "Luc, hurry. Gaspard's friends have found us. By the sounds of the earth, there are twenty or more."

The slaver breathed hard, his eyes pleading. "I beg you . . . let me live."

D'Arcy lifted Gaspard's head with the tip of the broad, well honed hunting knife. His silvery eyes narrowed when he shoved a dueling pistol in the slaver's clammy hand. "It is loaded. When your friends arrive, we will duel. I want them to see how well you die."

One

St. Louis, March 1846

"*Maman* ... Colette ... Yvonne ..." The sweeping
winds carried a man's feverish calls into the crashing thun-
derstorm. Busy travelers bustled over the gangplank from
the steamboat, huddling beneath woolen shawls and scurrying for shelter. The man's urgent calls were lost in the
sounds of mothers calling their children, men shouting orders, and the fierce storm. Lightning cut through the dark
clouds hanging over St. Louis, striking a tree near the swollen, rough waters of the Mississippi River. With a crash, the
burning tree quivered, tilted, then slid into the water, swallowed by the high waves. Thunder vibrated across the levee
as a huge mountain man stepped from the steamboat, carrying another large man in his arms. The Canadian, dressed in
frontier leather and fringes, ignored the mud soaking his
moccasins and the cold rain streaming down his grim,
bearded face. People moved aside as he passed, carrying the
younger man as tenderly as a babe.

In the darkness created by the storm and the spring's late
afternoon, the Canadian turned his head, scowling at a small

man who staggered beneath bundles and furs. The man smiled brightly. "Coming, Yer Lordship. 'Ere, folks. Make way. My friend is carrying a sick man needing shelter to die—"

He stopped, anxious as the Canadian shot him a dark savage look. "I . . . ah, he'll live, of course. He's wounded, but he'll live, I say. . . ." He hunched beneath the huge, leatherwrapped bundles and stepped into a deep puddle, trudging after the woodsman into a waterfront hotel.

"Hey, there—Woodsy—" the hotel clerk called as the Canadian passed by his desk. The woodsman turned slightly, carrying his friend up the narrow stairway. Behind him lay a path of mud across the parlor's Oriental carpet.

"Which room?" the Canadian demanded in a thick, rough accent, his eyes dangerous beneath his sodden slouch hat.

The clerk shrank beneath the contemptuous, threatening stare and issued a room number in a squeaking voice. He hurried up the stairway, quickly opening the door to allow the Canadian to enter. The small man with the bundles slid into the room, dumped his load into a corner, and disappeared.

"You will have your pay," the Canadian said in a rumbling tone, dismissing the clerk as he placed the unconscious man on the bed. "Bring hot water and fill the tub, *vite!* Bring broth and whiskey . . . a clean, fat whore who can be trusted."

The Canadian quickly undressed the younger man, lifting the bloody cloth away from his leg. The festering wound cut across the younger man's upper thigh, the ragged edges pushed apart by the hot, swelling flesh. "Luc, that is a bad one," he murmured gently, checking the cold, sweaty brow with his hand. "But you will fight and you will live."

With the strength of his fever, Luc gripped his friend's hand. *"Siam,"* he called, using the Chinook name for grizzly. "I should not have left them—"

"Your mother and sisters were safe in the ranch of your friend, Luc. It was their folly to leave."

"Bliss took them for a picnic—"

"Yes, it was Bliss's fault your family strayed from safety," Siam soothed.

Luc's black hair fell to the pillow. "I wanted to kill him. I regret he died before tasting my revenge."

Luc fought the cold shiver sweeping over him, replacing the fever's heat. His mind raced through the past. Sante Fe was too dangerous. A blend of Spanish and French blood, the D'Arcys were caught in the midst of a brewing war.

Siam murmured something in French—"Rest, my friend. Shh." Then in Cheyenne, "*Naaotsestse . . .* go to sleep."

Luc couldn't rest, the past clawing at him. He'd left the D'Arcy lands ten years ago for the rich fur lands of the Oregon country. Three times he had returned with Siam, a trusted friend.

Luc's marriage to Willow, a Chinook woman, had stunned his family. Upon meeting Willow, Jason D'Arcy, Luc's father, had demanded outright that Luc divorce her to keep the "blood of kings" pure. When Luc had refused, his father had banned him from the family holdings. Luc returned a second time after Willow's death, summoned by his mother, who was never strong. She wept and pleaded desperately, but a father's pride met a son's. In the end Luc returned to the wild country of Oregon to hunt and trap.

Then two years ago, hearing rumblings of war, Luc returned home. His father had been shot while protecting his family against Americans and Mexicans. On his deathbed, Jason D'Arcy had admitted his arrogant, foolish behavior and his sorrow. He asked Luc to deliver the family to Oregon country and safety.

When Jason D'Arcy died, Luc, Siam, the D'Arcy women, and a few servants set out for the rich Willamette Valley. His mother, mourning her husband and home, grew seriously ill. They stayed with friends near Fort St. Vrain, a trader's fort; his mother recovered but needed time to mend. She begged Luc to travel before winter closed the mountains, to claim the best farming lands and build a new home. Yvonne and Colette would care for her, and the family friends and servants would protect them.

Luc and Siam went ahead, purchased a homestead of 640

acres, and, with help, built a large, sturdy log cabin. The next March they crossed mountains with snowshoes, returning to the ranch near Fort St. Vrain. Luc had intended to unite his remaining family and bring them to their new home.

"Ah!" he cried out with the pain of his leg and the memory of his mother's violated grave. "Too late—Siam, we were too late by less than an hour. My sisters took that poison less than an hour before we arrived. They were still warm when we found them. Yvonne clutching this ring . . . Bliss's ring."

A man named Edward Bliss had enticed Luc's mother and sisters away from their friend's ranch for an afternoon of picnicking and ease. Now Bliss was dead, killed by the gang that mortally wounded Luc's mother and swept away her daughters.

Pain sliced through Luc like a hot sword. Before their dual suicide, his sisters had kept a journal. Yvonne had mourned her dead baby, Bliss's child. The slavers and men who had sold Colette and Yvonne's favors cheaply in Baton Rouge were dead now, all but LaFleur. Surging anger wiped Luc's sorrow aside. Five months were wasted, foraging for the white slaver's trail. Then word came that he was in St. Louis. Soon La Fleur would meet his fate.

Luc's leg throbbed. He fought darkness and pain. He would stand on two feet when he killed LaFleur, the last man.

In a low, swift curse the younger man raised to his elbow. "Don't take my leg, *Tsehe-neheto*," he whispered urgently, using the Cheyenne word for "my older brother."

Forcing a cocky grin, the Canadian returned, "One can make love as sweetly with—"

"Not my leg—" Suddenly pale beneath his tan and fever, Luc fainted back to the bed. He shivered with chills, and his jaw locked beneath his black beard. Rain had plastered his straight black hair against his angular face. Then his silvery eyes, bright with fever, jerked open. They were haunted, yet empty.

"They rest now, their honor avenged, Luc," Siam murmured gently. "Gaspard is dead. Your sisters and *maman* are at peace now. LaFleur will soon meet his fate."

Luc smiled suddenly, a stunning flash of white teeth across his dark skin and beard. "Are you my *maman* now, Siam?" he teased, then sank back to the pillow.

He cried out when the mountain man lifted and eased him into the hot water, allowing the wounded leg to soak. Minutes later Luc moaned as Siam arranged him carefully on the bed. The Canadian ordered the woman who had knocked quietly into the bed, warming Luc. Two servants slid into the room, emptying the tub. They scurried quickly, carrying in buckets of steaming, fresh water. Siam ordered the blond, plump woman to warm his friend as he applied an aromatic poultice of crushed leaves to the wound, then wrapped it carefully. "Hold him as a treasured friend who has lost his wife and his mother and sisters," the Canadian whispered huskily to the woman, gripping her searching hand as it slid down Luc's flat stomach.

"There's room in this bed for three, Frenchy," the woman invited with a wink. Her smile died when the big man scowled at her from the shadows of his hat.

He shed his leather clothing with elegant grace and slid into the tub of hot water, ignoring her. The slouch hat remained on his head. "I do not have the fine, gentle manners of my companion, m'amselle. Do not test my courtesy in this matter. I have none, they tell me. I do what must be done."

A fleeting expression of desire washed across the woman's painted face before she turned to her charge.

"He's hot with fever. You sure it ain't cholera?" she asked quietly, searching Luc's face in the shadows as lightning ripped through the sky. "There's plenty of that around."

"Luc fights his devils and the fever. If he loses his leg, he may lose the wish to live." Staring at his friend, Siam drank deeply from a pottery whiskey jug and settled into the tub to soak away the rain's chills. He closed his eyes, resting to save his strength. Luc groaned, warmed by the woman's plump body. He turned slightly, and Siam jerked out an order, "Hold the leg safe."

Obeying him, the woman soothed Luc in hushed whispers, glancing carefully at the hulking mountain man who rose from the steaming water. Ignoring the crashing thunder and rain slashing against the windowpane, he padded to the door and jerked it open when the clerk knocked. Taking the bucket of steamy water from the man who peered curiously at Luc, Siam nodded briefly. "Go."

"Ah, sir. There's the matter of payment. . . ." The clerk's eyes widened as the huge, naked man stalked to the bundles, delved into a leather pouch, and tossed two gold coins at him. Taking a last glance at the woman holding the feverish man on the bed, the clerk slid from the room, quietly closing the door behind him. "I'll bring the broth shortly."

Wrapping a heavy blanket around himself, the mountain man drew a chair to his friend's side, propped his feet up on the bed, and waited. "Luc deals with his demons," he whispered softly.

The Canadian lifted the whiskey jug, swallowed heavily, and wiped the back of his hand across his mouth. "He does not care if he lives. I do. Hold him closer. Whisper things a mother would tell her child. Make him want to live, woman, and you will be rewarded."

"What is in his hand?" she asked in hushed tones. "He grips it with his fist."

Siam lifted one lid and spoke slowly as if to himself. "A man's ring. Yvonne—his baby sister—held it in her grip just as tightly when she died." He closed his eye, the storm buffeting the hotel. Last August the air was hot, thick with dampness, and still. He and Luc had moved like shadows across the mansion's grounds, flattening to the huge trees laced with gray moss before moving closer to the lighted pillars of the mansion used for gambling and pleasure.

In the dirty room, reeking of strong perfumes and sex, Yvonne and Colette lay sweetly in death. They held each other on the huge bed where they had been forced by so many men. Beside them was an open bottle of poison and a sweet liquor. They had shared one glass; its shards had scattered across the polished floor, sparkling like diamond tears in the light of the lamp.

Now Siam stared at his friend in the shadows cut by the silvery glow of lightning. Luc bore Yvonne's jet black hair, her dark coloring and heavy lashes. Siam had been in love with Luc's sister; he wanted to kill every man who had touched her. A pretty, delicate flower, too sweet and soft for an ill-mannered woodsman, had borne a dead baby to another man called Bliss.

The woman in the bed gasped and huddled closer to Luc as Siam threw the jug against the wall. Thunder crashed and the room shook as the pottery shattered.

Glynis Goodman's hand paused on its way to her lips, the teacup steady despite the rolling thunder and the sound of something smashing against the hotel wall. She lifted her eyebrows and continued her conversation with Arielle. At times Arielle proved the current theories of the devil ruling persons with dominant left hands and red hair, though she preferred to call it brown.

Glynis sipped her tea. A dominant left hand was considered the mark of the devil by many. While the Browning family and servants feared Arielle's left-handed thinking and red-haired rages, Glynis did not. "Arielle, you are no longer the empress of a New York shipping company. In the West you are simply a woman, and men will not hop to do your bidding. Perhaps if you had not stabbed Mr. Smythe last year and ignited that awful scandal, we could be enjoying afternoon tea—" Lightning cut through the heavy dark clouds followed by thunder that rattled the oil lamp's glass chimney.

Arielle Browning pivoted from the window that overlooked the St. Louis street to face her companion, a six-foot, raw-boned Englishwoman endowed with absolute calm. Arielle gripped her full skirts with her fists, hiding them in the folds, just as a roll of thunder echoed like a cannon shot. Arielle's temper equaled the storm beyond the boardinghouse's small room. She scanned the lighted windows along the street and smoothed her thick auburn braids, coiled on

top of her head. She would not let her temper escape to be
mauled by the woman only four years older than herself.
With her mother, Glynis had been a family servant of many
years. She had a particularly keen habit of prying Arielle's
privacy from her, a habit she had honed through their childhood and adult years. Arielle resented Glynis's talent as
much as she did her freckles, which appeared with a splash
of sunlight.

Glynis Goodman looked over the wire rims of her small
glasses at Arielle and pursed her lips. "Stop glaring at me,
young woman. You may have the devil's own temper, but
you don't frighten me one whit."

Arielle smiled coldly at Glynis, who alternately sipped
tea and mended her mistress's voluminous petticoat. "You
and Aunt Louise are determined to blockade my plans to
take women to the western frontier. You perpetually throw
that one little incident concerning Mr. Smythe's indiscretions at my feet—"

"An indiscretion? The man was only courting you—"

Arielle slashed out her hand. "Glynis, he was shoving his
hand down my bosom, fishing at my person like a man
greedily seeking a fat piece of chicken...." She paused
when the Englishwoman lifted her eyebrows. "My fencing
foil was nearby. I simply defended my virtue. Why you and
my aunt insist that I caused the incident, I cannot understand."

The other woman shifted on the bed, adjusted the petticoat, seeking out a bit of torn lace, and began to patch it
with quick neat stitches. Speaking around the thread she
was biting off, Glynis said patiently, "Arielle, we can return
to the safety of the family estate, if you will simply apologize to your aunt. As your guardian, she is distraught that
you are undertaking a mission that is no light matter. You
had already invested your fortune heavily in this venture before she got wind of your caprices. We literally ran before
she closed the doors to your escape. You kept her dancing
this way and that so she wouldn't see your ploy. You may
be quite experienced in trading in New York, in shipping
and bargaining on the waterfront—which no proper lady of

quality should be doing, might I add—but you are taking women straight into Indian country . . . red savages and rough men who would—"

Arielle threw up her hands. "Will you stop? There are emigrants crowding the streets, all wanting to begin lives in the new territories. It is a simple business matter. I am taking my Percherons to set up a horse breeding farm; since they can pull heavy cargo, they might as well help supply a commodity needed in the West—"

"Not a cargo or a commodity—women, Arielle. Women and children. The trip is six or seven months in length. Hardships abound on the trail. Your famed Percheron teams made the trip from New York easily, with proper grain and grass. They might not survive the wilderness."

"My teams were bred for endurance. The Bordens say that the Zeus and his mares are doing nicely on their farmland, adapting to foraging for grass. The horses were hardy on our last visit to the farm. . . . I am not committing treason, Miss Goodman. I am a woman who has been running the family business since I was fifteen. I am now thirty-one, healthy, and perfectly competent to undertake this task. My brother, Jonathan, is at the helm of the family business, running it, and my aunt has nothing to fear. I will be successful on this venture to Oregon City—"

"You are headstrong and following your desire for Mr. Thaddeus Northrup, who enlisted in the army and was sent west five years ago."

"Let me repeat—I am taking good Percheron brood stock to begin horse breeding in the Willamette Valley. While making the journey, my horses may as well pull cargo— therefore, the women." Arielle jerked her chin up high. Glynis would not see that she had touched the real reason for the journey.

At thirty-one Arielle Browning had indeed charted a course for marriage with Thaddeus Northrup. She had decided on the matter after her best friend, a widow, remarried. Then there was Fannie Orson, her childhood arch rival, who married at fifteen and gave birth at sixteen. While Arielle longed for children and had yet to take her marriage vows, her childhood friend, Fannie, was preparing to be a grandmother.

Fannie waved her impending status beneath Arielle's nose like a flag. Fannie had tossed the word *spinster* at Arielle like a dueling challenge. After much stewing, Arielle had decided to accept the challenge. She'd been entertaining the thought for some time anyway.

Arielle fervently wanted marriage with Thaddeus and a bit of the wild freedom that the Oregon country offered an enterprising woman like herself. To marry Thaddeus was an undertaking that she was very capable of accomplishing. She had already traced him to Fort Leavenworth, where he had left the army to seek his fortune in the West. Arielle supposed his plans were to finance his family's stripped coffers since Thaddeus was sent money on a regular basis. The Northrups had borrowed heavily, investing in their only son's plan to begin business in the Willamette Valley.

Arielle couldn't expose her plans; to hunt Thaddeus across Indian territory and into the West would not be appropriate—even for those accused of using the wrong side of their brains for thinking, as demonstrated by dominant use of the left hand. She allowed herself a small, confident smile. At times it was wise to keep one's goals to one's self, like the new bust-improver she had hidden from Glynis. Researching a Browning trade route to the West and beginning a horse-breeding business were perfect shields for her purpose. Though Aunt Louise wouldn't admit the folly of cherishing romance, she softened a bit each time Arielle proposed taking brides to desirous husbands. Then there was the matter of Mr. Smythe and his fishing hand.

Arielle smiled again. Matchmaking was an age-old, honored occupation. She was merely inventing a new dimension to a marriage go-between. Of course, it was necessary to obtain her marriage without the aid of a matchmaker. By completing the task herself, she would save a tidy sum.

Thaddeus fit nicely into her plans. Always a gentleman, Thaddeus was handsome and reasonable. When they were children, he rarely mentioned her awful stigmas. Arielle straightened her shoulders. A dominant left hand and a

slight tint of red to one's brown hair was not an easy burden. Few men could handle them both. Thaddeus didn't
seem to mind her handicaps through their early years, and
Arielle had planned to acquire him in her early twenties.

She frowned. Shipping and business had pressed her in-
terests aside, and though Thaddeus squired other women
about, he always managed time for her. She felt secure,
cherishing the time they had together until the army ordered
him to the frontier.

A string of business mergers, shipyard problems, and tutoring her younger brother until he was able to take the
helm had prevented her from following Thaddeus sooner.
Now Jonathan was trained, running the Browning business.
He was also Aunt Louise's favorite child and had convinced
her that Arielle's venture would encourage the fur traders
and farmers to do business with Browning stores. Taking
brides and supplies to the men was a measure of goodwill.

Arielle plucked a thread from her skirt. She would follow
Thaddeus and reclaim him . . . marry him, she corrected.

She placed her palm on the cold windowpane, remembering Thaddeus standing straight and proud in his army uni-
form. His tailor had fitted Thaddeus's narrow, straight body
perfectly. His cornflower-blue eyes had warmed before he
bent to kiss her. The brush of his mouth across hers was
brief, almost brotherly, but she treasured it. A gallant man,
Thaddeus had ridden off proudly to serve his growing nation. She dreamed of him returning, of asking for her hand
in marriage.

His blond well-trimmed hair had gleamed in the sun the
day of his departure, his long face alight with the grand adventure of conquering the western lands. Their marriage
would be perfect and neat. Over all, Arielle wanted a tidy
marriage.

Arielle frowned slightly, tracing the window sill. Because
Thaddeus was devoted to his occupation, he had not courted
her properly. Once she located him, that would be much
easier, although at her advanced age, she didn't expect
courting or love. Thaddeus's understanding and calm would
blend well in their marriage arrangement. For his sake, she

would manage her left-handed thinking and red-haired tendencies. She would keep her hair from the sun, which tended to bring out the red lights, and work harder at right-handed skills for social occasions.

Glynis snipped a length of thread and inserted it into a needle, ignoring her mistress's glare. She looked up at Arielle and smiled tightly. "Don't worry, my dear. No one else knows your secret. You nurtured the idea of Thaddeus as a husband for years. When Fannie Orson announced her approaching status as a grandmother, you went white. I've always suspected a deep competition between you and Fannie. When she tossed her new coup in your lap, your telltale left hand went to your throat, a protective gesture. Surely you didn't expect me not to know. . . . You were heartbroken for a year, your calculations for marriage swept aside by a mere army order. Your aunt thought your devilish moods were because of business, but I knew the truth—Don't slash those green eyes at me, my dear. I've survived your tempers since we were babies, and Mother was your nanny."

When Arielle inhaled sharply, Glynis bent her head, her needle flashing. "Oh, yes, toss that indignant look at me—threaten to . . . what? Dismember me, wasn't it, last time? Or was it keelhauling? Yes, Arielle. You may appear cool and businesslike to your ships' masters, but I know what a tyrant you are and to what ends you will travel when determined to have your way. You picture yourself in love, a true romantic living on wisps of dreams, crusading off to reclaim your lost love."

"You forget your station, Glynis," Arielle reminded the servant darkly and was met with a bland smile. Swishing her skirts aside, Arielle sat in a small chair near a table and opened a large packet of letters. She sifted through the papers, which had begun arriving immediately after her advertisement in the St. Louis newspaper. She ran her fingertips across a woman's large, flowing script filled with dreams, and across a letter written by one woman and signed by another's X.

At the moment thirteen women and six children had

pledged to fill her three wagons over the Overland Trail to Oregon.

"Please do not lay Thaddeus at my feet, although I admit wanting to seek him out—merely for the sake of our friendship. My purpose for this expedition is supplying the demand for marriageable women in the Oregon country. The seeds and farming goods will make a small profit, but the ultimate reward will be in delivering these women to a new life. If I can run a shipping business, I can safely deliver the goods—women and children—to husbands in Oregon country. Toss in a few seeds and seedlings and you have a measure of profit. The safe transportation of these women is simply a matter of management, Glynis. Matters of the heart do not enter business."

She refused to acknowledge Glynis's correct thrust. When Thaddeus gave her his hand in marriage—Arielle rephrased that—when she gave her hand to Thaddeus, he would see that rumors of her hunting him down were stopped.

Thaddeus was what she wanted. A gentle companion and a good, stable father for the children she wanted to have someday. She could see them now, darling little blond children, waiting in a row for inspection before church services.

Taking her new continuous-flow pen in her left hand, Arielle scribbled a note on an applicant's letter.

" 'Matters of the heart,' " Glynis repeated. "What if these women are repelled by the very men who are paying their bridal price? Have you thought of that? What will you do when you arrive? What of your lot? Are you certain this whole venture is moral?"

"I am rising to a challenge. There is a great need for women and horses in Oregon country. The Willamette is good farming country and is likely to be conceded from the British soon. Therefore, both are necessary commodities. I will supply them. The applicants for husbands will be interviewed as carefully as the women. I see myself in the time-honored role of official matchmaker. This is still being done in the best of families."

"You are adept with your left hand, which shows that your thinking is not always conventional. Your temper is demonstrated by use, rather than the shade of your hair. Other than that, you are bullheaded and blunt, my dear," Glynis returned pleasantly. "And quite the match for that wagon master, Mr. Josiah Smithson. I'm certain you've found a scheme to meet his qualifications 'that these westward-ho wagons will not be manned by an unbreached, never-wedded female.' " She quickly bent her head to her mending task, shielding her smile from Arielle's glare.

Arielle crushed the list of applicants in her fist, tilting her head in a determined way Glynis recognized. "I watched that fine wagon master interview emigrants in the back of a saloon. He is a prime example of the outmoded man, unable to cope with a woman's business skills. Adept with my left hand or not, I have directed cargoes from England to Africa and back. Surely I can manage three wagons and a handful of women and children."

"You have managed the captains when in port and you have managed extensive paperwork very well. Smithson isn't pliable. Or your employee. There are other trains, my dear. Perhaps other wagon masters would be more generous."

"I find that an investment in quality is necessary in preparing for this venture. Mr. Smithson may be rigid in his belief that women are chattel, but he has experience and is considered the best wagon master by far. I like his idea of emigrants starting in St. Louis, practicing the Great Jump to Independence, and outfitting wagons after a taste of traveling. Though he has peculiar standards for his train, he chooses safe methods and solid men. I understand that he is greatly concerned about safety and the number of deaths caused by carelessness. Once he understands that I am serious about transporting wives, I am certain we will understand each other. He is the man I want."

"Ah," Glynis interrupted quietly, neatly tying a knot. "That is the key—men, my dear. Mr. Smithson chooses men."

"I can see why they are necessary, Glynis," Arielle returned with a sniff. "Yes, they are larger. Yes, they can lift more and for the most part are more experienced with weaponry. But a well-prepared woman with resources to purchase necessaries can manage just as well. There are men willing to work for their passage. I have made a promise to Sacha that I will arrive in Oregon City in the fall of eighteen forty-six with marriageable women and their children."

She paused, thinking of Sacha Eberhart. A trusted Browning employee of many years, Sacha had been eager to set up a company store in the Willamette Valley. Sacha was to begin trading goods with the settlers and natives eighteen months previously.

"My Percherons are expected . . . relished by some. I shall meet that promise."

Glynis nodded. "Of course you will, Arielle. You are determined not to fail, even though the challenges would frighten a mere mortal man. You are determined to thrust into the great American wilderness, carrying your charges through safely despite all odds. Sacha is a Browning company man and would not doubt your ability for success."

"Yes," Arielle agreed tightly. "I detect your grim humor, Glynis. However, I do choose Mr. Smithson's trains as they are the safest. He takes precautions, and I appreciate his forethought, strategies, and preparations. Yes, I like it. . . . Mr. Smithson will accept our applications here, and we'll join him in Independence later. We need the time from St. Louis to Independence to prepare the women for Mr. Smithson's interviews. At the Landing we'll purchase proper Conestoga wagons and supplies and join Mr. Smithson's train."

"Without a woman wagon master. Wagon mistress, really," Glynis interrupted wryly, taking a sip of tea.

Arielle glared at her. "In the morning I will return to Mr. Smithson's saloon office and approach him with my offer. No doubt he will require us to use the skills of hired men. I am prepared to pay them well. I am certain he will accept us as emigrants, despite his staunch views on the frailty of helpless women."

Then she crossed her hands behind her back. Glynis immediately recognized the familiar gesture. It was one Arielle used when she was not certain of the outcome of her plans.

Luc struggled against the waves of pain.

His wound had festered, poisoning his body, and now memories he had pushed back for years clawed from their locked den.

His fevers carried him to a time before his sisters' deaths. He had been married twice and both wives had died. . . .

Flames blazing in the family's huge fireplace lit Luc's father's still-handsome face. The firelight caught in Jason D'Arcy's blond hair, now touched with gray. Tall, lean men, father and son had faced each other with pride and arrogance, neither bending.

"You were a boy, not yet seventeen, married to an older woman," Jason had said between his teeth. "Catherine lied about conceiving your child, forcing you by honor to marry her."

He spoke in fluent, aristocratic French, his tone bitter. His ice-blue eyes met Luc's silvery ones. "You can't blame me for wanting to protect my only son . . . for sending you to safety in Oregon country . . . when one of Catherine's lovers murdered her and then turned the blame to you. Your mother would have died if anything happened to you."

"Is that the only reason you sent me away, Father?" Luc had asked coldly, slashing at the man who had spared little time for his family.

Jason's harsh face had tightened. "You are my only son. The D'Arcy name would have died with you."

For a time Jason D'Arcy slid back into the past. Luc clenched his lids shut, fighting the pain that swept him into merciful, black depths. When he surfaced, Jason D'Arcy's hand stretched across the years, snaring him back to the spacious study; the firelight blazed in the rock grate, creamy woven rugs spread across polished wooden floors.

Bitterness slammed into Luc's stomach, Catherine's taunts unmanning him. Once she had boldly seduced a young boy into a marriage that the D'Arcy family had protested. Young Luc, heated by lust and believing it to be love, soon found the bitter dregs of Catherine's well-used desires. Her taunts had sent him into duels and bordellos to prove his manhood, scandalizing the D'Arcy name. One night his wife lay in her bed, blood seeping from the fatal slash across her throat. Luc was just eighteen.

Her lover enflamed the crowd, and young Luc's father sent him to safety in the tall pines of Oregon. Within four months the murderer was discovered and hung. D'Arcy ordered his son to return, but Luc's pride kept him away.

The lines on Jason's face deepened, his eyes shimmering with tears. "Catherine scarred your heart, my son."

Luc had tossed down a brandy, then poured another, studying the amber lights. Catherine's cruel laughter swirled from the shadows, chilling him. Then a girl, with sleek blue-black hair and shy gleaming eyes brushed his life. "I married again. You refused to recognize Willow as a D'Arcy."

Willow. Her childbirth screams sailed through the years to slice at him. Then death stopped her cries, their child dying within her, and the echo of the silence shrieked inside his restless brain.

Jason's hand rested on Luc's shoulder before it was shrugged away. "Willow was a girl, my son. She worshipped you. Her life was gone before the marriage was tested. You have yet to love a woman, though I was wrong to deny your marriage. I was wrong to force you to hide until Catherine's murderer was found."

Luc had lifted an ornate gold chalice, studying the family crest. "It's a little late for that, don't you think? 'A red savage' was what you called Willow, wasn't it? How shocked you were by the flat shape of her forehead, a sign of her high birth. 'A heathen practice, flattening a baby's head by binding cedar bark to it,' you said."

Jason, elegant, strong, and proud, sank into the desk's chair like a feeble old man. "Why women fall at your feet, I don't understand. Perhaps it is because they are perverse creatures by nature. You are a hard man, Lucien. An unforgiving one."

"Perhaps."

Jason lifted his chalice wearily. "I wager that you will not die with a soft, loving woman at your side. I wager the D'Arcy name dies with you. I wager you will not find a woman to lighten your heart because you have declared it dead."

Luc raised his chalice, studying the fine tooling. "A wager? I have always liked your challenges."

His father had scowled at him. "Any woman who marries you won't be an angel. You haven't laughed freely since you were a boy. Catherine killed that in you. I damn her soul to hell for that cruelty."

"Catherine was in hell from the moment she was spawned." Luc had scanned his father's face. This was the man who held the D'Arcy name sacred . . . who had wedged a stake of pride into his son from the cradle. Who had forced him to run from a murdering mob . . . who had denied Willow as a proper D'Arcy bride. "I take your wager, Father. Before I die, I will marry an angel. The D'Arcy name will remain past my last breath."

Jason had snorted in disbelief, closing his eyes and downing the brandy. "Done."

"Done." The disbelieving last word clung to Luc now, echoing through the surging pain that sucked him into the black abyss. He cried out, hating the pain, the weakness—

"I will marry an angel before I die. I swear by the D'Arcy name."

Two
·········

The son of a French trapper and a Chinook princess, Siam was barely conscious and staked naked on the frozen ground when he first saw Luc nine years ago. A party of English misfits, driven by drink and hatred, soon sobered when Luc stepped into the light of their fire and slashed Siam free. Too weak to move, the Canadian had expected the tall, rugged woodsman to be one more of the pack. When Luc forced the men to place Siam on a thick buffalo hide and construct a shelter around him to the taste of a lash, Siam still distrusted the new man. Siam had waited tensely for more insults, while the English stacked food and wood at Luc's feet. He ordered the men to undress. Moments later they fled with their boots and their moccasins, the frontiersman standing with his rifle at his side.

Luc took Siam to his cabin, tending him while he trapped and hunted. Then Siam recovered and disappeared into the lofty mountain pines. Mountainmen told of *Siam Po-lak-lie*. The Chinook name for grizzly added darkness and gloom when he found and killed each man. One evening he appeared at Luc's cabin carrying a fresh deer kill. Since then the men had lived like brothers. Now Siam willed Luc to live.

In the hovering stillness preceding dawn, Siam dismissed the woman and paid her well. Luc's fever had worsened as the storm clung, probing the dark sky with fingers of jagged, silver lightning. Exhausted and having tried every healing herb in his pouch, Siam had decided to get the doctor. At seven o'clock in the morning, he had sent a servant to bring the doctor, who had refused to leave his card game and whiskey glass.

Luc had raved throughout the night, fighting the woman's attempts to calm his guilt; Siam feared he wanted to join his family in death. After dressing quickly in the sodden leathers, Siam gently brushed back the damp, sleek black hair of his friend and said quietly, "Luc, I must go for the doctor. Do you understand, *Na-semahe* . . . my younger brother?"

Luc nodded slightly, his cheeks above his black beard flushed with fever. "I must win the wager with my father. . . . Get me an angel," he whispered weakly.

"I will bring you one," Siam returned after a brief hesitation. He frowned, aware that in his delirium, Luc's mind had fastened to the past—the wager of capturing an angel before he died. He patted Luc's tanned shoulder, then left the room, closing the door softly. Luc should not be left alone, but Siam feared what could happen with the unsavory servants in the hotel. Determined to find the reluctant doctor, he turned quickly, padding down the shadowy hallway as though he were loping over an Indian foot trail. Downstairs a clock struck eight times, counting the precious hours, and Siam frowned. At the corner a woman's soft body collided with his, and he glanced down into wide green eyes.

Rippling reddish brown tendrils swirled around a pale heart-shaped face, and the loose braids on top of her head threatened to fall. The woman's head just reached Siam's chest, and for an instant her sputtering indignation reminded him of a small, furious red hen. Hens protected their offspring, and Siam glimpsed a woman who would fight for what she deemed precious. She wasn't Luc's sweet angel, but she would serve well to care for Luc. Siam decided this bit of feminine fury might just fight to keep Luc alive until the doctor arrived. He resented his lack of refinement, raised between races in a hard, take-or-be-taken life. But he had no time to debate the matter. Reacting quickly, the woodsman snared her slender wrist and dragged her back into the room.

Fighting the giant's grip, Arielle swatted at his broad, buckskin-covered chest. "Loose me! I will not be hauled about like a haunch of deer."

Siam released her wrist and pointed to the bed, the tall body of his unconscious friend outlined beneath the sheets. He realized he should be asking, but the chance that the woman would leave Luc now frightened him. He resorted to the path begun early in life, the path for survival—taking what he needed at the moment. The woman, gasping for breath, showed signs of being a talker; he had no time to listen. "You stay by Luc, woman, until I return with a doctor. He's been shot. I dug the ball out, but the wound is festering. I'll pay you for your time. Leave him or hurt him, and I'll hunt you down like a panther and skin you. That red scalp would make a fine trading piece."

Satisfied when her eyes widened, he nodded curtly. "The name is Siam, ma'am. Means grizzly in Chinook. I'm just as fierce when it strikes me." He locked the door behind him. Then the hallway was quiet.

Arielle straightened her blouse, simmered in her anger, and glared at the locked door. She swept a hand upward, smoothing a curl that had shaken loose and was bobbing on the nape of her neck. "My hair is not red—thank you very much, Mr. Lordly Woodsman." She tried the knob and found the thick door would not budge. "Very well, since you asked so nicely, my friend. Of course, I'd love to sit with ... Luc until you return. The alternatives are few."

Returning to the side of the bed, Arielle stared down at the man. A hard burst of rain hit the windowpane and streamed down the blue wavery glass in tiny rivulets. Lightning crashed, rattling the window in its frame, and the man resting on the bed shivered as though chilled. Arielle lifted the sheeting to cover his hot shoulder, then straightened and placed her hands on her waist.

Glynis would be gone for hours. She relished purchasing lengths of cotton, handkerchiefs, and thread as though it were a game. Until the frontiersman returned, Arielle was trapped with his friend, Luc.

Blood seeped through the cloth covering his right thigh. Arielle glanced at his strained features, then lightly probed the area to find a heavy, blood-soaked bandage fed by a gaping wound. "Your friend was correct not to leave you alone, Mr. Luc. He could have asked, rather than pirateered me for duty," she murmured softly. "For your sake, I pray that he returns quickly."

Straightening to stare closely at the bearded man, Arielle nibbled at her bottom lip and glanced at the spreading stain. When Luc groaned deeply and shifted as if in great pain, Arielle stepped back until he quieted. His hand moved restlessly on the sun-bleached sheeting, and Arielle noted the long slender length of his fingers. Her gaze moved over his thick wrist, up his arm to his tanned shoulders and the dark hair escaping the cloth covering him. A lean man, the cords beneath his darkly tanned chest shifted as he moved slightly. She suspected he had lost weight recently, as the arc of his ribs pushed against the taut dark skin.

Arielle folded her arms over her chest. Kidnapped by a woodsy in the hallway, locked in a bedroom with a wounded, feverish man, she should be frightened. Perhaps her left-handed thinking rejected fear. She'd wanted to smooth the expanse of warm brown skin with her fingers, testing its heat and power as she might do for one of her horses. She shivered and glanced at the gray rain. "Blast that hulking landlubber," she muttered darkly. "When our paths cross again, I will serve him a good sampling of manners. . . . Perhaps I should take a few nicks of his savage hide before running him through."

The wounded man cried out, fighting his pain as he tossed on the bed. The movement caused him to cry out again, then murmur feverishly in hushed, desperate tones.

Women's names flew across his hot, dry lips, and Arielle wondered briefly how many women had shared his life, his bed.

Exploring the room, Arielle found a clean towel. She soaked the end in water and drew a chair to the man's bedside. Gently patting the cloth across his hot face, she frowned when he avoided her care. "Blast you. I'm not courting you for my amusement, my good man. Lie still."

She gently swept back a straight length of black hair and noted the silver streaks at his temple. Closely cropped, his hair was thick and glossy against the pillowcase, contrasting the delicate embroidered flower patterns. A scar ran across a glossy eyebrow, severing it into a wicked peak. Another small scar broke the line of his molded bottom lip. Straight black lashes bristled above his cheeks, and suddenly Arielle found herself staring into light gray eyes. "I am in heaven," Luc said quietly, reverently, before closing his eyes. "Or Siam found my angel."

Straightening and stepping backward, Arielle placed her hand over her heart to still the rapid beat. "Blast," she whispered again, trembling.

Watching Luc carefully, Arielle twined a length of auburn hair around her finger and smoothed it with her thumb. The man's husky, deep voice held an accent she could not recognize. Surely he'd thought his love, another woman, was tending him. Arielle swallowed, examined the taut features of his face, and followed a drop of sweat running from his forehead. He stirred restlessly, seeming to search for something, reaching out his hand to grip the cloth over his wound. He cried out softly, and Arielle discovered her fingers rested on his shoulder. Muscles sheathed by hot flesh slid smoothly as he gripped her wrist. "Angel, stay."

Trapped in his fever, there was a rasp of arrogance in his voice . . . more of a demand than a question. His fingers caressed her wrist, yet kept it firmly encircled. "You are not a dream. You won't leave me, Angel. *You're mine now.*"

The deep, possessive tone lashed at her, lifted the hairs on the back of her neck.

Thunder shattered the sound of the steady rain, the panes

of glass rattling as the storm grew beyond the hotel room. The man drew her hand to his chest, and beneath her fingers rested a heavy medallion and too-warm flesh. Dark, damp hair tickled her palm. "Stay," he rasped, the deep tone suddenly uncertain and vulnerable.

Arielle swallowed the dry wad that seemed lodged in her throat. This man needed tending, and for now she was his guardian. Or angel, if he needed one to survive. "Mr. Luc, you must rest."

"You will stay," he insisted, this time more firmly. Was it anger that glittered beneath his sooty lashes, darkening his light eyes into a pewter shade? Or was it fever?

"Sir, I do not have a choice," she answered softly. Arielle tried to be kind, dismissing his commanding tone. "But you are to let me cool your brow with this cloth and tend you. You are frightfully hot. Your friend is searching for a doctor—"

"Are you married? Do you have children?" he demanded in rapid-fire order. His accent was thick, laced with French and threaded with other languages. Arrogance and command rang through his deep tone, the sound of a man who would be obeyed.

Startled by his intensity, Arielle blushed, shivering. "No."

"Then you are mine . . . my angel," he insisted feverishly, his fingers tightening almost painfully on her wrist. His deep voice was uneven, desperate, whispering urgently. . . . "My life slips away. . . . Lie with me. Let me rest my head upon your soft breast—"

"Loose me!" Arielle strained against the long, powerful fingers circling her wrist as they drew her palm to his lips.

"Men have died without a woman to hold, to comfort. I won't be one of them now that you are here."

His mouth was hot and dry, reverently caressing her skin. "So cool and soft. Your eyes are like a mountain forest . . . cool, green, beautiful . . . I knew you would be perfect."

"Goodness, Mr. . . . Mr. Luc. You are not behaving like a gentleman," she managed unevenly, aware that he was drawing her down to the bed.

"Lay with me, *mi mujer*. Then I can sleep. . . ." In a swift move Luc reached down, slid his arm under her legs and lifted them to the bed. He cuddled her in the cove of his body, one hand holding her wrists and the other seeking her breast.

Arielle struggled within the masses of her hair, the tangle of her skirts and petticoats, and the man holding her firmly from behind. Despite his illness, the man was incredibly strong, his arms looping around her. He sucked in a soft groan as her bottom struck his thigh. His big body tensed, his breath flowing through her hair unevenly.

"Mr. . . . Mr. Luc . . . you are to release me this minute," Arielle managed between her teeth.

In her lifetime she had never been held tightly against a man, cuddled and nuzzled—he kissed her ear, his breath flowing around the whorls—"*Chère* . . . Angel . . . sleep by my side. . . ."

"Blast! Stop this now, Luc. You have mistaken me—" Arielle began.

Warm, gentle fingers closed around her breast, smoothing it reverently. His tone reasoned, as if soothing a belligerent child. "Angel, shhh. It is only for this time, for this time when I fear to die without a woman. It is necessary, don't you see? I have no one but you now. You came when I needed you."

He shuddered, suddenly chilled. "My sisters, mother, father, all gone. I do not wish to meet death alone. It is a simple thing. A man needing a woman as he dies. . . . I am a mere man swept away by the beauty of the woman tending me. You are my angel. My quest is finished. With you at my side, I have a small measure of peace. Rest. . . ."

In the next instant Luc's breath swept through the strand of hair rippling over her temple, and his body relaxed as he slept. "Blast," Arielle said again quietly, not wanting to wake the man who held her as though she was his one dear possession.

The rain beat steadily against the windowpane, creating shadows of the rivulets on the whitewashed walls. Arielle lay stiffly in the tall man's arms, feeling his heart beat steadily against her back, his breath tickling her cheek. He was too warm; his body dampened the back of her blouse. *"Chère,"* he whispered softly, nuzzling her ear with his lips. Laden with tenderness, the dreamy, sensuous sound of his deep voice lifted Arielle's brows. "Mmm, *chère.*"

His hand gently closed on her breast, covered by the starched cotton. "You are a goddess, *mi mujer.*" Luc's voice was slow, sleepy, and rich with satisfaction. "My angel . . . beautiful."

She breathed lightly, forcing herself to lie quietly, as Luc's large hand opened on her wrists and captured her fingers. Lacing them with his, he squeezed gently and sighed. For the next ten minutes Arielle debated how to break his incredibly gentle but firm hold.

She'd never been held intimately, nor cherished as Luc had insisted. His rough jaw nuzzled her cheek, and a sleepy sigh escaped his lips. *A goddess . . .*

The man was hallucinating, snatching at past dreams that slid away from him in his fevers.

The key rattled in the lock, and Siam stepped quietly into the shadowy room with a smaller man carrying a small black leather bag.

Siam took in the scene in one slow stare, then grinned widely. "Women like my friend," he said quietly to the other man. "When he holds her, the pain—the rage of his hard life—is gone. He thinks of lovemaking, babies, and not death."

The doctor cleared his throat and avoided looking at Arielle's petticoats and ankles as he placed his bag on a chair and opened it. She kicked at the blankets, trying to slide her toe under an edge to draw it higher.

"Get this hot landlubber off me, Siam," Arielle ordered succinctly. "He's squashing me. Out of his head, dreaming of his wife, and thinking that I am she. . . ."

She moved and Luc groaned sharply. Siam shot out a huge hand to clamp around her throat. "You move and I'll snap it. You're hurting him."

Arielle glared up at Siam. "Remove your hand. I will not be pulled apart like a chicken's breastbone by two savages. Take my place if you want him coddled—"

She noted with satisfaction that a red flush rose in the Canadian's weathered cheeks as her barb struck home. "Doctor, would you please . . . ?"

"Emerson, ma'am. Dr. Emerson. I can treat the man's wound fine from where he's lying, if he's not stirred up. I recommend that you lie still until I'm finished securing the infected area."

"Shark bait," Arielle muttered darkly. "Doctor, surely you see that this man is making improper advances, even in his illness," Arielle stated before sinking her teeth into Siam's hand. He shook it slightly, trying to dislodge her, but she bit deeper, tasting the salt of his blood.

"Release her," Emerson said quietly as he eased Luc's large hand from her breast. "There, that is quite proper for the situation. The best we can do at the moment, I fear. Hold his hand, madam, because I fear he will not let you go without dear cost to you both."

"Mmm . . ." Arielle's grim sound reminded Emerson of Siam's bleeding hand.

"Release her, my dear savage, or I will not tend your friend. It is a simple matter of the Good Samaritan—this lovely young lady—trapped by a man needing a tender touch. I've seen it many times before in the fevered. They need to know a loved one is near, to lend a comforting hand in their moment of dire need. With the gravity of this man's wound, he is probably wandering through his life and his dreams, mixing them in his fevers."

The doctor hiccuped and blinked owlishly. "At this moment, my dear, you could be the woman he once wanted, a past love, or you could be what he wants for eternity. Whatever the reason, this man fancies you at a time when he needs you most."

He glanced at Arielle as Siam's big hand slid away. "My dear, it is for you to say. We can wrest you from this man who is needing a gentle heart in the midst of his fevers. Or you will stay because you are a kind woman." He paused, waiting for Arielle's answer.

Arielle licked her lips and held tightly to Luc's hand,

which had been sliding upward toward her breast. "Sir, I do not know either of these gentlemen—"

The weight of his large hand pressed against her breast, and Arielle flushed wildly. *"Chère,"* Luc murmured, breathing unevenly. With slow, straining effort, he lowered his cheek to rest upon her breast. He kissed the soft swell, and Arielle cried out softly in protest.

The small doctor smiled down at her flushed, indignant face. "Nonetheless. There is a need for a woman's soft body folded against this man who is lying near death's door. From the looks of him, he'll be at Gabriel's door soon enough. Would you deny him this boon, when you are not much indisposed?"

In the face of the man's gentle reasoning, Arielle scowled. "I am *much* indisposed, sir. But please continue your efforts to heal this man, for I long for my independence."

"Very well, I shall proceed to make him comfortable before he meets his Maker. Thank you, madam. You are indeed a kind heart."

Angel's scent and arms held Luc still while the doctor probed, working the matter from his wounded leg and applying a series of hot compresses. Covered with starched cotton, her breast was soft beneath his cheek. He caught the scent of violets and lavender, of sunshine dancing through a spring morning. Then the woman's scent, headier, beckoning, wove around him. He had longed for a woman like this, soft, fragrant, with a kind heart. He was awed to find her tending him at the very moment when the fevers tried to drag him into an abyss. His instincts told him that clinging to her, clinging to his dream of a life with her, would carry him through the worst. He cried out, clutching her tighter when the doctor replaced a hot compress. He clung to the sound of her heart, listening to the eternal beat. "Talk to him," Siam ordered, his rough tone veiled in the fiery distance.

Her breast quivered softly as she inhaled, and Luc clung to her heartbeat, fighting the black abyss that threatened to sweep over him. The fiery pain in his leg and the fever riding him surged, then crested, and he saw Yvonne and Colette lying in their grave, wrapped in each other's arms. Luc saw his mother's grave, torn by digging coyotes. He saw Gaspard's shock as the dueling pistol's ball struck his breast, saw the slaver crumble to the ground beneath the shadowy trees. Blue sulfur smoke rose in the morning mists, the swaying gray moss shrouding the trees. Gaspard's shot went wild, creasing Luc's eyebrow.

He cried out again, holding the sound of the woman's heartbeat in his head, concentrating on the racing rhythm. Gaspard's men loomed in the mists, and Siam's knife hissed through the still air, piercing the ruffles covering a big man's chest. There was a curtain of blood, a red-hot brand lying across his forehead. Siam pushed him on a big, fast horse, and they were racing away.

Months went by as they hunted for news of LaFleur, who had disguised himself and covered his flight to St. Louis.

On the steamboat a man shouted at a woman who reminded Luc of his sisters. He removed the man's hand from the woman's throat and a fight began. The gambler went down, and a shot rang out.

The shot echoed in his brain, the pain searing through his thigh.

"Shh . . . My dear, there . . . there . . ." A woman's soft hesitant voice whispered near his ear.

He clung tighter to her soft body, knowing that without it he would die. A Chinook death song swept from the shadows . . . *Tamala, tamala* . . . the tomorrows of forever . . . eternity. He pushed back the song, listening to his angel's strong, racing heartbeat. The sound filled his brain, and he clung to it.

Another wash of pain took him, and swirling into a dark abyss he called out, "Angel!"

"Shh," her soft whisper gentled the searing pain. "There now, Mr. Luc . . . soon . . . please drink this. . . ." The sweet sound of her voice eased the pain, her hand soft and cool against his forehead.

He allowed Siam to lift his head as he sipped the sweet liquor.

Colette and Yvonne had sipped another liquor, taking their lives. . . . He cried out, fighting the memory, clinging to Angel. He concentrated on her—soft green eyes filling her face, the scent of violets and lavender, starched cloth covering her rounded body. He saw her racing through the lush Willamette fields, saw her pluck a huge daisy. Then she was lying amid the white flowers and lush mountain ferns, looking at up at him with shadowy green eyes.

He wanted everything then, the softness that had never been a part of his life. He wanted this angel to hold him fiercely, to wrap him in her arms, closing away all the pain—

"Undress for me, my heart, my own," he whispered against her breast as she stroked his forehead. "Let me taste the sweet silk of your skin. Let me touch you as a lover, open for me—" he murmured, and she stiffened in his arms.

"That Luc. He makes love in his fever," Siam rumbled, and thunder rolled in the distance. Luc struggled to tell Siam to go to hell.

Suddenly he wanted children desperately, to carry on his parents' legacy. The deep need had been fostered since childhood—to marry a woman of his dreams, to carry on his heritage. Pain sliced through him again, and he held the woman, his angel, closer, desperate now to cling to life, to see his angel hold a D'Arcy child.

This woman held his wager in her small hand.

A soft woman. A sweet angel keeping him from death . . . the mother of his child . . . green eyes and silky red curls . . . cool summer glades and pale, sweet skin . . .

"He's developing a man's problem for certain," murmured another man as pain went spearing through Luc's leg. "Hard not to notice when I'm working on his leg."

"Gentlemen, how much longer?" Angel asked sharply, her fingers tugging at Luc's hair to draw him away from her breast.

Another fiery streak of pain cut across his leg, and he cried out sharply, the black weight pressing him down. He held Angel closer, his sweet talisman against pain and death—"Kiss me. . . . Take away this pain—"

"Sir!" Angel's sharp protest stopped as his lips found hers.

In the fever her mouth was cool and soft and sweet.

He tasted her gently, concentrating on the cool contours of her lips, pressed firmly together. He smiled tightly as another pain seized his leg, lessened by Angel's sweet touch. "A child's kiss, *ma chère*," he whispered, aware that one soft thigh brushed his amid the petticoats and sheets. Luc found her thigh, felt her stiffen as he trailed his fingers upward over her long, flannel drawers.

He'd expected silk and lace, and the practical cloth startled him.

He kissed her again, fighting the searing pain as the doctor began stitching his wound.

Angel's fist hit his head, a slight blow followed by Siam's rough grumble. A woman of fire, matching his passion . . .

Her belly was soft, and Luc saw his baby filling it, saw his son nursing at her breast.

"He's—" she began in protest, and Luc focused on her heart racing beneath his cheek. He wanted his seed in her womb, his son filling it.

He wanted a son. The desperate need to hold a child, a tiny part of him to go on forever, startled him.

"Almost done, keep him quiet," the doctor muttered. "Lie still."

"One sweet kiss, *chère*," Luc ordered against her throat, taking care not to hold her too tightly as the doctor took another painful stitch.

"Blast!" Threaded with anger, Angel's husky tone brushed across his hot cheek, cooling him.

He forced open his lids, pushing at them with his last bit of strength to see the woman who had lifted herself over him. Fiery hair caught the room's dim light, loose curls framing her face. The silky tendrils stroked his cheek, tormenting him with her delicate scent. Green eyes shaded with brown lashes looked down into his. Hands cool and soft smoothed his cheek, easing his fever and pain. "You should sleep," she whispered unevenly, gently.

Their eyes met and something ageless and deep passed between them. *This one will test my patience, my passion,* he decided. *But time runs away so quickly.* A piercing sweet tenderness curled around his heart, softening the scars he had protected, locked away. "Kiss me, *chère*," he whispered, running his hand to the nape of her neck.

She whispered something furiously, resisting the pressure of his hand as he drew her nearer. Then sweet and timid, her lips met his and lingered. Her breath crossed his face, the warmth of her skin easing his fever. Her lips were cool and untutored, and Luc closed his eyes, cherishing the sweet taste. He lay still, dozing, staying out of the shadows as she kissed him again, a mere brushing of her lips against his. Her lips quivered, pushed slightly with just a hint of hunger—

Luc closed his eyes, letting sleep come to him. He wanted to teach Angel how to kiss like a woman, not a child. He breathed slowly, his angel's body pressed against him, close and safe—and for a time Luc allowed himself to sleep as he had as a small boy.

Three
......

Luc damned his weakness, fighting his fever and pain. He dozed restlessly, awakening to Siam's quiet snore in lieu of the quickening heartbeat beneath Angel's sweet softness.

The pillow bore her scent, and Luc nuzzled it, fighting his rage and loneliness. He had never begged, his pride forged from centuries of breeding. Yet he craved the woman as he had not wanted another.

I want her softness and her fire, her outrage and tenderness. I want this strong, caring woman who will bend for the pain of others and fight for her pride.

Pale skin, heart-shaped face, reddish, tumbled hair ... kisses like a child's, passion like a woman's ...

He pushed away the hovering death song of *Tamala, tamala*. His weak body trapped his racing, lucid mind. He resented dying. Oblivion circled his family pride. His father's stark rage jabbed from the shadows, his wager won.

Luc fought Jason's rage and his own, forcing his brain to forage for gentler fare. *Tamala ... tamala ...*

He found sanctum in the soft, sweet turn of his angel's

lips. In her cool forest-green eyes, a drift of gold sparks swirled around the black irises filled with him. Sweet, tender, anxious eyes—

Angel enchants me. I resent losing my life and the woman I have captured.

Luc allowed his mind to drift, escaping the searing pain, dreaming ... He dreamed of loosening Angel's intricate buttons, of helping her with her dishabille, of the glow of her eyes as they danced—as they made love.

I would kiss her neck, seek her scents and sweet taste of her skin.

Luc shuddered, fighting away a wave of pain.

Damn. I'm not a boy to be seduced by a dream of never-ending love. Catherine has killed my dreams. She jeered at me, took her lovers into my bed, taunting me with her conquests. Love—or was it lust?—ended one way or another. I've never needed anyone for years, and now I beg for a moment with a woman who fights me. Unused to humility, Luc turned into the anger ... anything but the pain, the fever stalking him.

Luc wanted to play with his enchantress, to test her fire with his own. He shuddered, sinking into the pain, his tanned fingers grasping at the bed's sheets as he remembered the wager. His body arced against the pain. *He would win—he had found an angel.*

His mind fastened on the thought, locked it inside him, forcing his heart to beat until the next time he saw her.

"My kind heart, indeed," Arielle repeated darkly as she stripped the damp, wrinkled blouse from her and tossed it to the bed. She smoothed her camisole and thrust her arms through the merino wool vest, protection against the fierce cold. In the end, the two men had helped her slip from Luc's loose grasp, and he had protested slightly, exhausted by the cleansing and wrapping of the wound. A drop of laudanum in sweetened chamomile tea had helped him doze restlessly. "The man is a beast, grabbing at me as though he owned me. Look at my hair. It's tumbling everywhere after all my efforts to moor it in proper braids. Blast! I actually kissed him to keep him quiet. He wasn't helpless at all. He plucked me into his bed as neatly as he would a child. I have an idea that if he was not ill, the man would be most uncontrollable and arrogant. *He is very certain how to handle a woman's body.* I am positive that in his prime, he must have been a rake. I cannot abide arrogant, kissing rakes."

"Into his bed? You are quite rumpled—indeed you are glowing, my dear," Glynis said, easing her shopping basket onto a small chair. She stripped off her neat gray bonnet and cape, and placed them neatly on a wall hook to dry. She smoothed the cape's folds gently. "I hope you didn't take out your current frustrations with Mr. Smithson on that poor, wounded, dying man. The clerk at the desk tells me that the man has just a few hours to live. According to the servants, they are simply making him as comfortable as possible until he ceases. Apparently he comes from strong family ties, steeped deep in tradition and a heritage passed from father to son. One of the servants listened carefully to his delirious ramblings and reported it forthwith. He is the last heir of his immediate family, and he will die without a wife and children. The man is a blend of French and Spanish aristocracy, and those blood ties are age-old. I expect he fears he has failed—fears death before he can carry on his name."

"Outrageous. Bloodlines are not important, nor practical in this modern age."

"Arielle. Pray tell me that the bloodlines of your Percherons are not important. You fantasize about the mighty sire, the combat horse of knights in the Middle Ages. I have no doubt you dream of riding behind some avenging knight. You have said yourself that the strength and fighting will of these horses has been bred into them. Is it not possible that a man would feel honorably obliged to carry on his lineage? That the fevers burning Luc would open his lifelong dreams and wishes? The wish to create life that will carry on is eternal. To leave this world alone, without a mate to mourn your passing, would be terribly frightening, I should think."

Arielle patted her hair, nudging the willful tendrils at the nape of her neck upward. Though the fashion called for a center part with curls in front of her ears, her unruly hair re-

sisted attempts at order. A quick glance in the mirror
showed a froth of curling tendrils, which caught the light in
reddish tints. She foraged for the pins and the bow that had
come unmoored when she shared the dying man's bed. She
ripped the bow from her hair and tossed it to the bed. "He
was a rake. Just the same simpering, cooing sweet endearments that Uncle Charles used in his *tête-à-têtes*," she stated
flatly, sliding into a freshly pressed dress with Glynis's help.
She tossed a tortoisestone pin onto the bed and blew back
a curl from her eye. "Mr. Luc is quite experienced with
women, I assure you," she said in muffled tones beneath the
folds of the dress, working her way toward the top. "A gentleman would never clasp a woman so intimately."

Glynis watched with interest as Arielle's flushed face
emerged from the dress. The servant bent to adjust the
striped satin over the layers of crinolines, then straightened.
Arielle's trembling left hand adjusted the tiny buttons at the
throat, then lifted the heart locket from her neck to lie on
the starched cloth. "The man was feverish, calling me his
'Angel.' Angel, indeed. She's probably some woman he
knew quite well, from the way his hands wandered. Surely
any willing body would do. There was a woman's scent in
the bed, heavy and sickeningly sweet."

Moving to her charge's back, Glynis neatly buttoned
Arielle's dress. "The mountain man bought a woman of the
streets to warm his companion. Rather a practical idea, considering that Luc has demons at his heels and cherishes a
tender word. The image of that great hulking man holding
another man, almost as large, for warmth is another reason
for the harlot."

Arielle whirled to her, anger flashing in her green eyes.
"Are you quite certain, Glynis? Are you certain that Mr.
D'Arcy's bed held a . . . a woman of experience before he
drew me into it?"

Glynis's eyebrows rose, humor dancing in her blue eyes.
"Into his bed?"

The younger woman simmered in anger as she smoothed
the dress to her trim waist. "Stop tormenting me. He is not
a gentleman. Far too confident even in his fevers."

"My dear, he is dying. Surely you didn't resent giving him a moment of respite from his mortal wound," Glynis soothed, adjusting the large plaid bow over Arielle's full skirts and studying the effect. "In situations such as that, one must draw on the resources at hand. Mr. Siam simply considered you a resource to ease his friend—"

Arielle stared coolly at Glynis, who erupted in laughter. "If I did not know what a hothead, what an imp you can be when tried, you might frighten me. Please save that wintery look for others. Poor Sacha. How you frightened that fiesty family terrier. You terrified him until he took flight for the New West. Perhaps he is safer amid grizzlies and untamed savages."

Arielle's cool green eyes stared at Glynis for a long moment before she spoke. "If you are quite finished . . . I have decided to interview with Mr. Smithson. When I return, we can continue our plans." Then she whisked her arms into her coat sleeves, pushed her curls into a matching bonnet with a brim, and tied the bow at her jaw. She gripped her parasol and took a purposeful step toward the door.

"One more question," Glynis prodded, her eyes dancing when Arielle pivoted in a flourish of anger. "You are transporting women who want to marry men. The men want these women for purposes of dreams, love, children. Are these not the reasons that this Luc held you so closely in his arms, clinging to this world by a shred of basic instinct, a need bred into him from his first breath of life?"

Arielle's eyes widened. "Glynis, you are impertinent. He held me, placed his hand on my bosom and on my thigh. That was not love, but rather something else . . . more like a claiming," she finished, blushing. "Delirious or not, there is a tone in his voice, heavy with accent when he's desperate, and downright demanding and outrageously arrogant when he's not."

"Mmm. Perhaps the picture of love and children could introduce a bit of pure lust in a fevered man," Glynis returned dryly. "There is a process which links the two, you know."

In her haste to close the door Arielle's skirts were

trapped. When she retrieved them with a jerk, her companion laughed outright.

An hour later Arielle sat in the back of the dimly lit, smoke-filled room and watched the grizzled wagon master hold court. Mud clung to her shoes, and her crinolines and skirts were sodden with rain. Her new square-toed shoes were stretched and cold, despite the blazing stove at the front of the room. Applicants for the train approached the long table at the front of the room to be interviewed by the captain and his crony, a birdlike, ageless man. Smithson's bulk resembled carved granite, a huge man whose head seemed to sit on his massive shoulders. Dressed in a rough coat and brown trousers, Smithson was inflexible, announcing who suited his taste and casting others aside. Men with families were easily accepted, or young men heading west for their fortunes. When Smithson was likely to accept an applicant, the birdlike man spat a brown stream into a spittoon.

Arielle twitched her sodden hem away from her chilled legs. She had never really trusted men like Smithson's aide who wore their mustaches trimmed in the fashion of the day, tiny waxed upward curls. Smithson's fat gray sideburns were more to her liking.

As Arielle suspected, Smithson's actual "jumping-off" point, as the emigrants called the beginning of the Overland Trail, was Independence Landing on the Missouri River. To ensure that his quota of sixty wagons would be met, he had advertised in the newspapers for the St. Louis meeting.

Arielle toyed with the braid on her coat, thinking of the man who lay dying in his fevers. Luc D'Arcy would not be traveling to the West. He would not be delaying passage because of the impending birth of his child. She shivered, recognizing that Glynis's estimation of the man was probably correct—that he resented dying without a wife, a child to carry his name. Luc was a lonely soul, who had known little comfort in his life, and now wanted a sampling of tender care to meet his eternity.

Working near seamen and on the Browning family farms, she'd seen suffering and tended it with compassion when she could. She would do no less for D'Arcy, poor man.

Arielle clasped her gloved hands. She shared Luc's desire for children, and Thaddeus would be a perfect father. She had been far too busy dealing with business when he was near to nurture a relationship.

Luc's dark, feverish face swung into her mind, and she blushed, remembering his seeking hands. Thaddeus would never, ever explore her person without permission. A gentle man, reining his passions, Thaddeus would be a wonderful husband. Arielle's mouth tightened. Glynis would crow with delight if she once admitted that Thaddeus was her purpose for the journey.

Then, too, she rather liked the idea of matchmaking. With a new land to tame, men needed strong wives, and women needed husbands.

The wagon master shot a grim stare at four women who sat in the front row, then jerked out an order. His jaw flexed beneath the heavy sideburns, and beneath his bushy eyebrows his eyes were brilliant. "No doxies or tarts. No women who have never known the bounds of matrimony and the tethers of a good man."

The colorful plumes on the women's bonnets quivered; a thin girl held her skirts as she ran from the room into the gray rain. Another woman, her face hard with paint, rose slowly to her six-foot height, straightened her skirts, and gathered her patched cloak around her bulk with dignity. Walking proudly, she passed Arielle with her head held high, a wisp of dyed jet-black hair escaping her bonnet. A tear trail stained her white face powder, and a black jagged streak ran from her eyes to her chin.

The other two women laughed shrilly, slid knowing glances at the men gathered around, and swished from the room, arm in arm, as though on parade.

Smithson's booming voice shook the room. "By all that's holy, I will not have women aboard my train who have never married or ladies of poor virtue. Western lands need good females, strong women who will hold to a steady, righteous path." The wagon master hit the scarred table with his fist. "I will take widows and children aboard. They cannot help their lot in life. God will help them and so will I.

They will need a good marriage certificate in their hand and brothers or sons to help. If not, men can be hired for their passage price. Drunkards will not be abided. Those with first babies due soon are advised to wait until the infants are strong."

He glared meaningfully at the crowd. A baby cried, and a farmer placed his arm around his wife, gathering her closer on the bench. With a curt nod, Smithson lowered his craggy brows, stared at the crowd, and sat. "Next!"

Slowly pulling apart the tatted lace on her handkerchief, Arielle gritted her teeth, mentally circling Smithson and searching for his weaknesses. The man held to his rules rigidly, dismissing a young couple because the girl was heavily pregnant. "Next time," Smithson grumbled almost gently, "when the baby won't lay us up at the start. Put a few pounds on him. There are too many graves along the trail now."

Frustrated and damp, Arielle returned to her hotel room. Glynis tied a knot in her stitching and snipped the thread, glancing at Arielle, who punctuated her pacing with short, but effective seamen's curses. "You really shouldn't swear, Arielle. Keelhauling and skewering and slicing gizzards aren't skills your aunt would recognize as ladylike. Perhaps your temperament comes from her allowance of your dominant left hand. Really, every other child was made to write with his right hand. Yet your Aunt Louise thought you had talents that shouldn't be stifled. It was only after the Smythe incident that she saw the depth of your true rebellious tendencies."

"You've said enough about my left hand today, Glynis. You have omitted the obvious 'devil's mark' quote. Please refrain from mentioning my curse again."

Glynis ignored Arielle's hard glare and held the men's trousers she had been tailoring for Arielle up to the light, studying them. "I'm certain you'll deal with Smithson in more sensible ways. You can be quite devious when thwarted."

Arielle crushed a rolled paper in her notorious left hand. "I would appreciate your efforts on my behalf, Glynis. If you would spend your energies exploring Mr. Smithson's disgusting policies and trying to help my shipment of women to the New West, we would get on much sooner."

Glynis smothered a smile while Arielle paced the small room, striking the paper against her palm. "We've lost two women. They feared to leave the safety of their neighbors. One married a widower with five young children. To take a full cargo, I want to replace them ... and I think I know just the two women who would be interested in new lives."

She dug out her maltreated handkerchief and tossed it to the bed, ignoring Glynis's heavy frown. "When you are shopping, please stop at the Bull's Head Tavern. There is a woman there, big, raw-boned, gray hair, and wearing far too much paint. She may do as a candidate for passage."

When Arielle stopped to sip a cup of hot tea, her companion frowned. "When you're in a snit, you gulp tea."

Arielle smiled sweetly, drank heavily, and placed the cup to the tablecloth, not the waiting saucer. She plucked a tiny biscuit from a dainty plate and tossed it in the air, then caught it in her mouth with flair. Munching on it, she grinned impishly at Glynis, who shuddered with distaste. "My fine friend," Arielle said, licking a crumb from her lip, "you will be just the one to tutor any unlikely candidates for Mr. Smithson's train. You'll have three weeks of traveling to teach manners to our brides. By the time we reach the Landing, we will have a flock of perfect ladies."

Arielle debated how to bend Smithson to accepting her into the train. She studied the rain swirling down the panes, the heavy bolts of lightning shattering the gloom. The streets below the hotel were quiet, the emigrants, frontiersmen, and Indians clinging to their dry corners. Smithson was an unbending man, tossing out commands and sticking by them. As an "unbreached female," she had little chance to sway him. Glynis slept at her side in the high bed, used to Arielle's tossing and turning.

A man cried out in the night, the sound of pain skittering down the hall from Luc D'Arcy's room.

His angular face had strained against the fever, fighting the death creeping slowly toward him. She frowned as gunfire erupted in the street, quickly silenced. Luc D'Arcy's dream of wife and children would never come true. In the dark quiet of the night, she knew how much those dreams could mean, how the emptiness could stretch on while others grew warm on love.

Glynis sighed, and Arielle waited for her to awaken, to talk quietly and while away the sleepless hours. She blew away a curl tormenting her cheek and frowned at Glynis's nightcap. While Glynis's sleek black hair was easily tethered in braids and tucked beneath a lacy nightcap, Arielle's hair took to the dampness, curling wildly. With Glynis's help, Arielle was able to fashion a single fat braid. A calm woman, in charge of her fate since she had reached the spinster age, Glynis's perfection tormented Arielle. How like the servant to want to sleep when Arielle needed to talk—she lifted the tiny watch pin from the bedside table. Two o'clock in the morning and she hadn't designed a ploy to approach Mr. Smithson.

The man's cry came again, more desperate now, and loneliness welled within her, unexpected tears burning her lids. Arielle brushed her hand across her eyes impatiently. She would spend a few minutes with a dying man on the docks, despite her aunt's protests. In the morning she would check with Siam—

The muffled knock on her door did not surprise her. Glynis slept while Arielle eased from the high bed, sliding her arms into a wrapper. Siam loomed in the dimly lit hallway, his face grim beneath the shadows of his hat. "Luc asks for you. Will you come?"

She hesitated, sensing the grim determination of the mountain man and his fear. Clean shaven, Siam's dark skin was taut over his thrusting bones, his lips pressed into a tight, white line. Shadows slid through his expressive eyes. She had seen that shattering emotion in the eyes of others who loved a dying man. "Yes, of course."

Candlelight tossed shadows on the walls as Luc rambled feverishly about his sisters and his mother. He cursed a woman named Catherine, then cried out for Willow, his wife who had died in childbirth. He whispered intimately, coaxingly, forcefully, willing his young wife to fight, to push the baby from her. Then the deep, rapid burst of anger, of mortal loss, his dark fist gripping the white sheets. His pain and anguish swirled through the room, snaring Arielle. *"Tamala ... tamala ..."*

The man had fought and loved deeply, losing tragically. She briskly wiped away a tear that clung to her lashes and lifted her chin. Once long ago a fourteen-year-old girl was told her parents had died at sea. Young Arielle had Jonathan and a large family. Luc D'Arcy had no one. *"Nika Klootchman ... Talis ... Kloshe kopa nika."*

Siam translated: "Chinook. He says to his wife, 'My wife, beloved, I am satisfied ... it is enough.' Luc says he didn't need the baby, to fight for herself."

He'd wanted their baby desperately, but not at the cost of his wife's life.

He rambled through his vengeance, damning the whore-masters who had sold his sisters again and again.

He wagered with a man named Jason, determined to win.

Then the stark features softened, eased, as he discovered Willow was to have a child.

Arielle brushed away another tear, surprised at her lack of control. *Luc D'Arcy must have loved desperately.*

He calmed when Arielle sat in a chair near his bed, and whispered, "Shh. Rest—"

His hand shot out, claiming hers, linking his long dark fingers with hers. "Ah ..." His sigh was soft, sliding along her skin. "You came back. Yes, you are a caring woman, one who would come when she is needed," he whispered as though to himself. Then he spoke desperately in French, and she captured bits of words. "Lost the wager. I promised my father ... No D'Arcy name ..."

"Shh ..." Arielle smoothed his brow, carefully removing the warm cloth and handing it to Siam. The mountain man replaced it with a cool cloth as Luc's thumb began caressing the back of her hand.

He smiled whimsically, sadly. His eyes glittered fever-ishly beneath the long sweep of black lashes. "Angel, you will marry me," he commanded unevenly, through cracked lips. His eyes narrowed, pinning her.

His hand gripped her wrist, encircling it possessively with strong, dark fingers. His flat demand lashed out at her. "You little hellion! Do you think I wanted Siam to force you to hold me? I haven't wanted a woman in five years. Don't you think I'd want to fondle a willing one, or want her to hold me because she— Do you think I want to die? Madame, you aren't married, and I want you wearing my name when I die. You'll do well. You can strip it from you the moment I'm in the grave."

Fierce ice-cold gray eyes slashed at her, his lips pressing into a thin cruel line. Stunned by his sudden, raging anger, Arielle blinked, and in that heartbeat, Luc's lids closed. His fingers remained locked to her wrist.

Arielle took another cloth from Siam and patted moisture over the curved masculine line of Luc's lips. Her fingers trembled. She fought to remember that Luc was dying and that his demands were based on his fevers, his reluctance to slide away from life. "Place a cold cloth at the back of his neck. He should be shaved."

The Canadian obeyed, his big hands surprisingly adept as he placed a cloth beneath Luc's neck. "He is too restless to shave. I could cut him. This I cannot do."

The hulking mountain man frowned worriedly as Luc slid into unconsciousness. "He has had a hard life. The D'Arcys are a proud family. His father did not accept Luc's Indian wife. On his deathbed Jason D'Arcy recognized Luc's wife and unborn child, but it was too late for her to wear the family wedding ring. Now all his family is gone. The fever walks in his mind. He believes he has disgraced his father's wishes by not leaving a widow, a child behind him. He has broken a promise to his father—not a small matter."

Arielle fought the wave of sympathy; Luc had lost everyone. His poor, feverish, tormented brain scurried through the pain of the past, foraging for peace. She ached for the man, for the way he would relinquish life, foregoing the happiness he sought. She smoothed the rakish scar in his eyebrow, reminded of her grief when her parents' brigantine went down in a storm. "What does the doctor say?"

"I would not allow him to bleed Luc. Without bloodletting, the doctor says Luc will not make the night." Arielle stared at a thick white scar sliding along Siam's cheek and into his rough shirt; she sensed a deep mourning within him.

"You have made the right decision. I do not agree with doctors bleeding patients," Arielle returned, wanting to ease the doubt in the man's deepset eyes.

Luc slowly moved his face toward Arielle, his eyes closed. "Let me hold you."

"Shh. Rest." Arielle gasped when Siam scooped her from the chair and gently deposited her in bed with Luc.

"Stay," he whispered grimly, placing his hand on her throat, gently anchoring her beside Luc.

"I think not, you great buffoon." Arielle kicked out, her long nightgown hampering her thrust. Luc moaned quietly as her heel struck Siam in the groin. The mountain man inhaled sharply, staggering back slightly and holding his wounded area. Released momentarily, Arielle rolled from the bed and ran toward the closed door. "You great beast of a man. This isn't proper. You can't—"

Siam picked her up like a child and eased her back in the bed. Holding her wrists and her ankles, he glared down at her. "Perhaps I do not have the good manners to ask you. There is no 'proper' when a man dies—Luc is dying. He's asked for you, and he will have you at his side."

She breathed hard, slashing him with her eyes.

"Evil-tempered little cat," the mountain man rasped in hushed tones. "Lie still. If Luc wants you in his bed, you'll stay there!"

Fighting Siam with her eyes and muffled curses, Arielle heard Luc moan. He moved closer to her, his breathing labored. "Angel?" he rasped unevenly.

"She's here with you, Luc," the Canadian rumbled, his brows lowering fiercely. The glance he shot his friend was tender. "Lie still, you'll open the wound again."

"Angel?" The soft question hovered in the shadows as

Luc shivered, shaking the bed. His trembling hand lifted, seeking her cheek to smooth it with his thumb.

His heat burned her face, his skin fiery against hers. The rough fingertips quivered, searching her face.

A cold drop hit her throat, and Arielle glanced up at Siam. Tears filled the big man's eyes, glistening on his lashes.

"It is you, at last," Luc whispered shakily. "Angel." He cried out weakly, then fainted.

Arielle stared at the man sharing the pillow with her. Beads of sweat glistened on his forehead, catching in the lines spanning it. Pale despite his tan, his cheekbones thrust at his skin, his jaw covered with a black beard. His deepset eyes lay in shadows, his mouth trembling and gray. The Canadian's big hand moved across her to stroke Luc's rumpled black hair. "She's here, my friend. Your angel, she is here. Sleep . . ."

Siam's expressive, soul-filled eyes swung back to Arielle, demanding that she understand. "Hold Luc like a woman who loves him," he ordered quietly.

Luc's breath rattled in his throat, and he coughed violently. Terror clawed at Siam's weathered face, and Arielle closed her eyes. A dying man wanted to hold her; she could do little but give him the comfort of her body.

She thought of her brother. If he lay dying, asking for a woman to hold him—

"Angel?" Luc whispered rawly, desperately, as though he feared losing her.

"Shh," Arielle returned, slipping her hand over his hot one. "Shh . . . sleep."

"Arielle!" Glynis's soft cry came from the hallway, and the door swung open with her slight knock. Siam was on his feet, knife in hand, as Glynis pushed open the door.

"Goodness," she said tartly, slipping inside the room and closing the door. "Here you are again." She glanced at Siam, who moved uneasily near the bed, and crossed the room to stand at Arielle's side. Glynis studied Luc's features intently, then reached across Arielle to test his forehead. "Poor man," she said quietly. "Yes, it's the least you could do, Arielle. Though I would have preferred that you inform me of your endeavors. I was quite frightened."

Siam moved uneasily, shifting his great weight, and Glynis glanced sharply up at him. "You should take off your hat while inside, sir."

"Angel," Luc whispered unevenly, shivering beneath the quilt and gripping Arielle's hand painfully.

"Shh . . . I'm here, Luc. . . ." Arielle scowled up at Siam. "Although I preferred to sit in a chair."

"I see," said Glynis. "Mr. D'Arcy seems to prefer you in his arms. A little unconventional, but then, so is your left-handed thinking." The Englishwoman sniffed once and deftly scooped the knife from Siam's big hands to place it on a table. She patted her ruffled night bonnet primly and frowned at the hulking mountain man. "Really. You must ask properly next time for Arielle's presence in Mr. D'Arcy's bed. It isn't polite for a woman to be in the presence of two men alone in the middle of the night."

"Yes, madam," Siam rumbled sheepishly and hung his head.

"Very well. You were just doing what you thought best to help your friend. Next time perhaps you'll ask," Glynis said tightly, gathering her robe around her nightgown. "Although I wouldn't like this to happen again, mind you."

Siam cleared his throat and rumbled, "Yes, madam."

"This huge, misguided piece of blubber hefts me around like a bag of meal, Glynis," Arielle muttered darkly.

Her servant's expression darkened in the shadows, and Siam moved back a step. "Luc wanted her. She is a hellcat, not an angel," he finished flatly.

In the shadows Glynis's lips fought a smile. "That she is, Mr. Siam. I'm sure you acted out of need, rather than cruelty. Arielle has evil tendencies at times. However, I should not like it to happen again. Unless I'm quite mistaken, you're a man who acts from his heart, though you could temper your manners a bit."

When Siam ground his jaw and nodded, Glynis rubbed her hands. "Very well. I'm going down to the kitchen for a tea tray. I've always found tea soothing in matters like this.

When I return, we'll discuss the matter at hand logically. Arielle, please keep the gentleman quiet. He seems desperate for your attention. It's the least you can do for him, to spend a few quiet hours." With that she whisked out of the room, quietly closing the door behind her.

Siam's slow, toothy, triumphant grin shone in the candlelight as though he were a small boy who had just won a major battle. Arielle glowered up at him while she stroked Luc's hair. "Have you ever heard of the cat-o'-nine-tails or keelhauling?" she asked meticulously. She had fired captains who practiced the ungentle art and used her power to keep them from working on other ships. But Siam's victorious grin caused her notorious red-haired temper to smolder. Within minutes, the soft knock on the door announced Glynis's return.

Luc slept quietly, holding Arielle close to him. Without her corset and stays, separated from him by the light cloth of her gown, Arielle tried to ignore the tall, muscled body fitted against hers. The bed sagged toward his weight, forcing Arielle to brace stiffly against his side. Glynis placed the tea service on a table and bent over Arielle, tucking her beneath the quilt. "There now, you won't chill while we have tea. Mr. Siam, if you would sit, please. And take off your hat."

"We are not having a tea party," Arielle stated tightly, lifting her head to sip from the cup Glynis had offered.

"You lie still. Luc rests better when you hold him," Siam rumbled. The chair squeaked, protesting his weight as he sat.

Moving in the shadows, Glynis tightened her robe's sash and sat. She adjusted a starched and ironed napkin across her lap and poured tea. "There now. There are biscuits, Mr. Siam. Please make yourself comfortable. Arielle, I think we have nothing to fear from this gentleman. He is merely concerned for his friend. Unless I am quite wrong, their ties are deep, rather like brothers."

Arielle stiffened. "I am in sympathy with Mr. D'Arcy's plight, Glynis. Mr. Siam is acting to soothe his friend. But why am I included in this gambit?"

"It's quite simple," Glynis replied. "Mr. D'Arcy has taken a fancy to you. You are his unlikely candidate for an angel to ease his mortal wound. You have stayed with badly injured seamen before, eased their passing. Why is Mr. D'Arcy so different from those gentlemen?"

Arielle spaced her words carefully. "None of them forced me into their beds, nor touched me."

"Ah ... none of them were quite so desperate as Mr. D'Arcy. He is bound by his blood. He believes he is failing to achieve a standard set by his forefathers. To face death and failure of that great degree would be overwhelming, I should say. Apparently Mr. D'Arcy also blames himself for the death of his mother and sisters. He has lost a wife and a child," she whispered. "Surely you cannot deny him a feminine touch of kindness as he meets his fate."

While Arielle dealt with her sympathy for Luc's position, she was furious with Glynis's absolute calm. "In my prayers, Glynis, I wish for you to be harried, frustrated, anxious, and destroyed by doubt," she muttered.

Fumbling with the folded napkin, the six-foot, four-inch tall mountain man eased the white square across his soft buckskins. Speaking in hushed tones, Glynis asked, "I really wish you would take off your hat, but apparently you feel uncomfortable without it. Perhaps one should lay aside matters such as that now. How did Mr. D'Arcy receive his wound?"

Intent upon sliding his big finger through the cup's small handle, Siam frowned. "Fight."

"How?" Glynis persisted, adjusting her gown and robe across her legs primly.

"Glynis, will you stop chattering?" Arielle asked sharply as Luc's hand began sliding over her stomach. Beneath the quilt Siam had placed over her, Luc's fingertips traced her ribs, seeking each one despite her effort to squirm away gently. Arielle shifted slightly away, but he curled closer. "This man isn't sleeping a bit."

"As you were saying, Mr. Siam," Glynis prompted. "A brawl?"

"After cards. The gambler hit his woman for signaling wrong."

"Really? Luc's woman?"

"No. The gambler's. Luc's woman died, his baby in her belly, ten years ago. He has no woman. Many want him. But he has locked his heart. I think he would like to have this red-haired wildcat, though. The sickness has weakened him. . . . Few men would want to test her claws."

"Please be nice, Mr. Siam," Glynis soothed in her crisp, most English tone.

"She bit me," he muttered. Arielle opened her mouth, then closed it.

"Merely lessons in manners from a lady," Glynis stated. "Take heed."

Luc's big hands lay hot and callused on Arielle's stomach, spanning it easily. Next to her cheek, his breath was warm, his lips just touching her flesh. She edged away slightly on the pillow, and he followed, his hand tightening on her waist. One long leg, rough against her own, moved slightly until his toes found hers. He stroked them gently, caressing her insole with his foot. The intimate play caused Arielle to blush.

"Poor man," Glynis sympathized in the gloomy shadows of the room. "Wounded while defending a woman's honor."

"He's mauling me, Glynis," Arielle muttered, aware of her hot blush as Luc's bearded jaw pressed against her cheek. He inhaled slowly, nuzzling her ear. Arielle almost jumped free when his teeth nibbled her lobe.

"But did Luc win the fight with the gambler, Mr. Siam?" Glynis persisted, rising to help Arielle sip tea. The servant settled to pour more tea as though she were in the Browning parlor.

Arielle turned her head to protest and found Luc's eyes open. Dark in the shadows, they stared into hers. "Angel," he whispered in an uneven rasp. Trembling, his fingertips traced her face, skimming her features reverently.

Closing her lids, Arielle whispered, "Glynis, do something."

"*Chère*. Will you marry me?" Then Luc's eyes slowly closed, and he lay still, his breathing labored.

"He's been like that since he met her," Siam whispered

rawly. "Talking about marrying his angel. Leaving his name
with a woman. The D'Arcys have pride in their name, their
blood. He wants her to wear his mother's ring."

Luc began whispering unevenly. His face pressed against
Arielle's hair as though he needed her scent to survive.
"That's Cheyenne talk. Some Spanish," Siam muttered
roughly, looking away at the gray dawn poised in the window.

"Chère. Mi mujer . . . querida . . ." The words flew
against her hot and fast, his breath teasing the tendrils
around her face. Speaking in several languages, Luc's deep
voice wrapped around her, heating her though she didn't understand the words.

"Translate, please?" Glynis asked quietly. "He seems so
disturbed, so urgent."

"A man says strange things on his sickbed," Siam muttered, his hands wrapping around the small, fragile cup.
"It's best you don't know what he's saying."

"I insist," Arielle ordered curtly. "He is speaking to me,
isn't he?" She stroked his cheek, and Luc's head turned
slightly, his lips pressing against her palm. The kiss burned,
and Arielle jerked her hand away, rubbing it against the
heavy quilt.

"Sweet talk." Jerked out of Siam, the two words hovered
in the shadows. Then, clearing his throat, he glanced at
Glynis to save him. She smiled back serenely, gesturing him
to continue.

Siam scowled and drank his tea quickly. "She . . ." He
cleared his throat, then began translating: "Angel has sweet
lips, the lips of a virgin who hasn't known a man. . . . Against
him, her body is soft, her breasts full, and he longs to taste
them. . . . She would be hot inside when he gave her his
baby. . . ."

The mountain man translated as Luc continued, his deep
voice uneven and urgent. "Because he has no heirs, he
wants to marry her. He wants her to have his mother's ring.
For giving him peace now, he wants to leave her his holdings. Then—" Siam tilted his head, listening intently as Luc
spoke desperately in sweeping, hushed tones.

"He wants you to hold his head to your soft—uh . . . breast. He wants to taste—uh . . ." Siam glanced at Glynis, who looked at him curiously. He blushed above his beard. "Ah . . . he wants her to kiss him. To touch his dry lips with her tongue. She smells like flowers, like his life. Her skin is like silk, like a baby's. Yet there is blood in her, passion that he wants to taste—"

"Goodness!" Glynis exploded softly in the shadows.

"He's dreaming of his wife, of his time with her," Arielle protested flatly.

"No," Siam returned solemnly with a dark, foreboding frown. "He speaks of red hair and white skin, of green eyes . . . like a cool mountain meadow. Willow D'Arcy was a Chinook princess with dark skin. You are the angel he wants."

Luc's husky, uneven voice continued, stalking Arielle until her heart tightened, pounding rapidly. "He's wanting to marry you, madam," Siam said quietly, his black eyes suspiciously bright. "It's a small boon. . . ."

"*Chère* . . ." Luc's big hand captured her wrist, holding it tightly; his thumb caressed her skin. In a weak, uneven voice he whispered, "Marry me. Wear the D'Arcy name, if only for a time. . . . Give me peace."

Arielle frowned, looking up at Siam. "Ah . . . someone else, perhaps?"

"*You,*" Luc's deep voice demanded, his fingers tightening on her wrist.

Four
·············

Luc's eyes jerked open to the slicing daylight. *Angel should be with me, tending me.*

He hated the need that had made him beg, resented meeting a woman he wanted more than air when he was dying.

Catherine had played him like a marionette, introducing him to lust and then shredding his pride with her lovers.

Willow had been a sweet wisp of a dream, a girl, who softly touched his hardened heart, then was gone. He'd cared deeply for her ... but loved her as a woman, as the other part of his soul? Luc doubted that Willow had reached his scarred heart.

Angel stirred the ashes of his buried emotions, ignited his hungers for a woman. He'd been celibate for five years, his desire dormant until this small woman swept into his shadows.

Suddenly he wanted lovemaking desperately, wanted the celebration of life, the beauty of a woman flowing, heating in his arms.

His deep frown hurt. Angel bristled when she lay in his
arms. Luc wanted to cuddle his angel, to teach her how to
kiss. Part of him wanted to tease her, to play like a boy with
his first girl. . . . Part of him wanted everything a man
would take—

Luc's fingers curled into a fist. Another man would share
her life. Someone else would trim that dark temper, sample
her enchanting body, which she had held stiffly away from
his.

He stepped into the rage always prying, always lurking
near his thoughts. It was better than the pain that had reduced him to beg for a tidbit of her affection. Catherine's
cruel laughter knifed into him, her dismissal of his manhood
worse than stripes from a lashing. Then there was sweet
Willow, a girl he had begged to fight, to live.

He hated the fear that chilled him, his father's curse
swirling around his brain. He didn't want to die. Worse, he
didn't want to die dishonoring his father's last request. He
would not die without winning the wager.

Sunlight brushed his lids, warming his lashes, and reminded him that his heart still beat. He clung to the steady
sound, the rhythm, and promised he would not take the
D'Arcy name into death with him. *Angel would marry him.*

At eight o'clock the next morning Arielle plucked her
skirts aside from a puddle, then grimaced when she stepped
into another. She tilted her bonnet downward, avoiding the
curtain of snow sliding from the overhead roof, and
clutched her shawl closer. "Of course, the matter of marriage is out of the question. I have compassion for Luc
D'Arcy, but I cannot marry him. I will tend him when I
can."

Glynis adjusted her soft merino wool shawl over her coat,
protection against the bitter winter wind. The colors in the
paisley design fluttered vividly as though alive. "How kind
of you, Arielle," she murmured, and Arielle glanced at her
sharply to find a placid smile. Then Glynis offered quietly,
"Of course, wearing the D'Arcy name, you would be easily
accepted by Mr. Smithson. It is a simple, effective remedy."

"I'm certain there are other ways of making Mr. Smithson listen to reason—"

Arielle gasped as a woman dressed in a yellow India rubber cloak hurled into her. "Oh, please excuse me," the woman murmured in a low, soft voice, lifting her drooping pasteboard bonnet to expose a long, pale face. Steam clouded her round glass lenses, but her eyes were red and puffy as though she had been crying. "Please excuse me. I should have watched my step."

When she sniffed, huddling beneath the cloak, Glynis touched her arm. "We were just going into the restaurant. Would you care to join us for breakfast?"

The young woman sniffed, wringing her hands. "Lemon grass tea would be lovely now, perhaps with a bit of rosehips, spearmint, and eucalyptus leaf. I fear I'm taking a cold. One in my profession should never be ill, you know."

"Your profession?" Arielle asked while taking the woman's arm and steering her into the warm, cheery restaurant.

"An herbalist. I am preparing to travel overland to the Oregon land. The earth and climate are wonderful there for growing herbs. Along the way I will research the natives' remedies." She stripped off her dirty gloves and removed her steamed lenses. She held out a hand to a passing woman. "My name is Lydia Halfpenny, lately of Ohio country."

The woman stared at her, then swept on by with a worried backward glance. Arielle shared a smile with Glynis and took the narrow cold hand that Lydia had extended formally. "I am Arielle Browning, and this is Glynis Goodman." After removing their coats and bonnets, they sat near a window.

After their order was taken by a solemn woman with a florid bruise across her cheek, Lydia shivered. She looked out into the wintery street scene as she cleaned her lenses on a rumpled handkerchief. When the glasses perched on her nose, Lydia's smile wobbled. "You are kind. It is just that I am greatly distraught. I am on the adventure of my life, a dream. Now I find that single women—'unbreached, never been wedded females'—need not apply for passage with Captain Smithson."

She glanced at Arielle, whose gaze locked with Glynis's. "Is something wrong?"

"Mr. Smithson? The wagon master?" Arielle asked tightly.

"Yes. He has posted a notice in his meeting place. No single women need apply for his train. I have sold my poor dear mother's possessions to begin this new life, packed my lovely herbs and books and traveled from Ohio for this journey. At the moment I am foraging for any likely gentleman to be my husband. A marriage of convenience to suit us both. A practical idea garnered from long years of making do and foraging. Perhaps a widower who needs herbaling or who has children who need my skills. At the end of the trail we can deal with the marriage and go our separate ways if need be."

Glynis shot a glance at Arielle and murmured quietly, "How interesting. Foraging for a husband . . . a marriage of convenience. You would actually marry someone you didn't know?"

"Of course he must be appropriate and gentlemanly," Lydia returned with a sigh.

"So then," Glynis continued with a slanting glance at Arielle, who was glaring at her. "To acquire this gentleman's name and marriage papers, you would marry an unknown?"

Glynis poured tea and Lydia stopped, sipping delicately, tasting it on her tongue. She nodded. "Of course, I have always made do and foraged very well."

She sipped the tea again. "Pure undiluted green leaf tea. How lovely it would be to have a cup of beautiful chamomile, perhaps lovely red raspberry leaf," Lydia whispered wistfully. Her eyes widened when their breakfast arrived, platters of ham, bacon, and eggs with a mound of fried potatoes. "I am afraid my funds will not allow such a meal."

"Nonsense," Arielle soothed, pushing a plate closer to Lydia. "Please allow us the treat of your company. I would also like to discuss Mr. Smithson's policies with you."

"Horrid man," Lydia returned, carefully lifting away the thick slice of ham and bacon from her plate. She buttered the fragrant wedge of bread and spread apple butter upon it. "Lovely," she murmured dreamily.

Arielle frowned slightly when she noted the wrist of the woman who had returned with a fresh pot of hot water. Arielle touched it lightly. "You have been abused, I daresay. That mark was not here when you served us last. Nor the one on your cheek."

The woman's frightened eyes skittered away to the kitchen. "I have to go ... please," she whispered desperately in a lilting Irish accent and scurried back to the closed door.

"Arielle ... ?" Glynis warned softly as Arielle stared darkly at the closed door.

Lydia sipped her tea and ate ravenously while Arielle picked at her food. She glanced at Glynis. "I have never liked the practice of beating women."

"This is not your concern, my dear—" Glynis began as a woman cried out and pans clattered behind the kitchen door. Arielle firmly placed aside her napkin and stood. "Arielle ..." Glynis warned again, standing as Arielle walked toward the kitchen. "Do not—"

Arielle jerked open the door. The servant was crouching on the floor, a heavy-jowled man standing over her, his fist drawn back to strike. "Is there a problem?" Arielle asked lightly, moving toward the woman, who was shaking, her lip swollen.

"She sassed me," the man declared bullishly, the smell of whiskey heavy with the scents of fried ham and baking bread. "Told her to keep her brats away from here. Saw her slipping them food."

A boy of six peered around the corner of the door, holding the hand of a three-year-old girl. Both children were shivering, their dirty faces streaked with tears.

"Get back, you brats!" the man growled, raising his hand to strike the children. "Eating me out of profit. . . ."

Arielle swished her skirts away from the man's bulk. She bent to ease the sobbing woman to her feet. "There, there,

my dear." She faced the hulking man while drawing the
woman against her side. The children scurried to huddle behind their mother's skirts, their eyes wide with fear. "I will
pay for their food. You will not strike this woman again,"
she stated tautly.

"No woman tells me how to run my business—" The
man's giant fist drew back, and Arielle stepped in front of
the woman.

"Strike her and you will have to deal with me."

The man's piggish eyes blazed, his jowls quivering beneath his florid cheeks. "Then I will, by God," he roared
before a heavy pan smacked his head. He crumbled easily,
unconscious, and Glynis carefully placed the skillet to the
table.

She dusted her hands. "At times, Arielle, one must deal
quickly and efficiently with negative forces," she murmured
as Lydia swept into the room.

"Oh, mistress, mistress," the woman whispered in a
heavy Irish brogue. " 'Tis glad I am, but the master will be
killing me and my kin now for certain. I'm his servant, you
see. He has my papers in his pockets even now, preparing
to sell them."

"How much?" Arielle asked tightly. She bent to jerk the
folded papers from the unconscious man's pocket. She
scanned them quickly, jotted a note on another scrap, and
lifted her hem to unbutton a tiny pocket. Carefully placing
a gold coin inside the note, she stuffed the paper back into
the man's pocket. "There. Glynis, please deduct the sum
from our accounts."

"What shall we do, mistress?" the woman asked fearfully,
gathering her children closer. "I must work to pay our passage. Six more long years to finish my indenture, then I begin to pay the passage of my own sweet, dear departed
husband."

Arielle met Glynis's gaze, then patted the woman's thin
shoulder. "We are going to Oregon country. You are free to
come along. You will be a free woman either way. Your
name?"

"Mary O'Flannery. Alas ... my man died just after we

left the boat, you see. I sold our belongings to pay for poor Timmy's grave, and must pay for his papers, too."

"My name is Timmy, too," the little boy added in hushed tones. "Mam wants to go to Oregon country. She told me so."

"Shh, my lad. I have nothing to pay our passage. We cannot ask this good woman to—"

The heavy man groaned loudly, rubbing his injured head. Glynis snatched the pan and tapped him again. "We should go, Arielle."

"True. Glynis, please take Mary and the children out the back way. Lydia and I will recover our wraps and meet you in the alley." Arielle lifted her hem again and withdrew another gold coin and scribbled another note. "There. Payment for food."

She took a basket and stuffed it quickly, then handed it to Mary, who hesitated, her head down. "Mistress, I have no way to repay your kindness."

"Shh. Mary, you must go now. I fear another bump on the cook's head will permanently injure his beauty."

Within minutes Mary huddled with her children in the alley. Glynis stood in front of them, protecting them from the icy wind. When Lydia and Arielle arrived, Mary shook her head and lifted a small basket of clothing. " 'Tis all to our name, mistress."

Glynis took the basket. "Arielle, clearly this woman needs a visit to the emporium. Then . . . ?"

Arielle nodded, lifting her shawl to place around Mary's shoulders. "Yes. Lydia, are you coming?"

Lydia hesitated. "I fear I am a woodsy, used to country ways. There are those that say I am . . . unusual. Perhaps you should go on without me. I must see to my herbs. They are in a cold corner of the stable, and I fear they will be stolen. Thank you for your kindness."

Arielle took Lydia's arm and Mary's hand. "Glynis, we must act quickly. You take Mary and the children to the emporium while I help Lydia deliver her herbs to our room. We will then meet you in the emporium."

Two hours later Arielle smiled and lifted Mary's little

girl, Brianna, from her lap. "There. Lunch was very profit-
able and enjoyable with our new friends. So then, we have
an arrangement. Mary, you and your children and Lydia will
rest at the farm some distance away from the city. The kind
couple are keeping my livestock and would probably enjoy
sharing their home with you. Glynis will hire a man and a
wagon to take you there. I must stay and arrange for our
passage. Then we are off to Independence Landing, where
we'll buy our supplies for the trip and take 'The Long
Jump,' " she said, using the emigrant term for the Overland
Trail.

She slid her arm around Mary's thin shoulders. "Mary,
my purpose is to supply brides for the lonely men of the
wilderness. Lydia is considering the project. However, you
are both welcome without that purpose."

Mary gathered her children to her, smoothing their new
coats. "Mistress, there is no way I can repay your kindness.
If you will have us, we will be happy to be in your party."

"Good. Glynis will be bringing other women to the
Bordons' farm. Before we make this great journey, we must
be of one firm mind. I will not fail in this venture, nor endanger others who travel with me."

"Will there be boys and girls? And enough food?"
Timmy asked anxiously.

"Of course," Arielle returned with a grin, ruffling his
hair. "I intend to take full cargo."

Tamala . . . tamala . . . forever . . . Luc pushed away the
pain, fought it when it slashed back at him, and clung to the
thought of capturing an angel for his bride. Twice his father
had ruled Luc's life and took his bride; he would not now.
Luc concentrated on his steady heartbeat. He focused his
thoughts on strength. Once he was strong, he would capture
his angel. He drew in air, held it in his lungs, and let it
slowly flow from him. Again.

From the shadows Catherine's hard eyes gleamed, her red
mouth grimacing with venomous taunts. He shook loose the
specter pursuing him, the pride she had taken. Before he

met her in hell he would ensure that the D'Arcy name would remain a time longer—*Luc would win the wager.*

"Arielle, these ladies are willing passengers for our trip," Glynis said as the tall, raw-boned woman with dyed black hair and the young, thin woman from Smithson's audience entered Arielle's room that afternoon. "Tea?" Glynis asked, glimpsing the steaming pot and cups beneath a tea towel. "How nice."

Arielle folded away the papers she'd been studying. She rose to take the women's coats and hung them while Glynis poured tea. "Please sit," Arielle offered, aware of the wary, hard eyes watching her. "I think we're going to have a lovely trip. Glynis, I've just found that five more of our intended brides have changed their minds. The messages were delivered while you were out. Perhaps these ladies would know of other women who would want husbands?"

The large woman swallowed, clearly very tense. Then, taking a deep breath, she strode to a chair and eased into it. With a sweep of her hand, she gestured to the younger woman, huddling in the shadows, to come sit down. "Could be. But they be women like Sally and me. Name's Big Anna . . . uh . . . just Anna. I can fight like a man and drive mules or oxen. But Sally here, she's indisposed. Her man ran off and left her when he found out that there was a young'un coming. I never had a rightful husband. I want one. A good strong pilgrim or a tiny little one, makes me no never mind."

"And you," Arielle asked as the frail blond girl shivered, her eyes downcast. "What do you want, Sally?"

"I want my baby to have a father," she said quietly, wringing her hands. "I had none and I know the pain. If there's a man wanting me and my baby with marriage vows, I'll gladly have him."

"You'll have choices, Sally. There will be no forced marriages. I am prepared to see out my commitment," Arielle stated, handing Anna a cup of tea on a saucer. "There will be men waiting at the journey's end. But if you are not happy with any of them, we will wait."

Anna's rough hands shook, and the cup clattered. "I'm a mite jumpy," she stated flatly. "You sure there's men wanting the likes of an old mule like me?"

Glynis placed her hand on Anna's shoulder. "My friend, there are many men who would count themselves wealthy to have you as a wife."

Arielle studied Sally. "There is one wagon master whom I want. He is the most experienced but shows a reluctance to take women who will . . . be indisposed on the trail. I see this as a slight obstacle, one that can be overcome. But this wagon master has other reservations, and you must be willing to change . . . in appearance, and perhaps . . . give an appearance of a person other than you are. Glynis and I will help you—"

Anna leaned forward, her cheeks pale beneath the two bright spots of rouge. "I know that wagon master—Captain Smithson. You mean we've got to look like honest women."

"Yes. When we are interviewed at Independence Landing, you and the other women will give the appearance of widows. Well-mannered, gentle, obedient widows, who are genuinely seeking replacements—ah . . . other husbands. Anna, if you have friends who honestly want to make the trip with the intention of marriage, you will bring them here discreetly, one at a time, for interviewing. One loose mouth in the flock and the wagon master will catch wind of our ploy. They must be willing to learn the finer points of widowhood and wifery that Glynis and I will be teaching them. I want only those who are receptive to learning—and quickly."

She glanced at Glynis, then at the hardened older woman. "I see no reason to wait. Everything will be very quiet, Anna. We cannot endanger the safety and well-being of my charges." She smiled sweetly. "We will be on Mr. Smithson's train when he leaves on the last of this month or the first of April. Lady widows, the lot of us."

Glynis sipped her tea. "All of us, Arielle?" she asked dryly.

"Of course."

. . .

Later that afternoon Arielle sat at a crude table in the room Smithson used for hearing his applicants.

"A widow train," Smithson growled, shaking his massive head. "I support the idea of these draft horses—Percherons, was it? Farming country needs good draft horses. And taking trade goods west, using those powerful beasts to haul, makes sense. But widows . . . all widows?" he asked again, studying Arielle intently.

Dressed in "widow's weeds," a solemn black, she averted her face. Glynis's task to purchase over four hundred yards of suitable black widow material would not be easy. Then each woman needed a flannel petticoat and two cotton ones of at least seven yards apiece. Material for drawers also needed to be purchased. Arielle believed that Glynis's sometimes perverse nature delighted in listing her needs to clerks—and delighted in seeing their shocked expressions.

The captain continued. "So then, the intent of these widowed women and their children is rightful, lawful marriage in God's eyes and the eyes of man?" Arielle nodded, and the captain shook his head. "This venture is foolhardy. Women are weak and need men to protect them. You say you are sponsoring this venture, ma'am. When did your man depart this earth?"

Arielle wrung her hands and dabbed a handkerchief on her dry eyes. "Lately, Mr. Smithson. I have been so bereaved that I cannot count the days, the months, since my poor sweet husband passed away."

Smithson stroked his bushy sideburns thoughtfully. "I know of the loneliness of men in the new country. I saw a bit of it myself, Mrs. D'Arcy," he said slowly, reluctantly. "Women change the hard life, temper a man's ways a bit." Arielle swallowed, startled by the D'Arcy name she had desperately snatched under Smithson's wary eye.

"Oh, please, Mr. Smithson," Arielle pleaded, uncomfortable with the timid behavior she had affected since claiming Smithson's attention. "We would be so grateful. A widow's life is hard, and the children need fathers. Many of us want children. . . ."

She lowered her head as though blushing. "Please consider the plight of an unmarried woman, sir. She needs the protection of marriage, of a man wedded and bound to her. We have truly tried to find good husbands but could not."

Smithson considered her bent head, and Arielle hunched her shoulders while she waited for him to speak. She wanted to tell him that he was an officious, pompous ox of a man . . . that she had managed cargoes to places all over the world. Had managed *real* captains and pilots. That she had fended off business jackals and run a steady course for profits since the age of fifteen. Instead she sniffed and dabbed her battered, crumpled handkerchief to her eyes.

"Widows and children," Smithson said slowly, stroking his sideburns. "I'll want to interview each one here or at the Landing. One shrew or tart in the lot and you'll be taking another train, missus," he said finally.

"Each one a lady, sir," Arielle murmured shyly. "Each one wanting a husband. We have corresponded for many months, and I feel I know each one very well. We have formed the Society of Widows for the Purpose of Matrimonial Bliss."

" 'The Society of Widows for the Purpose of Matrimonial Bliss'?" Smithson repeated, tasting the phrase dubiously.

"I am the president and sponsoring several of the women until they remarry. When we correspond, we try to gather information on marriageable men. In that way, if an eligible bachelor does not meet one widow's requirement, perhaps he would suffice for another."

"You hunt husbands?" Smithson asked, astounded and a bit fearful as though Arielle was not carrying a full load.

"Oh, please, Mr. Smithson, do not be alarmed. Two of us have married and others will soon be taking their vows. When one lives in remote areas, perhaps on a farm, it is difficult to find marriageable partners. We help each other, and the potential groom—if he seems suitable to the introducer—must correspond to the likely widow. It is a poor world in which the widow lives, sir. Especially with the wars on the frontiers lurking nearer. But for the kindness of men like yourself, who understand the high value of marriage in this day, widows are doomed for unhappiness and dire consequences."

Smithson chewed on the idea, then slowly nodded. "Unusual, but perhaps necessary."

"Very necessary. You may not know, but there are horrid men who prey upon poor widows and turn them to a life of ruin. It is a hard lot without the protection and guidance of a good husband. My widows are honest women whose only purpose is to serve as some good man's wife, to tend his tables, and to help him in his toils. A willing partner to work at his side and share his burdens."

Smithson tapped his finger against a pewter mug.

Wilson spit into the spittoon, and the eerie sound echoed over the sound of the fire blazing in the stove.

"There will be fifty wagons in the train. No more than sixty," the wagon master said finally. "I'll want to interview your widows myself here or at Independence Landing. If you have not arrived with the women before the first week of April, I will strike your wagons from my list and fill the positions with others."

Arielle shielded her face with her bonnet and pushed a relieved sob from her smiling lips.

The wagon master continued: "Women take too many goods, missus. I'll need a reporting of each one's holdings. I've seen weeping aplenty on the plains. When the loads are lightened, women wail over each chair. The thought of three wagons of weeping women is frightening."

Arielle thought of Mary's basket of patched clothes and Big Anna's two tattered dresses and worn men's boots. "Not a one will cry for their discards, Mr. Smithson, I assure you. They'll all be looking toward marriage vows and rightful husbands."

"Then your personal interest in this matter is a husband," Smithson said slowly, eyeing her warily.

Arielle looked away shyly. "Ultimately. Though I am financially able to help other widows, I will require their future husbands to reimburse my expenses. My departed loved one was a businessman, and I learned much from him. I miss my departed, but . . ." she added with a wistful note.

Smithson patted her hand. "There, there. So then, your women—all of you—are needing traveling companions. There are no friendly pilgrims or families who would allow you to travel with them?"

"None, kind sir, that we can trust. Many do not want children. In many ways a widow is like an orphan, needing a strong hand at the helm. I have pledged myself to obtain the best and safest protection for the journey, and have chosen you, kind sir."

The birdlike man stepped from a shadowy corner and twirled his thin mustache. "Females are trouble. They'll forever be needing help. Can't tend a team of oxen, nor mules. They'll be men sniffing after them—"

"Enough, Wilson!" Smithson's fist hit the table and Arielle jumped. "They are honest, virtuous women, not doxies—" He glanced at Arielle. "Wilson is right. You'll need hired men. Good ones that won't run off when the trail gets rough or take another trail. You need men that won't"—his eyes sidled away, and his jowls settled down in his collar—"bother the women. Mind you, I'm not agreeing to your venture. I'll want to inspect each woman—er—talk with her, and then I'll want to see your wedding papers."

Arielle widened her eyes, her humble posture slipping. "Mine?"

"The other women can be discarded, but you are the mistress of the widow train—" Smithson paused, trying the words on his tongue. "I'll want your papers."

"I . . . I . . . they're in my trunk at the hotel."

"Bring them to me in the morning. I'll be leaving for the landing at noon."

At ten o'clock that night Arielle dabbed a cold cloth across Luc D'Arcy's hot forehead. Weaker than he had been in the morning, D'Arcy's coughs racked his lean body. His hand clamped hers, bringing it to his mouth. His lips were hot and dry, his breath uneven against her skin. He whispered weakly, a rapid mixture of French and Spanish and other languages.

Siam knelt at his friend's bedside, his darkly tanned face taut with emotion. "He wishes the D'Arcy name to stay on this earth after he takes his last breath. The family honor should not die with him. He says you are a strong woman who would bear the D'Arcy name well. He's wished for an angel, and now he has you."

Arielle fought the tears burning her lids, her fingers curving slightly to Luc's hot cheek. His flesh tightened across bold cheekbones, his beard damp with perspiration. While she planned her "widow train," Luc would not see the children he so desperately wanted . . . see a loving wife to bear his name.

He quieted when she stroked his cheek, his fever-bright eyes flinging open suddenly. "Marry me, angel," he whispered, then slowly closed his eyes.

Arielle brushed aside her tears. Siam's big hand weighted her shoulder. "I have never begged before in my lifetime. Not even for my own life, but now I do. If you would marry Luc, he could rest . . . die easily."

The big man's head bowed, his stark features grim. "I beg you now. Let Luc have this small boon. The doctor said he will not last the night. For some reason his fever has locked his brain on this last wish."

"No more than a few words, Arielle, and you will ease this man's passing," Glynis whispered softly. "No one, not even Thaddeus, could judge you in error." She touched the mountain man's shoulder. "Come, Mr. Siam, let Arielle make the decision that she must and soon."

Arielle pressed a damp handkerchief to Luc's hot face, studying the unconscious man, stroking his brow. While she would have Thaddeus and he would understand her compassionate deed, Luc was not expected to see sunrise. He mourned a young wife and an unborn babe. He had lost his mother and his sisters and had cared enough to avenge a woman's honor. If a measure of peace was what he sought before death, she could at least give him that. "A small thing to ask, Luc D'Arcy."

His face sought her palm, nestling there, the hard bones pressing against her soft skin. He was so vulnerable and had borne so much ... now to die without his last request answered—

"Yes," Arielle whispered gently. "I will marry you."

Five

·············

The second week of March, Luc D'Arcy turned to his side. Pain streaked through his leg, pouring upward until it hammered in his brain. The steady grating sound in the room proved to be Siam, sharpening his huge hunting knife, his thin skinning knife lying neatly beside a freshly polished hatchet.

Without his hat Siam's forehead was flat and high. Shaped by his mother when he was a child, it was the Chinook mark of distinction.

Siam grimly stroked the knife back and forth along the stone while rain battered the windows. Luc closed his eyes against another wave of pain, then opened them to the small vial of laudanum perched on his bedside table. He swallowed, aware of his naked, aching body beneath the rough sheets. The room's cold dampness weighted his blankets like a death shroud.

Death could not have him yet. Dim memories of a wager won swirled around him. Of deep pleasure easing away deeper torment. He tried to move, to push his body upright, but it would not obey.

73

The sound of the rain against the window and the blade rhythmically sliding along the stone continued while Luc rested. The scent of soup and medicine clung to the room, mingling with soap and musty, damp air. He longed for a warm, sunlit mountain meadow. . . . He dozed, aware of a dim light penetrating the heavy velvet curtains. In the street below a child cried out, a woman offered fresh bread, and a sea bell clanged two times.

Horses whinnied and mules brayed, a mother called to her child, tinkers hawked their wares, and the sound of ships' bells stirred the musty air of his small prison. Beyond his room, life called, and Luc listened, comforted by the sound of his steady heartbeat beneath his palm. The D'Arcy name was intact; he had cheated death.

Siam snorted softly now, his stockinged feet propped upon Luc's bed. Luc eased his hand to the mountain man's toes and pinched them weakly. Siam leaped to his feet, his knife in hand, his eyes still dazed with sleep, though his body crouched for a fight. He scanned the room, stepped back into the shadows, and was silent. The next moment he moved toward Luc's bed. "Luc?"

Pain speared through Luc's head, the wound in his thigh burning, itching. When the sudden attack eased, he noted with some satisfaction that the fevers no longer burned his veins and dampened his skin. He lifted his head slightly and was instantly sick to his stomach.

His friend hesitated, and Luc smiled grimly. "Now."

Siam eased his hands beneath Luc's arms, raising him slowly, gently to his feet. Luc breathed sharply, his bones seeming soft within his sagging flesh.

When he returned to the bed, Luc dozed, awakening to Siam's gentle touch. "Eat. Barley and mutton broth."

For the next day Luc slept and awakened to Siam's ministrations. "You have lost almost two weeks, Luc," the woodsman offered, spooning a barley and meat broth to Luc's lips.

"Was there a woman?" Luc asked, longing for the sweet scent of the woman who had shared his bed, held his hand,

and whispered encouragements—what was that she had said? *"My dear . . . my poor dear man."*

He scowled at the daylight passing through the window. He hadn't asked for her pity.

Siam smiled wryly. "She bears the D'Arcy name, though she believes she is a widow."

"Then it was true. . . ." Luc curved his fingers into a fist. He'd been weak, begging her to marry him in the face of death.

Begging her. Luc frowned, his pride nettled.

"You wanted more, Luc. But Mrs. Arielle D'Arcy was shy," Siam teased with a broad grin. "You thought to leave a D'Arcy *bébé* in her belly. You were unable to complete your quest."

"I don't need to relive my weaknesses, Siam." Luc pushed away the sleep that began weighing his lids. It was a good sleep, one of his body mending itself, and he slid into it easily.

When he awoke he glanced at the marriage certificate that Siam had requested. Luc traced the large impatient characters with their odd slant. A woman bore his name, and he longed to see her. Anger throbbed through him. *What woman would leave her husband?*

He realized that his anger was unfounded; she had married him because of kindness. Few women would have been as compassionate. Yet the anger remained, driving him as much as LaFleur's presence in life.

He had begged the woman, cried out for her. His pride had bent before death, and Luc resented the fierce, driving need. Yet the woman's absence annoyed him. A woman of conscience would have stayed to see him in his grave.

In the next two days Luc slept and ate, growing stronger. Siam unraveled the threads leading to the departure of Mrs. Arielle D'Arcy and Glynis Goodman. Arielle Browning D'Arcy had personally driven the heavy draft horses from New York. Five seasoned men defended her along the way, then returned to New York. Luc's angel commanded a new breed of draft horse, the Percheron imported from France. A

woman of means, Arielle planned to purchase trade goods
and Conestoga wagons before taking "The Long Jump."
Bound for Oregon country, they were expected to join a
wagon master at Independence Landing on the Missouri
River. They took with them a number of the town's accom-
modating ladies and over four hundred yards of black widow's cloth and enough bolts of petticoat and drawers
material to break a mule's back.

LaFleur, the slaver who had sold Yvonne and Colette,
lived near the waterfront. Siam had traced the thin, well-
dressed man to the shanty behind a warehouse. LaFleur
shared the hovel with his woman but had other prostitutes
from whom he collected on regular rounds.

For a week Luc pushed his growing strength. Two people
lodged in his thoughts, driving him—LaFleur and the
woman who bore the D'Arcy name. Luc resented her loss,
imagining the hushed scene when she informed Siam that
she must leave. There was a tear trembling on her lashes
and concern in her eyes, the woodsman had declared. Luc
spent long hours staring into the night, picturing a vision of
pale skin and soft green eyes. He remembered the silky russet curls scented of flowers and brushing his cheek. A compassionate woman, she had kissed him, and the sweet caress
lingered on his lips.

Luc resented the startling sensual tightening of his body,
the lack of control in his weakness. He'd wanted her desperately. *He had begged her.*

Luc crushed a tatted lace handkerchief in his fist. He
drew the scrap to his face, breathing the delicate scent
mixed with his. "She should have seen me in my grave," he
murmured darkly, rubbing the ache in his thigh and hunger-
ing for the woman who had become lodged in his mind.
The soft brush of her body near his tormented him.

"She is a strong woman, my friend, set on her course.
Travelers cannot wait to take the trail, or they will be lost
to winter. You cannot ask more than what she has given."
Siam scanned Luc's set expression. "Luc, be reasonable.
The woman married you to give you peace."

"I know." Luc turned his face into the pillow. "When I

am finished with LaFleur, I will find her. I want my mother's ring and to tell Mrs. D'Arcy that she is losing a husband as soon as legally correct. Don't worry, Siam. I will be a perfect gentleman. In fact, since we are going to the Willamette, too, maybe she would like our protection."

Siam chuckled softly. "She is difficult, but a good woman. Good women are trouble."

"She was my angel," Luc corrected with a wry grin. "I would like more of that stew, Siam, unless you are hoarding it to fatten your soft bones."

"Waugh—" Siam started, then roared outright. "So you are the hunter now, eh? We travel homeward to the Oregon country, and along the way Luc plucks himself a little red hen, eh? Take care, my friend. The plucking will not be easy."

Luc narrowed his eyes, staring at the candle beside his bed. "I don't relish the idea of facing a woman who heard me beg like a baby."

Arielle D'Arcy annoyed him. He didn't want dreams of her soft green eyes bending over him, nor the hunger stalking his weak body. He wanted to sever any reminder that he had begged for kindness. But first, he would thank her and do what he could to make her journey easier.

"Ah! The Dark Avenger who never smiles must not fall before a woman's soft touch, n'est-ce pas?" Siam teased, dismissing Luc's threatening scowl.

The next day LaFleur's eyes bulged with terror. He wiped his runny nose with the back of his sleeve. "You're him. The killer with silver eyes. Dark Avenger, they call you. Oh, mister, they say you don't have a heart, but please—"

"Oh, I have a heart. I hear you're good with a knife." Luc fought the urge to quickly kill this last man on his deadly trail. "I'm waiting."

LaFleur inhaled, some of his confidence returning. "Aye."

Ten minutes later an elderly woman covered LaFleur's face with a handkerchief. Filled with noise, the warehouse echoed LaFleur's last cry as his blood oozed into the hard dirt floor. "Naughty man. I saw him throw that knife at you. You were quicker."

She wrapped a shawl closely around her stooped shoulders, her hard eyes investigating him curiously. "Westerner?"

When Luc nodded, she stepped closer, peering up into his face. "You be going to Oregon country?"

"Yes." Luc placed coins in her hand. His leg throbbed, fiery with pain. Nausea slid up his throat, his muscles quivering. "See to him, will you?"

Her bony hand touched his arm when he turned away. "A minute of your time, kind sir. I'm only twenty-nine, dying of a disease LaFleur caused. I gave my little boy away to emigrants headed West. Simon was only three, and I wanted him to live better than what I could give him. He'd be five now and I'll have nothing to give him when I die . . . save one thing, his little kitten."

She smiled briefly and a shadow of her former beauty crossed her worn face. "Little Simon loved his kitten. How he cried when the emigrants couldn't take them—they had so many mouths already and to take my boy as their son was more than I could ask. Sir . . . would you take my son's little kitten to him and tell him that it's from . . . a woman who loved him very much? Just try, that's all I ask. . . . The doctor says I have two months at the most."

Luc wiped his knife clean and slid it into the sheath at his waist. His sisters had needed help, and he prayed that along the way a kind hand had helped them. It was a small thing to do for a woman facing death. He nodded and gave the woman more money, which she tucked in her pocket. "Here, kitty," she called, and a massive gray tomcat sauntered into the warehouse, tail high and winding around her legs.

The scarred tom's yellow eyes stared at Luc curiously, while one chewed ear drooped flat. A malodor spread over the dank air.

"Fart," the woman explained, beaming lovingly at the cat. She bent slowly, painfully, hefting the fat tom into her arms. Cradled to the woman's flat bosom, the tom hissed at Luc.

She kissed the tom's scarred head. "There now, Lorenzo. This kind man is taking you to Simon."

The tom hissed again, laying his scarred ears close to his head. When the woman tenderly gave him to Luc, the cat began clawing wildly.

On the first week of April, Arielle lined up the women near the three new Conestoga wagons. She, Glynis, and fifteen women and five children had been quietly living in a rented, poorly chinked cabin beyond Independence. Mr. Smithson held his meetings in the back room of the store, and Arielle intended to march her charges straight into his presence.

She smiled up at Big Anna, whose beautiful, shining gray hair lay in neat braids over her head. Sally, always near Anna, carefully draped a thick crocheted shawl over her loose coat. America Potts, an Italian woman with a small son named Gino and a dog, nervously arranged her dark skirts. Lydia Halfpenny peered through her lenses and smiled tightly beneath her black window's bonnet. Mary O'Flannery's neatly dressed children huddled, big-eyed, near her black skirts. Marie Dexler, a rotund, jolly woman of German descent, smiled widely. Nancy Fairhair, a thin blonde with wide, innocent blue eyes that belied her years serving men in the streets, straightened her shoulders. Eliza Smythe lifted her chin, angling it to conceal the tiny brand that ran along her throat. She tugged up the high collar of her dress.

Three other women firmly stepped into the line, their expressions wary and determined.

Harriet Longman, lately of a brothel from St. Louis, primly folded her hands in front of her. She straightened her shoulders and met Arielle's eyes with a steady gaze. Harriet had worked to shed her shame and walk with pride.

Biddy Lomax, an unsmiling, proud woman of African descent, had fainted when Glynis ordered the blacksmith to remove her slave bracelet. Biddy took with her a ten-year-old girl and a two-year-old boy, children of different white fathers. The girl, Liberty, her hair neatly braided beneath a bonnet, clung to her mother's dark hand as did the boy, Lion. Until Arielle purchased her papers, Biddy was owned by unkind New England travelers who planned to sell her children away. Though the children usually stayed with the mother, the tight-fisted, bloodless couple found Lion's poor health troublesome and had decided to sell him.

Arielle touched Biddy's smooth dark cheek. "There now, Biddy. You are a freewoman and so are your children. For the sake of the others and Mr. Smithson's sharp eye, perhaps you could shield a bit of the lioness that waits within you," she suggested softly. "You are off to a new land, where your children will be safe."

Biddy's expression softened. Her lips moved slightly, then again in a smile that grew stronger. "Yes, that is true, mistress."

Arielle returned the smile. "Freedom, Biddy. A whole land of freedom for you and your children. There you will have a husband that pleases you. He must please you or you need not marry," she added softly.

She stepped near Lelia Shelby, whose fear shimmered in her honey-colored eyes. "Lelia. Head up. Mr. Smithson doesn't know anything of our past, except that we were all married once . . . isn't that true?" she asked softly and waited for Lelia to repeat the thought that had been schooled into each woman. Lelia's father had sold her at twelve to pay for a coat for his new wife. Working hard during the day by plowing fields, Lelia was only seventeen and had buried three babies by three different men who had forced themselves upon her.

Desperate for a new life, the women set upon a course to change their lives or die by trying. While Arielle shopped for goods each day in town and returned exhausted every evening, Glynis spent hours tutoring the women, who sewed their widows' dresses. Each evening Arielle was met with women grimly determined to work into the night to become "ladies" and "proper widows."

Each woman sewed her own camisoles, petticoats, and drawers. At her height of usefulness, Lydia happily brewed, infused, and crushed herbs, blending them in cream and honey for skin masks, shampoos, and steamy water for cleansing. While she longed for fresh nettle, marshmallow, and dandelions, Lydia's patients looked forward to her ministrations and teas each night. The result of her efforts produced well-scrubbed, fresh-eyed widows cleansed of the effects of smoky taverns and poor diets.

Glynis worked quietly, firmly, teaching proper table manners, speech, and movement. Anna moaned, frustrated over the required dainty behavior and maneuvering voluminous petticoats, while Sally soothed her. Locked in a kindred spirit, a singular goal, the women encouraged each other.

Arielle's Percheron stallion and his mares shared the fenced pasture with five cows. The cows were chosen by Smithson's standards—four- to six-year-old ages and raised on Ohio grass—then two goats, and ten sheep. Each day for the past week Arielle would climb on a fence to reach Zeus's powerful back. The stallion's huge hooves pranced as he and a mare would easily draw the wagon into town. Recognizing a determined and wealthy woman, the town awaited her arrival each morning.

This morning Arielle demanded one last "promenade" to check the ladies' walk and management of skirts. Glynis inspected each woman, from the ties of her bonnet to her shoes. At Arielle's firm nod, the women lifted their skirts and stepped into the covered wagon, and Anna drove them to town. The narrow streets were packed, and Arielle decided to leave her wagon in the blacksmith's care with orders to check Zeus's massive iron shoes. Paid well for an order of extra shoes for each horse, the brawny man had immediately discovered Arielle's experience with draft stock. He didn't question her specific requests.

In the bustling city emigrants of all nationalities, many of African descent, mixed with Kansaw Indians who had crossed from Indian Territory. Mountain men, dressed in leather fringes and wearing caps of fur and eagle feathers, cradled their long muskets in crossed arms as they would a baby. Traders and bullwhackers from the Santa Fe Trail, which led into Independence, melded with river men and soldiers. Mules, horses, and oxen waited to be shod near a dozen blacksmiths' shops. The endless clang of hammer striking anvil rang out as a man hawked sausages from bison meat and fresh-baked bread. Children's faces peered from a wagon as a small train stopped in the street. Freight from Missouri riverboats was stacked against buildings. Dressed deer and pheasants hung in an open shop with beef, pig, and sheep carcasses.

Despite the excitement of the Overland Trail, tension raced around every street. Possible war with Mexico caused fear to lurk in every heart, the annexation of Texas just the year before, and President James Polk had won his election by advocating a policy of "Manifest Destiny." The Oregon Question, a boundary dispute between Britain and the United States, created cries of "Fifty-Four Forty or Fight." Though Britain was expected to concede the Oregon land, United States citizens threatened war if the boundary was not changed to fifty-four forty degrees latitude. California settlers wanted annexation because of suspected British intrigues.

Volunteers to fight for Texas came in small travel-worn groups. Cries of "Remember the Alamo" mixed with "Fifty-Four Forty or Fight." Painted with slogans, wagons rumbled through the muddy streets.

Smithson, noted for his caution, wanted his train on its way before the simmering pot of war boiled over to his emigrants. The wagon master had seen late-starting emigrants delay for warmer weather, drink away their savings, and look at lands already overgrazed along the trail.

Emigrants camped in tents near their Conestoga wagons; the wealthier rented rooms in the city.

The streets were muddy as the line of "widows" and children headed toward Smithson's interviews in the back room of an emporium. Stepping on the board porches in front of the buildings, they walked in a single line. Each woman carefully held her skirts against the revealing tug of the sweeping winds and tilted her bonnet against prying eyes. While the children swung sly, curious glances at a "stump speaker" demanding war with Mexico and Britain, their mothers kept their eyes firmly averted and clutched their shawls around them.

"The widow train is here," a man called out in a heavy French accent.

"Widow train ... widow train ..." the hushed words scurried along the boardwalks in front of the buildings and crowds gathered beneath the porches protecting them from the light rain.

Windows and doors jerked open and people gathered to view the women who picked their way, in an obedient single file across the street to the crowded emporium and Mr. Smithson's grim, battering interviews. Each woman produced proof of her marriage—a battered family Bible, a crumpled, blurred marriage certificate—and each wore a single gold band. Arielle's thick ornately embellished band was of Spanish design, weighting her slender hand. The design was well-worn, and she rubbed it often as Smithson battered away at the quiet, determined women, all very polite.

Arielle closed her eyes while Smithson attacked Anna, slashing, pushing, asking details of her husband, which Anna relayed with calm pride. Arielle pushed away the smile lurking around her mouth. Anna enjoyed drawing the fine picture of her farmer-husband, her ideal marriage, as had each woman, memorizing the details until they became part of her. Purchased from a tinker, Anna's worn ring was evidence of her twenty-year marriage.

Smithson slashed away at Lydia, Sally, Nancy, America, Marie, Eliza, Harriet, and Lelia.

When Biddy began to tremble at Arielle's side, she took her hand and found the woman clinging to it. "You'll be fine, Biddy. We are not leaving without you. Head up. You are a freewoman, and you are taking your children to safety and freedom," she whispered firmly. "Head up, now."

Smithson quietly interviewed Biddy without the prodding he had used on the other women. His questions to Biddy were direct after demanding to see her "freedom papers." "Are you traveling overland to participate in slavery of any kind?" When Biddy's eyes lashed at him, her face grim,

Smithson said roughly, "I will not hold with those transporting or selling slaves. How stand you with the other women? A servant, a maid?" he pushed.

Biddy's head went back, the satinette ribbons on her bonnet shimmering in the dull light. "I am my own mistress, sir. I want a husband, a good man to raise my babies. Mrs. D'Arcy will not hold for less."

"You have faith that Mrs. D'Arcy is a woman of her word?" Smithson probed.

"Yes. I would trust my children's lives to her. I *am* trusting her with their lives."

Smithson's massive head jerked down in a curt nod. "Done."

Then Mary and her children, who stood at her side, answered questions. The children huddled nearer her when Smithson began in earnest to tear apart her reason for taking the trail's hardships. Though she gave no other evidence of fear, Mary's face paled, and Glynis stepped forward. She placed her hand on Mary's shoulder. "I pray the hardships this woman has endured after her husband passed away will not continue, sir," Glynis said quietly, firmly.

Smithson's eyes jerked up to hers, and he blinked as though remembering something. A flush rose from his starched collar upward to tint his tanned cheeks. "Aye," he snapped, as though angry with himself, then added softly, "Missus, you are finished," and slipped a coin into Timmy's small hand and another into Brianna's.

When the small girl smiled shyly and curtsied prettily, Smithson's expression softened.

Glynis took the chair Mary vacated and folded her hands in her lap. "Well?" she asked Smithson. Arielle noted that tight note of displeasure before Glynis's temper struck. Arielle prayed Glynis would not whittle at Smithson and the "widows' " chance for a safe journey. "Begin," Glynis commanded regally, her eyes flashing.

"Vinegar," Smithson bit out. "You'll need plenty of it on the trail. The widows will need a woman with a stiff back who is willing to step forward when need be." Then he checked off her name briskly. "Mrs. Goodman, take care

who you decide to bite. It will not be me," he said in a low
tone resembling a growl.

He beckoned to Arielle, and she hurried to the front of
the room, easing her skirts aside the long fringed legs of a
westerner seated in a chair. Another big westerner with
broad shoulders filled the chair next to him.

When Arielle approached Smithson, Glynis stood by her
side. "The women and children are allowed, all proper widows. But your hired hands ... three wagons—three strong
men. Where are they?"

Arielle swallowed. She had worked, exhausting the
women and herself to portray Mr. Smithson's picture of
widows. Along the way she had forgotten the captain's demand that men accompany the widows. She bit her lip and
glanced at Glynis, whose mouth was pressed tight. Arielle
fought against her habit of clasping her hands together behind her back when faced with indecision. "I ... ah ...
perhaps ..."

"Out with it, Mrs. D'Arcy. I don't have all day,"
Smithson boomed, then glanced warily at Glynis, who had
raised her chin and met his eyes evenly from her six-foot
height. The wagon master cleared his throat and softened
his tone. "A widow train is not to my liking. You'll need
stalwart men, trusted men to see you through."

"That would be us," a deep male voice stated. The tall
westerners stood slowly, allowing the crowd to move aside
as they walked toward Smithson's table. Leaner than his
companion, one man limped slightly, his sleek black hair
tied at the base of his neck with a leather thong. His features were more honed than the other man, the dark skin
tight across jutting high cheekbones and his jaw angled
down to a square chin. Beneath his hat the Canadian's face
bore traces of his Indian blood, wide brows and straight
lashes, but the leaner man's eyes were the color of cold
steel. They seemed flat, devoid of emotion, framed by
glossy jet lashes, his brow line angling upward at the ends.
The lift of his head was arrogant, the curved line of his lips
tightening as he met Arielle's wide eyes.

It was a mouth she had seen before ... that daring little

scar on his bottom lip . . . A mouth that had kissed her pas-
sionately. There was no mistaking the medallion that had
warmed Luc D'Arcy's chest and now rested on the western-
er's shirt.

Wilson twirled his curled, waxed mustache tips and spat
into a earthenware pot on the sawdust-covered floor.

Glynis inhaled sharply, and Arielle felt the blood run
from her cheeks.

Towering above Arielle on either side in the smoke-filled
room, Luc D'Arcy and Siam stood in their fringed western
clothing. Each man held a black, broad-brimmed slouch hat
in one hand, a long rifle in the other. The Hawkens' long
barrels were covered by a leather-fringed sleeve. Smithson's
gaze slid over the men's belts, noting the walnut butts of
Colt revolvers and the thick antler handles of hunting
knives.

While Smithson slowly examined each man, Wilson spit
into the pot again. Smithson glanced at Arielle, who was
staring up at Luc's shaved face. "Your men?"

Arielle fought the flush creeping up her cheeks. She had
lain in this man's bed, snared in his arms. He had spoken to
her as no other man had, his hands had touched her. . . .
Standing upright, he towered over her . . . she barely
reached his shoulder. *A shoulder that was dark and gleam-*
ing smooth, that flowed into a wide chest covered by a
wedge of hair. She closed her eyes, willing away the image
of his flat nipple peaking through those black curling
whorls. When she opened her lids, Luc stood at her side,
leaning on his rifle.

When she had seen him last, he was slipping into death—
now a muscle slid beneath his dark skin and beneath the
lush raven lashes, his eyes glittered down at her. There was
anger there and a gleam of something that caused a tiny
chill to run up her nape. Arielle shivered, wrapping her
gloved hand around the hand that bore Luc's broad gold
ring. *Luc D'Arcy lived! His signature scrawled across their*
marriage papers with hers!

"Mrs. D'Arcy?" Luc prompted in a slow, softly dangerous voice, as though testing her wedded name on his lips.

The heated rapid mixture of languages, whispered desperately in his fever, swept through her brain. *Angel ... my angel ...*

She forced her head to turn, to nod in Smithson's direction. "Yes." The thin wisp of her voice startled her. With a word the woodsmen could end her plan to take the widows westward, and she would have a difficult time finding another wagon master with Smithson's skills. "Yes, they have been hired. Ah, Mr. Siam and ah ... Mr. ...."

Luc's fringed arm swept past her, the quick movement startling her as he took Smithson's hand. "Navaronne. Luc Navaronne."

Arielle stared at the clasped hands. Luc's hand was flecked with hair, broad, with strong fingers. Four deep scratches striped the dark skin. *Her breast had rested in the cup of his palm.*

"Mexican ..." Wilson muttered in the shadows, and Luc's eyes pinned him. The man swallowed, his rotted teeth showing as his lips pushed back. "Spanish name? You come up on the Santa Fe Trail?"

Luc moved swiftly, his feet noiseless on the sawdust-covered boards. When he towered over Wilson, he smiled coldly, and Arielle shivered again. "It is an honorable name. If there is a question of my loyalty and honor, sir, perhaps we could settle the matter now."

Wilson's thin face paled, his eyes widening. "Trouble with Mexicans. They want war," he muttered in explanation, his eyes snaking away toward Smithson.

"Where do you stand in the Mexican politics, Mr. Navaronne?" the wagon master asked slowly.

Luc's dark head lifted, his eyes cold. "With the United States. I will see Mrs. D'Arcy and her ladies to Oregon country. If war comes, I'll stand with my country."

"Do you trust them absolutely, Mrs. D'Arcy?" Smithson prodded, and when she nodded, shielding her face with her bonnet, he spoke to the men, "These women are widows. There will be trouble, and my men can't be caring for them when you quit. I'll want a fifty-dollar bond from each of you and another man. You'll get the money back when the women no longer need you. Done?"

Luc's hand reached past her, and coins dropped to the papers on Smithson's table. "The third man has not yet arrived. He will shortly. We'll bring him to you," Luc stated.

Arielle's heart raced and she clasped her trembling, gloved hands together tightly. She cleared her throat. Desperately hoping there would be a man who would want the post, she said, "He's a bit late, but a good man."

Somewhere she had to find another man. In a town desperately needing hired men to travel to Oregon country, she had to find one that could be trusted. She'd fought Aunt Louise for a season, worked herself into exhaustion, readying the company for her younger brother. Then she'd left New York, traveled with her dear horses through summer heat and raging winter to this point.

With wagons ready, prospective brides ready for passage, and Thaddeus just a few months from her, she couldn't allow the lack of one man to stop her. Nor the abrupt appearance of a husband she thought dead. She warily skimmed Luc's tall body from the corner of her eye.

As tall as Thaddeus, Luc's clothing hung on him, giving the indication that he had once been heavier. The width of his shoulders blocked out the room.

Of fair coloring, Thaddeus's slender hands did not have the strength of the long, dark fingers loosely holding the long rifle in its fringed leather sleeve. Arielle inhaled sharply, the air hurting her lungs as she remembered those dark hands touching her intimately—

Luc D'Arcy had spoken to her in several languages, translated by Siam. In every language he desired to make a child with her to carry on his family name. . . .

Arielle closed her eyes and willed him to go away like dandelion fluff on the wind. When she opened them, it was to a long length of fringed leather planted firmly at her side, a soft worn boot encroaching the shadows of her skirt. She eased slightly away from the infringement and from the scents of woodsmoke, leather, and animals, mixed with Luc's unique scent.

She remembered that male scent when she shared Luc's pillow, his hand claiming her breast.

He shot her a dark, smoky look, his light eyes shocking against his dark, devastating features.

A frightening cold draft quivered along her body. Luc D'Arcy had lived in hell, and now standing beside her, he seemed stripped of passion, of tenderness . . . a cold shell of a man.

Smithson's narrow gaze skimmed the westerners, locking on their dark faces. "I'd give my best team of oxen for more seasoned westerners. You don't see them having accidents with firearms like farmers." Then to Arielle, "If your third man is acceptable to these men, I have no problem with him. Wilson, give Mrs. D'Arcy the required list of goods and foodstuffs."

Wilson handed an envelope to her, glancing warily up at Luc.

Smithson checked off her name on the long list, made a notation, and placed the gold coins in a small locked chest. "Luc, we leave on the morning of the thirteenth. You will see that the wagons are properly loaded and the women prepared for the trip."

Arielle disliked being dismissed. She smiled tightly. "Mr. Smithson, of course I'll have everything at the ready."

"Mmm. Luc, women have a tendency to bring along gewgaws—furniture, pretties—freight that will have to be shed before South Pass," the wagon master continued, ignoring Arielle. "Make certain what they take—"

"Mr. Smithson," she persisted crisply. "The widows are in *my* caretaking. If you have instructions . . ." Too late she saw the wagon master's shrewd eyes narrow. He wanted easily managed women, and challenging him now could mean disaster. "Ah . . . yes. That will be fine," she ended softly, furious with herself for allowing the reins to be easily taken from her.

Luc's hard lips curved slightly, and Arielle inhaled. He mocked her ability to manage her widow cargo! Beneath her skirts, her heel found his soft leather boot. She found his toe and crushed it with all her weight. She wasn't in the mood to be taunted, nor intimidated.

Instantly Luc's face stilled, though outwardly his expression did not change. Something deep in his light eyes flared. "You have my word *and* Mrs. D'Arcy's." Spoken in his soft, slightly accented voice, the name ricocheted loudly around Arielle. "The ladies will be ready."

Smithson glared over her head to the commotion on the boardwalk.

Zeus whinnied and Arielle closed her eyes. "That would be my stallion. He doesn't like to be separated from me too long. I'm afraid he's probably uprooted the post he was tethered to and merely followed my scent. He has a habit of doing that."

"Great Jehoshaphat!" Smithson exclaimed darkly, staring out the window to Zeus, who stared back. "That is a horse?" He rounded on Arielle.

"He misses me if I'm kept too long," Arielle returned primly.

Smithson's jowls sank into his collar as he studied the small determined woman before him. He shook his head. "You and your men help the women across the river at dawn on Monday, then help with the rest of the wagons and stock," Smithson ordered, and Luc nodded. "I'll want to—" The wagon master shot Arielle a wary look, then spoke to Luc. "I need to speak with you in private tomorrow morning. There is a necessity of rules for women traveling alone. We will need to establish them apart from the women's interference."

Luc nodded again, and Arielle shot him a scowl she shielded from Smithson's sharp eyes.

Six
....

"Next!" Wilson yelled, stepping aside warily as Siam passed.

Arielle resisted Glynis's light touch, urging her from Smithson's presence. In her lifetime Arielle had planted herself firmly in front of any barricade to her success. When it was her desire, she managed to nick away at opposition and eventually succeed. In a few minutes the helm of her undertaking had been swept away from her by a towering, silver-eyed giant. She skimmed a glance upward to Luc's face. She didn't trust the amused gleam in his eyes. He nodded as if accepting her challenge. With a sweeping gesture of his hat toward the door, he indicated she leave the battlefield.

Arielle crushed the list of goods in her fist. She glanced at Smithson's intent frown, Siam's impassive face, and Glynis's amused but smothered smile. Brianna coughed and curled against Mary. The sound stopped Arielle from battling for possession of her train. Lifting her chin, she slid between Siam and Luc and hurried out into the street. The ladies filed out after her, and Arielle faced them, pasting a

91

cheery smile on her lips. "There now. We're ready for our adventure. Tomorrow we will bring two wagons into town and begin buying more goods."

She glanced at Luc, who leaned against the building, his firearm cradled in one arm. In the other hand he held the handle of a wooden cage containing a huge gray cat. The cat squalled, hissing and lashing out his claws between the cage's sticks, striking at the fringes on Luc's leggings. Siam stood, legs spread, face impassive at Luc's side. She looked back at Luc, found him studying her intently, and fought the flush that threatened to rise from her collar to her cheeks.

In her experience it was best to have matters out in the open. "Mr. . . . Navaronne . . . may I have a word with you?" she asked, directing Glynis to take the women back to the barn, safeguarding their health in the drizzling rain.

He nodded and Siam slid noiselessly from his side, taking the cat's cage and following the women. Timmy, open-mouthed and eyes wide, stared up at him and almost stumbled into the mud. Siam scooped the boy up without missing his stride and plopped him on Zeus's back. He nodded to the other children, who solemnly took their turn at being placed on the massive horse's back. Biddy's girl, Liberty, shied away from the tall man, who stood looking down at her. "Are you afraid?" he asked gently, smoothing Zeus's muzzle.

Liberty nodded shyly while she chewed on her braid.

"Sometimes I am, too." Taking great care to move slowly, Siam lifted her to the horse and handed her the cat, who was purring loudly, rubbing his shoulder against the cage. The westerner slipped Lion and the other children a lump of sugar candy. The anxious mothers hovered nearby, glancing at Arielle, then at Glynis. Fear leapt in Anna's world-wise eyes.

"Off we go," Glynis announced cheerfully. She lifted her skirts sedately to step across a puddle. The women followed her, sliding cautious glances back at the big man leading the huge horse. Arielle watched the "widows" climb into the wagon, and Siam began harnessing Zeus.

"Mrs. D'Arcy?" Luc's softly accented deep voice slid through the cold air to mock Arielle.

She whirled on him, furiously remembering how Smithson had tossed the reins to her adventure to Luc. "You. *You are supposed to be dead.*"

A woman eased by, her skirts brushing Luc's long leather-covered leg. He removed his hat and swept it gallantly in front of him in a bow. The woman giggled and glanced down Luc's buckskin-covered body. She raised her eyebrows to Arielle and behind her fluttering fan whispered, "He is luscious."

Arielle stared blankly at her, slowly realizing that the woman viewed Luc as a ripe fruit to be plucked into her bed. Flushing with the implication and the memory that she had been in Luc's bed, Arielle repeated under her breath, "You should be dead."

Luc's dark brow lifted, the aristocratic lines of his face clearly showing his recent loss of weight. The sinful peak of his scarred eyebrow lifted. "I live, *chère*. How could I leave my beautiful bride?"

Arielle scanned the bustling street and stepped nearer Luc, speaking in a hushed voice. "You're mocking me. This won't do at all."

"Won't it?" he asked easily. His gaze scanned her face, then eased slowly downward. The color of his eyes reminded her of dark, ominous thunderclouds.

"Stop looking at me like that," she whispered sharply, furious with the turn of the day.

"But *chère*, surely you are glad I have recovered," Luc drawled. Despite his easy manner, anger sailed along his hard jaw, locking in it. Screened by his lashes, his eyes were the shade of tempered steel, flashing, pinning her. "You were so caring, so tender when I was at death's door."

Arielle slashed out her hand in a gesture of silence. "Yes. Yes. Of course you don't have to die now, it's just that—"

Luc's other brow lifted questioningly. "Madame wife, these are not the words a groom wishes to hear on the lips of his bride. Though I am glad I do not have to die to please you, my angel."

The endearment caused Arielle's lips to part, her thoughts stopping in mid-flow. "Mr. . . . Luc . . . surely you see the folly of this arrangement. We must have the marriage severed as soon as possible," she said in a quick rush.

Luc straightened away from the wall slowly, looming over her. Arielle found herself looking straight into his chest. She forced her eyes upward, causing her neck to bend back. His voice was deadly quiet, and Arielle's heart skipped a beat. "For what reason?"

Arielle blinked at the passionate anger in Luc's expression. Unused to men standing close to her, she hesitated, then decided the matter needed a measure of tact. "Clearly you are not in a receptive mood. Perhaps you would like to discuss the matter after dinner tonight at the cabin. Keep in mind that I would reward you handsomely for a quiet divorce some distance away from here. We could take a short journey to another district perhaps, then the deed could be severed. In any case, you will not meet Mr. Smithson without me in attendance."

She looked up at Luc's intent face hopefully. "The deed?" he asked very softly.

"This rash mistake, this . . . marriage at your deathbed. Surely you know that I married you out of sympathy. . . ." Arielle floundered as Luc took a step nearer. A good foot taller than she, still lean from his illness, Luc loomed over her like a formidable wall. She could not see beyond the width of his shoulders, nor the silvery flash of his eyes as they consumed her. "You have recovered now . . . and, uh . . ."

Luc's eyes darkened, smoldering, dark with passions she had never seen nor experienced. A line creased his dark forehead, separating the thick straight brows. The skin over his slashing cheekbones tightened, his jaw flexing beneath the dark skin. The curve of his mouth pressed into a hard line, reminding her of the blood of Spanish and French kings that flowed in his veins. There was a fierceness there, too, startling her in its intensity. Her eyes skimmed down to his open shirt and found a vein beating heavily beneath his brown skin. The air between them seemed to heat, lightning crackling and thunder rolling. The rain dripped easily from the porch roof. She ran her finger around her buttoned collar, loosening the suddenly tight constriction.

"When you fought so hard to have me live—*make* me want to live," Luc corrected, "would you toss me and our marriage paper away like so much unwanted trash, *chère*?" he asked mildly.

Steel shot through the light tone, the quiet menace chilling her. His anger, tightly contained, raised the hairs on the back of her neck. Luc D'Arcy could be a very dangerous man. Perhaps she should use care in dispensing with him.

He was too large, his aura too powerful to dismiss easily. His hand tightened on his firearm, the knuckles pressing whitely against the dark, scarred skin. It was the hand of a man who did not relinquish his possessions easily. She remembered his delirious ramblings; he had stalked men, taking his revenge. Fierce, dark passions stormed his light eyes as they locked on her.

She remembered how desperately he fought for life. How he had captured his "angel." Severing their bonds required cool thinking. *Oh, why did she marry him?*

Arielle drew herself to her full height, resenting that for all her effort, the top of her head barely reached his shoulder. She straightened her shoulders as she had done often behind her desk when faced with a difficult task. Yes, Luc would not be easily managed. She quickly scanned his face, seeking a bit of warmth, and found none. She would use tact and reasoning, prepare her defenses, and then strike.

"I think," she said softly, carefully, after clearing her throat, "that after dinner would be a much better time to come to an agreement. Please join us."

He nodded, his gaze falling to her bodice, then lifted slowly upward to touch her lips. "A pleasure."

Arielle's heart raced wildly. Luc D'Arcy must be persuaded to annul the marriage. She thought of Thaddeus's cool blue eyes and Luc's smoldering silver ones and inhaled slowly. Taking care, she placed her hands behind her back and found Glynis looking at her with open interest. "A slight obstacle has arisen, Glynis. Nothing to be concerned about, really," Arielle said darkly.

"Really, Angel?" Glynis asked in a cool aside.

Luc shielded his anger beneath an easy smile as he watched her walk away. Her brisk step swished the layers of petticoats, her head high in the manner of a woman with a mission.

The little witch had tossed his pride back at him without a second thought. She would pay for that.

She wanted to dismiss him and the family ring she wore on her finger as though it was so much unwanted baggage.

He gritted his back teeth, remembering how Arielle had stood before Smithson's demand—small, very feminine, and submissive. Her scent had jarred Luc, the soft fragrance snaring the memory of her tender care. Why had he leapt to champion her like a foolish boy?

Fiery pain shot through his leg, protesting its hard use to arrive in Independence. It reminded him why this self-sufficient, bristling little woman wore his name. He had wanted to thank her for her kindness and offer his protection for the journey westward. As a courtesy for her kindness, he had intended to offer her a quiet divorce and his protection.

Arielle annoyed him. Delirious, locked in his father's wager, he'd spilled his pain at her doorstep, like a boy begging for a mother's soothing kiss. She'd strolled inside his darkness as no one had before. She'd touched a yearning warmth he'd hidden for years, and now she walked away as though dismissing him as so much extra ballast. He scowled at the cat, now draped across a boy's arm like a pasha holding court. Condemned to haul the cat westward, Luc likened the ill-tempered beast to the woman who was his wife. He'd wanted to crush that sassy rosebud mouth beneath his the instant he'd spotted her.

Luc stretched and tested his healing leg, rubbing it with a hand raked by the cat. He'd tied himself to a hellion who dismissed his claim easily. The thought lurked and nettled.

The D'Arcy ring had gleamed on her pale hand, the intricate design warmed by nervous fingers. His current tether on the stubborn, fiery little witch pleased Luc. There would be time on the trail to discuss ending their marriage. But first Arielle D'Arcy would sample well-deserved lessons in manners.

He jerked the reins of Siam's mule and horse from the iron circle on the hitching post, then his own. Walking slowly after the women, Luc returned Arielle's quick glare with an easy smile.

When she turned away the smile lingered, warming him. The unaccustomed warmth startled him. He wondered when he had smiled last. . . .

Luc followed the sway of her skirts and remembered the sweet curve of her thigh beneath his hand. When she stepped up into the wagon, assisted by Siam, a neat turn of slender ankle and dainty feet caught him. He had not thought about bedding a woman for five years. . . . *With Arielle—his wife—at hand, the thought was most entertaining.*

Glynis stepped back as Arielle lunged toward her. The fencing foil's blunt tip almost touched the embroidered heart on Glynis's padded vest. Lifting her foil, she smiled slightly through her protective mask. "My dear, your style is off when your temper rages. You are hacking away like a Cossack."

The sound of Siam's ax striking a fallen, seasoned tree continued in the early afternoon chill. Grateful for firewood they did not have to cut, the women were baking and cooking the evening meal, washing the woodsman's clothing with their own. In a happy flurry of grinding slippery elm bark to be used for poultices and teas, Lydia hummed and spread the powders out to dry. She was ecstatic that the woodsmen were familiar with herbal curatives and waved to Siam. The children perched on another log, eating freshly baked bread and staring wide-eyed at the giant woodsman. While he cut wood, he teased the children with animal calls.

"A bee, Siam. You sound like a bee—no a bear, a big,

mean bear!" they chorused, then were silent, waiting for another imitation. "A snake . . . a rattlesnake shaking its tail!"

Arielle kicked aside a wealth of petticoats and satinette skirt, her foil meeting Glynis's in slashes and parried thrusts. She ignored the trickle of sweat and the damp ringlets that had increasingly loosened from the ribbons and combs on top of her head. The dim light of the cloudy afternoon gleamed on the thin foils. Glynis stepped back, expertly meeting Arielle's quick, aggressive thrusts. "They discussed the Oregon venture as though I weren't in the room. Clearly Smithson will deal only with Luc and not a woman—myself. D'Arcy—Luc, did not defer. The whole attitude is antiquated beyond belief, Glynis."

They stepped together, skirts mingling, bell guards of the handles braced against each other. Glynis, though larger and stronger, lacked Arielle's dazzling skills and her anger. They pushed apart, and Glynis began a systematic offense to Arielle's defense. "Luc doesn't seem the sort of man who can be easily discarded. What will you do, Arielle?"

Free hands braced on waists, the women circled each other. Thrust and parry, Arielle lifted her skirts aside and raised her hand gracefully. "Diplomacy, my dear Glynis. D'Arcy will realize eventually that it is to his benefit to annul the marriage. I cannot see an honorable man doing otherwise. If necessary, I can wear his name until the journey is over. Since he is returning to Oregon country, we shall have time to resolve the matter to my satisfaction."

She slashed brilliantly at Glynis's defensive stance, ignoring a covey of quail that sailed from the bush near their skirts. "I do not trust the set of Mr. D'Arcy's—Luc's jaw, now that he has recovered. Too rigid. They are emotional beasts—males, that is. I've finished many a good business arrangement by watching that betraying male jaw. Nothing can disguise poor temper when it lodges in a strong jaw like Mr. D'Ar—Luc's. There's this back teeth grinding motion, which is easily detected beneath the shaved male jaw. Very feral . . . primitive. You should have seen this woman drool when she saw Luc. Luscious, she called him . . . luscious! A

term one would use for a succulent, sweet peach to be
squeezed and devoured!"

"I see," Glynis returned as they came together, resting
momentarily with their bell guards poised.

"He covers his evil tempers with a gallant's manners—Mr.
D'Arcy ... I mean Luc. Not at all like dear Thaddeus, who
is a gentleman through and through. Thaddeus's beautiful blue
eyes never reminded me of sparks from a fired flintlock. I
could never relax with a man like D'Arcy—wonderful how
exercise brings out one's base thoughts, unclouds them, isn't
it? Puts them all in a reasonable line."

"Dear Thaddeus?" Glynis questioned, advancing in a
ploy toward Arielle.

"Thaddeus is a gallant, courtly man. I fear there are rough
edges and tendencies beneath Mr. ... Luc's dark exterior.
He is far too near the uncivilized, predatory male sort that
I picture visiting brothels and lounging with hostiles."
Arielle grimly avoided Glynis's offensive, turned, and began
working fiercely away at her opponent's defense. Glynis
was always weak when forced to parry above her shoulder
and tired easily. Frustrated with an anger she did not want,
Arielle continued to force Glynis's arm high. "Mr. D'Arcy
will see things my way and shortly. He'll be gone with the
drop of a few coins."

"He dropped a few coins in Smithson's coffer. From the
ring you're wearing, I suspect Luc may have wealth in his
own right," Glynis reminded her between breaths. "There
are men who cannot be bought for coin, regardless of their
own circumstance."

Arielle's foil flashed quickly, raising Glynis's arm higher.
"Following us to the cabin with the horses and mules in
hand ... the women sliding glances out of the back of the
wagon ... as though they couldn't keep their eyes from him
... they don't understand men with evil tempers, as I suspect Mr. D ... Luc has. Yes, he has flintlock eyes when
he's angry, and I don't trust that jaw a bit, now that it is
shaved, exposing that fierce temper to the world. The man
doesn't use scents. One always wonders about a man who

doesn't use scents. Somehow the lack signifies a ruffian. My judgment was clouded because of his illness, or I would have seen his true character and let him die without the magnificent D'Arcy name tacked to my backside."

"Arielle!" Glynis protested between breaths as she defended the rapid thrusts. "You are slashing, hacking away at me as if I were a tree. I am not prepared to spill good English blood due to your frustrations."

Immediately Arielle slowed her foil and ended the match with an expert thrust to Glynis's unprotected embroidered heart. Arielle swept off her mask and dried her foil carefully, then replaced it in the velvet-lined case with its mate. Glynis untied Arielle's padded protector from the back. "My dear. We have a long journey, six or so months. If Luc is an experienced woodsman and Mr. Smithson respects his abilities, perhaps you are wise to delay severing the marriage until the journey's end," she suggested very carefully. "Exposure of our humbugging—our ploy to present our women as proper ladies—could mean disaster."

Arielle stepped free; she glanced at the man leaning against a huge oak tree, watching the scene. Luc seemed a part of the prairie, his leathers blending with the trees and sweeping ocher fields. She lifted her chin and pushed back a fall of curls that threatened her composure. She wasn't a helpless woman, and Luc may as well know from the onset that she could protect herself. Flushed with exercise, her curls resisting her trembling hands as she pushed them back, Arielle faced him, breathing hard. "Now would be a perfect time to begin negotiations," she stated firmly. "I want this matter settled quickly."

She slashed a glance at Luc. "I have always been a good judge of character, and I say Luc is a sinful man, Glynis. There was that heated byplay in his bed. . . ." She flushed and continued, "And there is just something of the predator in his eyes—a hawklike man, when he isn't amused at his private jokes. I really don't like the way he looks at me. I am a businesswoman, after all. A spinster protected by my advanced age."

She neglected to say that Thaddeus would never look at her so sinfully.

"Please be gentle with him, Arielle. Remember he's just recovered," Glynis urged as Arielle jerked her coat on and began walking across the field toward him. The six huge, mottled gray Percherons instantly lifted their heads from grazing and began ambling after her.

Luc kneaded the aching pain in his leg, leaning against the oak while its few, clinging dead leaves rustled above him. A red-tailed hawk swept across the blue sky and settled in the bowers of the naked, wintery oaks. When he surveyed his kingdom, hungry for a stray rabbit or mouse, his white breast shone against the dark sky.

Luc's wound had protested the urgent horse ride from St. Louis, which enabled them to arrive at Smithson's moments before the women. The first miles were agony. LaFleur's dying kick had damaged the wound. Beads of perspiration cooled on Luc's face as he watched Arielle walk toward him. He bitterly resented his weakness then.

She had left him, expecting him to die. But he had rallied and pushed back the rigid anger that she had not stayed to see him through the passage. At first, fighting his fevers, he had been bitter, unreasonable, raging to Siam that she had deserted him, taken his name and run. Only that dark need for revenge kept him going at first, to make her pay for ripping away his dreams. Then, realizing that she had acted from kindness, Luc wanted her near to thank her . . . to release her and offer his protection.

Today, she'd tried to dismiss him easily.

Luc pressed his lips together. No woman since Catherine had dismissed him, nor challenged his right to be where he wanted, doing exactly as he desired. Arielle Browning D'Arcy stuck pins in his intentions and cast his pride at his feet.

Then there was the urge to taste her sassy mouth. The need was unreasonable, considering his five-year abstinence from women. Perhaps fever had formed an illogical bond between them. Luc traced the curved body sailing toward him, shining in the black satinette gown. Leaves swirled around her feet.

He studied those delicate, quick feet, surprised that he was easily distracted by them.

He had taken women since Willow's death, using them as they had used him. It was an equal exchange to satisfy necessary hungers. "Arielle D'Arcy"—he repeated the name softly in the chilly April air, letting it warm him. This woman taunted him with her hidden passion, the soft body he knew lay beneath the layers of her boning and clothing. He had not wanted a woman this desperately in years. . . . He wondered distantly if in his youth he had wanted Willow as earnestly. Catherine's experience had blinded him to the appeal of sweet innocence.

Arielle's scent had clung to his bed, and Luc firmed his mouth. There was a dream that had floated with the scent, the dream of his body inside the fiery moist furnace of hers.

The fierce need startled him, his body taut.

Arielle's sharp tongue should have repelled him—it didn't. He kept thinking of how it would taste in his mouth.

She had hacked away at Glynis, wearing her down. Arielle D'Arcy was an opportunist, Luc decided, and a fascinating woman with secrets lurking behind her green eyes. She would not escape him easily.

He smiled slightly, enjoying the slight wind tossing her curls, the sunlight tangling in the fiery lights. Beneath the curls she pushed back in quick, angry movements, Arielle's heart-shaped face was pink with her exercise—or was it anger?

The giant, heavily muscled horses ambled after her like puppies. The big Percheron stallion nuzzled Arielle's stiff back, and she was forced to step quickly to keep her balance. Stopping to scold the horse, Arielle ran a loving hand across his huge muzzle and slipped her hand into her pocket. Immediately the five mares surrounded her, and she was caught in a tangle of supplying their needs. Her quick laughter and light scolding warmed the cold breeze sailing across the meadow. She patted each animal's throat, and the horses lumbered away to forage for winter grass.

Then she was striding toward Luc again, the russet curls bouncing, flaming above the black satinette gown. Luc watched with pleasure as her slender ankles thrust at the petticoats. A few feet from him Arielle slowed her stride and stopped abruptly. He watched, amused as her green eyes steadily met his. "I am glad you are recovered, sir," she said firmly, sincerely.

He nodded, wondering if that pale throat led to softer, sweeter fare. He relished the thought, the stirring of his body. Arielle had brought him back to life, and his need of her was a celebration he could ill afford. Pain waited in the shadows of life and laughter. Whatever the outcome, he would protect Arielle D'Arcy because of her kindness in his worst moment.

But he would not release her from their marriage just yet . . . not until he was ready.

She breathed heavily, as if calming herself, and the motion lifted her frilled bodice. "Luc. Surely you agree that we cannot have a marital alliance now. The terms—conditions—of our arrangement have changed." She began to slide the D'Arcy ring from her finger, and Luc's hand wrapped around her wrist.

"Wear it," he commanded, then softened his order. Again, she had startled him—he wanted his brand on her finger. Later he would reason with the stark need to possess her. "For the time. Smithson would spot the loss instantly."

Arielle looked down at his long, dark fingers circling her wrist, the near barbaric design of the ring on her pale, slender finger. She raised her cool gaze to his. "Do not have any illusion concerning this unfortunate . . . marriage."

Something fluttered inside her, shivering at the heat of his body enfolding hers. She glanced at his mouth and decided it was beautiful, perfectly molded.

The thought caught her broadside, and she shivered, deciding that Luc's smile had disarmed many women before her.

"*Chère,* I want no illusions between us," he returned, fascinated by the racing pulse beneath his fingertips. Taking his time, he drew her wrist to his mouth and kissed the fine inner skin. Her lips parted, her eyes widening until Luc felt himself leaning toward her, falling into the jade depths. "I want you."

She stared up at him, her lips moving silently, and again he felt her pulse leap. He eased his fingertip into a soft ringlet bobbing at her temple, studying the contrast of russet silk and dark skin. "Tonight after the evening meal, you will walk with me, *chère*. We will talk about illusions then."

She cleared her throat, stepping back and clutching her hands behind her back. Fascinated by the warring expressions of confusion and anger, Luc ran a fingertip over the frown lurking between her auburn brows. "Terms," he said softly.

"Terms?" she questioned, sweeping aside his hand.

He circled his thumb over the lingering warmth on his finger. "The terms of our arrangement. I wish them settled quickly."

She frowned, backing away from him. "Threats? You must know that I have the finances to support my venture. Extortion, perhaps? Somehow I expect nothing less."

Luc fought the wave of anger grimly. Few men had maligned his honor and lived. Arielle thrust at him without fear. He recognized the straightening of her shoulders as though she prepared to thrust her foil. She drew her body straight, as though preparing to launch herself at whatever stood in her way. Like a little fierce hen. It was a habit he would remember. There would be a time when she was not as brave, Luc promised. "Perhaps."

"You'll find the matter difficult, Mr. . . . Luc. Very difficult. I have been threatened before," she said. "I am a seasoned woman, not a girl, a spinster set in my ways."

"We shall see, Angel," he returned softly, stroking a fingertip down her hot cheek. He was fiercely angry, disliking the emotion and the woman who had evoked it. Her blank stare pleased him.

"Surely, you don't think that . . ." she began, then stopped, swallowed, and tried another route to end his insanity. "You know, I admire your courage, the love you evidently have for your family—for your family name,"

Arielle stated reluctantly. "It must have taken great fortitude to seek out your sisters, and to fight so desperately to live. Siam told me that you were protecting a woman from abuse when you took that ball in your thigh."

"Not a very wise thing to do, *chère*. I'd had my share of wine at the time," he admitted, enjoying Arielle's expressions. He touched the sunlight sparkling in her hair, and she swatted away his hand. Luc allowed the small defense, enchanted as Arielle chewed her bottom lip. She was clearly weighing issues as her green eyes slid off to the horses. He would enjoy touching this woman, challenging her perfect composure, warming her.

"Nonetheless, you are a brave man, Luc. You loved your family deeply enough to follow them into dangerous territory, to duel over their honor, and to hunt down the absent criminal. I would have done the same under the circumstances. But it would be foolhardy to think that this . . . bond between us could become a reality. Perhaps you are still touched with the fevers, your reasoning slightly awry," she suggested grimly.

"*Chère*, I am in a fever, but not from my wound. Rather from wanting to enjoy my bride," Luc murmured and enjoyed the swift rush of pink flowing up Arielle's soft cheeks.

"Clearly you are demented, no doubt a result of your illness," she said tightly. "No man would travel the earth to avenge his sisters, love his mother and sisters as you must have—do," she corrected, "then wish to force an unwilling woman to meet some obscure obligation."

"Would I not, Angel?" he asked carefully. Arielle knew exactly where to place her barbs, nettling him. Catherine's laughter hovered on the shadows of his mind, stalking him. "How do you know you would not be willing?"

Arielle's head went back, her eyes narrowing, the green color changed to emerald. "Let me warn you, Mr. D'Arcy, it would not serve you to anger me."

When she whirled away, her eyes shot him one last threat over her shoulder. Luc studied the sway of her skirts and the mass of curls bouncing with each step. Arielle D'Arcy would fight to protect her own, and the thought pleased him almost as much as the sight of her dainty ankles swishing briskly beneath the voluminous skirts.

He wanted to wrap his hand around that slender ankle, kiss the instep and work his way upward—

A dried leaf, shredded by winter, slid from the oak tree, and Luc studied it resting on the crushed leaves in the mud.

Willow had been quiet, submissive, loving him enough to ask that his child be cut from her so that his heir would live.

In his fevers Luc met Willow many times. A young girl racing across the meadow to greet him. Later as a quiet, shy bride standing beside her father as he accepted the bridal gift of Luc's horses . . . then swelling with his child, pride in her expression. . . . Later, she writhed on her bed of pain and weakly begged him to take the child at the cost of her life. . . . Once, on the riverboat, he thought he felt the brush of her hand against his forehead, and had wanted to join her. He'd wanted to leave the pain burning, swirling around him, and step into the cool, dark shadows with Willow. There was a child in the shadows, a son he had never held. He had cried out for his child, for his wife, wishing to hold them against the ache in his heart. *"No. It is not your time,"* she had whispered, floating away from him.

Then memories of her slid away as another leaf caught the wind: Arielle's pale face replacing Willow's dark one.

Luc rubbed his leg, cursing the weakness in him. Arielle's soft green eyes, and hushed, coaxing whispers had caused him to cling to life, then Willow had slid slowly into the shadows, a sweet smile on her lips.

He'd dreamed of Arielle then, lying beside him, pale, silky, warm in their marriage bed. Her fragrance floated around him, tantalizing and keeping him from the shadows.

For hours he'd hovered between life and death. Arielle's scent on the lace handkerchief she'd forgotten forced him to breathe. He inhaled the fragrance, wanting more, fighting the weakness.

When they were married, he was lucid, fighting desperately to remain propped upright against the pillows on his bed. In a romantic touch directed by Glynis, Siam had

placed scented candles around the room and found bundles
of dried herbs and flowers to brighten it. Seated beside him,
Arielle's hair was free as he had asked, a red mass of tumbling, candlelit silk. Her eyes were wide, concerned as she
brushed aside an errant strand of his hair, her palm gently
testing the fever on his forehead. "My dear, are you certain
this is what you want?" she had whispered when the minister stood at the foot of the bed. "There is time to change
your mind. I would not mind."

Her husky low tone had swirled over him, her face flushing when he stared at her for a long moment. "The D'Arcy
name must not die with me."

"There, there, my dear," she had returned in a soothing
whisper, adjusting the dress shirt that he wore. "Your name
will live, sir." After the hushed ceremony, she had bent to
kiss his brow, and Luc had turned to meet her lips.

She had tasted sweet and soft, allowing the small kiss.
Luc smiled wryly. Today Arielle's fiery anger replaced the
soothing tenderness he remembered at their wedding.

On her path to the cabin Arielle paused to toss back another heated glance, and Luc smiled grimly. Instantly he
fought the rising desire of his body, the hard thud of blood
in his loins. After Willow's death, then in the desperate
search for Colette and Yvonne, he had placed aside his
needs. Now they surged upward, pushing at his heart, his
veins. The buckskins stretched tautly across his hips, withholding the hard thrust.

He lifted an eyebrow, drinking in the sunlight traipsing
through Arielle's bright hair. The divorce she wanted would
have to wait.

The smile lurking around his mouth startled him. For the
present, he intended to enjoy the wager's booty—a certain
exciting, challenging, delicious angel.

Seven
....

The large, rented cabin provided shelter against the fierce prairie winds sweeping from the north. Arielle had decided against the town's emigrant hotel, not willing to expose the widows and children to "the possible attentions of rougher elements."

Then there was the matter of Anna's threat to dissect a local man's southward body parts. His leer at Sally had plopped him into the cold mud.

The cows and goats, easy prey for thieves and the other emigrants, were kept under a roof angling from the cabin. The animals provided a measure of heat. Each night horses and mules were hobbled nearby.

Double thickness of canvas coverings for the wagons had been waterproofed with linseed oil. They hung like giant sheets from the cabin's poorly chinked logs, retaining heat and modesty. The storage pockets, which lined the canvas, would be filled when the journey began. Tents would be purchased from town with the other goods. The aroma of chicken and dumplings, cooked earlier in the day, blended with scents of soap and hay and excitement. The women's washed clothing hung on ropes strung in one corner, and a basin, hot water, soap, and a towel waited outside on a plank braced by two large barrels. The men's clothing had been washed and ironed, and folded neatly in a basket on the plank.

Luc and Siam washed, then entered the makeshift room. While Luc's head was bare, Siam wore his hat.

A fire blazed in the huge rock fireplace. A rough table of boards had been covered by a fine linen tablecloth and china soup dishes with gold trim were stacked near the tureen covered with cloths to keep it warm. Heavy silverware spoons with ornate handles rested over ironed linen napkins. The scent of freshly baked bread wafted from beneath a towel. Nail kegs had been turned over for chairs, and the women hovered anxiously in the shadows while Glynis invited the men to enter their makeshift home.

Seated on an overturned long trough, which would later be attached to the bottom of the wagons, Arielle scribbled notations in a huge black ledger. She glanced up at Luc and Siam, snapped the book shut, and placed it inside a small trunk with a lock. She acknowledged the men with a curt nod as she rose, swishing her skirts away from Luc's leather leggings. "Gentlemen."

Luc bowed low, his hand sweeping his hat in front of him. His eyes caught hers, held them. He enjoyed her tense anger, her cool smile. "Mr. Siam," she said politely. "I believe you met everyone when you draped our poor walls—I compliment Luc on his practical idea. Timmy tells me you are as strong as ten men and that he is going to play your bird calls on his fife."

The Canadian's severe features softened, his eyes drifting toward Glynis, who was tying a napkin around Brianna's neck. He frowned slightly, his eyes clouding as though trying to remember something.

Glynis's gaze lifted at that moment, her half smile stilling on her lips, then dying slowly as a bright flush shot up her cheeks. She looked away quickly.

The women hovered uncertainly around the table, their

eyes avoiding the men's, but sending quick curious glances. America moved her toe beneath the canvas walls, edging away her son's dog. Dante was a medium-size, black hairy mongrel who was forbidden to attend their meals. He whined in the darkness beyond the canvas, stuck his head under the hem, and surveyed the dinner hungrily with beady eyes.

Lorenzo frolicked like a kitten, tossing Lydia's catnip ball and chasing it. Pampered by the women and children, the cat's yellow eyes taunted Luc. He sashayed by Luc, tail held high; the end was crooked from an old fight. When Arielle reached to scratch his ears, he leered at Luc, lording his favored position. "Lovely kitty," she crooned as the cat rolled to his back, exposing a fat stomach for her petting.

The sight of those slender fingers stroking Lorenzo's stomach caused Luc's body to harden, and he looked away. The traitorous cat had clawed Luc and brewed gas worse than a privy whenever possible.

Luc wondered grimly why fate had gifted him with the cursed cat and rampant, crippling desire for a woman who hacked away at his pride. She antagonized, annoyed, and intrigued him. He resented his body's aching, harsh reminder that it had been years since he'd had a woman. Fate had gifted him with a deathbed marriage, a feisty independent woman, and a cat that scorned him.

The unease cloaking his body reminded him of when he was a boy ready to jump into the first available bed. He inhaled and caught Arielle's unique scent. He forced it from his nostrils. If now was the time for him to return to lust, why with this annoying woman? His fingers curled into a fist, and he studied the new claw marks on his hand. God took His revenge in strange ways.

"I believe we can begin." Arielle eased her skirts aside a small barrel and sat. "Please sit, Luc . . . Siam," she offered, indicating seats near her. At the head of the table she lifted the lid of the heavy tureen and began ladling the food into bowls.

"Tea?" Glynis asked, pouring tea from an ornate silver service into china cups.

"Marie made crackers and bread, gentlemen. She is baking sweetcakes that will age properly on the trail, but tonight we have pie," Glynis murmured, frowning at Siam, who had not taken his eyes from her. She slid her hand to her throat, straightening the jeweled pin there. When her fingers moved away, they trembled.

After the prayer, hesitantly murmured by Lelia and coached by Arielle, the meal began and the childen's excited questions about the new country mingled with the women's uncertain eagerness.

Luc noted the women's eyes, the strained lines of their faces, and the curious mark on Eliza's throat, though she shielded it carefully. The mark was the brand of an overly zealous religion, placed on a fallen woman.

Anna handled the delicate china uneasily. At her side Sally looked at the chicken broth uneasily, gathering her shawl closer around her. Too formal and hesitant, the other women concealed their excitement with casual questions about Oregon country.

Arielle refused to meet Luc's gaze, jerking her hand away instantly from his when he passed the salt and pepper mill. The meal passed quietly, the children entranced by the men.

Siam's massive hand trembled when he held the delicate cup. His eyes skittered to Glynis while Lydia inquired about Luc's leg, suggesting a heated poultice of mashed potatoes when he retired. Lydia neatly noted the westerners' remarks about Indian herbs and cures, her narrow face animated and rosy. After dinner she prepared a tea of lemon grass and lemon verbena with rosehips and honey for Lion, Biddy's two-year-old boy. Suffering from a cold, Lion sat on his mother's lap, his eyes filled with the tall men sharing their table. "He's afraid," Biddy admitted softly, cuddling him closer as her daughter, Liberty, stood at her side.

"Ain't the only one," Anna admitted softly, her voice gravelly and flat.

"Fear is not a bad thing sometimes," Luc said. "It gives strength. You will need that to survive."

"We ain't weak women, Mr. Navaronne," Anna returned

quickly, her eyes hard. "We've seen trials that would test the strongest soul."

"Amen," Harriet Longman said quietly.

Luc studied Sally, who eased closer to Anna. The girl's fear slid through her blue eyes at the slightest noise. "You will make a lovely mother, Sally. But are you aware that Mr. Smithson wants no ... 'indisposed ladies of the later term' on the train?"

Sally nodded shyly, gathering her shawl closer. Luc noted that all of the ladies' shawls were new. That lengths of muslin and cotton lay propped on a table and several pieces of quilting scraps had been timeworn, a half-finished quilt spread over a frame. "The ladies sew. Busy hands soothe the excitement," Glynis explained softly.

"Sally will do fine," Anna said flatly, answering his question.

"She's recently been made a widow," Arielle added firmly.

"I think it would be best if she rested until we are on our way. She will need her strength," Luc continued softly, tugging on Sally's braid teasingly. His mind skittered back to Yvonne. Had a man protected her? He blocked out the deadly curiosity that could tear away his heart. This widow train would protect Sally; she wouldn't be left behind because of a baby. Under the protection of these women, Smithson wouldn't know that Sally's pregnancy was more advanced than he allowed. "In two months the baby will come early, isn't that right?" Luc prompted.

Sally smiled softly, warming toward him. "Yes. The baby will come early."

Luc stretched his leg, rubbing it. "Perhaps you will let me tend your son when he is here. It has been a long time since one filled my arms. It is a good thing to hold a baby. Then one sees the future and not the pain of the past. He sees his life continuing when he is gone," he murmured softly and inhaled slowly, spreading his hands on his thighs. "Mrs. D'Arcy, I must use my leg. Would you walk with me, please?"

Minutes later Arielle, dressed in her coat and shawl,

faced Luc under the chilling moonlight. "Navaronne?" she questioned briefly.

"My mother's name. Unfortunately, to claim my father's would place your mission in danger," Luc returned easily. "You are wearing the D'Arcy ring and the D'Arcy name. Therefore you are mine to protect."

Arielle's head went back. "Only for a time. I want no more talk of babies and 'seeing life continue.' Will you be able to ride to a remote area? I want no word of our divorce to endanger my cargo—ah . . . ladies." She tilted her bonnet against the hard, freezing wind and Luc's unsettling stare.

Shielded by heavy lashes, his light eyes touched her face, drifting and warming like a caress. His heat snared her, his body sheltering hers from the wind. Arielle stepped into the cold wind, stripping his warmth from her.

She didn't like the way Luc lingered on Sally's coming baby. It reminded her of his insistence that the D'Arcy name be carried on, and of his feverish ramblings, longing for a D'Arcy baby in his arms.

Her goal was to acquire—bear—a Northrup baby and all that went with it, though there was no reason to admit such to this bold man. She blamed Fannie Orson's announcement for intensifying her desire for marriage and babies before it was too late. From Luc's dangerous, hawkish expression now, he'd take that tidbit and devour it whole.

Luc stepped closer, enchanted with the night shadows making her eyes seem even larger in her pale face. "Madame D'Arcy, you will remain married," Luc returned softly. "I have no intention of renouncing my vows. Not just yet."

"Luc, please be reasonable. You were feverish—"

"I knew what I was doing. You did not have to tend nor marry me in St. Louis. Your tear dropped to my cheek, and I thought, there is a woman with heart . . . my woman. My last wish was to have a good woman at my side when I died. You are that woman and now my wife, though I lived." Luc's face was harsh. "I'm not quite ready to give you up, sweet wife. A perverse notion, considering your less-than-agreeable habits. I was angry at first, damning you for leaving me with nothing but a dream. Then I knew that others depended on you. You are brave, taking women of this nature on the trail. A woman with deep honor. Or a woman concealing a personal quest."

Arielle rounded on him, her auburn eyebrows jerking together fiercely. "What do you mean, 'women of this nature'?"

Luc stepped closer, his body shielding her from the brutal wind. His instincts told him to protect her whether or not she appreciated the consideration. He wanted no lies between them . . . nor space. Her scent drifted on the wind, swirling, enchanting him. She seemed determined to stay a distance away from him.

In his adult lifetime few women had avoided him. Enchanted by her delicate retreat, Luc recognized his hunter's instinct to pursue. He took a step nearer. Arielle eased back, her skirts wrapping around his legs. The seductive rustling of the material bound him to her. Luc wondered how many women would risk their fortune and life on a venture like Arielle's. Her expression intrigued him. Uncertainty shifted beneath pale skin with a whisper of freckles running across her nose. "They are women who know men. Mary has not yet become what the other women were. Lydia is a child in a woman's body, her mind filled with herbs and cures, not marriage to a man in Oregon country. She is an innocent. . . . I doubt that she has sighed in a man's arms. Except for Lydia, Mary, Glynis, and yourself, you are transporting fallen women, madame, not widows."

He admired the challenging, protective tilt of her head. This woman would fight to hold what was dear to her. "How do you know?"

He shrugged, too aware of her scent. "It is in their eyes. The brand on Eliza's throat, the fear in Sally's when Siam or I come too near. It is in how they look at Glynis to start the meal, to cover their laps with a napkin, to lift their cups. They are uncertain and ask her guidance with each look, even how to sit with skirts and straighten their backs. The knowledge sits on them uneasily. She has been training them to be ladies, madame wife."

The widening of her eyes when he challenged her with his possession pleased him. Luc noted the pulse at her throat, drawn to it as he continued, "Glynis touches shoulders to keep them straight with pride. You teach them to meet one's eyes when they would look away. Anna must not brawl on the journey. She cannot afford to break her nose another time. Perhaps she should use one of Lydia's ointments to soften the scars across her knuckles."

Arielle inhaled sharply and closed her eyes. Moonlight caught on the ends of her lashes, sliding away when she opened her lids and spilling into her eyes. "Your terms, Mr. D'Arcy? It is obvious that you have the upper hand at this stage."

He toyed with honor and dismissed it. Arielle had resurrected desire, sharper and more exciting than he had ever known. He wanted to explore her, savor the enchanting quick mind and agile body. Arielle struck something in him that he did not understand, a curiosity about life, the desire to live, to taste each day with her. In her presence shadows slipped away and his heart tilted happily . . . when he wasn't fighting his pride and the simmering anger that she—his wife—did not want him, could not stand his presence any longer than necessary. . . . He longed to torment her, infest her thoughts with him, making her long for him, as he had longed for her. . . . That he had thought himself long past boyish temptations did not please him. While he desired Arielle, he resented the carefully buried emotions she jerked from him. "I want you, madame wife. In my bed, my nightly blanket, for a time each night."

Arielle's eyes widened, her hand covering the betraying pulse. "Impossible!"

"Is it? We are married. I ask that you lay with me apart from the others. I would not take more than you would give, *chère*."

"I cannot. The idea is immoral, impertinent, and will not occur," she snapped, rounding on him. The silvery moonlight gleamed on her white face, shimmering on her trembling lips. "I will not oblige myself to an opportunist."

Luc stepped nearer, cupping her chin in his hand. "We

have a marriage between us, madame. I would not forgo all of the advantages. To lay with me beneath the stars for an hour or so each night will not compromise you. The others will think I'm courting you. And the small play will serve two purposes ... to protect the ladies from the failure of your mission and to let me enjoy you at my side again." He ached to become a part of her, to caress that pale skin and watch it heat in passion.

Her eyes lashed at him. "Preposterous."

Luc touched her earlobe, smoothing the unpierced, virginal softness between his thumb and finger. He had fought to survive and for revenge, and he had killed. To think that this small, soft creature would defy him when few men would amused Luc. "I think you should not fight too hard over this small matter, *chère*."

Jerking away, Arielle faced him. The set of her body reminded him of how she had faced Glynis earlier as a combatant. "You will expose me if I don't?" Challenge rang through her voice, her head high. "Are you an honorable man, a chivalrous one?"

The shadow of a soaring bird crossed his face. "Once as a boy, perhaps my honor was not perfect. As a man, my honor has never been questioned. I would be less than a man if I let my wife order me away. Perhaps you enjoy the chase—"

Arielle's slap to Luc's cheek was his first.

"Mon Dieu!" Luc swept her against him, folding her tightly against his body. Stunned by the sudden movement, Arielle gasped, her parted lips quickly covered by his searching ones. When she expected pain the heat of his mouth brushing against hers gently startled her, held her poised on the tip of pleasure and uncertainty.

He tasted of hunger. Or was it her hunger for him? Of a spice that she feared and yet could not resist?

Seeking the sweet cherishing of his lips, warmed by his arms, Arielle seemed to float nearer, her hands poised to push him away. Her fingers spread and stilled, and she hovered between the sweet tantalizing brush of his lips across hers and the reluctant need to free herself.

Luc's eyes were closed to her open ones, his lashes lush and long. Arielle felt herself floating into the warmth of his mouth, her lids closing slowly. His big hand stroked the back of her neck, seeking out the taut cords and soothing them while his mouth moved to seal hers firmly.

Deepening the kiss, Luc moved his hand inside her coat, stroking her back as he urged her body against his.

Despite the wintery wind, Arielle was too warm, a sleepy excitement beginning to shimmer deep inside her.

The tip of his tongue slid along her lips, gently wooing them to part. Arielle started when he insisted gently, entering her parted lips slowly, tauntingly.

A reckless, restless quiver of hunger leapt within her, and her heart skipped a beat as Luc traced the edges of her teeth. *"Chère ..."* he whispered huskily, hungrily against her hot cheek, his hands gently stroking her nearer.

A darker, headier excitement caught in the beat of her heart, urging it faster as Luc's heated face pressed into the cove of her throat. His lips whispered urgently against her skin in a language she did not know, his skin rough against hers.

Released from her braids, her hair swirled around them, and Luc caught it in his fingers, smoothing the strands from her face. The quivering tendrils webbed across her pale cheek like russet silk threads.

She shivered, her fingertips flexing against his coat, her body curved into his. Luc's heart beat heavily beneath her palm, his lips warming the taut cords of her throat.

The wind caught a strand of his hair, curving it against her hot cheek, snaring her gently to him.

Then Luc's mouth slanted against hers, tasting, feeding, his tongue sliding within to duel gently with hers.

Hunger exploded within Arielle, her mouth following his lead, matching his taunting game. Then Luc's hands framed her face, his eyes brilliant above hers. He smiled gently, his thumbs stroking her flushed cheeks. "You see, *chère*? Though you would be free, I cannot let you go just yet."

She blinked. "But I ... I have plans. . . ."

"I knew you would taste like fire and spice, like honey

and sunlight. Like enchantment and the wind sweeping away the night and leaving the golden dawn. There is heat inside you, Angel, that I regretfully must taste," he whispered unevenly, his eyes gleaming beneath the length of black lashes. A vein sliding down his throat pounded heavily as he brushed away a tendril from her lips with his fingertips.

She stiffened, her eyes huge and luminous in the shadows of the tree. "What are you saying?"

His lips brushed hers seductively. "Surely you must know how a man cherishes the moment of his wife giving herself to him," he whispered gently. "Though I cannot promise to remain as gallant after tasting your charms, my sweet wife."

Arielle inhaled, the wind chilling her nape where Luc had lifted away the masses of her hair, caressing it. She blinked. Her lips barely moved. "Wife?"

He lifted a sleek black brow. "Are you in the habit of repeating everything I say?" he teased, studying the heavy fall of curls in his palms.

Arielle breathed quietly, panic ricocheting through her. Her wanton behavior with Luc could not be explained.

She shook free and gathered her coat fiercely around her trembling body. "You must know, Mr. Luc Navaronne D'Arcy, that I can never belong to you. If you touch me again, I shall have to defend my honor. I am not a woman to be taken in by sweet words. Please do not approach any of my charges with this . . . this attempt at . . . at . . . "

He stared at her mouth. "Lucien. Say it. Now."

"Ah . . . Lucien." Was that her voice, the husky tone curling around his name?

Luc watched her with interest while she floundered, searching her reasoning powers to dispute his claim. She hated him for his patience, the amusement underlying his expression, and for the way her body was chilled without his. Then there was the matter of those damnable soothing hands knowing just where to stroke—

"An attempt at lovemaking with my wife?" he supplied gently, stroking a fingertip down the curl of her ear and tug-

ging at her lobe playfully. "I assure you, my wife, I am
ready to perform my husbandly duties."

The tease ignited her temper. No man had ever played
with her, nor touched her lightly. Shimmering in a fierce
need to strike him, Arielle managed unevenly, "Have a care.
I'm told I have an evil temper, and I won't have you interfering with my plans."

Luc grinned, a slash of white teeth in the darkness of his
face. "I welcome and await your passions, madame wife."

"Women," Smithson muttered the next morning at the local tavern. He pushed back the empty platter from his
breakfast of ham, eggs, and potatoes, then sipped his coffee
slowly. "Ah, that's good coffee. Not a bit of campfire soot
in it."

Luc lifted his pottery mug in a salute, nodded, then drank
slowly.

"Women, widows, and trouble," Smithson said darkly,
lifting his mug again and draining it.

Luc fought the smile lurking around his mouth, then gave
into it. Smithson frowned at him, drew out his clay pipe,
and filled it with tobacco. He stuck the pipe between his
teeth and looked at Luc from beneath his thick brows.
"Arielle D'Arcy is trouble. Red hair and green eyes. Full of
trouble. Runs out of her like this mug poured too full. Never
saw a redheaded woman who wasn't trouble. Give her the
reins, and the entire train will suffer. Are you in agreement,
Luc?"

"The woman has fire," Luc agreed easily, remembering
Arielle's furious last glance. He had ached throughout the
night, sleeping at one end of the cabin with Siam, while his
wife lay just feet from him. Little kept him from plucking
Arielle from her warm nest and carrying her into the night.
Before they parted, he would have her.

He adjusted his aching leg, resenting the conflicting,
strong emotions she evoked within him. She had acted
kindly, in good faith, marrying him on his supposed deathbed. He had intended to release her from the marriage easily, support her venture, traveling with her if she wished to

Oregon country. Until he'd met Arielle Browning D'Arcy for the second time, his goal had been to accommodate, to support her difficult venture.

Now that he had stepped within her net, his motives changed. *Lucien* . . . His name on her lips had seduced, enchanted.

Luc resented the excitement and the sudden burst of happiness tearing wildly through him. He resented her easy dismissal of his tenuous marriage leash. In his lifetime no woman had taken him lightly, not even Catherine. Luc drummed his fingers on the scarred table and cursed silently. A welcoming whore could ease a measure of his startling, awakened hungers, but empty pleasure would not last.

He had the uneasy suspicion that Arielle D'Arcy would become a thorn in his carefully shielded heart.

A small woman who commanded two-thousand-pound horses easily, with a soft touch, a gentle word, could not be taken lightly. The stallion, Zeus, was likely to be so well trained that when in harness, he disregarded mares in heat. His mares—Maia, Electra, and Taygete—were named for Greek mythological nymphs bearing children to Zeus. Calypso and Hera, also related to the god Zeus, were the namesakes of two more mares.

Inside his jacket pocket Luc's fingers smoothed the lace handkerchief containing Edward Bliss's ring. Arielle's handkerchief reminded him of a whimsical, sweet dream . . . that of an angel hovering close, easing his pain with her softness.

Arielle D'Arcy, proclaimed businesswoman and spinster—his widow—wished for good luck when she'd named the foals five years ago. The soul of a dreamer lurked within her, despite her claims.

He recognized the stance of her body, the lift of her chin. His angel was a lady with a quest that had nothing to do with her outright presentation.

". . . Too much will in the woman," Smithson continued. "The idea of the venture makes my knees shake. A trainload of women . . . widows . . . untethered women, hunting husbands. My knees go weak at the thought. They call themselves the Society of Widows for the Purpose of Matrimonial Bliss. Not a dress of homespun hickory among the lot . . . all seemed well heeled. The pack of them behaved like ladies, except that Mrs. D'Arcy. She doesn't like reins. I'll be the laughingstock of the frontier. Wait till Bridger and Carson hear this tale. Smithson, an experienced wagon master, the leader of a widow train. That's what the town is calling it, you know. The widow train," he finished sourly, squinting through the steady stream of smoke from his pipe.

Luc shifted, easing his leg to the roaring fire in the huge fireplace. He swung his thoughts from Arielle to the man at his side. He suspected Smithson had a reason to take the women when so many other applicants were begging to be on his list. "Why did you accept them?"

Smithson chewed on the question, then spoke reluctantly as he studied the glowing coals in his pipe. "Found it damn hard to refuse. My mother was a widow, a pretty one, hit by hard times. A half-grown lad, I had to battle men twice my size when they came 'round. Women should have a good man to protect them, keep them from disgrace. These poor creatures cannot help their lot, any more than my sweet mother could, God rest her soul. She'd skin me if I turned them away. Though I had it on the tip of my tongue until I saw experienced westerners ready to place good bond money at their sides," he said quietly. "I can count on you to finish the trail, straight to Oregon. You'll not take up the scent of this Mexican War and leave the train?"

"I will see the women safely to Oregon country," Luc promised slowly, remembering his mother and sisters, who had needed protection. "I have land there and nowhere else to go. You have my word."

"Work with 'em," Smithson said after a nod. "I've seen females' skirts tangle in a wagon wheel and take 'em down. . . . Slow way to die. Keep their hems away from the fires . . . the sort of thing a husband would tend to, like keeping the hot young bucks at bay. Sort out the feeble and take only the strong. Though from the look of them, each one is a healthy specimen and a lady. I admit to a feeling of being humbugged at first, but now I am relieved."

His eyes shot to Luc's face. "What do you think about that Mary O'Flannery? She's got a topknot full of red hair, for all her mild, wide-eyed manners. Disliked her on the spot. She's a troublemaker, bound for accidents and illness with others hovering around her and costing us good traveling time. But for her two tikes, I'd have ruled her out."

"All of the women are seeking better lives," Luc returned, remembering Arielle's furious pale face glaring up at him from beneath her bonnet. What drove her?

She took farmers' trade goods and stowed seeds, spices, and sewing goods into the bottoms of the great Conestoga wagons, covered by boards for safety. Buried in a board box of earth, seedlings stood in front of each wagon seat. Carefully checking the wagons each day and marking each shipment in her ledger, Arielle referred to her chests as "cargo." Satinette ribbons, silk thread, and carefully folded paisley shawls filled one chest. Cotton threads, needles, French lace, muslin, and blue drilling filled another with fashion issues of *Godey's Lady's Book*. Another was filled with patterned and plain silks of every color, then a box of colored parasols and a large cask of green tea.

The women's belongings lacked furniture, one set of cookware and pots serving them all.

Arielle's grim determination to deliver the women, trade her goods, and begin horse breeding concealed another purpose, Luc decided warily.

He stared into the flames, rubbing his leg. Each woman carried secrets and pain, written in the lines of their faces and in their eyes. He read desperate fear in each face, in their silence. There was an excitement, too, their eyes lighting when they talked about unknown husbands and the Oregon country. Mary dreamed of warm, safe beds for her children, of making butter from her milk cows, and cooking meals for her family—her husband. Nancy wanted a garden and hoarded a tiny tin of seeds. America wanted goats to milk, to make soap and raise chickens. She wanted her son to grow strong and healthy in the new land.

Marie wanted to wash and scrub her own home, and Eliza

wanted to raise flax for weaving and to spin wool from her sheep raised in the clean, fresh countryside.

"Each woman wants a husband badly," Luc said quietly and vowed to discover Arielle's needs before the journey's end. "They will follow directions."

Smithson tapped his pipe into the juices on his pewter plate. "Up at four in the morning, teams yoked and ready to leave at seven. Noon break and rest on Sundays. Wash and rest days when possible. The widows are to keep to themselves, away from the men, married or no. Any courtship, and there will likely be a great deal of that, will take place with my knowledge. For the duration, I want to be notified of any carryings-on. Which brings me to you. Yesterday, I caught a bit of byplay between you and Mrs. D'Arcy. Anything you want to tell me? Are you thinking of courting her yourself for matrimonial purposes?"

Luc met Smithson's eyes evenly. He had no thought of releasing Arielle before he settled what was between them. Nor would he allow her in another man's arms. Not just yet. He examined the thought of courting Arielle like an emerald—the color of her eyes—turning, delving out the facets. Courting, sampling Arielle was very appealing. "Yes."

"As I told you, she'll fight the rein," Smithson said, slapping his journal closed. "Though she's got wedding papers, she's got the headstrong look of an unridden colt. . . . Must have given her poor husband a devil of a time. Probably sent him to his grave. . . . Remember, go light on beans and rice. They take too long to cook. . . . Plenty of wheat flour, cornmeal, and dried fruit. Pack the bacon in bran to keep it from getting rancid. Mrs. D'Arcy has my requirements, but I'm requesting that you check her purchases and the amounts. Maybe it's best that you've set your eye on her. That way the other men will be safe from harm," he finished, rising to his feet.

He dropped coins onto the scrubbed plank table. "Keep a tight leash on that one, Luc. She signed her name with her left hand, and you know that the use of a left hand shows different thinking. I won't be losing my widow train because she decides to take another route. I know that Siam is helping the ladies, but where's your third man?"

"He will be here soon." When Smithson nodded and left the tavern, Luc stood and rubbed his leg slowly. Arielle had told him over breakfast that she would "have the third man beneath Smithson's mighty nose before noon." She had avoided looking at him and addressed Glynis. Lydia had involved Luc with her cures for his leg and "infusing teas for stamina," but he caught Arielle's slight frown when she looked at him. A patient man, Luc would enjoy the long trail and the exploration of Arielle's hidden fires. Last night she had tasted sweet, virginally curious, and he had fought to keep himself from demanding more, though before many more nights had passed, she would lay warm in his arms.

Slightly irritated that he had just noticed his five-year abstinence from women and the woman he desired wished to shed him like dirty linen, Luc frowned.

She could not be charmed, nor bullied. Luc's frown deepened. He had never wanted to bully a woman, but Arielle challenged him like a bristling porcupine.

His leg ached, reminding him of their meeting and his need of her then.

Had that need dimmed? Luc shifted uneasily in his chair. When Luc was a child, his father had punished him for weakness. The result was a man who let few inside his heart. Catherine had turned the lock. For a time Willow softened his life and didn't protest what little he gave her.

Arielle had stepped boldly into the heart of him, an angel appearing when he needed a soft touch. *"My dear . . ."*

Then she had whisked away, taking a measure of his pride and his mother's wedding ring.

His pride said she was his wife and that he desired the headstrong little witch. She'd challenged his honor and his manhood.

Through the window's wavery glass, Luc watched Arielle stroll down the sidewalk, Glynis at her side. His fingers smoothed the coins before he dropped them to the table. Arielle's skin was smooth, warm, then heating, her breath coming quickly though she held still in his arms. The russet curls had warmed his hands, spilling over them.

Arielle daintily lifted her skirt away from a puddle, and Luc glimpsed a trim ankle, sheathed in flannel. His strength had almost returned, though his leg ached, and his body was demanding Arielle's soft, pale one.

She stopped, stared into the busy street, and spoke to Glynis, who placed a hand on her mistress's arm. Arielle brushed it off and leapt down into the street, striding across the mud puddles, her white petticoats frothing in the sun.

Luc stepped outside just as Arielle slid between a small man with a whip and the bloody back of a tall, lean slave stoically gripping a wagon wheel. Luc's heart stopped, his legs closing the distance between Arielle's danger and himself.

The small man brushed her aside, snaked out the whip leisurely, preparing for another blow to the striped back of the slave. The man stood straight, despite his wounds. His big hands locked around the iron rim of a tall wagon wheel.

Arielle's dainty foot stepped on the whip. She bent to take it in her hand just as the man threw his arm into the blow.

In a flurry of petticoats Arielle's backside landed in the mud, and the man's blow went sailing out into the crisp air away from the slave. Glynis bent to help Arielle as a crowd gathered.

The small man whirled, his face florid with rage, and his shoulder caught Glynis's. She fell on top of Arielle, who shook herself free and struggled to her feet, her bonnet tilted to one side. She helped Glynis to stand, then her gloved fist shot out. The man's eyes widened with the blow to his jaw, and he drew his hand back.

Luc caught the man's open hand in his own and crushed it slowly, bringing the man down to his knees. Though the man needed chastising, Luc used the movement to relieve his anger for Arielle. Careless of her safety, she had reacted instantly, badly frightening him. "You are sorry, are you not?" Luc asked between his teeth.

His fear for Arielle had startled him, the need to throw

her over his shoulder and carry her off to safety barely
leashed.

"*I want that man.*" Standing with her feet slightly apart,
she pointed at the silent slave, his head held high. Arielle
shook her muddied skirts and grimaced with distaste. She
frowned at the man kneeling in the cold mud. "I know your
type. You won't understand anything but this—how much?"

When he didn't answer, she glanced at Luc. "I am taking
him, unless he refuses. You will have a price and his papers
ready for Mr. . . . Navaronne this afternoon." She nodded to
the slave, who looked coolly down at her from his seven-
foot height. "There now. You'll come with us and rest until
tomorrow. When Luc—he's my employee—has your papers, you will be free, though I would like to hire you for
our trip. Come along now, sir," she said brightly, smiling up
at him and touching his arm. "You need tending, and tomorrow you will be a free man."

The tall man straightened, then nodded slowly. While
Glynis and Arielle walked gingerly ahead, holding their
damp skirts away from them, the black man followed. Battered and dressed in rags, he walked straight with an air of
nobility.

Lifting his boot and placing it on the fallen man's chest,
Luc pushed slowly downward. Second to his distaste of the
man was his dislike of being addressed as Arielle's employee. He resented her leash and the overriding fear that
she could have been hurt. When the man lay full length in
the mud, Luc murmured, "I will expect you this afternoon.
Have his papers ready."

Eight

····················

The prairie spread out like a rolling green sea beneath the early morning sun. Wagons rolled easily, one by one, white cloth coverings rippling with each bump. Overhead the sky's brilliant blue spilled into the prairie's new green grass. Wilson, the wagon train's "pilot," rode ahead to prepare a campsite.

Timmy's fife cut through the excited air of the emigrants as they entered Indian Territory. Wrapped in "Oregon fever," the excited expression of the men contrasted with the women, who mourned farms and homes left behind. As they left the safety of the United States behind, each emigrant paused to look back, then turned, firmly facing the sprawling prairie and the unknown.

Smithson insisted that the widows follow the first wagon, an emigrant experienced in fording streams. Each day lots would be drawn for positions in the train, to equalize "eating dust." When possible, the wagons would spread out. At the end of the train, a band of poor emigrants from Italy pushed handcarts, doggedly following the large, heavily

127

laden wagons. Excitement traveled in the cold spring air like a heady wine, and the emigrants drank it freely. The day seemed like a giant carnival, and the train moved quickly. Songs sailed from one wagon to another, from women to children, then to men.

Arielle insisted on taking the reins of Zeus, Maia, Calypso, and Hera. Electra and Taygete followed behind the wagon as the spare team. The other emigrants shouted at their oxen and mules. "Giddap," "Haw," and "Gee" mixed with the excited cries of children. They scampered along beside the wagon, mothers warning them away from the massive iron-rimmed wheels. Anna drove the second wagon, expertly cracking a bullwhip over the two yokes of young oxen. The sound carried like a shot. Nancy followed with another team of oxen, carrying Browning trade goods for the Willamette farmers. The milk cows were tied to the back, a newborn calf standing unsteadily in the wagon. Dante shepherded a small flock of sheep led by a goat with a tinkling bell.

Lydia wandered happily beside the train, stopping to pluck stalks or dig roots for the basket she carried everywhere. She waved to Luc, and he returned the greeting, walking with one hand on Zeus's heavily padded throat. Arielle resented that big, hair-flecked hand on her stock; it spoke of possession. She also resented the way he'd easily lifted her up to the wagon seat, his gaze skimming her mouth, throat, and then her breasts. He'd held her there, her feet a foot above the ground, his expression hardening, his eyes dark with messages she didn't understand. Heathen, primitive desires that caused her heart to thump wildly. She had tingled then, her breasts suddenly peaking, thrusting at the practical cotton camisole and black dress. After Luc placed her on the seat, his hand had lingered on her thigh, his long fingers firmly finding the shape beneath the layers of petticoats.

Arielle remembered his kiss, the gentle seduction of warmth and pleasure. She had tasted a tenderness, too, the longing within him had curled around her.

Thaddeus had never kissed her, except that peck on her

cheek after a good game of whist. Arielle tossed her head, firming her mouth. Thaddeus, as a gentleman, probably had not indulged in realms of women, practicing the tantalizing technique. She frowned, uncertain if Luc's mouth did not border on sinful.

Seated beside Arielle on the wagon seat, Glynis sat straight. "Interesting," she murmured.

"Mmm," Arielle returned, distracted by the sight of Luc walking beside her team of Percherons. His broad shoulders strained at the seams of a dark red homespun shirt, tucked in at his waist. The ornately beaded belt at his waist supported his revolver and the huge knife. The butternut-colored trousers Biddy had mended for him ran into the tops of tall, fringed leather leggings.

He moved lithely, long legs easily striding over the prairie's new grass. At the slightest movement—a rabbit scurrying across the wide plains, a deer bounding away—Luc followed the movement with an alert jerk of his eyes. A dangerous, hawkish look shrouded him now, nothing like the man caught in his fevers.

He looked like a man who was going home, eager for it.

A child called out to him, and Luc waved, grinning boyishly. *That smile could charm a rabbit from a hole,* Arielle decided darkly. Perhaps if he'd exposed that dazzling, appealing grin when he was sick, she wouldn't be in her current entanglement.

Arielle pushed away the thought of that arrogant head resting on her bosom, heating it, and the rough scrape of his beard against her throat.

She much preferred Thaddeus's cool blue eyes and the comfortable way she could control the conversation.

Luc's eyes swung to her over his shoulder. The intensity beneath his lashes stopped her in midbreath, her heart racing. The unsettling emotions tangling within her were frightening.

Luc moved silently, quickly. His hand touched hers briefly when she adjusted the harness lines and the sight of the lean brown fingers closing over hers momentarily had stunned her. She didn't understand the heat in the man for a moment, nor the way her heart fluttered and her stomach knotted at the sight of him. Part of her wanted to touch the medallion, rummage through that dark hair covering his chest, and test the slow, hard pulse of his heart against her palm.

Luc reminded her of Zeus. The mares were easily controlled, but when Arielle rode Zeus, allowing his Arabian blood to rule him, galloping across the Browning meadows, she felt as free and wild as when Luc kissed her. The great stallion weighed over two thousand pounds and stood sixteen hands high, but when she rode him, the massive muscles straining beneath her, they became one. Sunlight shimmered, wove around her, in her, catching her for a time in the enchantment. The dangerous excitement of riding Zeus thrilled her, the wind sailing through her hair, the warmth of the sun blending with the stallion's heat.

Arielle tightened her lips. The excitement of riding a magnificent stallion with Arabian blood should not be compared to the delicate balance of friendship and respect that a woman feels for a man. A well-crafted marriage, artfully controlled day by day, required cool logic.

Thaddeus's presence was much more comfortable.

Her mind wandered when she saw Luc, and something inside her tingled and warmed. Arielle pressed her hand to her stomach and decided the reaction was caused by a quickly eaten breakfast. When Luc's open hand stayed on her stallion's strong throat, riding the muscles and caressing them, Arielle could not look away.

Her throat dried and her lips seemed to heat, the skin tightening on them as she remembered his hungry kiss. She closed her eyes. *To lie with Luc on his nightly blanket would be impossible.*

She opened her lids and studied Luc's firm haunches, his long legs striding beside her team, gentling them to the sound of oxen and mules nearby.

His mouth was beautiful, firmly molded, tantalizing.

She frowned. Thaddeus's lips were thinly molded, a proper manly line.

Luc's mouth was tender, warm, cherishing, fitting firmly over hers. . . .

She inhaled sharply, remembering that thrusting manly form against her nightgown. She dismissed the ache deep within her and scanned the rolling prairies, the wagon ahead of her team, anywhere but Luc's hard backside.

"I said, Luc is an interesting man. Clearly one who holds his promises. Did you know that he is taking Lorenzo to a poor dying woman's child? No small task, considering the cat has clawed Luc at every turn. . . . Yet he is determined to complete what he has begun. The children love Luc and Mr. Siam," Glynis said, her eyes sparkling, and as if on cue, Lorenzo squalled from his cage. He clawed and hissed at the chickens in the next cage.

Then she said, "Thaddeus is not a man that children love easily. I don't remember him letting a child wrestle him to the ground as Luc allowed Timmy last night. . . . Strange," she continued, looking straight ahead at the wagon in front of them. "I've never seen Thaddeus look at you like Luc did last night, either. As if he were hungry for you. Rather an interesting scene when he lay on the blanket beneath Timmy's conquering straddle . . . his eyes locked to yours. His had a distinct predatory gleam."

"Stop, Glynis. You are, as always, a gossip," Arielle said tightly.

"Of course," Glynis admitted airily. "I found it strange that when you moved around the area of their play, Luc's hand wrapped around your ankle. Quite a little struggle for supremacy, I must say . . . you with your red-haired temper bristling, and Luc's eyes teasing you."

Arielle dismissed the disturbing touch of his fingers caressing her ankle beneath her petticoats. "I find his many compliments strange. Like that statement about my hair. 'Coppery, sunlit silk,' indeed. No doubt he is skilled in debacle. Luc is nothing more than a gallant out to make a conquest, or a tormenting boy—"

Glynis's eyebrows shot up. "Really? He's got a gray hair or two and probably the experience with women to equal his years. He is quite the manliest figure on the train—

excluding Mr. Siam, of course. I heard Mr. Smithson direct
Wilson to leave Luc and you alone if you venture from
camp, as you are in the courting stage. Smithson feels the
westerners can meet any disaster. My dear, it seems as if
you already have a suitor to take you from widowhood.
How nice."

Arielle crushed the smooth reins in her left hand. "There
are matters that haven't been resolved between Luc and myself. I intend to put things straight as soon as possible."

Biddy peered through the opening, adjusting her skirts
over the chest of goods Smithson suggested they bring. The
small beads, cotton handkerchiefs, blue calico, and blue
drilling lay neatly packed with an assortment of the wom-
en's gaudy jewelry to be used for trading with the Indians.

In the wagon Sally rested amid a feathertick, quietly read-
ing *A Guide to Good Wifery*. Mary O'Flannery cuddled and
wrapped her shawl around Brianna, who had taken another
cold.

"Luc is a warrior and so is the black man," Biddy stated
quietly, her gaze drifting to the tall, former slave who
walked apart, his head held high. Dressed in a dark jacket
and pants, he had draped a red wool blanket over one shoulder and around his chest. Lydia offered her basket to him,
and he held it, patiently aloof, while she gathered several
stalks of dried grass. "Omar came from a great family, the
Zulu. His mother told him so, but he has forgotten everything else. I have heard of the African warriors, and though
he does not know the Bantu language, he comes from kings,
a great people. If he were in his land, people would kneel
at his feet. Mr. Luc comes from fine blood, too, I'm thinking. I bet there are women wanting him something fierce."

"I have heard enough about Luc, Biddy," Arielle said
slowly, firmly between her teeth. She tried to change the
subject—"These petticoats and skirts tangle badly when getting up on wagon wheels, even if one steps from a conve-
nient stump."

"Hmm," Glynis murmured thoughtfully. "They shouldn't
have tangled too badly when Luc lifted you bodily to the

wagon seat. My dear, you should have seen your face—you were positively stunned."

"But, Arielle—ma'am. A woman is safe with warriors at her side . . . in her bed," Biddy teased, grinning widely. "That Mr. Luc is one man dying to be in your bed for sure, ma'am. He'll be wanting to put a baby in your belly soon. All those poor lonely women without Mr. Luc . . ."

Arielle closed her eyes and counted to ten, while Glynis distracted Biddy by asking her to check the butter churning in a pot attached to the wagon's hoops.

"Yes," Glynis teased in an aside from beneath her bonnet. "All those poor lonely women. The daughter of that French farmer is entranced with Luc. She hasn't taken her eyes from him."

"Glynis. Perhaps we should change the subject," Arielle offered tightly. "Perhaps we should converse about Mr. Siam's sly glances at you and Mr. Smithson's evident interest in your well being. It seems that two gentlemen are very interested in you."

Glynis's lips parted, and she stared blankly at Arielle, who couldn't resist giggling.

Before dusk the wagons pulled into a circle, the tongues pointing outward. The chains of the harness riggings were attached wagon to wagon, forming a pen for the livestock, discouraging thievery in the night. Now the livestock grazed on new prairie grasses beneath the watch of the boys.

Arielle's arms and back ached as she stood staring at the westward trail. The other women prepared camp and tended the animals and Maia nudged Arielle's back, begging for a sweet. Arielle laughed and pushed back her bonnet. She dug into her pocket, supplying the bit of dried apple. "So, my pretty, you worked hard today. That naughty Zeus nipped at you. Don't pay any attention to him. I'll speak to him. I think we'll go for a walk now and graze a bit away from the rest of the stock." She leaned against the great horse's shoulder, resting her head against the solid muscle.

Arielle jumped when a cool finger slipped inside the torn sleeve of her dress, and Luc stood very near her back. Startled by the soft caress, Arielle stood still, her mind blank. His hand caressed the aching small of her back, and Arielle resisted the urge to lean into the wonderful soothing pressure. She closed her eyes, straightened her back, and prepared to move away, too tired to scold him. In the next instant Luc lifted her easily, placed her on Maia's back, and swung up behind her. His hands spanned her waist, holding her when she would have swatted at him. He bent to her ear and whispered, "Let me take care of you, *chère*. You are too tired. It was dangerous to fall asleep with the lines in your hands earlier."

She sat stiffly away from him, the hard warmth of his body enticing after the long day on the wagon's bench. "I didn't sleep much last night, wondering how to be rid of you. I barely know you, and you take liberties with my person," Arielle returned in a hushed tone as Mrs. Potter and the other emigrant wives glanced curiously their way.

Arielle lowered her voice. She was trembling with anger, at Luc and at the way she had wanted to rest in his arms. She was not a weak woman and didn't require cuddling. Least of all with a man who demanded that she lie beside him for a portion of each night. "How could any man so concerned about his mother and sisters act as you do? Where is your propriety?"

Smithson stopped talking to Siam and stroked his side-burns thoughtfully, watching Luc guide the great horse with a touch of his knees. The other five horses followed easily, ambling after their mistress. In the sweeping shadows of dusk, the wind chilled Arielle and she shivered, only to have Luc wrap his arms around her waist, trapping her within the merino paisley shawl. She tried to force them away, and against her ear he chuckled softly, nibbling at her lobe. "When a man is expecting his wedding night yet to come, perhaps he acts a little well warmed."

Arielle's eyes widened. She was no longer tired.

Her body was too aware of Luc's long one fitted intimately against her, his hard thighs next to hers beneath her skirts. "This is not proper," she said between her teeth, refusing to turn. "We are merely playing out a masquerade for the journey. You are my employee."

"Employee?" Luc's jaw hardened, a muscle jerking beneath the dark skin.

"Well . . . yes. Now, Luc, if you are going to travel a bit with us—until the divorce—we should come to the matter of your salary—"

His arms tightened, snaring her back against him. "I have a copy of our wedding papers. Siam requested them from our minister. Are you warmer?" he asked, sifting the pins away from her hair and lifting it in his fingers.

With a low rumble of pleasure, Luc fitted his chin over her head and drew her closer. He inhaled deeply, nuzzling her curls. "My little tigress. You are a strong woman, *chère*. Let me hold you, rest against me."

"I am not a happy woman," Arielle stated clearly when the horses began to graze on the new grass a distance away from camp. She held her body stiffly away from the warmth of his. This interlude with Luc would be the perfect time to straighten the matter between them. A slight rise in the prairie shielded them from the train. "I learned today that you spoke of courting me to Mr. Smithson. You will set that matter straight. You paid entirely too much attention to me at the nooning. It isn't proper for a man to be so attentive. The way you look at me is almost . . . primitive," she bit out. "As though you could . . . take a bite of me. I am a properly cured spinster after all."

"But I *am* courting you, my sweet dove . . . a natural thing for a husband to do," Luc returned easily, sliding from the horse. He grimaced when his feet touched the rich earth, and he limped a step before extending his arms up for her.

"Husband?" If only she hadn't seen his pain, remembered his fevers, Arielle thought desperately. She found herself plucked from the horse and tucked into Luc's long, warm arms. Her struggle to be free only served to draw her closer; the draft horses grazed close, breaking the sweeping fierce wind and enclosing them in privacy.

Then Luc was bending to her, his breath warm as it swept across her cheeks.

His mouth demanded; his hands opened on her back, urging her against his taut body.

Arielle tasted the heat, the hunger vibrating within Luc, the impatience of his hands.

Then her mouth was parting, her tongue tasting his as Luc deepened the kiss. Lost in the fiery hunger, the pleasure warming her body, weakening her legs, Arielle stepped into the fire.

She clung to his shoulders for support, the strong muscles sliding beneath her fingers.

Then Luc was closer, his hand moving between them, stroking the buttons on her bodice. Her heart leapt at the brush of his fingertips across her breasts, the gentle exploration to find the aching tip.

Arielle tried to cry out, to push him away. Instead her fingers clung to him as Luc became her world. Heat shot from his body into hers, filling her, energizing her, yet stilling, soothing, bringing that odd hunger to prey upon her. His teeth nibbled at her bottom lip, nipping it gently, the small injury exciting her further.

She ached, burned, needed. Then Luc's large hand found her breast, easing away her bodice, the merino wool vest, and the cotton camisole.

Caught on the pinnacle of exquisite delight, Arielle gasped and found her feet off the ground. Luc's lips burned against her skin, trailing across her breast to enclose her nipple in moist heat. Arielle cried out, a pulsating heat beginning low within her.

His face was hot against her skin, the wind whipping her skirts against her unsteady legs. She cried out again as tiny muscles deep inside her body tightened and melted with pleasure.

Luc gathered her close, holding her against him, stilling her with soft, sweet kisses that eased the urgent heat and soothed her aching body.

Arielle shivered once and stepped back, uncertain that her legs would stand apart from him. She was determined to place distance between his hard body and hers. She thrust out her palm when he stepped nearer, the dark skin stretched tautly across his high cheekbones, his eyes dark with promises she didn't understand. "You will stop this . . . play this instant, Lucien," she whispered huskily, her lips trembling.

"Lucien," he repeated unevenly, his accent curling around the word as though he were taking it from her mouth to his, "No other woman has spoken my name like you, *ma chère*."

When she flicked her bottom lip with her tongue, she found the taste of him. Luc's hands covered her breasts, soothing the aching hardness with light caresses.

Stunned by a touch she had never known, Arielle stared down at his hands, the long, dark fingers carefully smoothing her camisole and vest and buttoning her dress. Before she recovered from the intimacy, Luc smiled softly, the gentle expression a distracting seduction. "Now I know"—his fingertip traced across her swollen bottom lip gently—"my wife is a virgin or nearly so."

He took her trembling hands and bent to kiss her palms, his face hot against her skin. The gesture was reverent, his long black hair catching the wind as Arielle watched.

She tried desperately to assemble her thoughts. To put them in a logical line and strike out at him with the sharp tongue that had scourged sailing captains. She swallowed and tried, "You have breached proper etiquette—"

Luc's warm hand curled around her throat, his thumb smoothing her jaw. She shook free, smoothed her hair, and glanced down cautiously at her bodice. "I think . . ." she began carefully, "that you act quickly and take what you want."

"Take what we *both* want, *chère*," he corrected softly, sliding his finger through a curl. There was a sensuous curve to his mouth. His lips were slightly swollen, tinted by their heated kiss.

"Not I," she said firmly, backing away a step. "You are not my intended." She clasped her hands behind her back. Luc's gaze dropped hungrily to her bodice and the twin peaks thrusting against the layers of cloth. With trembling hands she wrapped her shawl around her.

Luc stroked Maia's muscled flank, his expression closing,

his gray eyes flickering beneath his lashes. A blue-black strand of hair slid along the rough stubble of his jaw and rested on the heavily beating vein in his throat. "You have plans for another?" he asked too softly.

She pressed her lips firmly closed. When it was time, she would wave Thaddeus's cool gentlemanly manners beneath Luc's arrogant nose.

Arielle forced her eyes away from the opening of his shirt, the wedge of black hair curling from his dark, gleaming skin. Her gaze seemed drawn to the intimate pulse beating at the base of his throat. She tried to think of Thaddeus's gentlemanly behavior. She took a deep breath as Luc watched her mouth. "Stop looking at me as though you were a hungry hawk waiting to snatch a fat field mouse and devour it," she ordered curtly, curiously drawn to the slow caress of Luc's hand across the Percheron's coat. "It isn't at all seemly for a hired man to act this way."

His hand paused before continuing. "Husband, Mrs. D'Arcy," he corrected. "If you wish, I can show Smithson our marriage papers."

"For the time, I expect you to act as my employee, obeying my orders. I pay well—"

Luc's dark scowl stopped her. "You are pressing your luck, Madame D'Arcy," he murmured quietly. The sound was too soft, accented and laced with danger.

"Yes. Well, I'll work on a contract for your services when I have time."

"Services?" Luc's smile was cold. "A husband is generally well paid for his . . . services."

Her hand rose to her throat, stilling the pounding heartbeat. She cleared her throat, backed a few feet away, and turned stiffly. Followed by her horses, Arielle walked back to camp. She shivered, her bonnet shielding her hot face as she bent to loosen the chain between the wagons. "Go," she ordered, and the great horses ambled through to join the other stock.

Smithson stood beside her when she straightened. "It's a nice evening tonight, isn't it, missus?" he asked cheerily, his gaze skipping to Luc, who had lifted Lion to his shoulders and was striding back to camp.

"Quite," Arielle returned, praying that her lips were not reddened from Luc's kiss. She didn't dare glance down at her bodice to see if it had been fastened properly.

"An easy day of it today," Smithson probed, puffing on his pipe. "Can't say as I was happy to see those huge beasts of yours prancing in harness. Fancy bits of horseflesh. Quite a sight to see a slip of a thing like you leading them around. What makes you think they can stand the journey? Maybe I should send Luc to fetch a proper team of oxen."

"My stock is well bred," Arielle snapped, tucking a curl Luc had loosened up into her bonnet. "Their stamina and intelligence are unquestionable."

Smithson snorted in disbelief, his eyes trailing after Glynis. "Smart woman, that Glynis. Calm . . . a proper widow. While Luc was courting you, she tended to the camp. Dinner is prepared already. The food was prepared yesterday. The ladies will have a hard enough time cooking later on. They've invited Wilson and myself to the mess and are washing and mending our clothes. An old bachelor like myself appreciates the refinements, you know."

Arielle smiled tightly as Lydia plucked grasses from her basket and held them out to Luc. Lydia beamed as though she had discovered gold when Luc inspected the stalks and nodded.

The French farmer's daughter walked toward him, carrying a large cup. Lydia, happy with her day's foraging, carried her basket to camp.

The Frenchwoman's skirt billowed around Luc's long legs, enfolding them as she handed the cup to him.

Caught midbreath, Arielle could not force her eyes away.

The intimate pose of his head bent to the Frenchwoman's blond one, the way they smiled at each other struck at her. Luc's low laughter tangled with the girl's mirth, floating merrily in the night air.

Arielle's fingers curved as though fitting around her fencing foil.

She wasn't jealous, not a bit. That the girl's hair was

neatly braided on top of her head, unlike Arielle's unruly curls, did not matter.

Luc was obviously the rake she supposed he was, placing his hot mouth on her breast and doing sinful things to her body. Within moments of kissing her he was flirting with another woman. "Dog. Shark bait. Cur. Fop," she muttered, turning away.

Arielle promised herself that if Lucien Navaronne D'Arcy ever touched her again, he would be missing fingers.

Later that night Timmy's fife music sailed along the wind, the wagon's canvas covers making a whipping sound. "In the next day or so we'll see bison, and I can't say how glad I am to have experienced westerners for hunters. Last year the farmers frightened a big herd, and the beasts nearly ran us into the sod. Ruined a wagon."

"I see the advantage of having experienced men along the trail, Mr. Smithson." Arielle fought the wave of heat claiming her when Luc smiled at her. It was a slow smile, laden with intimacy. Arielle firmed her lips, remembering his ability to forage at her clothing, then flirt with the neatly braided Frenchwoman. "I do not doubt Luc's experience," she said darkly.

"Perhaps you should consider leaving widowhood, Mrs. D'Arcy," Smithson said carefully, tapping his pipe against an iron rim of a wagon wheel. "It's apparent that Luc has his eye set on you. A woman should be married and tending a man. I see that you are not without a care for him. It's a grand thing to see when a man courts a woman and she blushes like you're doing now. Makes an old bison like me have a bit of the fancies. No need to ask my approval, missus. Luc is a fine man. He's already proved himself today when fording that river. The Joneses' wagon would have gone downstream if Luc hadn't jumped on the back of that strong ox. Took some fast thought."

"Yes," Arielle agreed darkly. "Luc is a very quick-acting man."

Nine

After their first day on the trail, the excited emigrants sat around their campfires or walked from wagon to wagon. Excitement quivered in the sweet damp April night, touching each heart; the journey had begun. Women baked bread and roasted rabbits over the open fires. Banjo and fiddle music blended, and husbands grabbed their wives for a quick jig that ended in laughter. Children played close to their parents, running between the tents. A mother called for her son, he answered reluctantly, and dogs barked at the deer and small animals foraging in the night. The scent of smoke and spring filled the air, the sparks of the fires sailing upward toward the stars. Livestock milled inside the barricades, unused to the confinement. Sleepy children nestled in their mothers' arms and inside tents.

Men smoked pipes and talked in earnest about the impending wars, their hopes for good crops in the fertile West, and the fall of the Mormon Nauvoo and Brigham Young's decision to take his people west. They spoke of the Kansaw Indians who had watched them pass. One bold horseman had ridden toward the wagon, demanding a fine blanket to match his tall beaver hat. Luc had urged his horse near the warrior and had signed with his hands in rapid, deft movements. The warrior nodded, and Luc tossed a blanket to him. Pleased with the offering, he had ridden off to join his band.

While the women moved around the camp, Wilson whittled a stick and glanced speculatively at the women. Smithson rocked on the wooden keg that served as his chair. When the children came shyly up to him, his eyes lit up. Lion stared at Omar with undisguised admiration, the tall black man standing regally apart, wrapped in his blanket and the night. Nancy Fairhair and Eliza Smythe milked the cows, while Marie hummed and baked her bread. She clucked over the buckets of milk, carefully placing a clean cloth over them. Mary O'Flannery rocked Brianna on her hip. Lydia beamed while she spread her day's harvest, cleaning and scraping roots, bundling grasses and herbs that she hung from string attached to the wagon hoops.

Arielle fought sleep, carefully logging in the day's journey while she sat at a small table. The contract for Luc's services was neatly folded in an envelope. When the time was right, she would discuss the matter with him. She nibbled on the fresh carrot Glynis had placed in front of her and sipped tea from her china cup. Because Arielle, Anna, and Nancy had handled the teams during the day, the other women prepared the evening meal, placing planks between two barrels and covering them with a tablecloth. Anna stayed near Sally, who was restless and pale, quietly stitching a gown for her baby.

Nightfall circled the camp as they ate, then prepared to sleep. Arielle wrapped her woolen shawl around her, leaned against a wagon wheel, and concentrated on Thaddeus. A true gentleman, Thaddeus would never attempt to hold her hand beneath the table as Luc had done. She followed Dante skimming around a restless sheep, driving it back to bed down with the flock.

Arielle jumped when a big hand weighted her shoulder, the thumb stroking the curve of her neck. Luc's clean scent mingled with soap, smoke, and leather. Heat warmed along her back as he stepped near. "Luc. Unhand me."

"Will you walk with me, *chère*?" he asked softly, tugging at a tendril at the back of her neck.

"I'm quite tired, Mr. Navaronne." She glanced at Smithson for escape and found him beaming. He nodded approvingly at Luc. "Go along now, Mrs. D'Arcy," Smithson said. "It's safe enough."

Arielle looked up at Luc and caught the grim set of his jaw and the flash of his eyes in the shadows. The set of his fingers around her upper arm denied her tugging away. Arielle inhaled sharply. "Perhaps now would be just as good a time as any," she whispered firmly, nodding to Smithson. She looked at Glynis, who was discreetly trying to put distance between herself and Siam.

The big Canadian was eager to lift and carry anything Glynis might need. He loomed at her every turn, his hair damp and neatly combed below his hat. The Englishwoman looked very uncomfortable, her glances at Arielle pleading and frustrated.

Arielle decided that Glynis could fend for herself. She plucked the envelope containing the contract and stuffed it into her pocket. Luc must be set straight and quickly. "Mr. Smithson, please tell Glynis that I'm walking and will be back shortly. She may go on to bed without me."

The captain snorted. "She's occupied. Go along now." With that he stood, stretched, and began making his way firmly to where Glynis sat sipping her tea. Brianna skipped beside him, then slipped her hand into his. In midstride the captain stopped and stared down at the little girl, who smiled impishly and lifted her arms up to him. With a chuckle the big man reached down and plopped her on his shoulders. Brianna pointed toward her mother, who was stitching, and Smithson walked slowly toward her.

Arielle stepped into the night, startled when Luc's open hand warmed her back. "You will unhand me now, sir," she said in a hushed tone, picking a way into the night.

Luc's big hand continued to ride the small of her waist, and Arielle waited until the night fully covered them from sight before she pivoted. She realized too late that while she had been placing her thoughts in a neat row, Luc had been skillfully guiding her behind a small stand of bushes. When she turned to confront him, her face met the breadth of Luc's wide chest. Stepping back, Arielle smoothed her hair with her left hand, then quickly changed to her right. She would not be accused of left-handed thinking when she sent Luc on his amorous way. "So here we are," she began unevenly, nervous beneath his intent gaze.

"Yes, here we are." Luc took her hand, raising and kissing the back of it. The moonlight swept his black lashes, tipping them in silver, and the heat of his mouth sent a shiver up the back of her neck.

Scents clung to him, soap and leather, coffee and animals. Shadows played around his face when he smoothed her cheek with his rough palm, his eyes gleaming as they traced her face. A flush she could not explain swept through her, her knees weakening. She swallowed when he rubbed the taut cords on the back of her neck, the caress both soothing and unnerving. The man seemed to know where to touch, what to touch—

"Goodness," Arielle whispered huskily, when she could speak. She drew her hand away and wrapped her shawl closer to her, stepping back. "Luc, at the onset of this journey, I think we must be perfectly honest with each other. While I am grateful that you have not exposed my ladies, I cannot allow you to foster the idea that I am . . . will be your wife—"

Luc's soft kisses sealed her last words, his mouth bestowing light and tantalizing bits of kisses across hers. "My adorable wife," he corrected against her mouth. She tried hazily to itemize exactly what was amiss with his statement and could not.

Though he had not touched her with his hands, his mouth drew her nearer, the sweet cherishing drawing her like honey she had to taste.

Like raspberry jam, she corrected on a heartbeat, with interesting little tangy textures of heat and hunger running beneath the stunning softness.

"You know ... I ... am ... a businesswoman, Luc. I have your contract in my pocket," she managed finally and found her traitorous left hand flat on his chest. "This ... ah ... venture ... must not be endangered...."

Luc's hands were soothing, so soothing, gently stroking her back and lower.

She wanted to run away, wanted to let her temper fly at his audacity.

She wanted to step into his kiss, press her advantage, and take the heat and hunger throbbing just below the surface of his hard, warm, tormenting lips.

She willed herself to stand coolly apart, to resist his tasting, nibbling, enchanting little kisses that were lengthening, seducing, melting ...

Her hair was free now, her left hand smoothing Luc's smoothly shaved jaw. His heat drew her, tempted her fingers to explore the tiny cord that had enchanted her earlier. His arms drew her down, slowly, inevitably against him. Then she was lying, facing him, and Luc's warm hands smoothed her waist, her bodice.

His deep voice rasped against her throat, his mouth burning her flesh. She wanted him closer still, wanted the movement of his lips downward, the gentle clasp of his hand on her breast.

Shivering, straining against her passion, Arielle tried to understand his words, the soft, seductive language, sweeping from him and swirling around her, heating her.

His hand cupped her breast, lifting it to his mouth, the burning heat enfolding her, and she cried out, afraid to move, afraid the delight would fly away.

But there was more, the delicate tugging of his lips, the spiraling delight that warmed the low intimate, quivering, shy aching part of her. She fought lifting her hips, fought the sounds that came from low in her throat, fought touching him ... and lost to the passion riding her.

Luc's hand was low on her stomach, the warm rough palm pressing against her intimately and she cried out again, stunned as his long fingers closed over her softness, caressing her gently.

"Ah, *chère*, you are so ready, so damp for me," Luc whispered roughly against her throat, his face hot against her skin. He shook now, bracing his weight from her, yet warming her with the length of his body.

Then there were urgent words, Luc's hands moving between their bodies.

Arielle wanted to move away, to rail at him for taking liberties. She wanted to move closer into the fire; her hands clenched his shoulders tightly.

His kisses were long now, heated and hungry, and she met them eagerly, learning the odd, tender duel of mouths and tongues.

Luc's fingers moved, easing slowly within her, and Arielle shifted away, suddenly frightened. "Luc, what are you doing?" she whispered, shivering, aching.

The fire burst into flame then. Tiny circling bursts of pleasure caught her, held her on the tip of delight. When she fell slowly, drowsy and exhausted, Luc wrapped her in his arms. She had never been cuddled, nor comforted. The cherishing, soft caresses and gentling words eased and softened taut cords within her. She snuggled closer, returning his soft kiss, and had never felt so cozy, despite the chilly night.

A heartbeat later Arielle breathed unevenly, aware that her head rested on Luc's shoulder ... that a blanket lay beneath them, covering a soft dry mat ... that another quilt lay over them and that between the layers of warmth, Luc's hard desire thrust intimately at her bare thigh.

Arielle's lids jerked open.

Her flannel drawers were down to her knees, her bodice was open, and Luc's big hand cradled her breast. His fingers played with the peak, rolling it gently.

Her eyes widened, her breath catching in her lungs. Each time his hand moved, heat raced down her body, and there was a distinct, undeniable, jerking ache in the moist heat between her legs. Arielle concentrated on the new sensation, dissecting it, tracing the cause. Each firm motion drew fresh tingles of pleasure deep within her; her body contracted in direct response to the movement of his hand.

Her lungs ached. She exhaled slowly, her breath blowing

away a strand of hair that had crossed her cheek and lips. She licked her lips, moistening them, and tasted Luc on the swollen contours.

Her hair spilled everywhere, and Luc's face nuzzled her temple, his breath uneven. He held her tightly, his long body trembling against hers. His hips moved against her, rocking firmly, his voice thick and uneven against her throat. "If I don't have you soon, madame wife, I shall turn into stone. Perhaps I already have." The smooth heated length of him branded her thigh, and she jerked away only to be hauled closer, his hand claiming her breast, caressing it.

When his teeth nipped her earlobe, Arielle batted at him, struggling furiously against him and the masses of her petticoats, skirt, and the blankets. "What are you doing?" she whispered desperately, her face hot with embarrassment.

She wiggled away only to be drawn back, Luc's big hand sliding smoothly along her thigh. "You have skin like silk, *chère*."

Arielle stilled for an instant, then pushed her hands against the muscles of his chest. She jerked her hands back the instant they touched the firm, slightly damp hair covering his chest. She rubbed her fingertips on her skirt, trying to dislodge the tingling warmth in the cold night air. "Sir, you cannot be serious. I am a businesswoman . . . a spinster."

"A passionate one, it seems," he returned with a hard, quick kiss.

"How dare you speak to me like that!" Arielle whispered furiously, fighting him. He chuckled, tangling in her skirts, rolling with her when she tried to scramble away. Catching her wrists in his hands, Luc lifted them above her head, while he carefully eased his body over hers. She bucked once against his weight, and Luc simply lay down on her, his desire resting intimately on her bare stomach. "Fiend. Cur. Great ox," she threw at him in a hushed tone. "Let me up, you great brute. You're squashing me flat."

Luc's grin infuriated, mocked her. He moved gently, demonstrating the slight brush of his body against hers. His fingers caressed her wrists, yet held them firmly, gently.

"Angel, how could I be so fortunate? Such a passionate woman I have married."

"Passionate?" she tossed back hotly, trying to escape the playful, nibbling kisses Luc was bestowing upon her breasts. "You great vast lout, don't you see? I am trying to escape your clutches. Stop that!"

When she squirmed, fighting him, the motion took her upward, and Luc's warm mouth found her navel, flicking into it with his tongue.

Arielle sputtered, quaked, and tried to assemble her defenses. Her fingers caught his hair, squeezing it between her fists, as he kissed the hollow of her hips. The rough scrape of his cheek startled her as Luc's hand scooped beneath her hips, lifting her. In one movement he nuzzled the soft mound of her femininity, then lifted her higher.

The intimate, light kiss slammed into her. A sudden fierce jolt of heat shot through her, quivering, tangling, stunning her into stillness. "Dear!"

The piercing sweetness lasted a heartbeat, shot deep into the aching core of her. Her body tightened, her mind racing desperately to find the sensible cause—then Luc was lying beside her, wrapping her tightly in his arms and the blankets. He rocked her like a baby, kissing her temples and stroking her back with trembling hands.

Arielle tried to breathe and to drag her analytical spinster's business mind from the mists of pleasure. "Luc," she whispered unevenly against his throat. "You kissed me . . . you . . . kissed me where no gentleman should ever touch a lady. . . ." She swallowed, running through the intimacy again, startled by the piercing pleasure. *The dark sinful pagan trespass on her person!*

He nuzzled her curls, inhaled their fragrance. "Mmm. But you respond magnificently—delightfully." His lips curved against her temple.

Unwilling to move away, she stared at the moonlit sky. Her thighs continued quivering with a reaction she did not understand, nor could control. "I cannot believe . . . Luc, you kissed me improperly. Sinfully."

He chuckled outright. "*Chère*, you are enchanting."

"Beast." Arielle swallowed, struggling for the clarity that marked her business dealings. She trembled, balling her fists against the stark knowledge that Luc had kissed her intimately. Surely the gesture hadn't happened, but it had—the fierce knowledge rested deep in her body, in her too-tight flesh. She struggled for sanity in a tossing sea of shaken emotions. Luc held her easily, her head resting on his shoulder. "Beast," she tossed at him again.

"Husband . . . I believe that no man has ever kissed your lips, or touched these beautiful breasts . . . sweet juicy apples. . . ."

"Apples? My bosom?" Arielle jerked to a sitting position, tossing back her long mane of tumbled curls and grabbing the edges of her bodice together. Luc raised a finger to lazily touch the escaping tip of her left breast and grinned when Arielle swatted him away. He lay on his back, arms placed behind his head, and grinned up at her, careless that his chest and stomach lay naked in the cold moonlight.

Arielle glanced at a shadowy movement low on his body. She suddenly realized that his desire ran strong despite his easy pose. She closed her eyes, fought the wild flush staining her cheeks, and muttered, "Have you no shame?"

"None." The lazy humor in his deep raspy voice caught her broadside, her temper rising.

Turning aside, Arielle tried to assemble her clothing, furiously pushing buttons into wrong places. She dismissed the lazy finger prowling the side of her throat as Luc sat behind her. His hands slid around her waist, curled around her breasts, and stayed despite her swats. "Shoo! You've done enough damage. I vow my camisole is torn."

"Not the damage that I long to do," he murmured dryly. "I will no doubt carry this pain with me to the grave." Leaning against her back, Luc rested his chin over her shoulder. His hands came around her front to skillfully fasten her clothing. He muttered something quick, passionate, dark, and very French against her cheek.

Stunned that he would touch her again, Arielle gaped at the large hands expertly, swiftly completing the task on her bosom. While her body refused to move, she watched Luc's dark hands slowly cup and massage the soft, aching weight. "Oh, my goodness . . ."

Arielle scrambled to her feet. She took a step, and her ankles caught in her drawers. When she toppled down on top of Luc, he grabbed her for a quick, hot kiss before releasing her. Arielle scrambled away a second time, turned away, jerked up her skirts, and knotted her drawers at her waist. She was shaking with emotion, her fists tightly closed, nails biting into her palms. She didn't dare turn toward him, remembering his naked state. Walking briskly toward camp, Arielle wrapped her shawl around her tangled hair. She would have her day, revenge at the sweetest moment— "Great mauling beast of a man . . . Improper, sinful letch . . ."

She prayed her knees would not crumble beneath her.

Later, in their tent, Glynis whispered crossly, "Arielle, please quit tossing and muttering. If your conference with Luc wasn't to your liking, you may clear the matter in the morning. Please, we need to rest for tomorrow."

"Great, hulking beast of a man, Glynis. He mauled me."

Glynis sighed tiredly. "You said he didn't hurt you. Arielle, my dear. A kiss has never wounded a woman. I have confidence that you will set the matter straight."

Arielle squirmed on her pallet, uncomfortable with her action in the heated scenario between Luc and herself. Her body was restless, aching, as though she could scale tall cliffs and never tire. Or take her fencing foil to Lucien D'Arcy, whittling away tiny pieces of his huge, dark arrogant body. She had scrubbed herself thoroughly with Lydia's lavender and oatmeal soap. Yet the scent that clung to her body since Luc's intimacy drifted upward from the heavy quilts. She squirmed deeper and jammed the coverings up to her throat. "By comparison to Thaddeus, Lucien D'Arcy is a playful boy, a great hulking man, who wants to play games. 'Adorable,' he called me . . . adorable. He cuddled me."

She fought the swift, angry rise of her tone. "He dared to cuddle me. Whispered odious, sweet endearments into my ear . . . as if I would believe them—not in this lifetime! The

man is dangerous and desperate, Glynis. He is after something. He has a purpose in this constant ogling, teasing. I
am a seasoned, practical businesswoman. Thaddeus is a
gentleman. Luc is not," she concluded, her fist ramming
into the feathertick pallet.

"So you have said many times, Miss Adorable. I would
so like to sleep a bit before four o'clock tomorrow morning," Glynis said and burrowed deeper in their quilts.

The next afternoon Arielle's temper clung to her like a
hot cloak. When she had checked the lines on her teams,
Luc had used the moment to press her against the horses
and his body.

The hard press lasted an instant and branded her with the
memory of his hard chest and thighs for hours. It reminded
her of his play the previous night. Arielle tilted her bonnet
to shield the furious flushes that pursued her throughout the
morning.

At the nooning Luc lounged on the blanket she had
spread to rest. He toyed with her fingers, despite her efforts
to tug away gracefully. She tried to ignore him, to gaze off
into the distance.

"Any proper gentleman would have known his company
wasn't wanted," she muttered later, watching Luc ride beside the front wagon. Riding in the saddle, in front of Luc,
Brianna grinned, and Timmy sat very straight and proud.

"He has a way with children," Glynis murmured. "My, is
that a herd of deer over there? When do you think we will
see those oceans of bison that Mr. Smithson says range over
the plains?"

"Don't change the subject." Arielle's body ached with a
strange taut tension. Her breasts weighed heavily with each
bounce, and her lower body tingled with that sinful kiss.

"My. How a body needs exercise when riding along on a
wagon," Glynis remarked and stood, bracing herself with a
hand on the back of the wagon seat. "Do slow down,
Arielle. I'd really like to walk like the rest of the women
before making camp tonight. To stretch my legs—"

Arielle squinted up at her, drawing the wagon slowly to

a stop. The other wagons continued past. "Are you certain you aren't avoiding my conversation concerning Luc's questionable character?"

"My dear, he could not help that he recovered. It is honorable that he wanted to find the woman whom he had married on his deathbed. It seems to me that he is acting as your protector after that scene at Independence. You could have been badly hurt when you attacked the man beating Omar. Luc clearly would have none of it. He has established himself in the widows' hearts. His actions are very honorable. You could have married later on and then discovered you were a bigamist. What he must have endured to travel so quickly, finding us at the Landing." When Glynis would have stepped down, Siam appeared, took her hand, and gallantly helped her to the ground.

Starting the horses again, Arielle's small revenge came at Glynis's expression of panic. She smiled tightly, thanked Siam, and began firmly striding on her way. Arielle grinned as Siam moved lithely after her. He walked beside Glynis, who tried to avoid him. She walked fast, slow, and stopped to visit. Siam remained at her side.

He bent swiftly, claimed a tiny flower, and offered it shyly to Glynis. At first the Englishwoman's expression was delight, which slid slowly into shock, then confusion. She pushed a smile on her lips and nodded. Siam smiled widely, apparently vastly pleased with himself.

A motion at her side startled Arielle, and she glanced up just as Luc stepped into the wagon box. He took the reins easily from her hands, despite her resistance. "Sleep well, Angel?" he asked as she stared at him furiously, willing her mouth to order him from her life.

"Of course not. I thought about your devious plans all night, Luc," she burst out. "You plotted the event . . . laid those blankets before you . . . you herded me into the night. You actually placed the feathertick on the ground in preparation to assault my person."

"Buffalo robe, *chère*," Luc corrected. "There is nothing so warm."

Arielle slashed out her untamed left hand. "Specifics.

Then the quilts on top of the pelt. Luc, you are guilty of planning the entire event."

The corners of his molded mouth moved as though a smile lurked within.

"The way you ... trespassed my person ..." Arielle fought the rising anger in her voice. She wanted to remain cool, to speak her analytical mind so that the "event" would never take place again.

She cleared her throat. "You are far too playful, Luc. If you don't desist, people will think you are courting me. Just sitting here beside me is enough to make tongues wag. Nothing can endanger my mission."

"Angel, stop fuming. It is natural that you want me. That you hunger for me," Luc said quietly, the creases at the corners of his eyes crinkling slightly.

She stared, openmouthed, at his profile. The wind caught in his hair, the dimming afternoon sun catching the blue-black lights. "I? I hunger for you?" she repeated when she could speak. "The thought never crossed my mind."

"Your breasts taste like honey. Your thighs are soft, and when they quiver, I want to sink into them," Luc continued, his eyebrow lifting as he leered teasingly at her over his shoulder.

Arielle blinked. She swallowed, sputtered, and finally managed, "Preposterous. Not me."

Luc laughed outright, his hand covering her knee. Then his smile stilled, and a dark sensual gleam replaced the humor. "I ache for you, my little bristling wife. To be in you would be to be in heaven. To lie in your arms, to rest between your legs, to kiss your lips and feel the heat begin in you is a thought that has kept at me all day. I fear I will explode with each dark look you toss at me."

"Gracious." Arielle swallowed again, tried to move her knee away from his caressing hand. "You are far too experienced with women's clothing, sir," she said when she could speak.

He shrugged, glancing aside at a herd of deer bounding over a rise. "I am a man. I have been married. Once I had sisters who needed tending. Yvonne could never match her buttons properly when she was young. As her older brother, I was given the task when *Maman* or the maids were busy. My father was meticulous about such things. One of his dark looks and Yvonne would cry." The sadness in his voice caught her. She pushed away the tug of sympathy, determined to keep on her track of putting Luc in his place.

"You touched me, Lucien. You touched me and you kissed me in a way that no gentleman should ever pursue," she stated firmly. "It cannot happen again."

"It cannot?" he asked as though challenged. "*Chère*, but it will and soon. You have a mouth that was made to be kissed. Your ripe breasts and soft buttocks were meant to be cherished. I can span your waist in the width of my two hands. You are a woman who was meant to be loved, to be tasted. A passionate woman."

"Passionate? I'm so passionate, Luc, that I could run you through with my foil if it happens again!" This time Arielle wrenched her knee free. She straightened her skirts primly. "You are taking advantage of my situation, Luc."

"Yes," he agreed, unbothered. "We are married, Angel. From the way my body aches, you have taken advantage of me."

"Why are you acting like this?" she demanded in a hushed outraged tone, then lowered her voice.

"How?"

Arielle's left hand escaped her control, slashing out a gesture of frustration. She captured it with her right hand. *She hated gesturing wildly.* "As though you were a hungry predator to my role as prey. It is unseemly . . . it is lustful."

"I took no more than you gave," Luc said thoughtfully after a moment. "Our children will be beautiful. Fiery, passionate children who will bear their mother's compassion. Only a compassionate woman would have undertaken changing women with a dark past into proper widows. Brides with manners."

"*Children?*" she echoed, while her mind placed Thaddeus's neatly combed boy and girl against a hoard of Luc's untamed children.

"The natural product of our lovemaking," he said slowly,

watching her carefully. When she flushed, reminded of his body taut and hard against her thigh, Luc grinned and dipped his head for a quick, hard kiss that burned her lips long after he had leapt to the horse tied to the wagon.

Ten

....

"Lift!" Luc braced his legs, straining with the other men to lift the wagon. The wheel slid free, the broken spoke was replaced, and the men lifted the wagon again.

He wanted the strain to trim a desire that Arielle had unleashed.

It nettled his pride that she affected him until he ached like an untried, hungry boy.

Arielle Browning D'Arcy turned up her nose and looked the other direction each time their paths crossed. He hadn't intended to pursue their marriage, but her defiance challenged him at a level no other women had dared. *Marriage to her would be hell. . . .*

Damn. Luc wanted her. The stark desire lashed at him, no less than the need to torment her, to hold and cuddle the little shrew.

There were easier women. Intelligent, warm, loving women who wanted the D'Arcy name. Yet he yearned for this starchy, little hotheaded wench.

Every sane thought told him that Arielle was trouble.

Every drop of his blood, every muscle in his body told him he wanted her more than any other woman he'd ever known.

She wasn't sweet. Any man with good sense would have run away.

Why the hell did he want to tease her, to see her green eyes light with laughter, her lips curve with a smile?

He wanted her. Wanted that shimmering passion and the tenderness he knew she could give.

He must be insane. There were easier ways for a man to die than at the end of a woman's lashing tongue.

Luc thought about that interesting little pink tongue and grinned. Marriage to Arielle would have certain advantages.

Buffeted by the prairie winds, the singular tree gave the much used campground its name, Lone Elm. Practicing what they had learned the previous night, the emigrants immediately began setting up camp. Latrines were dug, campfires started, and the stock that could wander or be stolen was hobbled for the night.

Arielle jumped when Luc sat beside her after the evening meal. She dropped her pen, and he caught it easily. She didn't trust the humor glinting in his eyes, nor the slow curve of his lips. When Luc was near, she wanted to rail at him, to hit him—Arielle took the pen from him with a distant smile.

"Walk with me?" he asked quietly.

"Can't. Busy. Sorry," she snapped. "Glynis, are you ready for our bout now?"

Smithson snorted nearby. "I'd think a widow would want to take a man's offer for an evening walk, rather than a sword fight with another woman. I've heard about your fancy play, Mrs. D'Arcy. If you're wanting a husband, I suggest you take what's offered to you. A nice walk would do you good. You're looking like you need the exercise . . . all tight and a bit testy."

He tapped his pipe and looked at her meaningfully when she parted her mouth to speak. Smithson continued, "In the morrow I'll not be expecting to hear much about ballast in a wagon from you. Nor any fine advice about matching teams."

Arielle almost choked when she saw the smile lurk around Luc's mouth.

That very mouth had kissed her with such heat that she burned . . . his lips had played with her breasts, hardening them, causing them to ache throughout the day—

"Thank you for your counsel, Mr. Smithson. *I* can take as well as give advice. But fencing is a habit I fear I must keep."

"You'd do better finding a proper husband," he returned grittily and shot another meaningful glance at Luc.

Across the fire Glynis sipped her tea, giving the appearance of an uneasy, cornered mouse. In her lap was a neat bouquet and at her side was Siam, who was working with leather and his awl. "Certainly," Glynis said, rising quickly to her feet. "Fencing now would be lovely. Ah . . . excuse me, Mr. Siam."

He rose to his full height, towering over her. "I'll come with you—"

"No . . ." Glynis's trembling hand swept upward over her hair. "No, that will be just fine. Arielle uses the exertion to relax after a day of fatigue. I fear I need the exercise, also. Thank you." She stepped gingerly around Siam's tall body, holding her skirts aside.

Within minutes the women slashed away at each other in the fading light. "Mr. Siam is becoming true to his namesake—huge and unstoppable, like a grizzly," Glynis said between pants. "He's lurking at my every turn. Whatever can the man want?"

Arielle blocked the thrust to her embroidered heart. She didn't want to think about Luc's wishes. She didn't want to do anything but work the temper from her mind and the taut energy from her body. She should be tired after the day's travel, but she wasn't. Rapidly wearing Glynis down, Arielle battled Luc in her mind. Her thrust to the Englishwoman's embroidered heart was too easy. "Again?" she asked from behind her mask as Glynis lifted hers.

"If you want to fight someone, *chère*, let me offer my

services," Luc said quietly and took the foil Glynis handed him.

"I cannot battle a novice, Luc. I would hurt you," Arielle returned airily. "I warn you, Luc. There is already one man suffering from my wounds. He was endeavoring to accost me and I retaliated. Learn from his mistake."

"I am frightened, but challenged, madame wife. I will try to survive your skills." Luc's raspy, low tone raised the hair on the back of her neck. Then he whispered away from Glynis's hearing, "But as my wife, there are more pleasurable ways to ease your mood in private."

Arielle pressed her lips together. She would teach Luc manners before the match was finished. "Put on the mask and the chest guard, and I'll give you a few lessons. I wouldn't want to hurt you."

"Please be careful, Arielle. Not everyone understands your fierce need for victory," Glynis warned. "I believe I hear Lydia calling me," she said, returning to camp.

Luc hefted the foil, balancing it in his hand. The lazy ease of his stance, his challenging gaze set her anger off again.

"En garde," Arielle returned, whipping her foil in the night air. "Pay attention. You see?" She placed her foil against the blade of his. "Fencing is a matter of offense and defense."

His greater strength easily pushed her foil aside, and he stepped nearer her, his free arm wrapped around her. Drawing her body tightly against his, Luc bent his head to an exposed area of her neck. He gently nipped her skin, shocking her. Before she could recover, he stepped back.

The emotions that had been riding her throughout the night and day surged upward, and Arielle slashed at his blade, careful not to hurt him. He defended the blow easily. She struck again, and Luc matched the quick series of thrusts. The sound of metal against metal echoed in the night. "You will learn not to touch me at your leisure, sir," Arielle said between her teeth.

Arielle kicked her skirts aside, lifting her arm higher. She plunged into a series of rapid thrusts, testing his skill. Luc

met each thrust expertly, easily. The thought that he invaded
her private arena infuriated her further. She fought, parried,
thrust, but Luc easily met her best efforts. Panting, sweating, and breathing hard, Arielle fought for her freedom, the
life she had planned. Used to laying her thoughts in a neat
row during a bout, she spoke aloud. "If you so much as
touch me again, I will run you through.... Your actions
border on piracy, and pirates must be taught manners....
Thaddeus is a gentleman, unlike you, and he understands
that a woman wants order and manners."

Luc stepped close to her, his foil crossed with hers. They
stood still as he swept an arm around her, locking her to
him. "Thaddeus?" he asked softly, carefully, searching her
mask.

Stepping back, Arielle parried his light thrust. Her right
arm was tiring badly. She changed to her left hand, which
possessed a more adept, dangerous skill. Plunge and thrust,
she followed Luc as he stepped backward. It was dusk now,
their blades flashing, clashing in the still, damp air. Luc
seemed unchallenged by her best techniques. She passion-
ately wanted to take her revenge by forcing him to ask for
a halt. "Thaddeus. My lifelong friend. A gentleman."

Luc eased around a small indentation. "Rabbit hole.
Watch your step, sweetheart," he explained as she followed.
"You are sweating. Would you like to loosen your cloth-
ing?"

"No, I would not—and I do not sweat!" Being reminded
that he had loosened her clothing the previous night set off
Arielle's temper and a fresh series of thrusts. The prairie
hung between dusk and night, their foils flashing. Air
caught painfully in her lungs, her arms ached, her fingers
locked in their grip to the handle.

Luc's cool dismissal of her skills angered her; her blows
grew reckless while his were casual and expert. "Tell me of
this Thaddeus?" he asked casually.

"I'm going to marry him," she snapped, concentrating on
penetrating his defenses.

Luc stepped inside her defense, drew her hard against him

again, and said flatly, "But you are married to me, madame wife."

Then he stepped back and Arielle swung into a fresh slashing offense, born of rich anger. "A mere legality. Easily rendered, just as I could slice that shirt from your body."

"You would like to see me undressed?" he drawled pleasantly, parrying her thrust. "I am honored that you hunger for the sight of my naked body. Though I must warn you, my wound is not that pretty."

She forced the breath from her lungs, blowing away a drop of damning sweat that clung to her cheek. In the moonlight Luc looked as though he had been taking a leisurely walk while she fought for each blow, ignoring his light question. "I am very angry with you, Luc," she whispered unevenly. "Thaddeus would never have touched me as you did. Nor given that improper kiss on my person."

His chuckle was low and mocking. "Thaddeus is not your well-warmed husband."

"Thaddeus is a manly gentleman. Pure of heart. He is not a rake, tormenting women at every turn."

"*Chère*, you are the only woman I 'torment.' Since you claimed me, my passion has been to bed you."

"You enjoy bedeviling me! Admit it."

"I do," he admitted easily with a slow, disarming grin.

Arielle barely heard his soft, deep voice as she worked fiercely to stand on her feet. Her blows were wide now, and at last Luc just stood, looking down at her as she swayed on her feet. "Ah! We are here," he said pleasantly, taking the foil from her numb hand and placing it on the ground near his.

Luc sank to a pallet spread with a patchwork quilt and tugged off his boots. He rubbed his thigh in a brisk, resentful movement, then favored it as he rose to his stockinged feet.

The sight of him flicking open his shirt buttons with one hand while he watched her, his feet locked to the quilt, stunned her. Arielle could not move, her arms aching, her lungs begging for air.

She remembered the buffalo that he had hunted and ex-

pertly herded near the wagons. When the poor animal was
tired, manipulated to the exact spot Luc wanted, he had
struck. Sweat clung to Arielle's forehead, her heart beating
heavily with her exertions. When she swayed, Luc caught
her in his arms. She looked at him blankly through her
mask. "Here?"

He eased to the ground, cradling her on his lap. Arielle
could not lift her arms to prevent him from removing her
mask and protective vest. "Beast," she whispered between
gasps as she realized he had snared her again to his nightly
blanket.

Luc chuckled and nuzzled her throat, pushing aside her
high collar with his teeth. His tongue flicked the sweat from
her jaw, and Arielle fought the immediate tingling that began in her lower body. She was too exhausted to fight when
Luc loosened her dress. When his hand claimed her breast,
she cried out softly.

Luc settled over her and drew the quilt over them. His elbows braced by her head and his fingers toyed with her
tumbling curls. In the night his eyes were tender. "You are
a fighter, Mrs. D'Arcy. But now you will let me take care
of you."

"Landlubbing pirate," she managed, suddenly aware of
his chest pressing against her breasts ... his hard thighs
pressing against her soft quivering ones through the layers
of their clothing.

Luc moved gently, covering her mouth with his. In a
quick jerk he drew her petticoats and skirts up to her waist.
They wadded between their bodies, but his desire rested intimately at the juncture of her thighs.

Incredibly, she moistened immediately to the gentle
thrust. He was trembling, bracing his weight from her, his
kisses sweet and hungry.

"Why are you doing this, Luc?" she whispered unevenly
as he trailed kisses to her ear, nibbling on it with his teeth.
She fought the tiny pings of pleasure racing through her,
pushing her hands against his shoulders.

"I desire my wife." His voice was deep, rich with ac-
cents.

"This is wrong." She desperately wished her breast didn't ache in his hand. She tried to push her wadded skirts downward—

His hand tightened gently on her breast, bringing it to his lips. Arielle cried out then, a poignant longing driving through her. He suckled gently, tasting her flesh, then treating her other breast to the heated moist pleasure. "Luc!"

Despite her aching body, her hips lifted as his descended.

The tantalizing movement caused Arielle to still. She fought repeating the lift of her hips and lost. Luc groaned deeply, his breath coming hard against her cheek. "Open your lips for me," he whispered huskily. "Let me in. . . ."

Fighting against her desire, the sweet madness aching low in her body, Arielle obeyed slowly. His tongue swept across her teeth, played with hers, and retreated. Enchanted with the repeated play, Arielle allowed hers to touch his lips. Luc inhaled sharply and let out a sound that resembled a masculine purr of delight.

He tasted exquisite, she decided, foraging the tip of her tongue along his mouth, dipping in it.

The delightful pressure of his hips pressing against hers didn't offend, but excited. Luc cuddled her closer, smoothing her breasts.

Arielle's flesh seemed too tight, too hot. She wanted to take, yet escape. . . .

Luc's hand swept downward, and then his desire pressed gently against the heated, moist entrance of her most intimate place. In the moonlight his features were taut and fierce.

While he did not hurt her, he frightened her then, the fierce demand of his trembling body thrusting against hers.

Arielle tensed instantly, pushing at his shoulders. "Luc! No, I can't."

The powerful steely warmth of his masculinity poised just within her stopped. Luc shuddered once, then rolled to his side, taking her with him.

Beneath her cheek, his heart raced, his hands trembling as they smoothed her back. "Shh, lie still," he whispered

roughly, pressing a familiar quick, hard kiss to her mouth.
"Lie still."

"You are ... huge." Arielle realized suddenly that she
had spoken her innermost thoughts.

Luc inhaled slowly, unevenly. Her head, riding his chest,
lifted and fell with each painfully slow breath. He stroked
her hair, kissing her damp forehead, his body rigid beside
hers. "You are hot. Wet. And probably very effective at de-
stroying what manhood I have left at this point," Luc muttered darkly.

Arielle blinked, the new thought striking her. His deep
voice was trimmed with resentment, and he had spoken too
frankly, his charm slashed away. The thought caught and
fascinated her like a rainbow of lights arcing from a prism.
True, she had methodically pushed her male business asso-
ciates to the ends of their tethers. Testing a man on that
level was good business. But arousing a man to such
passion—"Are you saying, Luc, that you find me ... interesting?"

"Beautiful. Fascinating as an elf and disastrous as a wanton without an idea of your allure or the damage you can do
a man." The words were flat, resentful, and trimmed with
Luc's unique accent. A series of curses followed, each spoken in rich, dark low tones that quivered on the clean wind.

Arielle considered the idea, turning it over in her mind
like a treasure, each facet to be carefully examined. Luc
shuddered in her arms, and she stroked his back as she
would one of her excited animals while she pursued her
thoughts. The caress gradually soothed him, and his breathing slowed. At the moment he seemed a great beast, vulnerable for a time, and needing her protection. She reminded
herself that he had recently recovered from a grave illness
and required tending.

*To rest against him was very comfortable. His warmth
was luxurious against the biting cold winds.*

Arielle stared at the stars overhead, lost in her thoughts.
She'd never considered herself beautiful ... yet Luc had
said she was. Her powers as an attractive woman had never
been questioned because she had never thought of herself as

a woman who could drive men into . . . "Such a heated fit."
She realized again that she had spoken her thoughts and
clamped her traitorous mouth closed.

Luc tugged up the quilt to cover her and cuddled her
deeper in his arms. His tall body framed hers as they lay on
their sides, his thighs cradling hers. He breathed slowly
now, wrapping her in his arms, his large fingers laced with
hers, his thumb caressing the back of her hand slowly.

Arielle considered the moment. In a swift change of
mood, Luc seemed almost companionable, a friendly
warmth in the chilly night. He nuzzled her hair and inhaled
slowly. "Peaches. You smell like ripe summer peaches . . .
what's that? A bit of cinnamon . . . a lashing of raspberry
preserves and honey? Do I smell honey?"

"I keep reminding myself that you have just recovered
from serious wounds . . . that perhaps your actions are born
of the unsteady emotions of an indisposed mind." Luc
grunted when her elbow jabbed his stomach.

"Indisposed, am I?" He kissed her cheek, nuzzling it like
a puppy wanting tidbits.

She tried to stop giggling but couldn't. "Luc . . . you . . .
must stop."

He tickled her then, his fingers finding the spot that had
lurked on her ribs for years. Only her brother, Jonathan, had
ever sought it out. Now Luc's fingers caused her to squirm,
giggling aloud. "Stop . . . oh, stop . . ."

"Say 'Please, Lucien. Please stop, Lucien,' " he teased,
sucking on her earlobe. She clamped her hand to her ear,
and he was gone, biting gently on her throat.

A shriek of laughter bubbled from Arielle's lips into the
night.

The echo plopped down into her heart, stunning her.
Luc's relentless fingers ran down her ribs, testing her.
"Lucien, please . . . please stop," she managed between gig-
gles.

"Aha," he crowed, rolling over and placing her on top of
him. "One day you will say 'Please, Lucien,' again and with
much less laughter, my lady," he said wickedly and leered
up at her through the darkness. Her grin stilled as Luc ten-

derly eased a curl behind her ear, his finger slowly trailing across her lips.

Arielle's smile slid deep within her, the pleasant moment lengthening, calming. Poured over him, she was instantly drowsy, feeling incredibly warm and safe. "Pirate," she whispered on a sigh.

"Not near as much a one as I would like to be," he growled against her skin. Taking care, he tugged the quilt over her and eased her head down to his shoulder "Rest, little one. Rest on me ... sleep ..."

Arielle tried not to doze, her left hand resting on his chest. Her fingertips smoothed the rough hair pleasantly. "You shouldn't say things like you do, Lucien," she whispered.

"Mmm?" He nuzzled her hair.

"Like talking about my ... my body like you do. It isn't seemly."

"Seemly isn't how I feel about you, my little fierce wife. I can't think of anything else but wanting you fitted around me ... me in you, and that tight heat around me like a glove."

"Impossible ... illogical," she murmured sleepily, dismissing Luc's soft chuckle as she allowed him to rock her gently against his long body.

Arielle awoke to Luc's light slap on her backside. His broad palm stayed to caress her naked softness. She moved and found her hand curled around his rigid desire. Jerking it back, she sat up, staring down at his wide grin. The moon was high overhead, and Luc's fingers were testing the folds of her moist, hot femininity. "Oh, my. Oh, my ..." she whispered after swallowing.

Visions of her dream whisked by her on the cold midnight air. Luc's huge body tangled with hers, his rigid desire buried deep—"Oh, my ... my ..."

"*My*. What an interesting word. My what? My dear? My lover? My beloved husband?" Luc teased and slowly sat up.

Arielle's eyes widened as he stretched, broad shoulders shielding the moon. She couldn't move as he bent his head and kissed her sweetly. He began straightening her camisole, her dress, and lifting her astride his lap, Luc raised her to kiss her breasts, suckling them through the cloth.

"Oh, my," Arielle gasped as longing speared through her.

Then Luc was standing, straightening his clothing and pulling her to her feet. In a flash he lifted her off her feet and suckled her breasts through her clothing. "Beautiful," he whispered against her bosom, nuzzling it luxuriously. "Perfection. Peaches. Ripe, soft, summer-sweet, tasty peaches."

Somehow Arielle managed to walk unsteadily back to camp. She lay awake for long hours, trying to place the night's events in a neat order.

They refused.

The next day the train swung away from where it flowed with the Santa Fe Trail and began its northward journey. The sweeping winds sailed through the staves of the uncovered wagons.

Luc rubbed the healing wound in his thigh, resenting the weakness and his grim, dark mood. His desire for Arielle hadn't been trimmed, but rode his body in a long, painful ache. Elyce DuBois waved to him as she walked along the French family's wagon.

He nodded briefly. To take Elyce would ease his body, but not his desire and fascination for the woman who was his wife.

He glanced back at the wagon Arielle insisted she drive and found her scowling at him from beneath her bonnet. He smiled slowly, displaying none of the urgency riding his taut body. Turning his horse around, Luc headed for her wagon, noting that Siam was driving another wagon with Glynis huddled on the far opposite end of the bench.

Luc scanned the wagons, the livestock following behind. Excitement danced over each face, a quick burst of laughter flying on the cold prairie wind.

Resting behind Anna in the wagon seat, Sally was covered with blankets, her face pale in the bright sunlight. Luc frowned slightly. The baby was coming too soon. She grimaced, writhing, her hands braced on the wagon stave, and

Anna turned to her instantly. The raw-boned woman met Luc's stare grimly in the distance.

She shook her head and flicked the lines over the oxen. "Giddup, you sons of—" She clamped her lips closed and straightened in the seat.

Arielle closed her eyes when Luc stepped into her wagon. She kept them closed, ignoring him. Sun danced on her dark brown lashes, firing the red lights at the tips. A rosy flush covered her cheeks, and her lips trembled. They parted instantly when Luc dipped his head to kiss them.

She pushed him away. Her green eyes glared at him, her palm shooting upward to his cheek. He caught her wrist, kissed the soft inner flesh covering the delicate blue veins. Arielle simmered in her anger, which delighted him. Taking the reins from her, Luc stretched his injured leg over the box and leaned against the back of the seat.

"Please make yourself at home," Arielle muttered. "You know you're making a scene, don't you? But then you don't care, do you?" She crossed her arms in front of her, wrapping the shawl around her coat and staring out into the plains. "There will be no more incidents like last night, Luc. You may as well adjust to that fact and move on to some other poor woman who may think your antics are interesting. *I do not.* And don't tell me you love me as rakes do until they have their way."

Luc remained quiet, fighting the anger that had been with him since her mention of Thaddeus.

"There? You see? Then that is the end of it, because I could never . . . never engage in a . . . marital process with any man who does not love and respect me."

"Love," Luc repeated hollowly. He watched a wagon pull to the side and the man dip into the grease bucket that hung along the side. The couple were newlyweds, lost in dreams and each other. Luc wanted this fierce woman at his side with every deep cord within him. He wanted Arielle's body and her quick battling wits at his side. He wanted the tenderness she kept locked inside her that would delightfully escape her control. But could he ask for love?

She glanced at his hand, soothing his leg. In a quick flip

of her hand, she tossed a crocheted afghan over his lap. Luc allowed the afghan to slide to the floor. He wanted her to touch him of her own will, to feel those soft, reluctant, trembling hands caring for him. Arielle glared at him, snatched the afghan up, and briskly tucked it over his lap and thighs. "You are hurting, Luc. Have the good sense to tend your leg. You surely strained it this morning when you helped lift the Emersons' wagon to replace that wheel."

Placing the lines in one hand, Luc took her hand and laced her fingers with his. "Tell me about Thaddeus."

When Arielle tugged her hand, Luc controlled her gently, firmly. "You will tell me, *chère*, and soon. I do not think I like another man in my wife's thoughts. Nor in our bed."

"This . . . bundling thing at night, Luc. It must stop," she tossed back, lifting her chin. The sun caught a russet strand that coiled along her cheek. "If you would desist, I'm certain your leg would heal much more quickly," she said reasonably. "If you don't, I'm terribly afraid I shall have to shoot you. Or run you through. Perhaps a properly placed nick to slow you down a bit."

Luc bent to kiss her again, this time harder. For just a flick of a heartbeat Arielle's lips softened beneath his, a teasing hunger riding beneath the silky surface. When he drew away, smoothing her cheek, Arielle gasped, "You are the kissingest man!"

Smithson's broad face turned to stare at them as he passed. "What's this?" he said with a smile, urging his horse to the wagon. "Courting? Perhaps you should patch Luc's shirt, Widow D'Arcy. He looks like a man who needs tending."

"I have just asked Mrs. D'Arcy to marry me," Luc said quietly, watching her flush and look away. She tapped her foot on the board flooring.

"Ah, I see," Smithson returned. "Well, then, the kiss was certainly called for."

"She wants to take care of me. Didn't you offer to do my washing and mending earlier, sweetheart?"

Her lips remained clamped together, then she smiled at Smithson. "Shouldn't we camp a bit later today, Mr.

Smithson? I think we could make better time if we hurried a bit. Perhaps you should check that lead wagon. It seems to me like the oxen are not a matched pair."

The wagon master stared at her blankly. "Woman, I have made the crossing twice before. Lost a wife along the trail because some fool decided to go faster. I suggest you stick to your mending and let men do the thinking for you." He stared meaningfully at Luc from beneath his eyebrows. "The sooner you marry this woman, the better. She's an interference . . . telling me how to match teams. . . . Good day, Mrs. D'Arcy."

That evening Arielle looked up when Luc tossed his clothing in her lap, covering her journal. "No," she said firmly. Picking up the garments between her thumb and index finger, she let them drop to the plank table by her tent. "I'm a businesswoman, Luc. I am tending my journal and my ledger. My talents with soap and needle are limited. I am formulating my plans, and I am not your intended. You are an obvious rake, a seasoned skirt tosser. But I am not susceptible to your games. Once, as a girl, I might have been, but now I am a spinster and safe from your dash and vigor. I seek gentler, more mentally rewarding moments than those you offer."

" 'Mentally rewarding'?" Though Arielle's quick mind delighted Luc at times, tonight he had definite plans to put their marriage on a better track. The thought that another man occupied territory that was rightfully his—Arielle's thoughts and designs for children, and therefore bedding a man—nettled Luc.

She nodded and the campfire caught the reddish lights in the braids that crowned her head. Luc watched the pulse in her slender, pale throat, fascinated with the rapid beat as she continued, "You must set Mr. Smithson right. The whole train thinks of me as your intended. This in indeed incorrect," she said tightly, snapping her journal closed and placing it aside.

He knelt beside her, taking her left hand and kissing the D'Arcy wedding ring. She reacted perfectly—startled, her tapered, pale fingertips curling. He pictured them on his back, digging into his shoulders as she began her pleasure beneath him. The thought hardened Luc's body immediately. "Smithson tells me that you argued about ballast in a wagon, *chère*. He isn't a happy man now. The word *landlubber* angered him. Would you like him to be even more unhappy when you don't walk with me?"

Her auburn brows drew together. "You won't tell him anything, Luc. You're not an unkind man. You've been watching Sally like a hawk all day. You've helped each woman when needed, and the children adore you. But not me. I know you for what you are . . . an evil, self-satisfying pirate, ready to toss skirts at the drop of a hat. I saw Elyce walk with you. Saw her touch your arm and the way you smiled back at her. You were fairly drooling in her arms," she stated hotly, rising to her feet. "I expected the two of you to fall to the earth and scorch the grass."

Luc gripped her elbow when she took a step, and directed her firmly into the night. "It pleases me that you notice other women when they are near me. Perhaps you are jealous?"

He admired the rigid, proud way she held herself. Arielle gasped when he looped his arm around her waist and lifted her from the ground. Carrying her by his side, her small boots flying beneath her petticoats, Luc hushed her protests with a kiss.

Arielle tumbled onto the pallet with him, struggling beneath his weight. "I'll scream, Luc. Smithson will—"

He kissed her again. "Marry us more quickly, my sweet peach. It's clear that you've set your net to seduce me."

She peered furiously up at him, blowing away a curling tendril on her nose. "I refuse to lower myself to a wrestling match, you great oaf. You're squashing me. How can you possibly enjoy tormenting me so?"

Luc began tasting her gently. He wanted to torment the woman who kept him in a constant state of arousal. After his long, hungry kiss she shivered, lying quietly beneath him. "I suppose you're right. Smithson would take this opportunity to force our marriage."

"Our second marriage," Luc reminded her, rolling to his side and tucking her against him.

"I'm really weary of this argument," Arielle murmured, lying still as he tugged the quilt up to her chin. "I ache in every muscle."

Luc eased her thick braids loose, spreading the frothy russet silk curls across his arm and nuzzling her cheek. He kissed her temple and cuddled her nearer. Soft and sweet against him, Arielle yawned. "I can't battle you tonight, Luc."

Luc smoothed her throat, letting his hand rest lightly on her breast. "Then we'll talk."

She turned her head toward him, her eyes huge in the night. "You mean, lie here, side by side, and talk?"

"Mmm." He wanted her badly, but the thought of a tender moment in Arielle's arms stilled him. He wondered if she knew her left hand rested on his chest. That her fingers toyed with the whorls of hair and smoothed him from breast to breast.

She studied him for a long moment. "I have to admit a certain cozy warmth. You are a very warm man, Luc. Much warmer than Glynis."

Luc forced the smile from his lips. He intended to get very warm with Arielle, but snuggling with her now was enchanting. He realized that he had never enjoyed a woman's presence as much as Arielle's. She wiggled her hips, getting comfortable on the buffalo fur covered by another quilt. "So you slip out here, fashion your pallet, then scoop me into your nest at the first opportunity. Great lengths for a man who has exhausted himself working throughout the day," she said thoughtfully. "You realize that we slept together last night almost until an hour before the train awoke? That was improper. Thaddeus would never sleep in such disarray—naked to the flesh. *Naked to the flesh*," she repeated in an amazed tone.

She stiffened as though realizing she had given away a secret. "No, I don't want to talk about Thaddeus. It's much too personal. Tell me about your family, Luc," she demanded. "Perhaps then I can better understand what drives you to such methods as instant kisses and wrestling bouts, treating me as though I were a child to be tickled no less. Yes . . . I want to understand," she said firmly, her breath swirling along his throat. "And this touching, hungry thing—touching and . . . and—"

She inhaled quickly when his hand slid beneath her camisole and molded her breast. "If I am to share my secrets, madame wife, surely you could ease my torment."

Over her clothing, her hand covered his lightly. "I'm not a young girl, Luc. Something is entirely amiss with this touching and kissing habit of yours. Tell me about your past, and then I will find a way to deal with your behavior," she offered thoughtfully. "It is highly irregular."

Luc stroked the smooth flesh beneath his fingers, cupping her softness in his palm. Memories of Willow swirled around him, then were carried away on the wind. "I cared for my wife," he said slowly.

"A Chinook princess?" Arielle allowed Luc to hold her closer.

He needed her softness, warm against him, he realized slowly. To keep away the fear, the despairing loneliness that had invaded his life after losing Willow.

A wolf pack howled in the distance, and the sound reminded him of his life. The warm woman in his arms kept the loneliness away. He locked Catherine in the past for now. He stroked Arielle's smooth breast and said slowly, "Willow died in childbirth. Our baby never left her body. They both died."

"The loss of a child or a loved one never goes away." Arielle's soft, sympathetic tone quivered softly in the wind.

Luc breathed easily, nuzzling the scented hair spilling across his chest as he stared into the night. He closed his eyes with the searing pain, the flashing memory of his family's death. When Arielle's gasp slid across his chest, Luc suddenly realized his arm had tightened around her. He held her fiercely for a moment, shuddering with the pain.

"Shh," Arielle whispered, stroking his chest. "Shh."

Luc fought against breaking into the memories he had blocked away, to keep the pain from wrapping around him.

He didn't want to share them, to let this small determined woman snare him back into the past, tearing at his life.

She rested her cheek on his chest. "Don't fear it so, Luc. Sometimes it helps to share one's burdens."

He frowned, wondering instantly who was the prey and who was the hawk. "You're like a mouse, digging away at a hidden piece of cheese, aren't you?" he asked darkly. He resented the intrusion into the past that rested quietly. "You would have my pain spread out before you like a feast."

She raised to her elbow, looking down at him. "Luc, I sat at your bedside for hours during your fevers. I know everything—"

"Do you?" he asked harshly, wrapping his fist in the masses of her scented hair, crushing the silky strands with the brutal emotions searing him. "Do you?"

How could she know the pain of seeing his mother's grave, her body desecrated by coyotes? Of seeing his sisters pale and thin in death when he had last seen them happy and alive?

How could she realize the guilt that weighed his every step and breath?

"I know that you are a proud man. That French and Spanish blood runs in your veins, and that you honor your family name above all. I know that you loved your wife and family deeply and that you grieve for them."

Luc resented that soft voice curling around him. His emotions were sharp, fierce. "Would you let me have your soft body, Angel? Will you take away this pain you think is driving me?" he demanded cruelly. "Do you know how badly I want you? To be inside you?"

. . . Just for a time, he wanted to forget . . . the release of his body into hers, the fever consuming him washing away the pain . . .

She paled in the moonlight. "It isn't possible."

Few women had barricaded their bodies from him when he asked. The thought that Arielle could burrow beneath his skin, take a portion of his soul in his fevers, and resist the pleasure they could share angered him. He didn't like the

anger over a woman, nor his raw emotions, usually easily
contained. "Not possible? Why?"

Embarrassed, she looked away. "I . . . you know that I'm
a spinster at thirty-one years of age. My heart belongs to another, Luc . . . and then . . . then you are much too . . . too
emotional . . . rather hot and hungry."

There was softening in the brutal emotions ruling Luc,
tenderness curling around his heart. Whatever experience
Arielle had had with Thaddeus, he hadn't aroused her. Nor
heard those soft little gasps curling from deep inside her—

She cleared her throat, a long tender line kissed by moonlight and fresh prairie winds. Her hair spilled around her,
dipping into the dress he had opened. "Then . . . you
frighten me a bit. One minute treating me like a pirate after
a wench, and the other tender and laughing . . . then this
frivolous kissing business."

When she inhaled, her breast nudged Luc's chest, and he
stilled, savoring the soft press, the pliant shifting that
brought her intimate fragrance wafting upward. The savage
need driving him, shifted and eased. For some unknown reason, this bit of a woman could enchant him beyond his
body's needs. The thought startled him. "Kissing?" he
prompted.

"Goodness. I've never been kissed or cuddled so much in
my life. I'm in a constant state of confusion. Not like myself at all. All in a matter of days . . . mere days, mind you."
She frowned down at him. "Is this kissing and cuddling
thing a family characteristic? Or fostered by some dark need
within you alone? I need to analyze the reason to bestow
such a variety of kisses and the frequency."

Luc carefully drew her head down to his, tasted her lips
in gentle nibbling kisses that she returned. "See?" she asked
breathlessly when she lifted her head. "That's exactly what
I mean. Kissing stops the flow of the mind. Strange . . ."

Enchanted when Arielle experimented with the lift and
slant of her mouth against his, Luc stilled.

"I think . . ." Arielle said unevenly moments later, "that I
would like to go back to camp now."

Eleven
....

The next night the train camped on a ridge between the Wakarusha Stream and the Kansas River.

After hours of Sally's suffering, her baby was born at midnight. The night wind whipped the small tent as the girl infant struggled for breath. Anna breathed into her tiny mouth and nostrils for a half hour, willing the baby to live. Sally watched, praying, begging for life, her hands clasped to her lips. She wailed softly when Anna shook her head and sadly handed her the dead baby, wrapped in a tiny embroidered blanket.

The baby's passing tore at each woman's heart. Mary and Biddy slid into their tents, cuddling their sleeping children close. Anna tried to comfort Sally, who would not let the baby be taken away.

The other women wiped tears away and retired to their tents for a few sleepless hours until the morning call. Lydia tended Sally, packing the heavy flow of blood, and urging her to drink tea or broth.

Lydia scurried past Glynis and Arielle and spoke quietly.

"Something must be done and soon. I've seen Sally's look before. . . . I fear none of my teas can make Sally want to live. Anna has threatened, cajoled, and soothed as best she can. It is for Sally alone now, and I do not like the look of her eyes. Dull, faraway . . ."

Arielle rocked, wrapped in her thoughts and her shawl. She was unaware Luc had taken her hand, and she had been clinging to his warm strength, until he released her fingers and stood.

He bent to enter Sally's tent, and after a half hour Anna emerged, carrying the dead child. She held the baby while Siam dug a tiny grave. The women emerged from their tents, each face pale, eyes swollen with tears. A farmwife, rangy and worn, stepped from the shadows. She placed a board shipping box beside the new grave.

"There's seven small boxes under the ground on our farm. Seven sweet babies who never drew breath," she whispered roughly, a silvery tear glistening on her shallow cheek as she walked away. Lydia placed herbs over a tiny folded blanket in the box and the baby was nestled inside.

Sally's cries cut through the night wind, followed by Luc's deep voice. The melodic, soothing tones changed, lifting in song, then speaking quietly.

By the four o'clock call Sally had quieted, and Luc emerged. He walked slowly to the campfire, staring into it while the women began the breakfast. Anna gave him a cup of coffee from the pot kept near the coals, then after an uncertain hesitation, she kissed him on the cheek. He nodded, watching the flames come to life.

At Arielle's side Siam said quietly, "He holds his grief. Always he thinks of his mother and sisters. Of Yvonne and her baby."

While dawn hovered on the ridge, Luc stood still, holding the tin cup of coffee, bracing his weight on his stronger leg.

A dove cooed in the still morning, and dogs began barking. A child protested awakening in a sleepy cry. Camp life began, men calling for oxen to step into yokes, cattle and sheep protesting the day. Roosters and hens squawked when their wooden cages were lifted and tied to the wagons.

Luc ran his hand across his face, the shadows of the sleepless night clinging to his eyes and cheeks. His beard was dark—Arielle realized suddenly that he had shaved each night before approaching her.

Marie Dexler placed a heavy quilt around Luc's shoulders, but he didn't move, lost in his thoughts. Arielle had never seen a lonelier man. Sally cried out his name, and he turned, his eyes meeting Arielle's. Luc's eyes were those of the damned—empty, hollow, dark with agony. His pain took her breath away.

Then he took a cup of broth from Marie and returned to the tent. He favored his injured leg, rubbing it.

Arielle and Glynis hitched the horses, and Arielle sat on Electra's back as the wagons began, their wheels rolling over the tiny grave to conceal it from scavengers, human or animal. In the lead harness beside Electra, Zeus proved his breeding and training, gauging his gait to hers. Maia, Taygete, Calypso, and Hera pranced behind Zeus and Electra.

"Sally ate a bit of meat," Lydia said cheerfully at the nooning. "That's a good sign. We have Luc to thank. The man has a kind heart and an unfailing will when he's determined to succeed. He's a wonderful storyteller, all the while tending Sally without the slightest embarrassment. As though she were his sister who needed him badly . . . in fact that is the truth. . . . I doubt that Sally would have responded for another living soul. He's cajoled her into eating, and the poor man's eyes were filled with tears when she cried those awful racking sobs. . . . Lovely man . . . kind, generous man. Nice knowledge of herbals, too."

When they camped again, Luc spoke quietly to Anna. Her bawdy laughter sailed through the evening air. The hard lines etched on her face disappeared in an impish grin, and she blew Luc a kiss. He snatched it from the air and blew it back. Anna shook her head and her finger at him. The teasing byplay caught Arielle in midstep. She frowned just as Luc caught her gaze. The smoky look held until she turned away.

Luc carried Sally near the fire. Wrapped in a blanket like

a sick child, Sally stared dry-eyed into the fire while Luc rocked her on his lap.

Biddy Lomax passed, her eyes wide and fearful as she gathered her children to her and huddled near Luc. She looked at Omar once, as though all her dreams had been torn away. She gathered her children against her, staring at the fire.

Omar stood straight and thin in the night, wrapped in his blanket. His shoddy boots had been replaced by tough sandals, and he braced a tall oak spear with a sharpened tip on the ground.

Smithson smoked his pipe near Arielle and watched Sally delicately sip broth, then doze in Luc's arms. "He's limping badly. Her weight on him can't help. He's not taken a moment for himself. Helped the Pearsons with that busted spoke . . . helped round up the cattle scared by the Indians. Then spent time with the girl," he remarked quietly. "Good man, that. I'd say a widow, like yourself, must consider his offer of marriage and soon. There's plenty of other women who'd want a man like that."

Arielle's fingers rested over her open journal. Her eyes kept skipping to Luc's worn face, the beard that now covered his jaw. She wanted to hold him, to allow his face to rest on her bosom—

The image of Luc's dark, bearded face against her bosom alarmed her. She shook her head, attempting to dismiss the urge to hold him close.

He looked like a boy needing care . . . like a man who fought his demons and suffered deep pain.

Arielle turned away, avoiding the sight of him and the growing pain within herself.

Luc had snared a part of her that she did not want to share. Not even with Thaddeus.

As though mirroring her thoughts, Glynis sipped her tea, then spoke: "He is a tender man, sharing Sally's pain. How he must have suffered . . . his parents gone, his sisters sold into bondage . . ."

"He lived only for revenge. Now I think he lives for something else," Siam said quietly as he worked beads into the moccasins he had fashioned. They were small, elegant, white doeskin moccasins with fringing. With his teeth he flattened soaked porcupine quills, which would decorate the leather. When Siam caught Glynis's eye, he smiled broadly around the quills.

Glynis, clearly flustered, stood immediately. Her embroidery hoop fell from her skirt, and she bent to retrieve it. Her skirts tangled around her feet, and she skipped a step catching her balance.

Arielle's smile died when she saw Biddy brush away a tear. Motioning to the woman, Arielle met her a distance away from the others. She noticed that Biddy walked as though injured, and beneath her shawl, her bodice was torn. There were marks on her throat. Arielle turned the woman's head aside to study the imprint of four big fingers. "Who did this?"

Biddy's eyes shut, tears squeezing through her lids. "I fell, ma'am."

"Biddy Lomax! You will not shelter a brute."

"He'll hurt my little ones, ma'am. He said he'd hurt my babies if I told . . . if I didn't meet him tomorrow night and give him what he wants again."

"Over my dead body, he will. I want his name and now, Biddy," Arielle demanded, fury boiling over her.

Minutes later she found Landon Jorgensen, a huge rough-tempered man, lounging in his tent. Jorgensen's wife, a frail, frightened-looking woman, had passed away before the train left Independence. He had been warned by Smithson to keep his distance from the widows but leered at them when he passed. "Mr. Jorgensen. Could I have a word with you, please?" she asked tightly.

"Evenin', Mrs. D'Arcy," Jorgensen said, emerging from the tent and taking her elbow. When she tried to tug away gracefully, his fingers tightened painfully. "There now. You missed your walk tonight with that fancy Mexican breed, Navaronne. So you came to the right man to take up the slack."

"I think not." Arielle dug her heels into the soft mud and jerked her arm away. "I understand you . . . touched Biddy."

Jorgensen laughed coarsely. "Not an hour ago I caught Biddy down by the stream. Tossed her skirt up and had her standing up, so I wouldn't get dirty. Now it's your turn. Before the trip is over, I'll have me a fine harem."

For an instant, nausea clutched at Arielle, soon swept away by her raging temper. "You admit assaulting Biddy? After all she's been through? I'll see you flogged, you shark bait." Arielle's slap cracked against his cheek.

Jorgensen's small eyes blazed, then he leered down at her. "High-nosed bitch. My wife fought, too—so did the others. You're no better. You tell anyone and I'll slit the throat of one of those brats."

He glanced at a movement in the dark and ordered between his teeth, "You've had your turn. Now I'm having mine, Navaronne."

"Mrs. D'Arcy is under my protection, Jorgensen. So are the other widows. Perhaps you should retire to your wagon," Luc said smoothly, though Arielle noted the soft accent trimming his words. His low tone roared with savage anger, barely concealed.

Jorgensen's hand jerked away to grab the knife at his belt. He wove it close to Luc's dark face. "Luc! Damned Mexican! Taking good land away from United States citizens, then grabbing our women, too. You think you can keep this lot of tarts happy in bed, Navaronne? You and that half-breed Injun and that black? There's plenty enough to share."

Luc's smile was cold, his teeth showing briefly in the black beard. While Jorgensen waited, jabbing the blade for effect, Luc leisurely unbuttoned his shirt. "Go back to the wagons, Angel."

"Angel?" Jorgensen laughed coarsely, his eyes wild. "This hellcat?"

Arielle fought her infamous red-haired temper. Her notorious left hand shook with the need to gut Jorgensen from stem to stern. "I am staying to defend my honor and those women under my care, Luc. Please leave. I am certain that Mr. Jorgensen and I can come to some kind of an understanding without your brute force."

Jorgensen placed the flat of his hand on her face and

shoved. "Ya. We can talk real pretty without you, Navaronne."

Arielle sputtered, then grimaced as her boots sank up to her ankles in a mud puddle. Her hair spilled from its moorings when she scrambled for balance. While she shoved the jumbled curls back, balling her fury and gathering power to launch herself at Jorgensen, Luc bent to kiss her. The kiss was hard, quick, and followed by a harsh order. "You stay put, little one."

"Well!" she sputtered, trying to find her scattered thoughts and blinking at the muscles rippling across Luc's naked back.

Jorgensen's blade slashed in the moonlight, the knife slicing the shirt wrapped around Luc's hand and forearm.

Her throat dry, Arielle watched, unable to move. Jorgensen's tall bulk moved slowly, while Luc's leaner body neatly danced aside the flashing blade. Jorgensen slashed wide, and Luc stepped in quickly, pounding his fists against the bigger man's stomach. Jorgensen grunted, doubled, and Luc's swift blow to his wrist sent the knife flying into the mud.

The back of Jorgensen's hand caught Luc's jaw and sent him staggering backward. Head down, Jorgensen rushed Luc, catching him in a bear hug and lifting him above the ground.

Arielle, frozen by the silhouette of the two battling men, launched herself at Jorgensen. She stepped on his calf, using it to crawl up his back. She swatted him with one hand while clamping the other around his neck. Jorgensen turned a circle, carrying Luc.

Fear raked Arielle as she glimpsed Luc's taut, pained expression. Luc's hand was gentler than Jorgensen's, but firm as he placed his hand over her face to shove her away. She dropped to the mud, backstepped to keep her balance, and stood, furious and unable to move. "I was helping you, you ungrateful beast!" she yelled. "You lout! Don't you know that the man is twice your size and that you've been ill?"

"Get out of the way," Luc managed between his teeth.

"You are my employee. I order you to stop this nonsense

at once!" Arielle shouted just as Luc's hands slapped against Jorgensen's ears.

The farmer roared, dropping Luc to grab his wounded ears. Glynis wrapped her arms around Arielle. Smithson, Siam, and Omar stood nearby. Smithson and Siam carried on a running dialogue comparing the techniques of both opponents. Jorgensen, a heavier, slower man, had a sneaky left hand that could stun an ox—or break a man's jaw. Luc, a lean, quick man, would have to wear Jorgensen's strength down. "Jorgensen once chewed a man's ear off in a fight. . . ." Smithson said thoughtfully.

"Stop them," Arielle ordered Smithson, who was calmly smoking his pipe while the fight's brutal blows sounded behind her. Fists slamming into body and flesh continued as Smithson blew a perfect smoke circle into the sky and watched it float away. "This first bit of the trail is interesting. Takes about two weeks for the fur to settle down. Maybe a broken jaw or two. From the looks of it, Luc has been in a few fisticuffs."

Arielle pointed at Jorgensen, who was doubling under Luc's methodical blows. The bigger man roared and charged, and Luc continued dancing around him, wearing him down. "That man . . ." Arielle fought for breath, the anger riding her. "That man, Jorgensen, had Biddy against her will."

Smithson stilled, no longer at ease. "When?"

"Not more than an hour ago. He was crowing about it like a cock rooster," Arielle bit out. She jabbed her finger in his massive chest. "If I were the captain of this train, I'd—"

"Madam, I am not taking advice on such matters from a hotheaded widow such as yourself. But Landon will be dealt with, and strongly so," Smithson returned, his jowls quivering beneath his bushy sideburns. "I won't have women accosted under my care."

"Your care? Why, you—"

"Arielle. Please watch your language," Glynis murmured after glancing warily at Smithson's jowls, sunk deep in his collar. "Remember you are a lady and a businesswoman . . . and *a widow*."

Arielle glared at her, then back at the fighting men. Luc
was limping, dancing aside, then pounding at Jorgensen.
Jorgensen's ham-size fist caught Luc in the jaw.

"Luc! Watch his left!" Arielle cried out, her fists jabbing
into the night air. Her skirts tangled around her legs as she
moved closer to the fight. Arielle bent, reached between her
ankles, grabbed her back skirts and jerked them to her
waist. Tucking the hem into her waistband to form pants,
Arielle circled the fight. "Luc, if you let him hurt you one
more time, I will never forgive you. *As your employer, I
have ordered you to cease fighting at once!*"

"Angel, get the hell out of here," he returned as
Jorgensen charged by, barely missing her. Luc followed, his
fist catching Jorgensen in the stomach. The big man grunted
and bent over, clutching his belly.

Arielle glared at Luc, who was dodging the other man's
fists. "Me? You are telling me what to do, Luc? How dare
you! How dare you brawl like a common cutthroat on the
docks with a gut full of whiskey!"

"Arielle D'Arcy!" Glynis's admonishment was covered
by Arielle's continuing, angry dialogue.

"Luc. Stop this at once . . . watch his left, you landlubber.
Blast! It's sneaky."

Luc's battered face was grim as he concentrated on
Jorgensen's wild, wide blows. "Angel, if you don't get out
of here this moment, I will be forced to paddle your backside."

"What?" Arielle stopped in midstride, her fists poised
with the last jabs. "What? You are threatening me as though
I were an ill-behaved child? Me? A businesswoman?"

"I think they will be married again soon, no?" Siam murmured, standing close to Glynis.

"Yes, well . . . we shall see," Glynis returned in a distracted tone as she moved a step away.

"Brute!" Arielle accused Luc. "Great brutish lout of a
man! Who do you think you are?"

"The man who will claim you, *chère*," Luc returned
calmly, methodically circling the bigger man with quick,
pounding jabs.

"Blast! You will not! Thaddeus is a gentleman, not a brawling brute. I wager he's never engaged in fisticuffs in his life. *He* is a man who uses reasoning. I want my children to be well mannered, not savages at war."

"Perhaps he does not return your affection," Luc said between deep breaths.

Arielle sputtered, then asked darkly, "How dare you? Of course Thaddeus has affection for me. He'll have more after I acquire him."

Glynis shook her head. "Oh, dear."

Stunned and winded, Jorgensen hovered like a wounded buffalo before he crumpled into the cold mud. He lifted his head once, groaned, and fell unconscious. Luc watched him for a moment, then bent to kiss Arielle again.

Her hand went to her lips and came away with blood. "Oh, Luc. You're bleeding. Oh, your poor, dear bruised face."

He wrapped his hand in her hair, smoothing the silky texture with his thumb. "You, madame, must learn to obey."

Her eyes widened. "Obey?"

"Love, honor, and obey," Luc murmured softly. "Are you going to tend my 'poor, dear bruised face' with kisses? I will let you acquire me very easily."

He leaned closer, his eyes smoldering beneath the shadow of his long lashes. A vein throbbed heavily in his throat; the muscle crossing his jaw tensed rhythmically. "Don't . . . don't ever do that again."

"What?"

"Give me an order in front of the others . . . in that tone." The trimmed, softly contained savagery in Luc's soft tone, his accent slipping around the words, stunned her. One eye was swelling shut, but the gleam was fierce, predatory, and very outraged.

She swallowed, licked her lips, and tried not to remember what she had said during the heat of the fight. She glanced at Glynis and the men, at Biddy huddling near the wagons. "Oh, dear," she said. "Oh, dear."

While Smithson and Siam moved past her to collect Jorgensen and drag him away, she looked up at Luc. He stood there like a battered warrior demanding his woman to tend his wounds. There was a wary question in his eyes, an arrogant tilt to his head.

Part of her ached to cuddle and soothe—part of her wanted to tear at him for interfering.

She settled for a slap. Not a full-fledged slap, because she didn't want to hurt him more.

His head jerked back more with pride than with pain. Gone was the playful, lusting man, replaced by one whose anger shimmered along her flesh. His voice was deep, trimmed with his accent. "I will want to hear more of dear Thaddeus."

Mary O'Flannery emerged from the shadows to touch Luc's arm. "I am so sorry . . . but Sally is crying for you."

Two hours later Sally slept in the tent like an exhausted child who had cried away her soul. A distance away from camp Luc lay on his back. He stared at the clouds sweeping across the night sky. The air was heavy, the brewing storm matching his dark mood. He wanted the time apart from the rest, to calm the savage urge to take Arielle Browning D'Arcy . . . to slake his body in her small tempting one.

When he'd seen Jorgensen snare Arielle's arm, Luc was startled by his fear for Arielle.

He braced against the thought slamming into him, stronger than Jorgensen's fist.

He'd never needed anyone, not in his basest needs of heart and soul. He'd cared for Willow, but not the fiery, stormy elements that Arielle managed to rip from him. . . .

He ripped aside the poultice of comfrey leaves Lydia had applied for bruising and scarring. Letting the cold, damp air play across his chest, he thought of Arielle. Fearless, raging at him one minute to watch Jorgensen's sneaky left, then her wide concerned eyes stroking his face as though her fingers were moving over him, softly, tenderly.

He'd wanted to carry her away and lose his pain in her arms. He frowned at a deer herd foraging at the stream. In his lifetime, he'd had women leisurely, never a swift, demanding, savage mating as he'd wanted at that moment.

Arielle could raise his passion as no other woman had. He wanted to bury himself in her, wrap himself in her heat and softness.

He didn't like the savage cloak of needs.

Luc's jaw hurt as he gritted his teeth. His wife wanted to "acquire" another man.

Arielle caused the darkness and the years to slide away. A whimsical bit of pale flesh and red hair, a scent like no other woman, and green eyes that could look like cool ponds one moment and blaze fiery gold the next. Luc frowned, remembering her light slap.

If ever he wanted to lift a woman's skirts and plunge into her soft, quivering thighs, it was Arielle at that moment.

Luc closed his eyes. Never in his lifetime had he ever treated a woman with less than courtesy. Yet Arielle tormented a part of him that no other woman had touched.

His passion for the ill-tempered little shrew was as unexplainable as the tenderness and joy. *"Poor, dear face,"* she had said. Why did the endearment curl in him like a small treasure to be hoarded?

He inhaled slowly. She was his wife and yearned for another man.

Luc absorbed the thought, disliking the immediate anger. Long ago he'd barred those deep emotions from his heart and mind—his revenge on his sister's tormentors had been fierce but controlled.

Arielle tilted that control, sweeping aside Luc's safe barricade.

With Arielle—his wife—the tempest frightened him. Each movement of her body enchanted him, each expression dear to him. He waited for her wildly gesturing left hand and the quick proud lift of her head. Then there was the fierce gentleness with which she tended each charge, the softening of dark green eyes, the tender curve of her mouth—

The woman is a witch, he mused darkly.

The bruising on Luc's ribs caused him to grimace. He eased deeper into the buffalo hide he had covered with a quilt. The quilt bore Arielle's clean intimate scent, and he grabbed the soft padding in his fist, bearing it to his face.

Luc closed his eyes, absorbing her scent, letting it cure him.

The cold night air carried a sound from the cottonwood and willows. Luc's hand tightened on his knife, and he lay still as a woman approached him. Elyce DuBois crouched by his pallet, smoothed her hand over his jaw, and smiled seductively. She handed him a mug of whiskey and sat on the pallet while he sipped it.

Luc read the desire in her eyes, in the poise of her body. The rich curve of her breasts pushed against the thin night-gown.

He closed his eyes, letting the whiskey warm him, and Elyce slipped into the pallet, snuggling against him. She spoke soothingly, in French, telling him how she wanted him while her hands smoothed his hair, his chest.

Luc absorbed her heat, the soft scent of her body, already damp. He wanted a woman, needed the savage release. . . . His palm brushed Elyce's lush breasts, and he thought of Arielle . . . the scent of her hair, the coiling tendrils clinging to his jaw.

Elyce's lips trailed across his bruised ones, her hips rhythmically nudging his hard ones. He wanted what she offered. . . .

Luc pushed her away gently. She smiled wistfully, then her hand found him, stroked him. "You are wounded, *mon cher*. Let me cure you."

Her mouth was hot against his skin, traveling toward his belly—Arielle's lips were tangy, hungry, soft . . . Luc inhaled, then caught his breath with pain. "Go back to camp."

"But . . . I will pleasure you," she insisted with a frown.

He shook his head, stroking her silver hair away from her cheek.

Elyce's full mouth tightened, the line between her brows deep. "If you are waiting for the fine widow, you will wait forever. She has her heart set for another. She toys with you, *cher*."

When Luc did not answer, she leapt to her feet. The night

wind carried her threat back to him. "You will want me and I will laugh at you."

A bird trilled through the night, and Luc closed his eyes. "Siam, are you so bored that you watch my lovemaking from the night?" Luc asked, closing his eyes against the desire for Arielle.

"Your trysts are not very interesting." Siam slid into the clearing and sat on a fallen log. He took off his hat and rubbed his flattened forehead. "The people wake in two hours. There has been no sleep this night. What do you think about Glynis? Why is she always running from me? My heart quivers each time she smiles. I treasure the scent of her body. Glynis said my scar does not frighten her, but she has not seen my head. I would cut out my heart if she asked me. When I told her so, she ran from me . . . she looked at me as though I was mad. . . . Maybe I am . . . crazy with love. Have you ever seen such a lady? Such a beautiful princess?"

Luc smiled wryly. For the first time, aloof, quiet Siam had found love. He did not know the pain of losing a woman. "You frighten the Englishwoman."

"What? I? I have looked at her with love in my eyes. Surely she can see that I love her with my heart, as well as my body—" Siam looked away, the darkness concealing his blush. "To touch her hand is magic. To kiss her feet would be joy. Her body—"

He cleared his throat, then continued huskily, "Each day I give her gifts. The bunch of sweet grass a warrior gives a maiden he is courting. The moccasins soon. A beaded belt . . . She is a goddess . . . a moon goddess driving me insane with—"

"You are stampeding her, Siam. Play with her, like snaring a rabbit. Slowly. Come closer. Wait. A game." *How much longer could he wait for Arielle?*

Siam began to laugh, echoing Luc's dark thoughts. "You tell me how to treat a woman. Tell me, Luc, each day you grow worse, your mood darker. You have never had this problem before. Women fall at your feet, no? Climb into your bed at the crook of your finger. What is wrong with my friend now, eh?"

Luc turned his head and lifted his eyebrow as he smiled ruefully. "My wife loves me."

Siam roared with laughter, doubling with it. "So that is why you sleep alone, eh? Out here, like a pouting child. I think at last there is one who claims your heart, my friend."

He stilled, surveying the cattle milling near the wagons. "The Omaha say a white man left pale-face babies in their camps. A tall blond officer charmed two maidens. Now they pay for his pleasure with their pride."

Siam stared into the night. "Do you think I am too old to dream of children, my friend? Of Glynis as my bride?"

"Dreams are for the having," Luc said quietly, wondering if Arielle would ever come to him of her own will.

"Your woman sleeps alone," Siam stated quietly. "Glynis is sleeping with Sally tonight. Anna sleeps elsewhere. She has a cold and is afraid she will infect Sally."

Twelve
....

Minutes later Luc ignored the pain blazing in his ribs and concentrated on the sleeping woman he carried in his arms. Siam, guarding the pallet, moved into the night when Luc approached carrying Arielle. She protested the cool quilts and burrowed beneath them while he slipped off his clothes.

She snuggled into his arms, and Luc slid her gown upward, the need to take her thrusting at him savagely.

Beneath his, her lips were silky, soft, and warm. They began to lift to his, slowly. The sounds coming from the depths of her throat were hunger, enjoyment, and his lips lingered against that warm, fragrant neck. He savored each soft purr rising from her throat.

Luc inhaled the scent of her hair, nudging her thighs apart to lay within them.

Her nipples peaked, their taste sweet as she whimpered, her hands reaching for him.

He smiled against her breast when she stiffened, her hands jerking away from his back. "Luc?" The drowsy sound slid through the two o'clock hour.

"Luc?" she asked again, this time sharply. "Exactly what are you doing here?"

"Holding my wife." He was too tired, too aching to argue, watching her eyes round in the night.

"You aren't wearing a stitch of clothing."

"Not a bit."

"Oh! . . . Nor am I," she whispered suddenly. She gasped as Luc's fingers tested her warmth slightly. "Oh, you mustn't! I . . . stop that . . . I can't think properly."

Luc kissed her breasts, roughly savoring the soft quivering flesh, the nubs brushing against his cheek, soothing him. Heat rushed through Arielle, her heart thudding rapidly beneath his cheek. Her small hand pushed against his shoulder, then her fingertips closed over it slightly, possessively. "I . . ."

"Chère. I need my woman with me tonight," Luc whispered unevenly, tasting the heat in her mouth with his. "Tonight, do not play with me." He fought the savage need to bury himself in her, to forget the pain of the past years. He trembled with the fire, forcing himself away.

"Luc . . . you're upset . . . the night has been too—oh!" she cried out softly against his shoulder as her body jerked beneath his. Her thighs quivered along his, and he saw the startled question in her eyes, knew that she fought the pleasure circling inside her body.

He wanted her desperately, to feel her sheath tightly glove him in pulsing, moist heat. His body ached for release, screamed for hers. His heart cried out for her sweet shield against years of pain. . . .

Then Arielle's lips raised sweetly to his. Giving gently, softening. Her fingertips fluttered along, then smoothed his taut, damp shoulders. "You were magnificent tonight, my dear. Simply magnificent," she whispered unevenly, her tongue licking at his bruised lips. "Thank you."

Luc savored her play as she kissed his bruised face. His pain floated away as Arielle's soft lips trailed against his jaw. She nuzzled his beard and giggled softly, squirming beneath him.

Despite his raging need, her delight stilled him, and Luc

listened, enchanted while she repeated the play. He nuzzled her throat, and she squealed softly, her body flowing beneath his.

No woman had ever enchanted Luc as much as this woman, his wife.

The thought stunned him, and he braced on his elbows looking down at her. "Witch," he whispered tenderly.

Arielle's mouth curved with laughter, her eyes sultry with it as she traced his swollen lips with her fingertips. He nibbled on one, and she grinned impishly. "Hungry?"

"Wench," he returned with a grin that pained his jaw.

"Barbarian. You have two black eyes, Luc. One is swollen shut. You'll be a beauty in the morning." She placed her hands on his ears and tugged him gently down for a kiss. "A kiss for Biddy's knight. Though you know I don't approve of fisticuffs."

Luc slid his hand to her breast, cupping it, sliding his thumb across the peaked nipple. Arielle's kiss had eased the savage need, soothing him. Suddenly tired, drained, Luc eased his body from hers. He was pleased that her hand stroked his shoulder, almost a caress. "You could cure me," he offered, the hopeful leer hurting his mouth and jaw.

He had the woman he wanted, the scents, the soft body, and the whispering intimacy of Arielle in his arms. The thought pleased him immensely as his body relaxed, sleep tugging at him.

"Lydia will help you in the morning. I'm afraid I'm not skilled at healing—oh!" Arielle squirmed when Luc placed his head on her breasts.

He sighed, nuzzled the gentle flesh beneath his cheek, and pressed his face between her breasts, absorbing the scent, the beat of her heart, the silky skin. He rested there, comforted by her warmth.

He must have dozed and awoke to the beat of her heart, the soothing play of her hands over his back.

Her breasts were soft and fragrant, pillowing his head. Arielle inhaled sharply when he kissed them, covering one with his hand.

He had never needed anyone like this ... as if her body were a part of his, her heartbeat matching his.

His woman's breast in his hand was a good feeling, a magical charm against the years of despair and the pain in his body. Luc slid into sleep, comforted by the gentle rocking of her body, the stroking of her timid hands on his hair, his face.

In the morning Arielle turned her head when she saw him and walked quickly away to harness the horses. Her blush enchanted Luc, and he stepped between the Percherons with her.

Her green eyes shimmered with golden sparks of anger, lashing at him. "Shame on you. Smithson caught me returning to camp this morning. I told him that I was checking on your injuries."

Luc ran his fingers along the flushed, silken line of her jaw, and she swatted them away. "None of that."

She frowned, peering up at him and tilting her head to study different angles of his face. "How are you feeling, Luc? You look horrible. . . . Don't you ever fight like that again, do you hear me? You could have been badly injured."

He grinned, delighted by her concern, and ignored the painful bruises. "After a night cuddled like a baby in my wife's arms, I am fully restored."

Her eyes rounded. "I never cuddle."

Enchanted by the sudden change of her mood, Luc bent his head to kiss her.

Her mouth was soft, lush, and he tasted it like a fine wine, cherishing the delicate contours, savoring them, testing her warm breath flowing unevenly into his mouth. Her body eased slightly, softly against him, her eyes dreamy when a shout drew Luc away from her.

The second call widened Arielle's eyes, her cheeks flushing. "Beast," she whispered unevenly, her eyes flashing. "Rake. Leave me be. Surely the DuBois girl is more to your taste. I see her trailing after you every day. It's sinful. You are a flirt, Luc D'Arcy. But I am immune to your charms."

She shot him another blazing glare, then stepped between the horses and away.

His grin hurt, and Luc stopped the chuckle preying inside him. For all her indignation, Arielle's lips had gently, firmly responded to his.

The Jorgensen wagon was left behind. Jorgensen ran after them waving a doll. "African witch! Pins in a doll with a piece of my hair and my shirt. You can't hex me, I'll whip you—"

Jorgensen's heaving chest suddenly met the sharpened tip of Omar's spear. The farmer's eyes rolled up to the warrior's impassive face. Jorgensen backed away, tossing the doll into the bushes.

The wagon wheels screeched during the day. Arielle forced her eyes away from the women hovering around Luc. Lydia tended his cuts with yarrow, a styptic herb, and Marie baked him a special sweet roll with cinnamon and honey. Anna kissed his battered cheek and giggled girlishly at his sweeping bow. Nancy filled his coffee cup and blushed when he lifted her hand to kiss it. Biddy fried a special skillet of potatoes and precious eggs, seasoned by a thick wedge of smoked ham. She placed it in front of Luc with a grand flourish. Harriet and America quickly washed his clothing and hung it to dry on the back of a wagon.

"Disgusting," Arielle muttered when Eliza slipped him a square of Lydia's lavender soap. "They are fawning over him."

Elyce DuBois walked next to Luc's horse, her hand on his saddle. She laughed merrily up at him, and Luc returned a grin.

"Absolutely disgusting," Arielle repeated, seated on Taygete's back. She lifted her chin, loftily absorbing the rolling prairies. While the mare moved smoothly beneath Arielle, her body tightened with an emotion she didn't understand. She had awakened to Luc poised between her legs, his desire pressing intimately against her.

He was a warlock, she decided darkly, flushing when she remembered the quivering, tightening pulse of her body

around his fingers, the humming chords heating her as his
mouth suckled at her breast.

*For an instant, only an instant, she wanted him fiercely
enough to deny everything she had worked for, planned to
achieve, to acquire. She wanted that hard, pulsing staff
within her, taking away the fierce, burning ache—* "Blast!"
Arielle muttered.

Then she remembered Luc's poor, battered face. Her fingers ached to stroke his bruises, her lips to soothe them.

Her breasts ached this morning, taut and swelling, almost
painful to the touch, and each motion of the horse beneath
her touched an unpleasant ache.

She would not be another trophy for Luc's charm. She
would not fall before that devilish, dangerous charm and
those smoky-hot-hungry eyes.

"Arielle, stop speaking to yourself," Glynis ordered
tightly as she tried to ignore Siam, who had taken the harness lines from her fingers. She looked at him pointedly
from the shadows of her bonnet. "That is quite close
enough, Mr. Siam."

They ferried across the Kansaw River and camped along
the banks of Big Soldier Creek. Replenishing their stores,
they traded tobacco, powder, and lead with the Indians. The
land stretched out into prairies and small groves. They
crossed streams and Big Blue Creek, then came to the Re-
publican fork of Blue River. War parties of the Kansaw Indians passed, carrying Pawnee scalps.

Each night Glynis and Arielle battled each other fiercely,
their foils crashing in the dusk. Unknown to them, two tall
westerners watched from the shadows.

Sally clung to life, growing stronger each day under
Luc's cajoling care. Lydia cooked fresh dock and dandelion
greens, a change from the meat diet. Fat from roasting wild
turkeys drizzled into the cooking fires of dried buffalo
chips. Gathered by the women before camp each night, the
"buffalo wood" burned hot and lasted longer than wood,
burning with no odor and little smoke.

While other women protested touching the chips, lifting

their noses at the task, the "widows" did not. They had survived with little and few helping hands.

The second week of May the Platte River spread out before them, a winding river of sand through marshy islands. Antelope grazed in the lush grass, and buffalo herds covered entire hills, leaving deep paths from the surrounding bluffs to the river.

The excitement of "Oregon fever" had dimmed, the travelers settling into a hard, daily routine. Cholera struck, and despite Lydia's help, a mother and two children died within a day. A grandmother died within a few hours of her daughter.

Messages from other travelers were written on bleached buffalo bones. Indians left directions with stones piled exactly or grass bent and bunched in a certain way.

Luc and Siam hunted buffalo each day. The emigrants watched, learning, as the meat was jerked, the hides cured if possible. Arielle fought watching Luc, her body tightening at the sight of him. Broad shoulders and rippling muscles strained to lift a wagon while a wheel was replaced; the powerful arc of his body drew his trousers against hard haunches, and she found her palms moistening unexpectedly.

The wagons needed constant repair. The dry axles screeched despite heavy swabbing of grease.

A farm boy standing on a wagon tongue and bracing his hands on the rumps of the oxen fell. Crushed by the massive wheels, he died slowly, another grave disguised by the wagons as they continued westward.

Two weeks after the death of Sally's baby, she laughed as Luc wrestled on a blanket with Gino, America's son.

Arielle ignored his wink but flushed, smoothing her hair. The bit of feminine vanity enchanted Luc, who lay beneath Gino's conquering straddle.

She'd been too wary, sidestepping him, to the amusement of Smithson. "You've got her noticing you now, boy. Give her time to think about the matter. She's mulish and needs time to come to terms with the idea."

Luc had to agree. Pushed too hard, Arielle could later resent their marriage and the children he wanted from her. His pride was nicked, he decided. His wife had set her bonnet to "acquire" Thaddeus, the picture of gallantry.

When he blew her a kiss, she jerked to her feet, her journal falling to the ground. From where he lay, Luc enjoyed a view of her slender ankles and the sway of her skirts around her hips. She turned suddenly, caught his smile, and scowled fiercely at him. Luc grinned when she stuck out her tongue at him.

He lingered on the thought of that pink tongue, its sweet taste and delicate foraging, then lunged to his feet.

While Siam grimly stared at the fire, Smithson tamped his pipe and sipped the tea he enjoyed with Glynis. "By Jesus. That D'Arcy woman is driving me to the brink," he muttered. "Today, it was 'Smithson, we're lagging. Perhaps the teams aren't properly matched after all.' "

He clamped his teeth around his pipe stem. "Though I will say the woman knows horseflesh. She'll run a fine breeding farm, if the Indians don't get 'em first. Those Percherons follow her around like immense puppies, scrambling for her affection like smitten swains. Glynis says the breed comes from the days of knights—war horses bred to carry the weight of armor and the jaws and ears of the lively Arabians. Those big draft horses make a right nice dowry, eh, Luc?"

Luc didn't like the idea of himself tagging after Arielle like one of her pets. Nor did he like the picture of his wife in another man's arms.

The second week of May, Arielle tapped her toe to the fiddler's music, watching the couples swirl around the campground. Wilson had selected the campsite between the North and the South Platte rivers. The next day would be a "wash day," a time to rest and prepare for another long trek. Buffalo and deer meat hung in strips over a scaffold, drying over a slow fire.

Glynis sat nearby, her darting needle catching the light of the campfire. She jerked Arielle's torn petticoat, preparing for another rip, and began muttering. "Siam is over there, watching me with those liquid deer-brown eyes of his. . . . I feel like a rabbit before a wolf—Don't you dare look, Arielle! Today he told me I was a goddess—a goddess! Don't you think there is something sinful about that?"

"Glynis, don't be melodramatic. Siam is smitten with you and clearly has you all aflutter," Arielle returned, closing her journal. She had just been subjected to another of Smithson's lectures concerning passing up marriage offers at her advanced age. Smithson nettled and pried, spreading Luc's finer points before her like a tasty meal to be devoured.

Arielle tapped her pen on the journal's blank page. Luc's charm matched only his wit and his bravery.

She disliked and distrusted his charm, his easy manner with people and animals. She distrusted the way he disregarded her notorious reddish hair and her left hand, when everyone else knew the obvious dangers of such burdens.

He stunned her with hungry kisses, each more devastating than the last. Yet he hadn't taken her to his nightly pallet.

Arielle allowed herself a tight, pleased smile. Perhaps Mr. Lucien Navaronne D'Arcy had finally learned that she was interested in another. She was a smart-thinking businesswoman after all, not susceptible to charming rogues.

He could be a savage. She'd seen that dark side of him with Jorgensen.

She'd tasted his dark, elemental hunger for her. Luc D'Arcy possessed primitive tendencies when forced to shed his veneer of charm and civilization.

Arielle closed her eyes, trying to force away thoughts of Luc. They seemed to tighten her whole body into one knot. She longed for Thaddeus's calming presence, the ordered gallantry of his company . . . the predictability and restraint of his molded character. When she acquired him, he would be perfect as a husband, a father—

Luc would be devastating. She would spend her life breathless from kisses and cuddlings. Then his raw male arrogance would challenge her every minute—

"Jean-Pierre—Siam—smitten with me?" Glynis's question held a note of panic. "The man is comparing my eyes to silver, he's dared to . . ."

The older woman's hand rose to clutch at the collar over her throat, a protective gesture. She cleared her throat, lowering her voice. "Today, Arielle, that Canadian told me I needed no clothes to be beautiful. . . . Arielle, he said the word *breasts* . . . actually spoke the word to tell me that 'the most beautiful vision' of his life was the way the sunlight touched my face, my breasts. . . . My bosom, Arielle, is not a topic I want discussed. How much milk I will give a baby to make it strong is not debatable, nor his concern. Then he ogles my hips—*ogles my hips!*" she repeated indignantly.

"One must learn to dismiss unwanted admirers, Glynis," Arielle said, distracted. Luc's head resting on her bosom while he slept was a memory that had sprung to life easily. She found herself lingering in the moment, her breasts sensitive immediately. She resented the aching need to hold him, a battered warrior demanding her kisses.

She'd actually . . . cuddled him! Rocked and shushed him!
She'd found her hand locked gently within his more than once, Luc's bigger warm fingers laced intimately with hers. His dark skin contrasted with hers, bringing to mind instantly his dark face against her breasts. He'd needed the comfort she could give.

Then there was that sinful kiss low on her body.

She actually ached for the sweep of his hand—the possessive, too intimate sweep of his big hand over her sensitive flesh.

Her thighs jerked together, quivering beneath the layers of her skirts.

She found her gaze straying, latching on to Luc like a hungry hawk. Her ears caught his deep tone, listening for the accent to thicken as it did when he was excited or . . . *aroused.* The word brought images of Luc's lean body, poised above hers, the cords of his shoulders and arms standing out in relief, trembling with the intense need driving him.

Each day his eyes slid down, then up her body like hungry, caressing hands. He seemed to be waiting, his bruises clearing quickly while the "widows" hovered over him like hens with one chick.

His mouth had curved sensuously, sloping almost wistfully when he stared at her mouth. She licked her dry lips.

"He is the kissingest man," she murmured, then clamped her lips closed, surprised she had spoken.

" 'Dismiss unwanted admirers,' indeed," Glynis muttered, draped in her own thoughts. "Fine one you are. Luc takes every opportunity to touch you, to help you up and down from the wagons or your horses. He kisses the back of your hand, and the whole train wonders when Smithson will marry you. Clearly you are under siege, Arielle, and not doing very well at dismissing Luc. You have confidence in his abilities, respect his kindness toward our charges, and act in every way like a woman being courted by someone she desires."

"You know the danger of Luc exposing my façade, Glynis. One word from him, one flash of the marriage papers beneath Smithson's nose, and the whole adventure— the broadening of Browning shipping and trading—will be thrown to the winds." Arielle leveled her best quelling stare at Glynis, who returned it evenly.

"A match, my dear?" Glynis asked between her teeth.

"Heavenly," Arielle returned, slapping the journal closed.

Then Siam was kneeling beside Glynis, his eyes worshipping her. He had shaved, his skin glistening in the campfire light. Beneath his hat, his hair curled on his broad shoulders. He wore a linen shirt, cut full in the sleeves, and embroidered with beads. In one hand he held a small package, wrapped in leather, and in the other a bouquet of daisies and yellow prairie flowers. "Goddess of my heart, will you walk with this poor ugly man?"

"Goodness, Mr. Siam, you are not ugly. You are the most handsome man I have ever known!" Glynis exclaimed, her eyes widening as he grinned broadly. She flushed, clearly uncomfortable when she realized what she had said.

"I have a gift for you." Siam's deep voice was musical, his eyes beaming into Glynis's. "I would die for the picture of your beautiful face bathed in moonlight."

"Mr. Siam, you mustn't speak so!" Glynis exclaimed, a blush rising from her throat to her cheeks. Her bright eyes darted to Arielle, who was grinning. "Clearly, we must speak in private."

When Glynis rose to her feet, Siam took her hand and placed it on his arm. Glynis's backward glance at Arielle was fearful as the big Canadian proudly walked her from the camp. Siam's manner was that of a gallant promenading a highborn lady.

Arielle was forced to deal with her dark mood alone. Luc had disappeared once the camp settled down, and she refused to ask his whereabouts.

He stepped into the circle of the wagons, dressed in a white shirt that Anna, Lelia, and Harriet had sewn for him during Sally's illness. America, Eliza, and Mary had embroidered an intricate arrangement of tiny blue and yellow flowers in rows down each side. Styled by America, the shirt skimmed Luc's broad shoulders, the full sleeves rolled back at his forearms. On another man, the shirt would have seemed feminine, but Luc's dark, masculine looks offset it perfectly.

Luc's hair gleamed, the firelight flickering on it and the curve of his slashed eyebrow. The night wind riffled his hair, playing with it like a woman's fingers—

Arielle's hands clenched her pen as she remembered that hair flowing through her fingers, not soft or silky, but stark, masculine, with a will of its own. His scent—a unique dark, mysterious tang of danger and excitement, of seduction— lurked in the crisp strands.

Nothing like the scent she wanted near her for a lifetime. Not like Thaddeus's safe bay rum.

The firelight gleamed on the hard angle of Luc's jaw, and she realized he had just shaved.

Her neck tingled, remembering the almost pleasant rough scrape of his beard. She fought for the memory of Thaddeus's jaw and lost.

Arielle warmed beneath the weight of his silver eyes as they locked to her across the huge bonfire.

His bold stare snared her in wild, stormy emotions, her

body tingling, empty, heating—Arielle was startled to find her hand at her throat, her pulse racing beneath her fingertips like that of a frightened rabbit.

Elyce clung to Luc's arm, laughing, smiling up at him, and a tight bitterness unfurled in Arielle's stomach.

Lydia, concentrating on her basket of herbs, stumbled and stepped on Elyce's foot. The Frenchwoman's beautiful face changed into a mask of fury, spewing venomous threats in her language. Lydia went pale, trying to apologize as Luc swept her beneath his arm. He bent to kiss her cheek and straightened, speaking to Elyce in low, rapid French. She blinked, paled, and forced a smile at Lydia, who was sobbing.

Elyce's features were taut, her smile pasted warily on her lips. She glanced at Luc, who looked arrogantly down at her with a coldness Arielle had never seen.

When Elyce moved away with the dancers, her eyes pleading with Luc, he bent to kiss Lydia's cheek again.

The herbalist began to smile and soon engaged in plucking herbs and roots from her basket. Luc tapped her nose with his finger playfully, and Lydia laughed merrily.

Arielle remembered his tickling fingers and ground her teeth. She frowned, discovering herself toying with the intricate design of the D'Arcy ring.

Nelson Bancroft, a young rancher wanting a wife to help him start ranching near Marcus Whitman's mission, asked her to dance. Though Arielle had never danced to the lively fiddle music, she nodded.

Not long after the dance began, she found herself staring at Luc's chest, the columns of blue and yellow flowers flowing down it.

He spun her around, then another man caught her, the women moving back and forth in a line, clapping their hands.

Nelson grinned at Eliza, his new partner, and she beamed up at him.

Luc's hands caught Arielle's waist, lifting her off the ground as he spun around. His eyes sparkled, challenging her.

"Wicked, wicked man," she muttered, stepping close to him as the dance prescribed.

"Angel, you are delightful," Luc said, grinning as he lifted her off the ground.

"I am a grown woman, not a child to be tossed around, Luc," she whispered sharply.

"*Chère*, patience. When we are alone, I will let you toss me over your shoulder." His lips formed a kiss. "You may 'acquire' me tonight."

"Burn you at the stake is more like it."

Luc laughed outright. When the dance was done, he lifted her hand to his lips, kissing the palm.

There was something in him tonight, something lurking, savage and strong, hovering too near—he spoke in rapid French and another tongue, stepping close to her.

Arielle shivered beneath the large hands that smoothed her loosened braids. "I am not in a good mood, Luc. I suggest you keep your distance. At the moment I could run you through with my foil."

"You are a passionate woman, my angel," Luc returned slowly with a grim lift of his lips. "But I am losing patience."

She smiled too sweetly. "Perhaps Miss DuBois is more suitable. Undoubtedly she has kept you busy every night for the past two weeks."

His eyebrows shot up. "Elyce? What do you mean?"

She enjoyed having the advantage; Luc was clearly puzzled, scowling down at her. "I mean that you and Elyce are clearly . . . ah . . . warmly involved."

He took a step toward her and she retreated. "Go on," Luc said too softly, in a voice trimmed with his unique accent.

Arielle stopped, suddenly aware that her back was against the wagon. Luc's broad shoulders blocked out the campfire and the dancers. "You, sir, are making me very angry."

For an instant temper seared his silvery eyes, darkening them into the shade of pewter. His jaw flexed rhythmically, his hand tightening on her braid. "Perhaps if my wife were warmer, Elyce would not be so tempting—"

"Ah! She is tempting, then," Arielle crowed. "Admit it. She is French and beautiful. Much more suitable to you than myself, a sensible businesswoman."

Luc's sensuous mouth tightened, his dark eyebrows almost meeting in a fierce scowl. "Sensible? You dream of one man while married to another." Luc's voice was very deep, clipped with his accent.

"Married. Hah! We are in a temporary state, soon to be severed," Arielle returned, crossing her arms over her chest. Her knees quivered unsteadily, and she realized that she had seen Luc near death, delirious, and then charming, laughing. *She had never seen his fiercely savage mood turned toward herself.*

She should have been frightened. She wasn't.

She wanted to tear at him—to avenge poor dear Thaddeus. She scowled back, undaunted. "I have no intentions of letting you—of—" She cleared her throat.

He moved quickly, clamping a hand to her waist. He lifted her feet from the ground and stepped into the darkness beyond the camp. Once there he placed her on his shoulder and ran for the cottonwoods rimming the river.

Luc placed her on her feet. Arielle wanted to hurl herself at him. She wanted the pleasure of revenging her sleepless nights and the primitive emotions she couldn't rule. She pushed back the curls that bobbed near her nose.

Luc scowled down at her. "Why do I want you? You?" he repeated darkly, as if questioning his sanity. There was a rapid burst of hot, fluid French, mixed with other languages.

She smiled sweetly. "You don't. You want Elyce."

"I do?" he questioned dangerously.

Undaunted by his too soft tone, the accent rising softly, almost melodically in his deep voice, Arielle lifted her chin. She could control her anger . . . she could batten it down—fury stormed over her like a wildfire. *Why should she care if Elyce touched him whenever possible?*

Luc's large hands wrapped around her throat, his thumbs lifting her chin. She tugged at his wrists, refusing to relinquish control.

His kiss enchanted, warmed, exquisite in its fashioning. A

brush of warmth across her lips. Again. Tasting, tilting, deepening.

Arielle tried to think, to breathe, to force her languid body to move away from the seduction of his mouth. "You . . . are . . . incorrigible," she managed in an uneven whisper.

"You are enchanting, exquisite, delightful," he murmured, deepening the kiss.

She tried to breathe, her body catching fire. "Not you," she whispered, her treacherous fingers clinging to his shirt.

A carefully fashioned pocket tore, the sound ripping through her as desperately as the fever heating her languid body.

She leaned against him, too weak to stand away.

"Angel," Luc murmured, his lips demanding. "So sweet, so sweet—"

She answered his demand, clinging to him as his fingers floated over her bosom, teasing, tormenting. Then his hand took her breast firmly, gently possessing.

She clung to him, wrapping her hands in his hair, her arms around his neck. Then the soft pallet was at her back. Her body quivered, balancing a lifetime of celibacy against the hungers raging inside her.

As if years of waiting came unfurled, Arielle trembled, arcing her hips against his hand. The cold night air struck her flesh, soon to be replaced by his foraging fingers, gently easing into her. Cloth tore, another rip, and Luc's masculinity lay within the quivering cradle of her thighs.

"Magnificent. Sweet. Enchanting . . ." Rich with emotion, Luc's heavy accent swept across her hot cheek. "*Chère*, your maidenhead—" He thrust gently, and pain streaked through her.

Arielle bit her lip as Luc stilled, kissing away the tears lingering on her lashes. The rumors of women whispering about their marriage beds snagged at her. Luc was not beastly; indeed he was sweet, withholding himself with what appeared to be great restraint. She had waited a lifetime to step into the fires, to unleash her emotions—"If you leave me now, Luc—" she threatened unevenly. "I would see this bit of rough seas through. I am not a weakling."

His flesh surged, naked, hot against her secret place, and Luc trembled. "So damp, tight—Angel, this time it will hurt . . . I cannot wait—"

At first the fullness was ecstatic, easing. When Luc's mouth slanted hungrily against hers, she wanted more. . . .

Searing pain cut through her, her cry caught in Luc's mouth.

His eyes were silvery in the moonlight, gentle, caressing. "My sweet little one . . . it could not be helped. . . .

Shaking now, Arielle forced herself to lie still. She wanted this desperately, this feverish deep heat that Luc had begun. Shattered by the softening within her, the moist enclosure trembling, gloving Luc's heavy manhood, Arielle dissected every nuance of her body joined to his.

Rich, lovely, she thought, watching the play of emotions across his taut face. Whatever happened he could not leave her now.

She wanted every nuance of what she sensed Luc offered her, every deep thrilling sensation.

His thighs were rough within hers, his body taut, trembling with a desire she had only tasted. Perspiration beaded Luc's upper lip, his chest rising unevenly against her suddenly sensitive breasts.

His palms cupped her naked buttocks, caressed and lifted her higher gently, and the ultimate pleasure of his fullness startled her. "Damn," he cursed softly, his hand trembling, smoothing her softness.

He looked so shattered, so distracted, that Arielle couldn't help but giggle.

"Damnation, Angel. This isn't funny," Luc bit out, clearly upset. "Tossing up your skirts and entering you like an untutored boy wasn't my plan."

His charm had slipped, and nothing was so endearing as Luc struggling for control.

She ached to unleash that control. Gently Arielle lifted her lips, teasing him as he had tormented her. She licked the rough side of his throat, testing the uneven pulse running beneath the damp skin.

"Angel!" Instantly Luc plunged deeper, quivering, locking her to him.

The deep pulsing of his body into hers startled Arielle as he groaned softly, easing down into her arms. Helpless, vulnerable in her arms, Luc groaned again, his great body lax and heavy on hers, his thighs quivering.

Arielle stroked his back much as he would one of her horses, soothing them after a long race.

He really was very sweet, trying for control and losing it.

Because he was sweet in his dark confused mood, lying over her, caressing her thigh, Arielle kissed his ear. It was a tasty ear, dark and mysterious, she decided. She flicked her tongue in it, floating along in her happy, mellow mood. Yet her body still ached, taut with an emotion she did not understand.

Why was this fierce longing—craving—aching so harshly within her? What sort of woman would want to . . . to participate, to engage in a battle of . . . ?

"You're squirming, Angel," Luc muttered darkly. "If you don't stop, the second time won't be better than the first."

"You sound disgruntled, Luc. I'm certain you were adequate."

He tensed, his caressing hand stopped. "Adequate?"

"In the mating. Remember, I breed horses," she mused, frowning. Luc's body was growing, filling her again. The incredible sensation caused her to tighten immediately around him. She gasped, savoring the intimate pleasure, tightening again.

Luc groaned harshly, pulling away and leaving her empty. "You are a disaster, madame wife," he stated ruefully, sitting upright. He tugged her into his arms and looked down at her in the moonlight, lifting away her masses of hair, watching the moonlight slip through the strands.

It was pleasant, soothing, she decided as Luc continued to play with her hair. "Do you hurt?" he asked finally, cupping her hips beneath her skirt.

She mentally examined the slight twinge. "No more than a brisk ride would cause—" She blushed when he arched a brow.

"A ride," he repeated flatly, unbuttoning her dress. "You compliment my skills as a husband . . . as a lover," he murmured mockingly.

Arielle closed her eyes, the roaming of his hands luxurious against her skin. Cherishing, molding, testing . . . she snuggled deeper in his lap, resting against him. On an impulse she lifted her head. "Lucien, how do you feel about my dominant left hand?"

"This small thing?" he asked, taking her wrist and bringing her fingers to his lips. He kissed the D'Arcy ring, then each knuckle, suckling her fingertips. "I love the shape, the taste of each finger."

Taking her hand, he pressed it between his thighs, holding her palm against the hard length when she would have drawn away.

"Amazing," Arielle managed when she could speak.

The silky skin shielded the hardness that had been within her. She fought the curious notion to stroke and cuddle his great throbbing shaft, trembling as he gathered her closer. "All that—"

She explored his heavy thighs lightly, entranced by the hairy muscular shape so different from her slender ones. She touched the scar on his right thigh, caressed it softly until Luc groaned.

"To the hilt, sweetheart," he whispered unevenly against her temple. Luc's unsteady breath brushed her cheek, and he groaned, his hand trembling, caressing her breasts, sliding to flatten against her stomach. "A perfect fit."

Arielle's eyes flung open. She framed Luc's jaw with her hands, peering into his eyes. "Did I hurt you, Luc? Oh, how it must have hurt . . . you poor man . . . you were admirable, sacrificing your pain just because of my . . . my—" She swallowed, tossing out the word on the wind. "Lust. Oh, dear. I'm nothing more than a wanton, slaking my thirsts on you, you poor man."

"Torture," he whispered, breathing hard and ripping away his shirt. He tore away the knots of her petticoats with trembling fingers. "I'm disabled for life."

"Oh, no . . . You were magnificent. Wonderful—" Arielle

shook aside the folds of her dress as Luc drew it over her head. He tossed it aside and drew her into the snug blankets beside him. "I can never forgive myself."

She was desperate now, weighted with guilt that Luc would never be able to—she wondered about his hampered abilities. When Luc's lips prowled down her throat and his hand claimed her breast, she stopped thinking.

Thirteen

· ·

The next day Luc sat on his heels beside his mother's grave. The hard, fast trip from the wagons had not eased his savage need for revenge, nor the futility of his grief. He tore away a weed clawing at the rocks covering the grave, just as he wanted to rip away the mistake of leaving his family.

He scanned the small iron fence enclosing the grave. The blacksmith had placed an ornate *D* on the tiny fence and on the red stone gleaming in the noonday sun. Clouds raced by overhead, and a band of Cheyenne walked their ponies on the horizon, winding toward him.

Siam eased away from the tree he had been leaning against and walked leisurely to Luc's side. Both men noted the blue spots on the leader's face, a sign of his coups against the enemy. Red lines shimmered on his arms and legs, signifying coups, and the intermixed yellow lines counted the number of horses he had stolen. All twenty warriors were painted elaborately, their horses's tails knotted for the war trail.

Wounds were circled with black, lines radiating outward

in a prayer that the sun would come to heal. The coup sticks and shields were decorated with feathers and scalps, the horses' eyes circled for clear sight. The marks of their different societies gleamed on the horses and their riders.

Luc rose slowly to his feet as the war party approached. The chief, a fair man frightened for his people, nodded to Luc. He raised his right hand to his neck, palm outward with the index and middle fingers touching. He lifted his hand until his fingertips reached his face, then lowered his hand.

"Friend." Luc returned the signal.

The chieftain nodded again, then signaled the signs for heart and sick. "You have counted coup, Torn-Heart?"

Luc acknowledged the chief's name for him with a nod. The Indians across the territories had placed their choicest maidens at his bidding. At first disgruntled that he chose not to marry, they had accepted his "bleeding heart."

The war chief's red feather, signifying he had been wounded earlier, shone in the dim light. "The man, Bliss, lives. He wears a blue coat with gold buttons, but he has no soldiers. Men took him in a wagon to Fort Laramie. A Shoshone woman bore his child, then he went." He signaled to the west.

Luc's hand rested lightly on his knife, despite the rage sweeping over him. "Bliss is dead."

"He lives, Torn-Heart. He laughed at the woman when she begged to go with him. She drowned the baby and herself. There is another woman with his child at this fort named for the dead man, Laramee."

Siam cursed, low and savage, then placed his hand on Luc's shoulder.

"I will find Bliss," Luc promised too softly, his heart chilling.

"He does not wear the name Bliss, but carries another. You have a woman now? A son?" the chieftain asked.

Luc inhaled, his thoughts jerking to Arielle, soft and pliant as she snuggled against him. Suddenly he wanted her with him. Arielle, determined to bring each woman safely across the great land, full of life, swept away the shadows

in his life—the image of his child nursing at her breast
eased the pain again. "I have a wife. She is new to our marriage bed. A son will come."

Sharp Knife nodded, the other warriors following him as
he urged his horse away. "That is good. The woman will
heal your heart, warm your bed at night. A warrior with a
brave heart needs a woman to tend him, or he becomes
empty, bad."

Siam watched the war party wind over the slight hill.
"There will be word of Bliss at the fort."

Luc plucked another encroaching weed from his mother's
grave, fighting the rage inside him. He crushed the weed.
Bliss lived.

He closed his eyes, his stomach contracting painfully
with emotions, as though slammed by a giant fist.

Luc fiercely wanted to hold Arielle against him.

Revenge, taking the lives of Gaspard's men, had also
taken a part of his soul. For a time he'd placed the Dark
Avenger in his past. He'd tasted life and the future in
Arielle's arms. . . . Now there was one more man—

He tossed the weed away and stood, watching a coyote
slide into a thicket. *Bliss would not live long.*

Arielle jerked her blanket higher that night, and Glynis
held tight to her side. "Arielle, stop this eternal tossing. It
has been a long day, and tomorrow we will be on our way
again. Please let me rest."

"I will run him through," Arielle muttered to herself as
the rain pelted the covered wagon.

"Mr. Smithson isn't worried, nor should you be," Glynis
said with a yawn. "I'm certain they are fine and well, at-
tending to Luc's family business."

"Family? When he was ill, he grieved badly for the loss
of his family. He has no family . . . it is Elyce DuBois. You
should see them together, flirting so thick you could cut it
with a knife. Elyce and her giant udders. *She* would never
need a bust enhancer. . . . She runs after him like a hungry
mare to his stallion . . . and what does he do? Turn her
away? No. It's all sweet talk and laughing between them."

"Luc strikes me as a man who would not wander from his marriage vows."

Arielle twisted the D'Arcy ring weighing her finger. Luc had taken her gently, returned her safely to the wagon, then was gone in the morning.

She wanted to be cuddled, to listen to that deep, exquisitely melodic voice whisper urgently to her. Arielle punched her feather pillow. She had given Luc her most precious gift, and he had ridden away at daybreak.

She brushed the tears away from her lashes with the back of her hand. Luc had strained to go slowly, embarrassed when his body denied his reins. His efforts were endearing, his caresses fevered, his hands trembling.

He had whispered dark, passionate, stormy words, puctuated by hungry kisses.

Arielle flopped to her stomach and clutched her pillow tightly to her breasts. "Apples . . . peaches," she muttered, her breasts sensitive from Luc's restrained lovemaking. She closed her eyes, reliving the gentle caresses, Luc struggling for control.

Her lips curved into a smile. She ached deep inside, yet Luc's stunned expression was almost worth the venture. She stroked the pillow, wishing for Luc's strong chest, his heart beating slowly beneath her cheek. She smoothed the hidden chafe marks on her throat, a reminder of Luc's lovemaking.

Thaddeus. The name dropped into her thoughts like an ice-covered rock.

She shivered, huddling beneath the quilt. Her fist gripped the feather pillow. She'd begun the venture to claim Thaddeus, and Luc now filled her thoughts.

"Arielle, I hear something outside the wagon. . . . Zeus and the mares are restless. Shh." Glynis faced Arielle.

Zeus pawed the ground, and a man's voice murmured in the night. Arielle grabbed the man's trousers Nancy Fairhair had fashioned for her. She thrust her legs into them while she lay on the pallet, then jerked on a shirt Anna had patched for Luc. It fell to her knees. "Arielle, please don't—" Glynis whispered as Arielle took her foil from the case and tugged off the protective blunt tip.

"Nonsense. I knew I would have to act in moments like this when the trip began. In the wilderness one must protect one's possessions." Arielle slid from the wagon, the cold mud oozing between her toes. Then she saw the two men. They were easing her horses from the camp with neck tethers, walking beside them. She whistled low and the six horses jerked against the ropes, backstepping, turning toward her.

The men held the ropes, their bodies glistening with paint in the campfires. "Stop!" Arielle called.

When the men pulled away hard, Arielle whistled again. The horses nickered and ambled back to her, dragging the thieves. One of the men lurched toward Arielle, his fist raised to strike. The fine point of her foil pricking his chest stopped him. "I really wouldn't," she said quietly. "I've been having a bad night, and you could suffer the consequences for my lack of sleep."

"Bitch. You think this toy will stop me? It won't," the man snarled, grabbing her foil. His fingers came away dripping with blood, gripped by his good hand.

"Smithson!" Glynis cried out sharply. "You hulking land-lubber, get yourself aft."

Arielle glanced at her friend. "You are in a temper, Glynis. Your language is shocking. One would think you possessed a dominant left hand and a cap of red hair."

"Arielle, must you?" Glynis asked between her teeth. Her foil caught the faint light. "Do you need my help?"

"Not at the moment. Perhaps later," Arielle returned, carefully watching two men lurch from the shadows, stalking her. "Shame on you, painting yourselves like Indians," she tossed at them, noting their pale skin and boots.

"Give that pretty here," one of the men ordered, stepping close with his knife raised.

"En garde." Arielle nicked his wrist and danced back. She lifted one leg, then the other, grinning at Glynis, who peered anxiously around the wagon covering. "Glynis, these trousers are marvelous. They don't hamper at all."

"That's enough, Mrs. D'Arcy," Smithson said calmly, his

pistol leveled at the two men. "You've done well," he said reluctantly.

"The cause of my success, Captain Smithson, is that I am wearing trousers," she stated. "I think I will be wearing them hereafter."

"Fine," he returned easily. "Loose, practical trousers would suit all the women."

"Goodness!" Glynis exclaimed worriedly, looking from Smithson's set face to Arielle's triumphant grin. "Arielle, should you?"

"Of course she should," Smithson returned as the men from the other wagons gathered around. "We're not far from the fort. We'll take these fine specimens there for judgment."

A half hour later in their wagon, Glynis muttered, "Trousers. Your aunt Louise would be mortified. Your willful behavior reflects poorly upon me . . . dismissing everything you were taught, wearing mens' trousers, indeed."

"Shh. Glynis, that little bout trimmed my temper, and I'm really sleepy."

Smithson's deep tones rumbled outside their wagon, blending with Luc's melodic voice. He was angry, Arielle noted as his accent trimmed his words. She frowned when he cursed, *"Mon Dieu,"* his tone dark.

Another man chuckled, and Glynis sat up. "That is Mr. Siam. He laughed outright! I've never heard him laugh. How delightful! It's a lovely laugh, full-bodied, deeply pleasured—"

Arielle tugged her down, drawing up the quilt over them. She wasn't certain how she would react to Luc just yet, resenting the energy she'd shed on the thieves. She wanted her left-handed thinking and her red-haired temper in place when she saw him again. "Shh."

After a half hour of tossing, and both women punching their pillows, Glynis swept back the quilt, sliding into her dress. "I must speak to Mr. Siam. He left those beautiful moccasins for me this morning. I can't accept such a gift. . . . Oh, they were so beautiful though."

"Shh. Glynis, lie down. Tomorrow will be soon enough

to thank him," Arielle whispered urgently as Glynis stepped out into the night.

The Englishwoman ignored her, calling into the night, "Oh, Mr. Siam, could I speak with you a moment, please?"

Arielle lay stiffly waiting, her fists locked to the blankets. In the morning, when her thoughts were in a neat row, she would face Luc and demand a divorce. The wagon creaked and Arielle flopped to her side as Glynis slid into bed beside her. Tomorrow Luc would pay for his infidelities—

A calloused hand covered her mouth as Luc's tall body curved around hers. He bent to nuzzle her neck, kissing it. Snared to his large body, Arielle refused to lower herself to the indignity of a struggle—until his hand left her mouth to slide down her throat, then possessively cup her breast. "Loose me, you lusting, indiscriminate rake!" she whispered unevenly, kicking against him and tangling in her nightgown and the heavy quilts.

Luc pressed her to her back, his expression fierce in the shadows above her. "I thought we dispensed with our little battles last night, my sweet wife," he said in a low, heavily accented whisper. "You will not face men like you did tonight again, *chère*. You could have been hurt."

"I was fully capable of handling the situation. . . . Why are you here?" She tried to move the wrists he had locked in one hand.

"To lay with my beloved wife for a few moments," Luc stated between his teeth. "To taste her welcoming kisses—"

"Well! Go to Smithson, I don't care. I will not be used at your will, dispensing—whatever—upon demand."

His scarred eyebrow lifted. Deep lines of fatigue rested on his face, the shadows beneath his eyes dark. The fierce expression in his eyes held and startled her. The mouth that curved sensually last night pressed into a thin line. "Perhaps I need the comfort of my wife's arms, the warmth of her bed, the tiny locked box she calls a heart. Perhaps you would bed me if I were on my deathbed, or if I bore the name 'Thaddeus.' But I don't, my love. I'm simply a man needing what you hoard so well."

His lips sank into hers, a fiery kiss startling her with its intensity and hunger. He tasted of desperation, of anger, and Arielle's mood lurched out of control. She tugged at his hair, locking her fingers in it, fighting the rising need.

Luc raised his head, his expression harsh. "You little enticing witch."

"How dare you! You stayed away all day. After last night the least you could have done is—" She faltered, uncertain what Luc should have done. "Then you appear and expect me to—"

Luc watched her, his fingers toying with a soft, fragrant curl. "Yes? I definitely expect my wife to welcome me."

"You've been gone all day," she threw back.

"You missed me?" Luc countered tightly. "Tell me you missed me, you little savage. Tell me you want me," he demanded.

"Never." Arielle lifted her chin only to have Luc's warm finger trace the contours.

"Tonight, *chère*, I fear I cannot wait for your gracious acceptance of our marriage bed," he warned between his teeth.

"Beast," she countered, blowing away a tendril clinging to her lips.

"Obviously. But I will not be denied your charms, Madame D'Arcy. You are my family now—my only family—and I fear I must warm myself at your hearth." Luc bit the words, his expression grim and harsh. He ripped away her bodice, staring down at her breasts, touching them with his trembling fingertips.

Arielle had braced her body against his assault, determined to remain cold to his touch. Luc's hand cherished, his expression changing from fierce to a soft gentle reverence. He closed his eyes briefly. "My child at your breast will be a beautiful sight. You are a beautiful, passionate woman, Angel."

Then he bent to taste, and Arielle bit her lip to quiet the pleasure. "You can't just—" she began as Luc stripped away her long drawers.

Arielle closed her eyes, fighting to remain cold beneath him. She should be angry . . . she *was* angry. "Of course, you're much bigger, you beast," she whispered between gasps, her fingers curling into fists. "Your victory is expected."

The lines of fatigue on Luc's face shifted, lightened into a disarming, boyish grin. "You long to fight, *ma chère*. Why don't you?"

"I am a lady, you sprawling length of bilge water," she said icily, trying to cling to the words as desire rocked her body, heated it. "Surely you realize that a lady would never welcome such ... heathen advances."

"No?" he mocked, brushing his lips back and forth across hers.

Arielle trembled, heated, fighting the desperate need warming her thighs, moistening—"Fine," she said tightly as Luc nibbled on her ear. "Fine. You're toying with me, Luc. I could retaliate."

"Mmm?" he challenged, moving her breast gently in his palm. Her body contracted as he laved moisture over her nipple. "Beautiful."

She shivered, her fingers splaying through his hair. "I could hurt you, you know. Drastically so. I once ran my foil through a man's hand when he made inappropriate advances."

Luc's low laughter rumbled against her neck. The rich sound caused her heart to beat unevenly, her fingers to still, to tremble before they smoothed his hair. He looked down at her with tenderness, his thumb smoothing her cheek. The soft gaze warmed into a boyish grin.

In the next heartbeat Luc was nuzzling her throat, his beard tickling.

Arielle squirmed, fighting the laughter bubbling out of her. When it did, Luc lay back. "I won."

"You did not."

He stretched out lazily, closing his eyes. "You may kiss me."

"What?" Arielle sat up, clutching the blanket to her chest. Luc tugged her down and settled around her. "You're enormous," she said finally. She silently admitted that Luc was very comfortable, tangled with her. She had longed for his teasing throughout the day, waited for it, and now her restless energy slid into quiet happiness. Luc rocked her pleasantly, companionably, in his arms.

The night slid by them, the livestock restless as wolves howled in the distance. A baby cried, and the wagon creaked beneath them.

"I went to my mother's grave," Luc murmured drowsily after several moments. His hand cupped her breast, smoothing the shape delicately. "She would have liked you."

Arielle's heart tore a bit, softening. Luc had lost so much. . . . "Shh." Arielle smoothed his hair, her body pleasantly tangled with his tall one. She was angry with Luc moments before, and she fought to balance her emotions. True, Luc had missed a few gallant points . . . like telling her where he was going—to visit his mother's grave was admirable—then exhausted, he had returned to her.

She turned the thought in her mind, probing it. She liked Luc returning to her . . . sharing his life in this quiet, companionable moment.

The night wind fluttered the wagon's cover, enclosing them safely in a shadowy, warm nest.

He lay at her side, anchoring her with his hand and a long, heavy leg across hers. He whispered slowly, caressing her breasts gently and resting his fingers between her thighs. He rubbed her gently. "You must ache from last night."

Fatigue weighted his accent as he nuzzled her throat. "I missed you today," he murmured sleepily. "I am glad you are here, *ma chère*."

"Lucien, you can't sleep here . . . we can't—" Arielle stopped when she heard Luc's gentle snore, his face resting against her throat. His long eyelashes fluttered against her skin, and he sighed deeply.

Awake for hours, Arielle forced herself to breathe slowly. Luc's damp, clean hair clung to her cheek, and she realized he must have bathed before coming to her. Clearly exhausted, Luc slept deeply, heavily, against her.

Arielle listened to his breathing. His heart pounded slowly against her. "Angel," he whispered dreamily, pulling her deeper into his arms.

She stiffened, her body still soft and quivering from his lovemaking. She shook him gently. "Luc, you must go."

He nuzzled closer, kissing the side of her throat. He cuddled her, smoothing her body possessively, gently, then settled back at her side and slept deeply. Arielle listened to the gentle wind, the raindrops striking the wagon cover, and closed her eyes.

The single tear left a warm trail as it oozed from her burning lids.

She could not care for this man, nor long for his touch. She would not.

Then she rested her cheek against his and closed her eyes.

The next morning Luc's cold gray eyes met hers across the morning cookfires. "You will not wear trousers, Mrs. D'Arcy," he stated abruptly, oblivious to the other women.

Arielle braced herself, squaring her shoulders. There was that arrogant tilt to his dark head, the muscle flexing in his newly shaved jaw. Possession rang through his tone. She smiled tightly as he approached, broad shoulders blocking out the rest of the party. Her betraying left hand found its way to her untamed, reddish curls, smoothing them self-consciously. She desperately longed for neat, smooth braids as she looked up at him, trying for a fearless expression. Luc's smoky gaze strolled down her pleated blouse, covered with a woolen knit sweater. The angle of his smoothly shaved jaw hardened as his eyes brushed her belt and the dark, loose cotton trousers. "Get them off."

She lifted her eyebrows and smiled sweetly. Perhaps she had been mistaken about tending Luc's bruised heart. "Take them off here? The ladies would be shocked. Smithson would go into convulsions."

Luc's hand slid along her arm, his fingers enclosing her wrist, his thumb caressing the back of her hand. He said something that sounded ominous, an obscenity in swift, dark French, and whispered harshly to her, "My wife does not wear trousers. Nor does she face thieves alone. You could be *enceinte* now, *ma chère*. You wear that"—his eyes raked down her legs—"this obscenity, and men will go mad with desire."

"What?"

He loomed over her, blocking out the interested women. "You are a luscious woman, Angel. Perfect breasts, a tiny waist I can span in two hands, and generous hips. A goddess. These trousers, this abomination, with your milky skin and hair touched with fire—" Luc glanced sharply at Anna nearby, who was smothering a giggle. She burst out laughing, smothering it when she turned away. Beneath her shawl, her shoulders jerked suspiciously.

Arielle shot her a burning stare. Luc's choice of words might have been appropriate for lovemaking with a beauty but not herself. Still, they tingled around inside her like little gold bells. Determined to hold her own against the intimidation of his larger body menacing hers over a small point, she returned under her breath, "I am a functioning businesswomen. Men don't . . . desire me, not at all. In fact, I purchased a bust enhancer to improve my figure. Once I am certain Thaddeus is nearby, I will ask Lydia to stain my hair a decent shade, Glynis will help me into my new stayed corset, and with the bust enhancer, Thaddeus may find me slightly attractive." Arielle watched with interest while Luc pressed his lips together, the set of his jaw grim. She backed a step and he followed.

Pressed against the wagon, Arielle looked up the distance to Luc's stormy eyes. There was no evidence of the tender man grieving for his family in his fierce expression. Nor the gentle cuddler of the previous night. She noted the betraying, clenching muscle sliding down his cheek. "If you color your hair, you will have to deal with me. I don't recommend disobeying," he stated tightly.

"Disobeying? You are issuing me an order? By what right? Remember, you are *my employee*," Arielle shot back, disliking craning her neck to look up at him. Then when Luc spoke fluently, darkly, she ordered, "None of that. If you want to argue, do it in English."

Between his teeth Luc said in a heavily accented tone, "No doubt you affect every man as you have myself. Driving them slowly to insanity. Yet I desire you. I would like to take you now, this moment. I am very hard, madame wife. Painfully hard. No doubt the result of slipping into my wife's boudoir like a thief for a few stolen minutes. A month in bed with you would not purge the need I have of you. To ride horseback at this moment would undoubtedly cripple me. *Take them off. You are my wife and will do as I say.*"

Unable to stop, Arielle suddenly found her eyes drawn down to the bulge pressing against Luc's trousers. She barely kept her left hand from reaching toward him. She looked away quickly, shielding her blush with a long swathe of rippling hair.

"My hungry, passionate little angel. You will pay for that," Luc whispered gently, trailing a finger down her hot cheek. He scowled at Anna, who was openly grinning. The women stood in line, their heads up. Each woman wore loose trousers.

The emigrants clustered nearby. Women and children's eyes widened as the "widows" began breaking camp, harnessing horses. Men looked away, their gazes returning with curiosity. Smithson passed by, patted Luc on the shoulder, and nodded. "Practical addition to the ladies' wardrobe. Scavenged them myself from the rest of the train until they can make their own. When need be, they'll change back to skirts. But none of these fine widows will be losing her life because of skirts tangled in wheels."

Luc closed his eyes as Siam grinned. The men exchanged a rapid mixture of French, Spanish, and quick hand signs before Luc strode toward the livestock. "What did he say?" Arielle asked.

"My friend says that he wants to get drunk . . . but for his marriage vows, he would sleep with the first woman who welcomed him. He says if he is crippled, it is your fault."

"Nonsense. Luc is an emotional man, too fiery by far. Too emotional about the slightest thing. Perhaps he should list his thoughts on paper, rather than tossing them about with such . . . such passion. I've found that notation takes the edge off emotional heat." She took a breath and continued, "It is my theory that Luc is attracted to me because I tended him in a moment of need ... and this ... attachment is what mars his common sense. This stubborn attraction he has for me is unreasonable."

"To some, he is feared as the Dark Avenger, who has no heart."

When Siam's gaze slid to the slight reddish patches on her throat, Arielle quickly tugged her collar higher. She blushed, remembering Luc's devastating lovemaking, his shaken expression later. "Dark Avenger, indeed."

Siam shrugged eloquently, his liquid soulful eyes locked on Glynis, who blushed. "My brother has met many trials, much sorrow in his life, and always he keeps his heart guarded. Now you make his heart glad, and he fears for you. You are the first woman to upset him so. The rest have not been permitted in his heart, not even his wife."

Siam sighed wistfully. "Is not Glynis the most beautiful lady on earth? When she calls me Jean-Pierre, my heart goes wild like a dove fluttering against the wind."

"Jean-Pierre?" Arielle asked, fascinated as Luc gave her a hard, dark look while he harnessed the oxen to the other wagons. Zeus stood at his side, conferencing with his human counterpart. Both of French extraction, no doubt their viewpoints concerning the feminine peculiarities agreed. Arielle sniffed. No doubt she was the subject of the dark mutters and low nickers. Zeus nodded companionably when Luc spoke; the great stallion's intelligent eyes and the set of his ears seemed animated with human emotions.

Siam inhaled deeply. "My father named me Jean-Pierre. ..." His dark eyes swung down to her, his frown anxious. "Angel, I must know. How can I make myself better for her? I do not know these things that soften women's hearts. I am but a poor, rough man who is used to taking what he needs. Glynis makes my knees weak ... for her I must learn these new things. Luc says I must go slowly, snaring her like a frightened rabbit—is that what he does with you?"

Arielle fought her sudden anger. Luc had snared her with

tenderness. He kissed her sweetly as though she filled a missing portion of his heart. "Did he say that to you?"

Siam nodded. "Luc knows women. I do not." He flushed and looked away, uncomfortable, then shrugged.

"Oh, he does, does he?" Arielle asked, placing her hands on her hips.

Distracted by Glynis as she smoothed her trousers, clearly uncomfortable with the new garment, Siam nodded. "Women fall at his feet. Many want to wear his ring ... have his children."

A wave of dark heat crashed over Arielle. She whistled for the horses, and they walked toward her, nuzzling her hand for sweets. Arielle patted their muzzles and frowned. "He has many conquests, does he?"

Looking down into Glynis's starry eyes, Siam did not answer.

The last of May the wagons wound past the landmarks of Solitary Rock, Chimney Rock, and settled into the ruts near Scott's Bluffs. They fought each rock, passing discarded furniture and chests that stood like weathered monuments along the trail.

The needs of survival filled each day, demanding every bit of strength. Arielle's Percherons easily pulled the wagon, prancing a bit in their newly fitted shoes, a process in which Arielle took meticulous care. She reluctantly admired Luc's handling of the great hooves, trimming them, sanding the rough edges, and even managing Zeus, who could be a demon at that time. Omar repaired the harnesses and lines with meticulous, inventive skills, proving to be more valuable every day. Luc and Siam helped the pilot, Wilson, determine camps and provide fresh meat. The matter of repairing broken spokes and wagons became routine. Cholera struck swiftly; life or death was determined within a few hours. The wagons passed wagon wheels stripped of metal rims and learned that the Indians used each discarded piece for arrowheads and weapons.

Each night Arielle fell into bed, asleep immediately. She awoke each morning with a prairie flower woven in her hair. At breakfast Luc held her hand beneath the table, a gentle trespass Arielle savored. If caught between the harnessed Percherons, Luc would steal a long, sweet kiss. If she touched his cheek, he nibbled her finger, his eyes heating. Deeply tired, drained, Arielle would rest against Luc's strength in the shadowy night, her breast gently cupped in his hand.

The gentle bond grew. Now Arielle did not protest when Luc rested his hand on her shoulder. The companionable touch comforted and strengthened in the long, difficult journey.

One night Luc helped a young boy repair his guitar. Then Luc carefully, gently folded the guitar into his arms. Wrapped in concentration, he placed long fingers carefully, exactly over each string. He rummaged through chords slowly, closing his eyes. The music's tempo slowly began to build, pounding from his almost savage skills.

His mouth tightened into a cruel line, his black brows drawn together. The music beat into the evening camp, the women gripped by the fierce, emotional intensity.

Luc's music tasted of sweeping Spanish passions, soaring, falling, eloquent in the delicate plucking of the chords. Then tempestuous and erotic, the beat pounding from Luc's strong hands. A strand of hair crossed his brow catching the beat as his fingers swept expertly over the strings, the cords on his forearms standing out in relief. Sweat gleamed on his forehead, the music pouring, throbbing from him.

Then Luc stopped, his fingers gripping the instrument. His eyes pinned hers, forging into her, demanding, fighting against an inner pain. Arielle realized her pulse raced beneath her protective hand, the emotions swirling between them.

She'd seen a part of Luc, stepped into a past he didn't want revealed, nor touched. He'd shared something with her, a deep pain that was too intimate, too dark for others. The tenuous bond between them had released his awful, unknown secret for a moment. He bitterly resented her intrusion. Slowly, in control now, Luc handed the instrument back to the boy and stood, sliding into the night shadows.

"I have been with him for nine years. I did not know he could play," Siam murmured quietly.

Arielle followed her left-handed thinking, or was it her heart? She found Luc a distance away from camp, head thrown back, gazing at the starlit night. Wrapping her shawl around her, she stood behind him. "Did I frighten you, Angel?" Luc whispered rawly.

She knew he referred to the music throbbing from him as though it was part of his life, his breath, his emotions pouring into the air. She touched his arm, wanting to soothe, to understand what dark shadows drove him. "No. How did you know it was me?"

"Do you think I wouldn't know your scent? A woman who lured me back from death with the same stubborn determination that refuses to acknowledge our wedding vows?" His tone was flat, hard. "*Ma belle*, your scent is unique. A blend of flowers, sunlight, exotic woman flesh, and the ultimate scent of horse. I'd know it in heaven or hell, and tonight it's hell."

Arielle frowned and mulled the curious mixture of compliment and insult.

He loomed over her, harsh features etched in the moonlight, broad shoulders blocking out the night. His hand wrapped around her throat, lifting her chin with his thumb, stroking the soft flesh. "You're not afraid to stalk my shadows, to enter the darkness where I dwell, are you, my angel?" he drawled slowly, watching his dark hand caress her pale, pale flesh.

"Should I be?" she whispered as Luc's light eyes skimmed her face. She rested her hand on his heart, absorbed the painful racing into her palm.

The next heartbeat Luc swept her into his arms, crushing her against him. His tall, lean body shook, his face pressed against her temple. He held her desperately, shuddering, pressing his bones and flesh against hers as though making them one. She held him, her hands smoothing his long, taut back. "Shh . . . shh . . . there now, my dear. . . ."

His fingers shoved through her braids urgently, loosening her hair, burying his face in it. The rising, damp wind whipped the strands around them as his lips played gently over hers, tasting, supping. His tongue moistened, delved, thrusting boldly into her mouth until her mouth answered his delicately. Luc nuzzled her ear, nibbling on it until her fingers clenched into his back and her body flowed into his. "You witch," he murmured wryly. "Are you taming me to hand like one of your great horses?"

"Hmm. I'd have a time of it, if I tried."

His smile curved against her neck. "Come with me. Let's talk of babies nursing at your breasts—many babies—of fields to be plowed and colts to be foaled . . . of which way you prefer to make love. There are several—"

"Wicked man!" Her pinch on his lean backside earned her a tickling. When she squirmed and giggled, Luc bent to plop her over his shoulder.

She yelled—not too loudly. She didn't want the whole train viewing her like a sack of grain tossed over Luc's shoulder. She cursed and Luc lifted her over him, pushed his face beneath her loosened shirt and nibbled on her belly. "I'd like to fill this soft, warm place with a baby and soon, *ma chère*. But not tonight. I'm afraid your offer will have to wait."

"Oh! You landlubbing beast, you ox . . . !" Her body jerked when Luc's hard face pushed beneath her camisole, tearing the fabric. His mouth suckled on her breast.

Arielle stopped squirming. Stopped breathing. Luc's hot open mouth swept to her other breast, and a seam burst open. Buttons popped loose. Gently nibbling her nipple, Luc managed to scoop her legs over his shoulder. His muffled tone burned her belly, his tongue flicking into her navel. "Mmm, it's interesting under here."

The stubble on his chin grated her smooth flesh as he pushed her trousers downward, kissing the nest of curls between her legs.

"Luc!" Shocked at his play, unable to do other than moor her hands at his muscled throat, Arielle squeezed her eyes shut. Her body tensed, moistened, and heat poured into her veins.

"Fine grazing on my wife's body," Luc stated with an arrogant grin as he eased her gently to the ground and straightened her clothing. He fingered a button hanging by a thread and slid a finger inside her torn camisole. The hard length rested between her breasts, caressing them. "Glynis is apt to scold you, my sweet little sorceress."

"Sorceress? I am a practical businesswoman ... I'll sew it myself," she snapped, very aware of his prowling, taunting fingertip. Annoyed that part of her wanted to leap on Luc and bear him to the ground, while the other part wanted to slap away his cocky, knowing grin, Arielle drew her shawl around her. She faced him with dignity, her hair wildly catching the damp breeze. "You are less than a gentleman," she stated tightly, uncertain if her legs would carry her back to camp.

He bowed gallantly. "At your service, madam wife ... anytime."

Arielle simmered in her temper, aware that amused, Luc waited for her answer. "I wasn't asking for stud. I'm certain your children would have too many untamed characteristics."

His laughter followed her into camp.

Arielle did not sleep that night. Whatever haunted Luc needed a gentle touch. She wasn't certain she could face the passions ruling him at that dark moment, the pain surging from him into his fingers and out into the night.

An hour before the shot awoke the camp at dawn, Arielle fell asleep with one last thought: Luc needed her in a desperate way she couldn't yet understand. Tonight he had exposed his dark soul, swept her into it, and allowed her to tempt him away from the pain he'd kept so tightly wrapped inside. A bond wove between them, twisting, strengthening, as it tantalized, seduced.

It frightened her.

At Fort Laramie, a trading fort, another wagon train was resting and trading with the Indians. The emigrants gossiped, traded, and prepared an evening social. A fiddle, harmonica, and banjo player played a lively reel, the fort's whitewashed adobe walls gleaming in the firelight. Furniture had been taken from wagons, and rocking chairs

squeaked to the music as the dancers circled the huge bonfire.

"The Society of Widows for the Purpose of Matrimonial
Bliss ..." Emily Donally murmured in her soft, southern,
and slightly derisive tone as she eyed Arielle. She considered the title thoughtfully, glancing at the dancers. "How
wonderful. We have two widows who refuse to go back
East—their husbands died in an encounter with a drunken
mountain man. He'd gone wild swilling the bile from a buffalo. . . . Perhaps these poor unfortunate women could join
your train. Captain Smithson has a high reputation."

Her fan fluttered. "I hear Captain Smithson approves of
ladies wearing trousers for safety. How novel!"

Arielle sipped her mulled apple cider, enjoying the qua-
drille. Women happily served cakes and coffee, excited
about the social. Though the emigrants would rest for the
long climb westward, tonight was for pleasure. Plans were
made for Lydia's special class in flower and herbal beds. As
an herbalist, she would lecture on tips for hair coloring and
on softening agents against the effects of time and weather.

The "widows" were discreet, tending their new manners
with fluttering fans and shy smiles.

Clearly uncomfortable, but determined to succeed, Siam
loomed at Glynis's side. She wore the white decorated moccasins; her hand rested on his stiffly held, crooked arm. In
an aside she had informed Arielle why Siam always wore
his hat—his high, misshapen forehead was a sign of his
high birth from his mother's people. Glynis thought the pale
flat expanse was beautiful and was honored that Siam
would share his heritage with her.

Luc smoked a small, thin, dark cigar with a group of
men, clearly savoring the tobacco. He leisurely blew smoke
rings, his grin slow and devastating at something one of the
men said. Dressed as a gentleman in a pleated shirt, which
Anna had carefully starched, a tie, and a dark suit, Luc was
handsome.

He was much too popular, much too charming. Arielle
disliked the easy manner in which he met and socialized.
Her lips tightened when Luc raised the lady's hand extended

to him, kissing the back with polished gallantry. Arielle lifted her head, scanning the dancers, the clusters of people infested with the party air.

Smithson finished dancing with Mary and strolled up to Arielle wearing a boyish grin. He nodded. "You should be dancing with your beau, Mrs. D'Arcy. It wouldn't hurt to smile a bit at him, maybe share a dance."

Mrs. Donally's fan stopped fluttering. "Beau?"

Smithson nodded to Luc. "That fine gentleman there wants to marry this woman. She's mulish, bossy, outspoken, can't sew or cook. But she's got some good qualities, if I am pressed to mention them. I am certain those qualities are what draw a highly marriageable man like Luc Navaronne to her. He's got land in Oregon country and wants a wife and children. I'd say from the cut of him, he's got a fair penny in his pocket. Not a bad catch for any woman."

"Gracious!" Mrs. Donally exclaimed, her eyes swinging down to Arielle. "If you're worried about a proper ceremony, we have a minister, and the ladies would love to help with a wedding. I don't see how you can refuse Mr. Navaronne for a minute."

Arielle inhaled. "This is a private matter."

"But, my dear, with your advanced age, is it wise to turn down any offer whatsoever?" Mrs. Donally asked urgently, slapping her fan closed. "Pray reconsider. From the rest of the company, not your loyal 'widows,' you have a reputation of being a hotheaded woman, a slightly savage one who faced and captured thieves single-handedly. I understand your reputation has gone to the Indians, and they are calling you 'The Little Fire Warrior.' The incident alone could deter men from asking for your hand. Within the male breast beats the need to protect and comfort a poor helpless woman. With your rumored attributes, you might seem to be—ah—a hellion? Though I apologize for the use of the word."

"She is left-handed," Smithson offered lightly as an explanation.

Mrs. Donally's sympathetic expression matched her tone. "Oh, no, my dear, surely not red hair and a dominant left hand. You are marked, my dear. Don't you see? You are extremely limited in assets and time. You must marry the first man who asks. I strongly encourage you to accept Luc's generous offer and quickly so."

Arielle frowned at Smithson, who was rocking back and forth on his heels, watching the dancers and smirking. Arielle defended herself. "Luc has an evil temper, Mr. Smithson. At the moment he is dancing with every woman in sight, which proves my theory that he is a rake."

The captain's massive chest lifted as he inhaled. "You would bring out the worst in the best of men, Mrs. D'Arcy. As to dancing, he is merely politely obliging their wishes. I pray that you have the good sense to bait your hook for Luc before he retracts his offer of marriage."

Mrs. Donally leaned closer and shielded her whisper with her fan. "My dear. Perhaps you could try a bust enhancer."

Fourteen

....

The Nez Percé girl pointed to her one-year-old daughter's matted, swollen eyes. *"Silu komain. Ilatama,"* she said, looking from Siam to Luc. Luc acknowledged her words for "eye sickness" and "is blind" with a nod.

Seated on a blanket outside her tipi, the girl looked much older than her fourteen years. Her chubby, lighter skinned daughter hugged a leather doll tightly, cowering against her. The little girl smiled shyly at the men, though she could not see from her matted, closed eyes. Her mother's young face hardened as she scanned the walls of the adobe fort. The sound of the water rushing by almost swallowed her quiet words. "You want to know about the father of my child?"

She indicated that they sit. When Luc dropped coins onto her blanket, the girl snatched them eagerly. She quickly described the officer who matched the description of the man Luc sought. "I find him someday," she stated harshly in her language. "I kill him. My name is Kahno, prairie-hen. But when he enters my mind, I am *pishakas*—bitter. I was a pretty girl with many suitors when my father brought his

233

trading furs here. This man with ice-eyes and corn-color hair knew magic to capture me. He did not want me later . . . nor his child. He said he always made sons and that I had slept with another."

Kahno lifted a piece of cooked pork from a dish and tied it to her daughter's wrist with a thong. "New teeth," she said proudly. "Strong. Pretty."

Her black eyes clouded as she scanned the white-barked aspen trees shimmering in the early morning sun. "This white man takes only women who have known no man. He has one woman, then goes to another innocent like a hungry bee tasting all flowers," she said darkly. "I found him with a girl three winters younger than me."

She shrugged. "So. He has many Indian girls. Smiles at the white women, eats at their tables. Then he gives whiskey or guns to the fathers of these girls and buys them . . . for a time. My heart bleeds for the women he seeks, always hungry for more."

"His name?" Luc asked, his hand outstretched to accept the baby's chubby one as she toddled into his arms. "Was it Bliss?"

Kahno spoke sharply, jerking the baby away from him. The baby cried, clutching her leather doll. Kahno forged the name with a thick accent and lashing hatred, "Thaddeus . . . Northrup."

The heavy signet ring Yvonne had managed to hide from her captors rolled in Luc's palm. Kahno stared impassively at it, then nodded. "His. He took from me to give to another. The wind says that he bartered for his life . . . that he gave the woman wearing his ring, her mother, and sister to traders. The woman already carried his baby."

Luc nodded, rising to his feet. The hair on the back of his neck lifted, his body cold despite the bright sunlight. The man who claimed Arielle's hopes had traded away his mother and sisters' lives. Luc's fingers curled into a fist, the ring burning in his palm. He hoped Thaddeus Northrup knew how to die well. "I will send a woman to heal your baby's eyes."

"Healing Woman with Glass Eyes?" Kahno asked

sharply, then nodded. "Good heart. She talks with the people, learns their healing ways, listens to the earth, the wind. The Fire Woman is a warrior but has a good heart."

"I've used the eyebright herb many times. Eyebright washes will heal those pretty eyes in no time," Lydia said soothingly, dabbing a square of clean cotton over the baby's heavily crusted lashes. Siam acted as translator, seated by Glynis and holding her hand.

Lydia rocked the toddler, allowing her to touch her glasses. When the baby's lashes were clean, Lydia instructed Kahno about application of the herb and to keep the child away from smoke.

The baby pushed away from Lydia and scrambled toward Luc, locking her arms around his leg. Luc chuckled, lifted the girl, and tossed her lightly in the air. The baby giggled wildly, clutching at him and nestling cozily in his arms. Luc cuddled the baby closer, kissing her fat cheek, and she returned the gesture, giggling and slipping her finger in his mouth. He allowed the inquisitive little finger to prowl to his ear and touch the scars on his eyebrow and bottom lip.

He met Arielle's wide eyes over the baby's glossy hair. The deep bond ran between them, and he wanted children from her. The idea of bright-haired, green-eyed imps with gesturing left hands caused him to smile. Arielle flushed and looked away from his intent, probing stare, clasping her hands on her lap. The sunlight caught on her hair, red tendrils gleaming over the dark.

Thaddeus Northrup stood between them. Luc's stomach lurched when he thought of Arielle sharing Northrup's bed. His mother and sisters had died, a baby—his nephew—never drew breath because of Thaddeus Northrup's—Edward Bliss's weakness. The morning wind, kissed by flower fragrances and birds chirping, chilled the nape of Luc's neck. Luc kissed the baby again. She settled sleepily in his arms, toying with the medallion on his chest.

"A good man." Kahno spread her hands, studying them. "He wants you, Fire Woman. It is in the ways his eyes touch you. Wants many babies, a good life with you. To laugh, maybe. He is known as Torn-Heart, a good heart. All this is in his eyes ... not like Thad-deus."

"What?" Arielle demanded, her face paling in the bright sun.

Luc cradled the baby closer. Arielle's freckles danced over her pale skin. Her expressions changed like the wind, first shocked, then incredulous. "Thaddeus? Was there another name, Kahno?"

The girl's face tightened. "Spears-Maidens," she said harshly. "He tells others to call him Captain Northrup. He puts babies in Indian girls' bellies, then goes. One kill her baby, then herself."

"Oh, dear," Glynis murmured, her tone sympathetic.

"It isn't him ... not Thaddeus Northrup," Arielle whispered, her hand at her throat. "You must be mistaken. He is *not* the father of your baby. People at the fort say he passed through, that he was wounded and needed to recover before going west. But I am certain, *Thaddeus is not the same man. You must be mistaken about the name Northrup. He would never leave a woman under these circumstances.*"

Kahno stood, facing Arielle with dignity. The Indian girl spoke in swift, biting Nez Percé language. "I say it is so. He is a weak man seeking pleasure. He plays a game and does not recognize the half-blood children he spawns. There are more women, more babies scorned by the people of both races. That is the reason he must die."

Arielle looked at Siam to translate, and when he shook his head, she asked, "Luc?"

"My dear," Glynis soothed. "Please don't. I don't believe Siam or Luc wants to translate. From Kahno's tone, her feelings are bitter and vehement."

"Luc?" Arielle persisted, placing her hand on his thigh, her shimmering green eyes begging him. The movement caused her combs to slip, her single fat braid sliding down across her breast. She looked like a hurt child; he refused to hurt her more deeply.

"No." Luc watched her stand, stare blankly at him, and gather her shawl closer for protection. She nodded stiffly, flexed her lips in an absent smile, and hurried toward the rippling creek.

The wind blew her skirts against her, and outlined against the blue sky, she seemed very small and alone. She stumbled, squared her shoulders, and disappeared into a stand of box elder trees. Luc handed the sleeping baby to her mother and walked after Arielle.

He found her beside the swiftly rushing stream, staring at a stand of swaying rushes. She accepted his arms around her, drawing her body to his, accepted the gentle swaying. "I know it isn't the same man, Luc. Our families have been friends for years. It just isn't so!"

He wanted to take the pain tearing her, to kill the man who had caused this shattering moment. Arielle turned to him suddenly, wrapping her arms around him—

The gesture startled Luc, this docile, needing woman, held him tight, her damp face pressed hard against his throat as if seeking shelter. "Luc, I know Thaddeus. He isn't the demented man she describes. . . . Thaddeus could never have caused that look on a woman's face . . . so much hatred," she whispered unevenly.

Her fingers dug into his back, clutching desperately. "We were childhood friends. When my parents died, Thaddeus consoled my brother Jonathan and me. Oh, Luc . . . he helped me to survive those years, always laughing, daring me to fight Aunt Louise. He couldn't have left a woman who was carrying his baby. Could he?"

Luc looked down into her tear-stained face, kissed her damp lashes, and folded her closer against him. He wanted to say that the childhood friend she remembered was not the man who had caused so much grief. He stroked her shaking shoulders, kissed her temple, testing the rapid pulse there. "Angel, let Lydia give you her tea. With rest, you will be able to think straight."

Luc raised her chin with the tip of his finger, kissed her lashes, the tip of her nose, her sweet, trembling lips. "Shh, *chère*. The worst of the storm has passed. Shh . . . sleep with these thoughts . . . turn them over."

"Kahno is blaspheming the Northrups' good name,"

Arielle whispered shakily, firmly. She rested her head on his shoulder, allowing him to support her weight. She began to cry so softly, he thought she was shivering.

A part of him tore away, a sliver so tiny that it fit easily in her small hand.

"I don't believe it, not for a moment." Her tears slid along his throat, her muffled sobs stabbing his heart. Struggling with his tangled emotions, Luc closed his eyes, tucking his chin over her bright head. He wanted to protect her from harm, to wipe away the shattered expression, and bring back the enchanting, lilting laughter. Glynis stood at the top of the stream's embankment, her face concerned. Luc nodded and she waved, soon shielded by Siam's bulk as he placed his arm around her shoulders.

"Angel," Luc whispered against her hair. Thaddeus Northrup would have another debt to his account—that of hurting Arielle. "Tomorrow will be better. You have done so much, giving new life to these women who love you. Look at Anna. She laughs now, and Eliza walks with her head high. Mary is growing strong, her children, too. Then Biddy and Omar. Each woman is confident."

He smiled, nuzzling her scent. "Your 'Society of Widows for the Purpose of Matrimonial Bliss' has given them something—pride forged with a future. . . . So many lives are changing for the better because of you."

In French Luc told her of his admiration and pride for her. That no one could ask more of her than she had given . . . that the man she mourned would die and that he wasn't worth a heartbeat of time. That only a woman of great kindness and courage would have married a dying man, giving him peace. He spoke softly, reverently. Arielle rocked gently against him, still locked to his body. "I don't know what you're saying right now, and I don't care," she whispered against his throat, digging her fingers into him. "But just keep saying it, Lucien."

A mourning dove cooed in the bushes, a chipmunk chattered as he ran up a tree. Luc told her of his hopes, his dreams of a true marriage, of children and the future.

She gave one last sob, shivering against him. "Luc, whatever you're saying, your heart is racing. . . . If . . . if you don't tell me what Kahno said, I'll find someone who will."

He smiled slowly, sadly. "Are you threatening me, *ma chère*?"

"Yes . . . Her face, oh, her face, Luc. It was so fierce— what did she say?" Arielle's arms slid around his neck as he scooped her up and carried her into the shelter of a willow stand.

"I'm not a child," she grumbled as he eased to the dry warm sand and cuddled her closer on his lap. Luc leaned against a tree and stroked her hair, enjoying the sun-warm tangle of curls twining around his fingers. "Tell me," Arielle demanded after accepting his handkerchief and blowing her nose. "I can always keelhaul you for disobeying an order," she whispered after another sniff and settled back against his chest.

Luc explained slowly, watching a fish lazily tread the rushing stream. He carefully omitted the name "Bliss," which circled his thoughts. Arielle listened, her fingers wrapped in his.

"Lucien," she whispered slowly, lifting their laced hands to study them. Fascinated by her play, Luc watched as her slender fingers toyed with his darker, larger ones, caressing the scars, flowing lightly across his palm. "Thaddeus isn't the same man. He is a man of high morals."

Luc pulled her closer, then leaned back against the box elder's trunk. Time skimmed through the shimmering new leaves, sunlight sliding along the cottonwoods bordering the stream.

High on the embankment, Glynis's clear gray eyes found Siam's sad brown gaze. "Arielle has always worshipped Thaddeus. She tossed away his boyish pranks, though some of them were quite cruel and she reprimanded him severely. Then when they were older, no one wanted to tell her of his indiscretions. His parents always paid off the girls' families. His ways have cost his parents their hard-earned fortune. They sent him enormous amounts when he left the army to go west and begin business in the Willamette. Bliss and Thaddeus are the same man, aren't they, Jean-Pierre?" At his curt nod Glynis wiped away a tear that had been shimmering on her lashes. "Luc will kill Thaddeus, won't he?"

In a movement that showed little practice, Siam placed his arm around Glynis and drew her to his chest.

The wagons left the next morning, a sweeping cold wind penetrating the wagon covers and their clothing. The emigrants had passed one-third of the way to Oregon country.

Arielle grabbed the harness between the lead horses, Zeus and Maia, tugging, cajoling the great Percherons to pull the steep, rocky grade. Since they left Fort Laramie two weeks ago, she spent every minute working feverishly to keep the Nez Percé woman's accusations at bay. Fatigue clawed at her every muscle, her mind jabbing, scurrying away from the dangerous topic of Thaddeus. Lying at Glynis's side each night, Arielle strained for the sound of Luc's deep, accented voice outside the wagon. While she couldn't explain her emotions, she longed for his damnable cuddling and soft, fluent French. They had eased the blow of the Nez Percé woman's accusations. The first week, his kindness bordered on brotherly. A solicitous "You must eat. Get some rest." The start of the second week he showed a bit of ill temper when she counted his pay into his palm.

That evil clamping jaw motion, and dark thundercloud color of his eyes matched the fierce line of his eyebrows. When his hand clamped over her wrist, and he poured the coins back into her palm, his smile wasn't nice. He gave the odd impression of being at the end of his tether . . . a curious thing since she had tried to pay him very well.

Arielle noted Zeus's teeth as he chomped at the bit, straining to haul the wagon upward. Thaddeus's bottom teeth lurched a bit forward. The result weakened his chin and jawline.

A man's strong jawline, such as Luc's, could show a temper and an overbearing personality. He shouldn't have yelled at her during the buffalo stampede at Mineral Springs. Employees didn't yell at employers. Let alone roar to everyone that only an idiot would have tried to turn that

buffalo herd. Arielle began jerking the harness impatiently
and muttering to herself.

"How would I know that the whole brown hill was covered with buffalo? Any beast with sense should have turned
away with a few shots. Luc acted outrageously. Riding
down like some savage and plucking me up like a chicken
didn't help my dignity. *I am a businesswoman with valuable
cargo.* How dare he yell at me?"

That singular event snapped her determination to ignore
several facts:

Her weakness in Luc's arms stood out like a lighthouse
beacon in thick fog.

She should never have collapsed into the simpering, sniffing helpless female he expected.

That she had been cuddled in those strong comforting
arms in her moment of need drove her harder. Luc's dark
scowl when she ordered him to stand aside while she took
the team up the dangerous grade caused a little thrill of victory.

She reveled in that dark scowl. She pitted her weight
against the harness, urging the horses upward. Dealing with
Luc was merely a matter of balance: She was his employer
and unfortunately legally wed to him until she could obtain
a divorce. Once he realized the hand in power, he would be
more reasonable.

Luc's tall body loomed at the top of the grade, his shirt
stained with sweat and clinging to him. Arielle closed her
eyes and swallowed. She would not fall to his beauty, man-
liness, and grace. Thaddeus needed her. She needed the cool
stability of a man she had known as a friend, not the tumul-
tuous passion—reckless desire, she corrected—that Luc
could arouse in her. Stability and control in her endeavors
was her goal. Thaddeus would provide the well-ordered life
she wanted to lead.

The woman was wrong about Thaddeus!

A rock slid beneath her boot, and she scrambled for foot-
ing. A wheel spoke broke and the wagon dipped sharply.
She yelled, cursed, threatened, and crooned, and the six
draft horses responded, surging to the top.

"They would damn well drag that wagon to the moon if she asked them," Smithson muttered, straining opposite Luc to get his double teams of oxen to fight the hill. "That's a scampy little miss you've set your sights on, Navaronne. Hey-ah, go bully!"

A barrel skimmed down the rocks, bounding along beside them, and a young bullock went down to his knees. "Up! Anna! Give them more slack!" Luc called, pushing his shoulder against the muscled ox, bracing him as the animal righted.

"Good God's breeches," Anna shot back, panting. "I'm on my way to get a husband. This little bully boy isn't slowing me down!"

The other women, dressed in their trousers, carried goods to lighten the load, fighting to the top of the hill. The third wagon, loaded with goods, was the last. The emigrants watched the young oxen sidestep in harness, swaying their great horns side to side and braying. Omar, a dark, lean silhouette against the basin's light sand, touched them with his spear. Luc and Siam began down the hill with the other men, and Arielle called, "Watch out for rocks! Coming through!"

The six draft horses sank low on their back haunches, their front legs stiff as Arielle walked behind them, keeping the lines clear as they descended the grade. Luc started toward her, his heart beating painfully with fear, and Siam jerked him aside. The men fell together on the sharp incline, and Luc struggled to his feet. "Stop," Siam snapped and stood.

"Let her be," Smithson said quietly, his hands on his hips. "She's been fighting something since Laramie. That sassy little general's mouth has been much too quiet. Let her go. Missed her noise. She's small and wiry, just the sort to scramble out of harm's way without skirts hampering her. Those great beasts of hers obey her every whisper. She'll be fine."

Luc caught a flash of white beside the trail and heard Lydia cry out. She slid down a small embankment, clutching a tiny plant to protect it. When he reached her, she grinned up at him, dismissing the long grating cuts on her arms and the blood seeping from her stocking. "Look. A perfect little specimen of safflower. It was growing next to an open tin from some hapless emigrant. Some poor herbalist must have mourned losing his catnip and chamomile. Oh, how will he survive without his horehound?" she questioned urgently, her glasses askew.

She righted them when Luc helped her to her feet. "Whatever is Arielle doing?" Lydia asked with a frown, peering at Arielle and the six horses at the bottom of the hill.

"Getting herself killed. She's been trying to do that since Fort Laramie," Luc said between his teeth as he picked a safe path over the rocks to a large flat one. *Since she discovered the chips in Thaddeus's fair image.* "Stay put."

"Oh, dear. Are you certain I can't be of use?" she asked worriedly. When he shook his head, Lydia sat, hoarding her find and watching Arielle's struggles.

Luc moved cautiously down the rocky grade, his hands damp with the sweat of fear. Within sight of their mistress, the contented Percherons grazed while the oxen brayed to the others at the crest of the hill.

She glanced up as Luc stepped close. "What do you think you're doing, Mrs. D'Arcy?" he asked, trying to push away the fear clinging to him. He wanted to wrap her in his arms, to protect her from the pain riding her for the past two weeks.

"Taking my cargo with me. The oxen are exhausted. They can pull the wagon, but not the cargo. They're so badly frightened now that hooking another team to them will only make the matter worse," she said, climbing up to the wagon bed and surveying the contents gingerly. "If you take the harness lines off my horses, they can be used to strap goods on their backs. With a lightened load, the oxen won't balk."

She looked so small, so determined to succeed, and there was another element lurking in her clear green eyes. That of a woman who had lost her dreams and who fought to keep them. Luc framed her face with his hands. "Angel, go up the hill and wait for us."

"Nonsense. I won't have Smithson say I can't handle the responsibilities of my cargo. We'll bundle the loads on my horses, and the oxen will pull the hill."

On impulse he bent to kiss her sun-warmed lips, savoring the brief soft taste. He watched her warring emotions, the flick of her tongue over lips he had just tasted. Then before she had time to deal with the kiss, he explained his plan to get the "cargo" to the top of the hill. Arielle shushed Zeus when he nickered nearby, and the massive stallion obeyed.

"A *travois*!" she exclaimed later, studying the result of Luc's suggestion. "Of course, the Indians use them on horses and dogs. A perfect solution," Arielle repeated later, looking at the long poles lashed to the horse's huge leather collars. The poles would drag on the ground behind the animals, smaller branches across them. Small wooden crates and barrels were lashed on top. "Luc, you are very creative."

He stopped in midstep and turned slowly. Stunned by her delighted praise, Luc stared at her. He had kept his distance for the two long weeks, letting her sort out her thoughts. Arielle's victorious grin stilled as their eyes locked. She looked quickly away to Omar, who was urging the now obedient oxen up the steep grade. "I appreciate your efforts on my behalf," she stated quietly, formally, as Luc stood by her side.

Luc eased away the jumble of curls from her face, enchanted as she blushed. Arielle shivered once, then stepped aside. "We must go. Captain Smithson will call me a laggard, and I may have to set him straight," she murmured.

Her green eyes flashed, and she angled her head up, staring coolly at him. The Arielle who he knew had returned, her wounds mending. While Luc appreciated her weighing the matter of Thaddeus and had given her time and quiet, he wanted her in his bed. His eagerness to sink into her tantalizing warm body stunned him. He inhaled sharply. She was his wife; bedding her was a fact. He took her hand, lifting it to kiss the back of her fingers. "Will you walk with me tonight, *chère*?"

Her slow nod caused his heart to sing. Luc pushed away the sudden light-headed feeling.

He'd missed sparring with her and her confused expression while she tried to control her gesturing left hand. She must have forgiven him for rescuing her from the buffalo stampede.

He traced the sway of her hips beneath the abominable trousers. He'd never yelled at a woman, and remembering his tirade annoyed him. His heart had jerked to his throat when he saw the mountain of buffalo head toward the wagons. Siam, Wilson, and the other men had acted quickly, effectively, turning the herd at the last minute. Arielle hadn't blinked at his tirade, just angled her head up to his, her lips pressed together tightly. "Should I thank you? You're making a spectacle of yourself, you know. I did the logical thing, defending my property. The shots turned the herd, didn't they? And by the way, please make your comments all in English. I want to understand every word perfectly. I've rarely had an employee address me in such a variety of languages."

At the time Luc had been too incensed to argue. Collecting the shards of his temper, he had forced himself to walk away.

Now, watching Arielle's rounded backside as she strained up the mountain, Luc frowned. He didn't trust the angle of her head a moment ago when she looked up at him. It reminded him of her controlled temper after the stampede, like a covered pot simmering on a stove and about to boil over.

He decided to pick a bouquet of flowers for their bed that night. Perhaps the Bonhommes, a French family planning a western vineyard, could be persuaded to part with a bottle of their best hoarded wine.

They camped on the banks of the Sweetwater River in the last days of June. The animals grazed on the grass between the river and a granite stone an eighth of a mile long, which jutted against the night sky. Emigrants carved or wrote their names on this massive stone, Independence Rock, climbing to the top and scanning the sprawling blue-green sagebrush that would lead them to South Pass. After supper Smithson stepped into Luc's path as he walked toward the stream to bathe. "Nice night, eh, D'Arcy?"

Luc faced him slowly. "How long have you known?"

Smithson puffed on his pipe. He peered at Luc through the smoke. "Fort Laramie. I'm a cautious man, one who likes to ask questions. Seems you used our layover not to rest, but to track the servants of a family who met with ill times. I chatted a bit with an elderly Spanish Indian some miles south of the fort . . . a leathery, quiet man dedicated to maintaining a certain grave north of St. Vrain. Seems the blacksmith was paid to make a fancy 'D' for an iron fence."

" 'Ill times,' " Luc repeated slowly, watching the silvery stream wind around the rushes and willows. He crushed the length of toweling in his hand. One man had caused disgrace and death in his family. Northrup would pay.

"The trail leads to you, Mr. Lucien Navaronne D'Arcy," Smithson said, slapping his pipe against his hand and tossing the hot ashes away. "I know of you from my visits west. Now you will tell me why you practice the deception of courting Arielle, when you are actually married to her. I've grown to admire and like that little sassy bit and her brood of misfits. Rather fancy myself a knight of her poor widows, taking them to better times. Well?"

A great owl swooped across the moon as Luc turned to meet Smithson's gaze evenly. "I was dying. She married me to give me peace. Now I want the marriage. She doesn't."

"So she believed you were dead until you appeared at Independence Landing. That's why she was momentarily muddled at my interview."

Luc fought the memory of Arielle's less than glowing welcome for him, her bristling refusal of their marriage. He remembered her clear green eyes flashing as they looked up at him earlier. She hadn't fought his suggestion to walk later. She hadn't resisted his kiss. Arielle was an intelligent woman. Their marriage could work once she thought of him as a husband and not an employee. The sight of her determined expression as she poured those coins into his hands nettled his pride. She had put dreams of perfect Thaddeus behind her, and soon Luc would be tasting that sweet little mouth, cuddling her warm soft body to his—"Yes. She thought I was dead."

Smithson rubbed his jowls thoughtfully. "So . . . then she was a widow, and she wasn't humbugging me, and to protect her—that's why she was so stunned when you stepped up at the Landing, wasn't it? To protect her, you used another name. I should have recognized the D'Arcy name. . . . You've got a name out here, lad, a good one. Men respect you and you're a thorn in the side of every mother with an unmarried daughter. I reckon that what's done is done, and it's best to leave it to you and Mrs. D'Arcy to work out the matter."

He grinned and clapped Luc on the back. "She's a hard-headed little biddy. A good thinker for a woman and takes good care of her flock. Keeps their poor grieving minds busy with tasks—handwork, making tablecloths and so forth for their new homes. That's good. I've got my eye set on a likely widow. I've had some success in turning her head. Come to me if you need advice concerning Mrs. D'Arcy to recognize you as her husband. Try saying something about her womanly beauty—"

Smithson hesitated and frowned. "Well, ponder the matter. If you try hard enough, you'll eventually find something passable about her. Embellish whatever small beauty she may have."

Luc nodded tightly. Smithson's antidotes annoyed him. In his youth Luc could slather charm when necessary. But for years he hadn't wanted to turn a woman's head. Now that he did, the woman was his wife and, in the mind of others, his employer. Smithson had treated him to advice as though he were an empty-headed boy.

"Thank you," Luc said tightly. "I will do my best."

Fifteen

·····················

"Well, embellish. Go ahead. I'm waiting to hear about my womanly attributes." Arielle's crisp order stopped Luc's cupped hands, water dripping from them. He braced against the stream running swiftly through his legs and began sluicing his body leisurely. She stood on the moonlit bank, her hands curled into fists. Little kept her from launching into the water and pummeling him.

She swooped to gather his clothing, clutching it to her. He had cost her a measure of pride; taking his clothes could exact a small revenge. Accosting a man occupied by bathing was a novel experience. She had to wait until Smithson was out of range to confront Luc, and in the meanwhile he had stripped and entered the water. Opportunity was not a commodity that Arielle, as a businesswoman, dismissed. While the camp was busy with the evening meal, she would discuss the matter of their relationship.

Standing in the moonlight, Luc's naked body glistened with silvery streams of water. He shook his head, water flying away. "How long have you been standing there?" he asked, continuing to rinse the soap from his chest.

She couldn't speak, caught in the male beauty before her. The moonlight flowed over broad shoulders and padded muscles, tracing his narrow hips and heavy thighs down to the water flowing around his knees. Arielle braced herself, inhaling and drawing her body to its fullest height as she was accustomed to doing when she addressed a wayward employee. She wouldn't let the sight of his naked body deter her from her mission. She wanted sweet, cherished revenge, the beauty and the glory of besting a man who had diminished her honor. In her lifetime no one had yelled at her. If Luc was not brought under control and soon, he would begin to have outrageous ideas.

She would have to apply reins to his ideas. She would control Luc's tendency to dominate, much the same as Zeus when he tested her powers.

Luc turned slightly, raising his cupped hands to spill water down his chest. In profile his back rippled and gleamed. His chest flowed into a flat stomach, then surged into heavy thighs. She avoided the shadows lurking between his thighs as he began walking toward her.

Arielle backed away a few steps, her throat suddenly dry. Then Luc loomed over her, his mouth curving in a grin. He took the clothes away from her clutching fingers, tossing them to a bush. "I . . . I . . ." she began, wringing her hands. Where was the anger she'd stowed away all day? Luc deserved a trimming, and now was the perfect chance.

"I am honored that you wanted to see me without clothing, *chère*," Luc murmured as she took another step back.

His hands curled around her throat, lifting her mouth for his slow, seductive kiss. "You need a bath."

"Mmm?" Lost in the sweet, gentle brush of his mouth across hers, Arielle forced her lids open.

"Let me bathe you, Angel," he whispered unevenly, his mouth warm on hers. "You smell like a horse."

She drew away from his kiss. "I what?"

"Smell." Luc bent and stripped off her boots while she braced her hands on his back. The water-slick muscle rippled beneath her palm as she hopped on one foot, then the other. "Undress."

Arielle's hand fluttered to her throat, covering the high, buttoned collar. "I think not."

"I have seen everything, Angel," Luc warned tightly, scooping a bar of soap from a rock. "I want to have my wife in my bed, not an employer who stinks like a horse."

"I am your employer . . . and I am not beautiful. Those fine words may turn another woman's head, but not mine. My features are elfin, other than a strong jaw and a bit of a nose. And freckles now that the sun has touched me."

"You are my wife and you are beautiful to me, though I don't know why." With that Luc lifted her, carried her into the stream, and let her drop.

The icy water took her breath as she went under the surface. Arielle floundered for balance, came sputtering to her feet, and shoved at him. Her hair slid down in front of her face, her braids unfurling with the water's weight. While she struggled for breath, pushing her hair away, Luc's large hands soaped her blouse, cupping her peaked breasts in a quick, possessive gesture.

She lashed out a hand, and he grunted painfully, the blow striking him between his legs. "Why I think about you every minute, I don't know," he said after a succinct, biting curse. "There are easier women."

Arielle shivered, wading a few feet away from him. She rubbed her left hand, the one that had touched him intimately. "You are demented. Only a man without his wits would have yelled at me after that stampede."

He waded to her, water streaming down his body. He smiled tightly. "Perhaps I was worried about your life, sweetheart."

"You needn't be. I've been taking care of myself and others all my life. I am quite sensible in the face of danger—"

"You are in danger now, madame," Luc murmured, inserting his fingers into her belt and jerking her to him. He unlashed the leather strip, tugging her wet trousers and drawers down her hips. In a quick motion he bent, grabbed her ankles beneath the water, and pulled them upward.

Arielle went down, only to be drawn up quickly. While she sputtered, swatting at his hands, Luc quickly unbuttoned her blouse and stripped it away. The camisole slid over her head, and Arielle folded her arms over her breasts, shielding them.

She shivered, shaking the sodden, dripping curls away from her face. She blew the stream of water dripping steadily from her nose. "Beast. Lout. Landlubbing—"

She spat the soap foam Luc had smeared across her lips. "Why, you—"

"I have never met—" Luc determinedly scrubbed the soap bar over her hair, laving it thoroughly while she gasped for air. He spoke as if to himself, punctuating his words with a rapid flow of French, Spanish, and other tongues. "I have never met such a beautiful, contrary woman. Waspish, tormenting, devilish temper . . ."

"I am not beautiful." He plunged her head beneath the swiftly flowing surface, jerking her upright, and wrapped her in his arms.

His kiss was hungry, hot, and slightly bruising. His hands caught her buttocks, lifting them, until his desire rested between her legs. "You are beautiful. Desirable. And driving me into permanent crippledom."

"Ah . . . Luc . . . perhaps we could talk about this when we're both more calm," she offered, uncertain as how to handle a fully demented male, an illogical one that obviously wanted her. She tried reasoning. "We're tired. Perhaps in the morning over coffee."

Luc's warm face burrowed into her throat, his body trembling. "Coward."

Arielle stilled. She inhaled once, sharply, then exhaled slowly after realizing that her breasts were flattened to his hard chest. The hair there sensitized her nipples.

Despite the chilling water, warmth began to flow through her, tugging at her inner depths. Luc's manhood arced heavily against her stomach, bobbing insistently with each ripple of water.

Curious and afraid, Arielle fought her wandering left hand. Fought it stroking Luc, curling around the wonder of his strength. Luc groaned, his eyes closing. "Take me in you, *chère*."

She swallowed, unable to unfold her fingers, to loose the silken, warm steel in her palm. "I . . ." Then slowly, irrevocably, her hand drew him into her.

Luc's hands on her waist tightened as he watched. When his length rested fully in her, Luc closed his eyes and folded her gently into his arms. They stood locked together as he bent to kiss her. His tongue played with hers, and Arielle leaned against him, trusting his solid warmth.

For a time the night air filled with fresh scents of sage swirled around them. An animal scurried along the bank, and in the distance a child cried out.

Luc's tender, sweet kisses trailed down her throat, his hands cupping, caressing her breasts, urging her closer. "I missed you," he whispered unevenly against her ear.

Arielle slid her arms around his neck, wanting to be closer, filled with his heat and length, with the tenderness that had suddenly settled over them. For now it was enough to stand, locked with him, warmed by him. She had never wanted to be kissed, to be held and cherished, but Luc had changed her. She nuzzled his shoulder, experimenting with kisses across the heavy pad of muscles. He shivered, drawing her closer.

Anna's call sounded nearby, her boots crunching against the sand. Luc gritted his teeth. "Anna. You are disturbing my bath."

She laughed outright, her footsteps halted. "Too bad. Luc, have you seen Arielle? She's missing."

Luc eased away a wet strand from Arielle's cheek, bending to kiss her lips. His fingers tightened possessively on her hips, jerking her to him.

He thrust quickly against her, shuddered, then drew away slowly, leaving her empty and aching. His hand massaged her softness gently, lingeringly. "She's here."

Anna laughed again. "Thought so. Here's some clean clothes for her."

Moments later Arielle allowed Luc to button up her blouse. She resented wanting more cuddling, more sweet passionate words, and Luc's warm, hard body. She ached, remembering the fever from their past adventures and wanting it now. She glanced upward and found him staring hungrily at her breasts. He traced her jaw, sliding a finger downward and hooking it in her bodice. "Stop trembling. The water was not that cold."

"I am mortified. Simply mortified. What will my ladies think?" she muttered from the confines of the towel he had wrapped around her head, turban-style.

"They will say that you are being sensible for once. I had different plans for tonight. There is something about you, Angel, that tosses away my good intentions," he said grimly, scanning the huge rounded granite boulder surging against the sky.

Arielle glanced anxiously back at the campfires. "What plans?"

Luc patted her bottom as they walked toward camp. Arielle stopped in midstep. "What are you doing?"

"Not what I want to be. I will be lucky to survive, *ma chère*," he said darkly, disappearing into the shadows to emerge in camp from another direction.

"Damnation, Mrs. D'Arcy! There are savages lurking about. When you decide you want to leave camp, you will take Luc with you," Smithson ordered sharply, facing her when she stepped into the wagon circle. His thick brows stood out in the moonlight, his frown fierce. "I'll deal with you later."

Sally's protesting scream quivered in the night air. Another woman cried out angrily, and Arielle ran to the small gathering, pushing her way through the crowd to the center. Sally clutched a newborn baby in her arms, facing another woman just as frightened and tearful. "She's mine. She didn't die. You took her!" Sally cried out. She glanced up at Luc, who had just placed his arm around her shoulders. "Luc, tell her this is my baby. That she shouldn't have stolen my little baby."

"Sally," Arielle began, easing toward her. "This is her baby. You will have more babies after you're married ... when we reach the Willamette," she whispered softly.

"Luc, tell them. They'll believe you!" Sally cried, huddling against him. "This is my baby."

"Give the baby to its mother, Sally," he urged gently.

"Give me my baby!" the woman cried out, clutching at Sally when her husband held her away. *"That crazy woman's got my baby!"*

Luc spoke softly, firmly. "Sally, we talked about how your baby went to heaven. How you would have other babies ..." He glanced at Arielle—the look held a command.

She understood. The towel wrapped around her hair shifted, and she slid it away. She did not try to comb her fingers through the wild mass of curls. "Mr. Smithson. This matter could be better settled without a crowd. Sally will return the baby." She touched the mother's arm. "You must understand how upset she's been."

The woman rounded on her, her face vivid with anger. "You widows. You put your men in the ground, and then you come after ours ... come right after our children. The men can't think half the time, lusting after you in those abominable trousers. You think you can walk off with our men, then our babies?" Her slap caught Arielle's cheek, snapping back her head.

Arielle ignored the burning imprint of the woman's hand. She caught sight of Sally's rounded eyes, of Anna's dark anger as she pushed her way through the crowd.

Luc's hand caught the woman's hand as she pulled it back again. "No."

Sally's voice was strained, very uneven, and hushed. "Here's your baby, ma'am. I'm sorry I took her. Please don't hurt Miss Arielle," she whispered before she gave the baby to her mother. Sally's fingers slid reluctantly away from the baby. She clasped her hands to her chest. Horror filled her eyes as milk stained her bodice, evidence of her dead baby.

Arielle squared her shoulders, standing between Sally and the other woman. She ignored the curls tangling along her cheek and spoke with quiet dignity. "Please accept our apologies. I will see that a measure of our regret is delivered to your wagon tonight."

The woman stared coldly at her. "See that you do."

Luc's hand curved around Arielle's chin the moment the crowd dispersed. He lifted her cheek, studying the reddish tinge before kissing it. She jumped back, glancing to see who had seen the tender gesture. Smithson stood nearby, his arms crossed over his massive chest, a grin pasted on his broad mouth. She tugged back her improper left hand from where it had attached itself firmly to Luc's belt.

His fingers smoothed her damp hair, returning to lightly caress her cheek. The seductive, gentle motion trapped her in something she didn't understand. The warmth in Luc's eyes drew her nearer. She couldn't move, her breath trapped in her lungs . . .

Later, she would wonder how much time passed before she looked away from Luc's dark gaze. From the yearning and tenderness in it. The campfire surged, ashes spiraling to the night sky, and part of him eased into her heart. When his fingers slid to lace with hers, she allowed the gentle trespass.

Smithson whistled happily as he passed with Mary's hand on his arm.

"Shoshone," Siam signed as the men swung up on their horses. "Your woman is facing a Shoshone war party. Do not fear. They will surrender."

Luc gritted his teeth, urging his horse into a fast walk around the sandy, sagebrush-filled stretch. Early that morning Wilson had needed help for a burial party, the burned wagons and dead oxen several days old. Siam and Luc helped bury the dead, noting the Arapaho sign. They stopped to speak with weary, seasoned California men traveling eastward. When Luc and Siam returned to the wagons with a fresh antelope kill at midmorning, Arielle was gone. The wagons wound away from them, headed for South Pass, while Zeus's heavily shod tracks led back toward Split Rock.

Luc and Siam rode quietly, scanning the sand and the

broken sagebrush twigs, following the tracks of a dog and a boy, covered by the deep hoofprints. Siam glanced at Luc. "If you are blaming yourself for questioning the California men about Bliss, for taking too much time hunting the antelope, you must not. She is a strong woman."

Luc gripped his saddle horn, scanning Arielle's boot marks where she had walked alongside the horse. The boy was riding now, holding his dog. Shoshone tracks crossed Zeus's. Then moccasin prints circled Arielle's boots, and the boy had jumped from the horse. The boy fought, his small boots digging in the sand. They were deep as though he carried his dog. Drops of blood dried in the sand as though the dog had fought and fallen to be rescued by his young master.

The war party had covered its tracks leading down to the Sweetwater Canyon. A waterfall thrust through the rocky gap, and the scent of smoke mixed with sage. The party made camp just over a small mound.

At noon they found Arielle and the warriors sitting around a trading blanket. The men's faces beneath their paint were impassive, while Arielle appeared to be sitting at the head of a business meeting. Gino tended the cooking fire, turning chunks of a big snake as Luc and Siam rode slowly into camp. Dante was held in a huge warrior's arms, who petted him gently.

Luc made the sign for "peace" and "friend," and the chief, Stone Elk, returned it. He gestured toward the roast meat and indicated they be seated for food.

"Oh, hello, Luc. We're doing nicely. These gentlemen are listening, and that is always a good sign. Please sit down," Arielle said lightly as though she were inviting him into a business conference.

"Big Horse Woman talks much," a warrior said darkly in Shoshone. "Hurts ears."

She nodded, smiling benignly. "I'm sure he's told you that everything is going fine."

Luc signed that Arielle was his woman and the boy was his son. The war chief nodded gravely. "Take her. She is much trouble."

Arielle passed by, thrusting a wood trencher filled with roast snake into Luc's hand. She shot a wary look at the Indian chief, who nodded and beckoned them to eat. "I've got everything under control, Luc. It's just a matter of palavering," she said brightly, using the term for talk. "Don't say anything. I'll have us safely away from these good men in due time," she whispered, rising to her feet.

A warrior snapped angrily in Shoshone, and Arielle glared at him.

"Sit behind me." Luc jerked her down. The warrior's questioning of Luc's skills to make his wife obey was not a small matter. If a man couldn't make his wife obey, he lost stature. Gino sat by a tall warrior, clearly worshipping him.

"I've already bargained with them," Arielle stated smugly.

"You like this woman?" Stone Elk, the chief, asked Luc, who fought his rising anger. Arielle straightened her back and laced her fingers together on her lap. Her confident smile incensed him. He knew that very little kept them from harm.

Luc nodded. This morning he had taken his ill temper out on Siam, who grinned widely. The night of Sally's baby theft, Arielle had fallen asleep over her journal. Luc was left with the hard edge of desire.

"You are Torn-Heart and Siam. Your prowess is known by all. The people say you take no more wife. Yet you take this evil-tempered one? This Big Horse Woman?" Stone Elk signed.

"She is not much, but she is my woman. The mother of my son," Luc replied.

"What did he say?" Arielle asked in a hushed voice, touching his arm. "Tell him that he will be rewarded when we are returned to camp. Since you are here to translate, perhaps you could start negotiations for trading furs. Ask them what they want most."

"They want peace. They fear the flood of whites."

"The woman and your son can go. Big horse will stay." Luc translated, then added, "You will let me handle this."

Her green eyes widened. "I shall? When this entire venture is at my direction, my expense? When this man dares to suggest that I would part with my poor pet? When every woman on the trip is under my care?" She tugged her blouse down at her waist and raised her chin. The long thick braid dipped along her breasts, and Luc wound it around his hand, jerking her close to him.

He pushed his lips into a tight smile. "You're in no position to bargain, Mrs. D'Arcy. You will act obedient. If you don't, you're endangering all our lives, perhaps the train."

"You forget—I have my foil," she returned, drawing back on her braid. Her chin angled out at him, the sun catching fiery sparks in her hair. "I've provided lunch, if not eating it. I'm afraid roast snake isn't my favorite dish."

He tugged her closer and wondered in a flash of anger why he allowed this small woman to nettle him. A captive white woman could be taken as a wife or raped and killed easily. Arielle had little idea of the methods they could use to make her obey. Fear shot through Luc, startling him. This nasty-tempered little hellcat had dragged it out of him. "Perhaps Gino might want to see his mother again. He could get hurt while you're defending us."

"Oh, of course. Very well, go ahead. Bargain."

A warrior spoke quickly, asking how many sons Luc had with the woman. Arielle blushed when he translated. She studied the horses tied to a line strung between pines.

Stone Elk's warrior tossed sage branches into the fire, and the sparks shot high. He sat and the chief began speaking with dignity. Gino slid into Siam's lap, his eyes drooping. Luc translated the story the chief wanted told, a Shoshone and Arapaho legend. "A strong, bad spirit took shape as a huge beast with tusks. It ravaged this valley, and the people couldn't hunt or camp. The Great Spirit, through a prophet, told the people to destroy the beast. They attacked him from the passes. He thrust upward with his tusks, ripped open the mountain, and disappeared. He has not been seen again."

"Wonderful folklore," Arielle whispered, stroking Dante's head as it rested in her lap. "But I think we should be going. Please extend our thank-yous for their hospitality."

Stone Elk smoked his long pipe slowly, thoughtfully. He passed it to Luc.

Arielle nudged Luc's backside with her toe. "Now is no time to dally, Luc. The wagons are moving."

He continued to smoke leisurely, the custom of friendship. She inhaled sharply, the impatient sound carrying to him. In the next instant she was on her feet, whistling.

The men leapt to their feet. Zeus whinnied, nodded, and walked toward her, dragging the horses' tethering line behind him.

The warriors yelled, their horses sidestepping, rearing, bucking. Zeus kept walking slowly to Arielle. He stopped and waited patiently after she fed him a sweet from her pocket. Arielle swept Luc a sidelong glance. "What are they saying? Goodness, they're upset."

Siam's hand rested on his knife, and Luc stepped in front of Arielle. "They think you're stealing their horses. For a woman to count coup or steal their horses would be the ultimate insult. Mrs. D'Arcy, you may have to miss your rattlesnake dinner."

Her hand touched his tense arm. "Luc, you won't fight, will you? I order you not to."

Mad Bull, the fiercest warrior, strode toward them, his hatchet raised. Luc leapt aside, stepped behind Mad Bull, and jerked his arm high. The Indian dropped the hatchet, pivoted toward Luc. His war cry split the air, cut short by Luc's blow to his stomach. "Siam, keep her out of this."

When the short fight was done, Luc struggled to his feet, spat blood from his tongue, and faced Stone Elk. On the ground between them Mad Bull groaned. Stone Elk smiled and said, "The woman is your punishment, Torn-Heart, for not taking another wife quickly. You will pay well. I like her, but maybe not as a wife."

"I ordered you not to fight," Arielle muttered, riding behind Luc later. She tightened her arms, leaning her cheek against his back. Luc took a small pleasure from her choice of riding behind him, rather than on Zeus with Gino. "You could have gotten hurt. Let Siam and Gino go on ahead. I don't want Anna to see you bloody. She'll blame me. She's worse than a broody hen with you."

"There now," she whispered later while she dabbed a damp handkerchief to Luc's bottom lip. He closed his eyes against the bright summer sun and listened to a bird sing in the wide expanse of sagebrush.

His head resting on Arielle's lap compensated for his aching night. She stroked his brow and allowed her fingers to be held against his chest. He liked those restless fingers, that curious left hand rummaging through the hair on his chest.

Arielle D'Arcy, his wife, was easing away his pain and replacing it with something he didn't want to give her. In little or no time, he would be following her around like one of her oversized horses.

During his youth and for a time after his wife's death, Luc had charmed his way in and out of female hearts. *The unique thought that he was being tamed to Arielle's small hand shocked him.*

He tried to ignore the gentle brush of her breasts against his cheek. *She could be lying beneath Stone Elk's warriors now . . . or dead.*

Luc trapped her hand with his, studying Arielle's determined frown. "You could have been killed. You don't leave the wagons without my permission after this."

He recognized the tawny sparks in her green eyes, the cocky tilt of her head. Her betraying left hand lifted to smooth her curls. "Are you giving me an order?" she asked lightly.

"I am."

Arielle jerked a whorl of hair on his chest and scrambled to her feet. "There I was, feeling sympathetic for your pain, and what do I get? Orders. You forget your position, Luc. *I* am your employer."

Rising slowly to his feet, Luc dusted his hat against his thighs. He fought for control, refusing to rub his injured chest. Arielle's talent for bringing him from a dreamy mood into simmering anger wasn't appreciated. Luc never lost control, with an animal . . . with a human . . . with a woman.

"Do you have any idea, Luc, how you are usurping the confidence that these women have in me? I was well on my way to bargaining for our safety."

"You were well on your way to being dragged into the sagebrush." Luc plopped his hat on her head. "Wear that. You'll burn. Or turn into one big freckle."

Arielle pushed her hands at his chest. The hat slid down to her nose. She tilted it back. "How dare you taunt me! I've tried everything to cure them, including wearing blood of a hare and of a bull, manure paste, and distilled walnut water."

Luc fought the chuckle rising in his throat and lost. "I adore each one. With your hair tucked under that hat, you look like a half-grown boy. Except for these—they are beautiful." He touched the crest of each breast with the tip of his finger, slid his thumbs into his belt and braced his legs. Teasing Arielle was a delight, sloughing off the years and making him feel sixteen with his first girl.

While he had shared what other women offered, he wanted more from this small, determined woman. Arielle enchanted, amused, and fascinated him as no other woman in his lifetime.

She had no idea of his passion for her, of the tempting idea of jerking down her ridiculous trousers. Luc's body hardened as he thought of those silken legs wrapped around his waist, her body tightly gloving him.

Arielle simmered for a full minute, her fists at her side. "I refuse to dignify your actions by retaliating—"

Luc could not resist bending to steal a quick kiss from her pouted lips. It pleased him that Arielle stopped talking, staring up at him. "You are beautiful, *chère*. Any of Stone Elk's men would have bedded you ... perhaps all of them."

"Nonsense. I'm past my girlish years, a spinster."

"My wife, and no longer a spinster. We could have made a child," he reminded her gently, bring the D'Arcy ring to his lips and kissing it. "Tonight we will finish what we started last night, *oui*?"

She stared at him, then blinked. "Why are you insisting on the ... procedure?"

"The procedure? Ah! Making love to my wife." He lifted a brow, enchanted by her blush. "I want my wife. She is— you are a desirable, passionate woman. Say *'Oui, Lucien.'*"

"Oui?" Arielle repeated. Luc kissed her again. Startled, Arielle stepped back, then fell into a huge sagebrush. She scrambled out of blue-gray branches, straightened her blouse, and dusted her bottom.

He chuckled, delighted by her expression. Arielle turned on him, her green eyes bright with anger. "I understand your motivation for . . . for pursuing me, Luc. For insisting on this sham of a marriage. If you want money, I will pay you well. Unfortunately, my aunt controls the family coffers, and as my . . . husband . . . you would receive a pittance. Not worth your time, really."

Luc stared at her, his amusement gone. His lips still tasted of her sweet softness. A heartbeat ago he enjoyed her tender, soothing care. She amused him, caused him to live again, caused him to think of children. "Madame D'Arcy. Is it not possible that I want that warm, soft body beneath mine, that I want to hold you and keep you as my wife because you suit me?" he asked, resenting that his last words were shouted.

Sixteen

....

"I want to have a baby," Glynis whispered dreamily as the women sat listening to Timmy's fife. The evening campfire of sagebrush blazed near Three Crossings— where the wagons crossed the Sweetwater three times. Gray smoke lifted into the clear starlit sky, and Glynis's wistful gaze followed a mother taking her children to the tent-covered latrine.

Arielle entered the day's events in her journal. A grandmother had died, wishing for a son who lived in Oregon country. Three hours later her three-year-old granddaughter caught cholera and followed her into death. The tired emigrants pushed their wagons and stock in the daily routine to survive. Men, curious about the women, stared boldly. Arielle wrote a bleak, stark admission—"This day I am glad for the men accompanying us. A trespassing remark was made to Eliza by a married man. He has apologized after discreet visits by Smithson, Siam, and Luc. The men each caught the rumor at a different time, and only later discovered that each had visited the improper man. I must admit

I alone could not have been as effective. These incidents are decreasing as we progress."

She noted the excitement of the emigrants when they first sighted the snowcapped Wind River Range. Everyone but Glynis, who had been unusually quiet that day, and now she spoke of a baby. "Glynis, are you feeling well?"

"A baby," the Englishwoman returned firmly. "I'm only a bit older than you, Arielle D'Arcy, and I fancy holding my own dear child. I've decided that Siam will make a perfect father. The ladies are giving me tips on the hows of capturing him. He's so fragile that one wrong move could frighten him away."

"Glynis!"

The servant straightened her back, her gray eyes clear and defiant as she met Arielle's. "Luc was very worried about you. The poor man has had enough sorrow in his life without losing another wife and perhaps a child, if you've conceived. You could have been taken captive today, that fine red mane—oh, yes, Arielle, don't deny it . . . you have red hair—could fly at the end of a scalp lance. All that I would remember was you flying off on Zeus's bare back, a lifted foil in your notorious left hand. It was quite a scene . . . red hair blazing in the hot sun, flying behind you like a flag. I could see your Aunt Louise faint. Poor dear Luc. You should have seen the terror on his face! He has been a wonder with the ladies, instilling peace in their hearts when there was pain. Each is blooming, becoming more aware of their human worth and dignity. Perhaps you should relent and consider Luc as a proper husband."

"Glynis!" Arielle snapped the journal closed. "That is enough. I've listened to Luc's and Smithson's lectures—surely not you, too."

"I refuse to waste my energies when they can be better used on a more tender heart. I wish to inform you that if Siam is in the mood to be seduced, I shall endeavor to oblige him. I wish to strike while the iron is hot—while his opportunity to escape my net is minimal." Glynis blushed, standing and smoothing her skirts with trembling fingers. "There are times when one must act in one's own behalf. I choose to do so now. Good evening, Arielle. I will see you before dawn."

Glynis walked to Siam, smiling seductively. She paused, touched his boot with the toe of her moccasin, then walked into the night. Siam blinked into space, then stared at his boot. A huge, boyish grin slowly spread across his dark face before he pivoted and entered the darkness after Glynis.

Harriet leaned against the wagon, wrapping her shawl around her, as she spoke to Arielle, "Your man is hurting, honey," she said quietly, rocking herself. "He was sick with worry today. The Indians call him Torn-Heart because he's lost so many loved ones. Maybe you'd better tend him a bit. Smooth his feathers."

Arielle glanced at Luc, who was holding Gino on his lap. The boy slept deeply, exhausted by his adventures and recounting his exploits.

Luc's eyes lifted immediately as though he had sensed her stare, and their eyes locked. Arielle tried to swallow, willing her racing heart to slow. With the day's growth of beard on his jaw, his eyes biting into hers, she absorbed the man Luc could be when angry or challenged. Harsh cheekbones caught the firelight, which glistened in his black eyebrows and hair. Cruelty lodged in his mouth, a mouth that had once tempted hers sweetly, lips that could slide into a devastating grin. Tonight Luc's impassive expression reminded her of his sorrow and of his revenge. She saw him now as Smithson's seasoned, proven westerner, as a man who kept his heart buried. Who kept his possessions.

The thick D'Arcy ring branded her hand. Wrapped in his arms, she had experienced Luc's gentle, teasing side . . . and his passion.

Smoothing the worn quilt wrapped around her, Arielle longed for the gentler, teasing Luc. After he gave Gino to his mother, Luc walked toward her. Arielle stood, uncertain and yet unwilling to turn away as he approached. She gathered the folded quilt that had been around her shoulders closer, gripping it painfully.

His wary expression curled around her heart—like Zeus

when he had acted unruly, then wanted a petting. Arielle's heart tilted, warmed, as Luc stopped in front of her.

His head lifted with pride, thunderous eyes lashing at her within his impassive, dark face. His eyes locked with hers, fierce, demanding, the impact taking her breath. Then they dropped to her bosom. His jaw tightened, the cords in his throat standing out in relief. Then with a nod, he stepped into the darkness.

The cold night wind swished through the sagebrush, swirling the fragrance around Arielle as she followed Luc to a distance away from camp.

He stood, hands on hips, legs spread, a solitary figure in the vast wilderness.

Arielle plucked a tiny branch of sagebrush, shredding it. She had no experience in salving male pride. However, Luc had risked his life to return Gino and herself to safety. Prudence demanded that she did not offer extra pay just now, but she would note the matter in her journal.

Arielle frowned, her fingers stroking the stitches on the worn patchwork quilt. She had been at the helm of her own life's ship since fifteen. She had mothered Jonathan for years because of their parents' dedication to business. She had acted as provider, supporter, and protectress. With the exception of Glynis, few people had claim to caring and protecting Arielle. To allow Luc to take a bit of her independence was not easy.

She tossed the sage branch away and dusted her hands together. The unique task of smoothing Luc's ruffled masculine feathers seemed to have fallen in her lap. Arielle stepped around the massive sagebrush, her boots crunching in the rocks and sand.

Perhaps she shouldn't have tossed the idea of his acquiring her family's wealth at him. Luc's pride was deeply ingrained.

Arielle paused, tilted her head as she studied his foreboding, broad back. She had never feared approaching a man, especially a man engaged in an operation with her. She admitted that Luc was equally devoted to the safety and dreams of each woman on this adventure.

Except hers. When Thaddeus's name dropped into her conversations, Luc's body stiffened, his face hardening. His jaw clenched, and his silvery gaze darkened into steel. While he had taken the Nez Percé woman's identification as truth, Arielle clung to the hope of an error. Thaddeus was a part of her childhood, of home, and until lately, she had cherished plans of marriage to him.

She frowned. While she had begun her quest for Thaddeus under pressure of Fannie Orson's impending grandmothership, did she want him now? Living with Luc, working with him, and spending the nights in his arms had changed her. She wore his ring. Each day she wondered what waited at the journey's end. Whatever happened, she knew that Luc now filled her days, her thoughts and dreams.

She hadn't thought of love at her age. Yet every chord within her reacted when Luc was near and in a manner that poets had relayed for eons. Was it possible? Did she love Luc?

She stood a little behind him, uncertain now.

Arielle touched his arm; the cords and muscles contracted beneath her fingertips. She swallowed, drew herself straight, and voiced the apology she had been turning around in her head. "I . . . I am sorry for your inconvenience of the past days, Luc. It was thoughtless of me to follow Gino without informing Smithson or taking help. I . . . feared for the boy. Thank you for coming after us."

He nodded, his features set and harsh above her.

"I have apologized, Luc," she prompted gently, willing him to speak. Peacemaking involved both warring factions, and Luc's thinly pressed lips didn't soften. Then there was the niggling desire to hear his deep, softly accented voice.

Arielle bit her lip, rummaging through the rescue, searching for a tidbit to foster conversation. She tightened her fingers, determined to smooth the coldness Luc spread between them. "I shouldn't have thrown my family's money at you, Luc. It's a habit, I suppose. There have been a few suitors with that motivation. I learned to disarm them effectively."

Luc looked down at her over his broad shoulder. His eyebrow lifted.

Arielle shivered in the cold contempt he'd tossed at her. She wanted Luc's teasing amusement. Shielding her face, she placed her cheek on the hard pad of his upper arm, resting against his strength and warmth, much as she would lean against Zeus's power. She was tired, exhausted now, startled by her need to be near Luc, to be held against him safely.

She rubbed her cheek against his rough shirt, soothed by the hard muscles beneath it. She closed her eyes, resting lightly against his tall, hard body. "You frighten me, I suppose," she whispered.

She wanted his blasted cuddling, the sweet kisses to ease away her years of loneliness. Her temper simmered a bit, since he had laughed outright at something Anna had said earlier, and now he was ominously silent. Arielle firmed her lips. She could adapt to teasing. It was simply a matter of practice. "*Oui,*" she whispered, nuzzling his arm. "What a nice word."

"*Oui.*" His uneven, deep tone whispered slowly across her skin.

"*Oui,*" she returned, lifting her head. Luc stared down at her, his eyes flashing in the moonlight. She touched that betraying, tightly clenched muscle in his cheek, soothing it.

His rough skin tempted her fingertips as they prowled across his cheekbones, then down to his firm mouth.

"What is it you seek tonight, Mrs. D'Arcy?" Luc asked carefully as her fingertip explored the mysterious corners of his lips.

Enchanted by the shudder that rippled down his tall body at her touch, Arielle traced his strong throat and the intriguing bit of hair escaping his opened collar. He placed his hand over hers, flattening it to his chest and a heart that pounded under her palm. The idea that Lucien Navaronne D'Arcy, a man who could charm women easily, was affected unreasonably by her touch excited Arielle beyond caution. She hadn't intended to jerk the hair on his chest that day, and memory of his outraged expression caused her to grin. To soothe the damaged area, she nuzzled his broad chest, inhaling the scents of soap and the particular enchanting, taunting scent that was Luc's alone.

He inhaled as she kissed the small injury, exhilarated by her brave play. "What are you doing?" Luc asked, his voice trimmed with the lurking accent that escaped when he was deeply affected.

Arielle wrapped her arms around him, smiling against his chest. Affecting, disarming Luc was a very enjoyable task.

His heart raced beneath her cheek, and she grinned, holding him tighter. "Brave, are you?" he demanded roughly before picking her up in his arms, wrapped in the quilt.

"Courageous," she tossed back, daring him with a kiss on that firmly closed mouth.

His arms tightened, his scowl down at her fierce. "Are you flirting with me, Angel?" he asked tightly.

Her lips pursed to say "no," then the tantalizing excitement swept over her. She'd never played, and Luc responded beautifully to her first attempts. *"Oui."*

She placed her palm over his heart and took encouragement from its racing beat. Luc muttered a curse, gathering her tighter as he ran through the sagebrush away from camp.

Arielle clung to his neck, letting her giggles escape. Suddenly she was free, the burdens of a lifetime sailing away into the faraway mountains.

"Demon," he whispered in a heavily accented voice as he allowed her to slide down his body.

"Beast," she returned easily, her arms still looped around his shoulders, her hands smoothing his hair. She loved the teasing play, loved the savage hunger lurking in his eyes, the heavy set of his thighs against hers.

She wanted to explore Luc. To taste, to forget every dark worry that had plagued her life, the struggle to succeed, to prove that she could master the tasks before her . . .

There was something else. A dark, hungry passion storming out of her, the need to find the passion—Arielle shivered with it, her fingertips flexing on Luc's strong nape.

His desire rested against her stomach, thrusting against

the confines of his clothing. She resisted the urge to slide her hands over Luc's chest, his rapidly beating heart, the clenched flat stomach. Then her left hand lightly brushed his belt and lower, hovering over the hard length she wished to explore. Luc cursed exquisitely in French and several other languages.

Challenge, daring, and desire caused Arielle to step back. While desire heated her, there was also an incredible tenderness for Luc, the need to soothe, to ease his dark mood.

Arielle met his eyes, then allowed her left hand to flow inside his shirt, stroking his chest. His dark eyebrow shot up. "Angel, I warn you. This is not the time to play games."

The challenge in his deep heavily accented voice caught her. Taking a deep breath of courage, Arielle leaned forward and kissed his chest. Luc's hands encircled her arms immediately. "Mrs. D'Arcy, I am shocked," he murmured, humor lacing his tone.

She grinned against his chest. Shocking Luc was most enjoyable.

His fingers slid inside her blouse, flicked open the buttons, then rested in the place between her breasts. "You don't need a breast enhancer, *chère*. It would be an abomination to change these."

"Really?" She had always wanted to flirt, she discovered. With Luc, it was delicious, tempting.

His eyes dropped to her bosom, peaked by cold and excitement. The stark hunger in his expression caused her to shiver, her legs weakening. Her hands tightened on his shirt, and a button tore away. She gasped, biting her lip, aware of the damage and yet enticed. She met his eyes, wrapped both hands in the fabric, and jerked them apart.

Luc's eyes narrowed, and he placed his hand on her breast, running his thumb slowly across her hardened nipple. Then he began to smile devastatingly, and her heart lurched. He bent to kiss her gently, his lips cherishing hers. "*Chère . . .*" His deep, husky sound spoke of longing, of hunger, of the shimmering emotions that tangled between them.

In the next instant Luc flicked open the quilt and placed

it over the sand. He tossed his jacket aside, then ripped away and discarded his damaged shirt.

Arielle met his eyes, her heart racing as he reached for her belt. They undressed slowly, savoring each touch, each sweet kiss. Their clothing fell away as Luc drew her into his arms and lowered her to the quilt.

She wanted him. Wanted the tender tasting of her mouth, her face as his hands trembled, flowing over her breasts, her hips. She cried out and clutched him as his fingers entered her. "Touch me," he demanded harshly, his mouth suckling her breast. When she did, slowly smoothing his silken steely power, Luc closed his eyes, his body surging into hers.

Resting over her, waiting, Luc's face pressed against her throat. His uneven breath caressed her skin, warming it. He waited, she sensed, her hands stroking his rippling back. He thrust down then, burying himself deep in her moist heat. Locked to him, Arielle stroked his hair, the arch of her foot exploring his bulky calf. She cared deeply for this man, admitting her fascination with his great body, so vulnerable in her arms . . . waiting, demanding.

Suddenly he lifted, framed her face with his large, callused hands. His expression was fierce. "You won't leave the wagons by yourself again, is that clear?" he demanded roughly. "I want your word."

She gave it instantly, followed by a gentle kiss. "I promise."

The fierce determination eased within him, his hair flowing through her fingers. She loved touching him, the heavy thrust of his desire locking them together as one. His heart beat against her breast, his weight welcome on her softness. Luc's hand shifted, cupping her hips, lifting her higher, and she cried out against his mouth.

They fought the fever, then gave themselves in it. She bit her lip against the throbbing pleasure, the circling, tightening of her body as he plunged and withdrew. She protested, her teeth finding his shoulder as the fiery warmth flamed higher.

Luc's raspy, uneven deep voice curled around her, urging her on in languages she didn't understand. His tone spoke of primitive passions, of possession and tender yearning. She gave herself to the flow of his voice, the surge of his powerful body into hers, the wild, sweet power of meeting each hungry kiss, tasting his skin and becoming one with his heart.

Sometime later, Luc drew her closer to him, his hand cupping her breast. She listened to the slowing beat of his heart, the sound no less comforting than his callused hand stroking her back gently. "You're noisy," he teased against her hair, kissing the tumbled curls on her temple. "You scared the rattlesnakes away."

"Rattlesnakes?" The stories and warnings of the danger raced through her, her eyes jerking open.

Luc chuckled, holding her closer when she squirmed to lie over his body. "So I am to be their dinner while you save yourself?" he teased, his tone softening, lowering sensuously.

Glynis's soft laughter blended with Siam's just as Luc drew Arielle closer. He lazily caressed her breast, drawing it to his mouth. Arielle stiffened. "Stop that. If we're in danger—"

"*Ma belle*, the only danger is you," he said quietly, kissing the hardened tip, gently biting it. Her body contracted immediately, his length filling her again with the sense of coming home. She tightened around him, pulling him deeper, testing his need until Luc groaned and turned her beneath him.

She forgot about rattlesnakes, Glynis's voice, and everything but Luc's sweet kisses, his body surging into hers.

Thaddeus Northrup. The name burned into Luc. While trading at Bridger's Fort for "Indian fixens" of furs, food, and clothing, Luc questioned the band of Snake Indians for information. Traveling without soldiers, a blond army captain had courted a young girl, took her violently, and then left immediately. The girl had followed on foot and had fallen prey to a bear.

Luc followed Arielle as she walked past the crude mud and pole trader's fort. Her horses ambled after her. Luc

smothered a smile. He was no better than her pets, waiting
for that secret, impish smile curling her soft mouth. He ran
his fingers over the shirt she had patched. The stitching
looked like a child's despite the hour of Arielle's concentrated attention, her teeth worrying her lips. She'd glanced
at him when he stroked the back of her neck with his finger.
Her eyes had blazed immediately, jarring him with sensual
excitement. Her blush was more devastating than the sudden
lurch of hunger in her willow-green eyes.

He traced antelope running across a clearing into a stand
of cottonwoods, then swung to the Snake boy proudly carrying gleaming, wet trout to his mother. Luc acknowledged
his needs, the hunger for Arielle's soft, agile body. The desperate need to lose himself in her scent, her fiery heat. His
child could be nestled in her womb—Luc rubbed his healing thigh. He wanted Arielle as his wife, and he wanted
children.

Arielle was a practical woman. She would realize the advantages of their marriage. His intense sexual need of her
startled him, each coming together more fiery, more sweet
than the last. His gaze swept over her neat dress, locking to
her breasts, and his body strained against his trousers.

Luc frowned. With Arielle these last few days, he had
lacked control. The need to be in her, to be locked with her
in the desperate, fevered lovemaking was intense. A long,
slow simmering look from those dark green eyes sent him
hardening against his clothing. He wanted long, slow lovemaking, but the hard days took their toll. Time was running
out for them, and they both sensed that when the journey
ended, they must face what they had begun.

*Whatever happened between them, Thaddeus Northrup
would die. Once the women were safe, Luc would hunt and
kill him.*

The Hudson's Bay Company's Fort Hall provided relief
with fresh provisions, trading only for cattle or money. Protecting its interest, the company encouraged emigrants to go
to California with tales of Indians and hard crossings on the
Oregon route. The Columbia River and two crossings of the

Snake were noted for losing men and cattle. The distance to the Willamette was too great, leading to famine and death. Smithson acknowledged the dangers politely to those who wanted to follow the California route, then ordered Wilson to shoot anyone who left the train. The captain packed up his wagons after three days of rest and struck out for Oregon country.

Luc carried with him the dark knowledge that Northrup had deflowered two Snake maidens. In retaliation the Indians had reportedly taken three white girls, who now had half-blood children. Throughout the next two days Snake men followed the wagons, curious about the famed "Widow Train."

Carefully preened, the warriors shouted at the women and performed horseback-riding tricks. The women were fascinated, but warned to keep their eyes from straying to the Indian men. One tall, pockmarked brave rode straight between the wagons, turned, and dropped furs beside the wheels. He spoke to Siam and Luc, roughly demanding a woman when they had many. There were white women in his camp, he said. They were scrawny, crying, and bore weak babies. He wanted more women, more children, because of the tribe's continuous warfare with the Sioux, Crow, and Blackfoot. According to the Indian, Big Horse Woman's sturdy women would adapt to the hard life better.

He motioned to riders in the distance. Three women, each holding dark-skinned babies with glossy black hair in their arms, stood looking at the wagons.

Dressed in loose cotton shifts and leather leggings, the girls were pale beneath layers of grease and soot. The thin babies, wrapped in the blankets that covered their mothers' heads, mewed weakly.

Luc translated for Smithson. The captain grimly shook his head "no." The men grimly swung up on their horses. Without turning from the warrior's threatening scowl, Luc recognized the heavy hoofbeats of Arielle's horse. Taygete's mottled gray bulk easily pushed into the space between Smithson's horse and Luc's as though they were toys.

"Siam says that this man has stolen white girls," Arielle stated.

Smithson inhaled slowly, grimly. "Get back to the wagons, Mrs. D'Arcy. Leave this matter to men. It requires cool thinking."

"Get back, Angel." Luc disliked the tall leader's flaring interest in Arielle's slender body.

"*I want these poor, unfortunate women.* I have trade goods. Lucien, do something," Arielle ordered imperially.

He pushed the smile lurking around his mouth away. Arielle's soft mouth circling his name was a seduction. He wondered if she realized how she had begun using it—when her emotions ruled her, when a matter was dear to her.

Luc turned to the task before him. White women who had been taken captive and bore children were often treated unkindly by their own kind. Many of them left their half-blooded children. These girls, their blue eyes stark with fear, cuddled their babies closer. Luc had already decided that the girls were going with the train, his decision made easier by Arielle's arrival. This was one time he didn't mind saying, "Yes, boss."

Her emerald eyes jerked to his face. "You are impertinent, sir. I leave you to your task. Do not return without these poor women," she ordered, turning Taygete back to the wagons.

Luc studied her squared shoulders, the huge slouch hat, and the single swaying braid bouncing at her hips. A determined woman, Arielle would fight for her beliefs and those she loved, just as she protected Northrup.

Then she loved a dead man. . . . Not even she could prevent Northrup's death. . . . Luc turned to his task with deadly intensity, bargaining for the girls.

That night, while the women tended the girls, Luc slipped from camp. He wanted time alone to balance his emotions.

The thought of Arielle in Northrup's arms, his bed, caused every muscle in Luc's body to tense. He'd slashed at Anna, who wasn't affronted. She told him in short terms that perhaps he needed to trim the edge off his temper. Anna suggested that he toss Arielle over his shoulder and run into the wilds. The idea appealed to him. He doubted Arielle would agree.

While the women hovered and tended the recovered girls and babies to the alarm of the other travelers, Luc slid into the night with a bottle of whiskey.

He'd purchased the bottle at the trader's fort. It was a luxury he had never used since his boyhood and Catherine. He needed that brief, blinding obscurity. *". . . acquire Thaddeus . . ."*

A dead man would be hard to acquire.

Luc lifted the bottle high, toasting a great horned owl swooping across the sky. He struggled to his feet, aware that no amount of alcohol could trim the anger and frustration within him.

After midnight Luc walked by the wagons containing the recovered girls, who refused to be separated. Mackie Logan, a seventeen-year-old farm boy who desperately wanted his first experience with a woman, stood against the girls' wagon, one foot raised to enter.

Luc stared at the boy's backside and decided he was the same when it came to entering Arielle's bed. He disliked the comparison. He blinked away the throbbing that had begun at the back of his brain and jerked Mackie's belt. Hard.

The boy reeled, found his balance, and stared wide-eyed at Luc, mouth agape. "Sir . . . I was just . . . I was just going to . . ."

Mackie's eyes widened more when Luc jerked the front of his shirt. "Let's just take this discussion away from camp, shall we, Mackie?"

"But, sir . . ." Clearly frightened, Mackie's eyes darted around the sleeping campground for help.

"Uh-huh. I know what you were doing." Luc disliked his snarling temper, and distantly realized that he wanted to climb into Arielle's tent just as badly as this boy wanted to enter the girls'. The thought didn't help his dark mood. Arielle had reduced him to following her around like one of her horses, waiting for a sweet. *". . . acquire Thaddeus . . ."*

"Hello, Mr. Siam, sir . . ." Mackie said hopefully, attempting a wobbly smile as Siam approached.

"Let the boy go, Luc," Siam said quietly, grinning at him.

"Damned foolishness, leering at sleeping women," Luc stated, gauging Siam's bulk against the boy's. Siam would serve better to withstand his temper. He smiled tightly, his head throbbing.

"Go along, Mackie," Siam murmured easily. "Luc will feel better in the morning, eh? He'll probably want to discuss life and women with you in a calmer mood."

Mackie scrambled into the darkness after one last look at the two big men facing each other.

"I'm not in the mood for talk," Luc began darkly. "Let's take this discussion someplace where it won't be interrupted."

"I don't have time. Glynis is waiting. She says ladies shouldn't be made to wait, Luc. Sorry," Siam stated, his grin widening.

His big fist was the last thing Luc saw.

Seventeen
....

"Outrageous!" Mrs. Mueller dragged her water-soaked skirts out of the spring after the dangerous crossing of the Snake River. Smithson had announced a rest and wash day at the campsite. He had also announced his marriage that night to Mary.

"You are fostering a sinful condition, Mrs. D'Arcy," Mrs. Mueller muttered, pushing her soaked, drooping bonnet away from her face. Just a moment before she had ordered Arielle to shed the unfortunate girls and their babies. Mrs. Mueller had made the mistake of enforcing her dictum, her bony fingers locking to Arielle's shoulder. "You've taken those three Indian tarts to your bosom."

Arielle turned slightly next to Mrs. Mueller. Her shoulder bumped the sodden, indignant woman and sent her reeling clumsily backward, arms flailing for balance. She landed on her backside with a splash. "Oh, Mrs. Mueller. I am so sorry," Arielle cooed, wading into the stream. "Here let me help."

"You should," Mrs. Mueller spat indignantly, her hand

outstretched to Arielle's. "Oooh!" she cried as Arielle stepped back and the woman fell back a second time. Her skirts swirled around her in the stream, her wet bonnet covering her face.

Arielle smiled tightly. Mrs. Mueller had provided an outlet for the frustration that had been building since one of the rescued girls mentioned Thaddeus visiting their camp. "I really don't have time to swim today," she said sweetly and walked away from the sputtering woman.

She glared at Luc, who overlooked the scene from the bank. He looked like Smithson's prized westerner . . . long, powerful legs locked at the knee and sheathed in fringed leggings, flowing into narrow hips and upward to broad shoulders. The revolver tucked into his belt and the huge knife sheathed on one leg had already proved his skills. He stood silhouetted against the endless blue sky—big, powerful, and thoroughly confident in his manhood. "Don't," she ordered. "Just don't."

Luc's dark skin tightened over rugged, jutting cheekbones. The quirky muscle jerked beneath a jaw covered with a day's growth of beard. His dark lashes framed his light, smoke-colored eyes. Now there wasn't an ounce of softness in him, the charm locked away. He nodded curtly, the sun casting blue lights in black hair. "Yes, boss."

Arielle threw up her hands. She would not rise to any argument with him now. She tried to walk back to the wagons with dignity, dismissing the sloshing in her boots with each step. Luc had kept his distance once Thaddeus's name erupted. His manner had shifted slightly, though unnoticed by others.

She had never trusted his motives for keeping their marriage, though in every other matter concerning the safety of the women, the wagons, or stock, she trusted him explicitly.

If anything should happen to her, she had already stored away a note gifting Luc with her stock . . . the Percherons loved him, and he tended them expertly.

Arielle sniffed, shivering from the icy water. She would have to deal with Luc and the D'Arcy ring. She sniffed again, jerking her sodden handkerchief from her apron

pocket. Luc was dangerous, effective, and beneath his
charming manners lurked a will of granite. "Boss," she muttered, nettled by his reference to her issuing orders.

Lydia hovered over the various creams and scents she
was brewing for the wedding festivities. The three women
traded from the Indians hovered near her, obeying every
word. They were clean now, but the slope of their shoulders
evidenced their shame. Each day the other emigrants
snubbed the women, and several indecent remarks had been
made. Anna wanted to fight, and tears shimmered in the
women's eyes as they clutched their babies close.

Arielle dressed quickly, needing time to herself and uncomfortable with the fuss the women were making for the
wedding. The swirling, lazy gray river provided the quiet
scene she needed to soothe her nerves. The willows swayed
with the damp wind. Behind her, children laughed and
played. Her horses stood on the bank like sentinels while
she skipped small, flat rocks across the surface. A large rock
splashed in the swirling eddy. Luc stood nearby, his bearded
jaw flexing slowly.

Head back, weight slanted to one long leg, thumbs looped
in his belt, Luc's smoky eyes held hers. If only he hadn't
caught her crying over the girls' mention of Thaddeus. If
only his stance wasn't so dangerous, so ruthless. Despite the
passion they had shared, she didn't want Luc prowling
through her uncertainty about Thaddeus. Whatever he kept
tightly locked inside now was deadly. She resented his secret when they had reached the ultimate bonding of bodies
and minds.

"Step aside," she said, pushing past him, afraid that he
would see her tear-stained face. She couldn't abide weakness, and he'd caught her in her lowest moment. The reminder of how he'd cuddled and soothed her at Fort
Laramie stung; the weakness would not be repeated.

"Yes, boss." Luc's head went back, arrogance in the de-
ceptively lazy stance of his lean body. The steely tone
locked in her bones, taunted her to her very essence.

He caught her flying left hand before it reached his face.
Jerked to his lean, hard body, Arielle fought, immediately

aware of Luc's arousal pressing at her stomach. She was exhausted, dusty, frustrated by the sheer rocky cliffs keeping her from seeing Thaddeus. She wanted to lean against Luc, let him hold her tenderly. His cold silvery eyes swept over her face, his mouth firming into a cruel line. Rising out of the dark stubble covering his jaw, his cheekbones slashed against dark, weathered skin. He released her hand slowly. "Cool down, Mrs. D'Arcy," Luc ordered darkly, then walked toward the bank.

He crouched by the water, scooping water up to his face with cupped hands. Arielle inhaled, took a step toward him that was stopped by Luc's "Don't. I'm not in a good mood right now. There's very little stopping me from taking my wife. A small compensation for watching you brood about Thaddeus."

Arielle stopped in midstride. The exhaustion of the journey had drained her every day. The reminder of Luc's tender, passionate lovemaking curled in her. A bit of gentle, seductive play would serve well now, not the determination she read in his steel-colored eyes.

Luc stood slowly, stretched, and turned to stare at her. The rage and hunger in his stormy eyes caught and held her, drying her throat. "Well?" he asked, walking slowly toward her.

"You're upset," she stated unevenly as he threw his hat to a bush and began stripping away his belt.

His smile wasn't nice. "Really? Now why would I be upset? My wife is plotting to acquire another husband more suiting her tastes. You have been plotting to 'acquire Thaddeus,' haven't you? This should be interesting since I have no plans to relinquish my marriage vows. In fact, I have decided to devote my energies to giving you my child. Starting now."

Arielle's deceiving left hand flew to her throat as Luc loomed over her. "Impossible," she managed through a dry throat.

"Is it?" he asked tightly, light eyes blazing in his dark, impassive face.

She stepped backward and found her back against a cottonwood tree. "Before I lay on another deathbed, I want a child and *we are married*, Mrs. D'Arcy. Though you tend to forget that when you're craving Thaddeus, or when you're pointing out that I am 'your employee.' The experience of being an employee and your husband isn't sitting well at the moment."

Alarmed at Luc's menacing tone, she touched his arm. "Luc, you won't endanger my venture, will you?"

"Hell, why not?"

She noted the bruise on his cheek. "Oh, Luc. What happened?"

He trapped her seeking fingers, pushing them away roughly. "That is not your concern."

"I could make it my concern. As my employee, you are under my protection—" she began, the words drying on her tongue as Luc's big hand collected the material covering her chest.

He jerked her to him, his face inches from hers. "You want to protect me?" he rasped disbelievingly, spacing the words. Then he fitted his hard mouth over hers and took it hungrily.

In the next heartbeat he was striding away, jerking on his belt. The tense set of his shoulders and curt nod to Sally stopped Arielle from calling out to him. She tested her swollen lips with her trembling fingers, aware that his fierce kiss had slid into a seductive brush of his warm, hard lips.

"Oh, dear," she whispered unevenly, willing her knees to stop shaking.

"Sage and sand," Smithson muttered two days later as he scanned the wide expanse past Salmon Falls. The last days of July baked the hot earth, draining the worn livestock and the emigrants. Mary lifted a precious cup of water to the wagon master, and they shared a tender moment before he drank. Since the wedding, Smithson had acted like a groom half his age.

He leaned back in his saddle; as the wagons passed one pulled to the side. His hand rested lightly on Mary's bright head, her hand on his leg. "Barren, godforsaken country. No grass for the stock. We'll have to push on ... Can't stay here with the Parkinsons until they die or recover. We've made them as comfortable as possible, left what water we could spare and gathered enough sagebrush and greasewood for fire. It's up to the Lord now."

"He'll need help." Luc urged his horse toward the isolated wagon. "I'll stay."

"Cholera, man. You could die," Smithson said, his gaze glancing off a sun-bleached, weathered chest of drawers along the trail. "Wilson has gone on ahead, buying a bit of peace from the Indians and selecting tonight's campground. We've got to push through this country, or we'll lose more than stock."

Luc watched the wagons glide into the sagebrush, dry axles shrieking. The emigrants were quiet now, exhausted and determined. Lydia no longer embraced the wonders of sage, the curative teas, and likening it to European tarragon, absinthe, and mugwort. She plodded wearily behind the wagons with the rest of the women. Marie baked bread for Arielle's horses, which they ate stoically in lieu of grass.

Smithson rode his horse to the back of the column, shot a dying cow, and met Luc's eyes. A covey of quail burst into the blue sky as Luc nodded. He understood the dangers of cholera and of a wagon alone. The captain slapped his dusty hat against his thigh grimly and returned to the wagons. Siam left Glynis's side and loped back to stand in the distance. He stood, legs apart, the timeless image of a powerful westerner. Then he was gone.

Anna had stuffed a basket of food, and Luc carried it to the Parkinsons.

The young parents, a boy of three, and a girl of five lay in the shade of the wagon, their stock hobbled nearby.

In the next hour Luc worked feverishly to keep fluids in the Parkinson's bodies. The mother and father tried desperately to help their children, their own faces drawn, cheeks sunken. The children cried pitifully, doubling with pain. Luc dabbed Mrs. Parkinson's dry lips with a damp cloth and glanced up at a slight noise.

Arielle seemed very small in the tall sagebrush as she

walked into the camp. "Go back to the wagons. Take my horse," he ordered tightly, fearing for her. He knew that she would not be turned away even as he spoke.

"When I am ready," she returned calmly, kneeling beside him. Her hand touched his arm, taking the damp cloth. "Tell me what to do. Lydia sent herbs for healing and strength, but first she said we must get them past these first hours. She has confidence that if anyone can accomplish the task, it is you." Arielle's soft, green eyes lifted to his. "I know you will save them. . . . Luc, please let me help."

Mrs. Parkinson cried out in pain, writhing on her pallet. Arielle patted the cloth over the woman's hot brow, smoothing her hair. "There, there . . ."

"You're the widow-woman . . . the one taking the widows to Oregon country," Mrs. Parkinson rasped weakly. "Reckon I made enough trouble for you—why are you staying?"

"You need help," Arielle answered simply, her eyes locked to Luc's grim ones. "I am no less a samaritan than Luc."

For the next three hours Luc and Arielle offered what comfort they could to the Parkinsons. The boy slid into death, and Luc buried him in a dresser drawer according to his mother's wishes. She lost the will to live, and Arielle battled to infuse it in her, reminding her of her daughter, her husband . . . Slowly, reluctantly, Mrs. Parkinson's glazed eyes began to light. "What's that noise?" she managed through dry, cracked lips.

A cat yowled in the darkness, like a long-lost soul seeking its mate; the second yowl was nearer. Arielle grinned and winked at Luc, who closed his eyes. The third yowl sounded nearby, and Lorenzo strolled into camp, tail high. He hissed at Luc on his way to Arielle, leaving an odor in his wake.

Arielle giggled as she fed the cat, the delighted sound lightening Luc's current disaster. "He loves you, Lucien. Say 'oui,' Lucien."

She cuddled the tom and grinned over his scarred ears to Luc's dark scowl.

"I am cursed."

"He loves you. . . . You can be sweet. How many men or women would keep their pledge to take poor Lorenzo to his master? Few, I think," Arielle stated softly, her eyes glowing. "Thank you for your kindness for my brood, dear Lucien. You have dedicated yourself to making them feel like proud, strong women with places to fill in a man's heart. Every one of my charges is half in love with you. I am more than half. *Oui.*"

The sweet curve of her lips coaxed his, and Luc found himself falling into her cool, shadowy green eyes.

The moment hovered in the still night, caught on the sagebrush smoke, and swirled around them. Drawn to Arielle's softness, clinging to it, Luc gave himself to the tender kiss, lowering his mouth to hers.

She met his lips, her own parted, brushing featherlight against his. "My dear," she whispered gently, her eyes filled with him. Her hand lay along his rough jaw, gently stroking it. "My dear, sweet Lucien."

Luc placed his hand over hers, closing his eyes. He could do with a lifetime of Arielle's slightly callused hand stroking his cheek. "You shouldn't have come back."

"Do not ask less of me than you do of yourself," Arielle returned in a whisper. "You must take a sip of water now and then, my dear. The Parkinsons and the mules will need you to survive. I need you."

Luc tested the tenuous moment, sliding his thumb along her cheek lightly. He found himself falling into her cool green eyes. "So you think I need an angel by my side?"

"Yes. Unfortunately, all you have is me."

Luc allowed the smile surging inside him to curl around his lips. Arielle was not an easy woman, but he'd rather have her at his side than any other female. He respected her strength and the ability to turn disasters into challenges. The bond between them was deep, passionate. Yet he had seen bonds severed that were just as deep. *Thaddeus's death could cause the tenuous bond to be cut.*

At three that morning the family had passed the crisis, taking small, but nourishing sips from the beef and marrow broth Luc had made. They slept heavily at dawn. Luc stud-

ied Arielle, sleeping sitting up against a wagon wheel, a
quilt drawn to her chin. In the next moment he was folding
her into his arms, drawing the quilt over them both. Arielle
snuggled against him, her breath flowing across his throat.

Wearily Luc closed his eyes, allowing the curling tendrils
to flow around his face. He gathered Arielle closer, needing
her soft warmth.

Her dry lips found his cheek, kissed it lightly, then again.
He turned his head slightly, and their mouths met, tasted leisurely, tenderly. "Lucien," she whispered on a dreamy sigh,
sliding her arm around his neck.

He stared grimly at the new dawn, laying pink over the
sprawling sagebrush. If they survived the journey, Thaddeus
stood between them.

Luc and Arielle pushed the mules that day as the Parkinsons rested inside the wagon. The next night they camped
near a deserted wagon, a reminder of emigrants who had
pushed too hard in poor grazing land, exhausting their stock.
Weather had dimmed the letters painted on the wagon: "Oregon Bound." When the recovering family and the mules
were settled that night, Arielle dropped fully dressed into
the pallet beneath the wagon. When Luc joined her, she
snuggled against him, one slender leg resting between his,
her cheek on his bare chest. "Mmm. You need a bath," she
murmured pleasantly, adjusting her softness into his lean,
hard body.

He found himself smiling and plucked a bit of sage that
had tangled in her hair. Arielle's soft curves, her breath
flowing across his chest, eased his past and swept away the
strain and fear of the day. To settle by her side each night
would be heaven. He allowed himself to rock her and picture them snuggled in the massive D'Arcy bed at his farm.
He toyed with the curling ends of her long, thick braid, one
he had woven long, exhausting hours ago at dawn. "And
you don't smell?"

She sighed drowsily, snuggling more comfortably against
him and pushing her face into his throat. Her lips moved
against his flesh, and pictures of that pink mouth against his

dark skin sent desire skimming down his body. Arielle did not help the matter by stroking his flat stomach as though he were Zeus. The thought settled on Luc uncomfortably, fueled by Arielle's drowsy, "Did I ever tell you how comfortable you are horizontally, when vertically you are absolutely all muscle and bone? I can't conceive of sleeping apart from you . . . my dear Lucien. . . ."

In the next heartbeat she slept soundly, and Luc was left to deal with his thoughts. A lifetime ago he'd needed her to die. Now he needed her to live. She gasped, protesting his tight hold. Slowly Luc forced himself to relax. For a time, at least, his wife clung to him, needing him as much as he wanted her.

The next day stretched endlessly, the mules exhausted by the steep grade that slid into the Snake River. Arielle expertly obeyed Luc's instructions, the Parkinsons holding on to the possessions piled high within the wagon. Mrs. Parkinson lost a tin filled with scrap thread, crying softly as it swept lazily away on the gray river. The camp that night provided good grazing, and after the Parkinsons were settled, Luc bathed in the creek nearby.

"I hate dirt," Arielle stated flatly as she stepped into the rippling water. "I've walked with it in my boots, eaten it, drunk it, and worn it like a second skin. I feel gritty from the top of my head to my toes. When we get to Oregon City, I'm going to spend a week in my bath."

She began furiously rubbing the thick bar of the Parkinsons' lye soap over the borrowed shirt of Luc's and her trousers. She sat, teeth chattering, and leaned back to wet her hair in the stream.

Despite his exhaustion, Luc fought the chuckle warming him. She looked like a small, determined boy . . . until the cold water caused her breasts to peak against the wet cloth. Arielle scrubbed, fumed, muttered, and cursed. She glared at him, tossed a thick wet strand away from her face, and jammed her fingers into her hair. "There's nothing more maddening and lecherous than a naked man leering at a lady in her dishabille, Luc. Turn around."

He waded to her. "Why don't you take off your clothes?"

She grimaced, spitting out the soap. Her eyes skimmed away from Luc's aroused body to a fish breaking the water's surface for a juicy insect. "My clothes are dirty. I'm dirty. I'm just saving steps."

"Ah. I see." He bent to rub the soap in her hair, holding her nape and easing her backward to rinse the long strands.

"I have died. Heaven is here. Amen," Arielle murmured, closing her eyes and trusting herself to his care. Her lips curved sweetly, clearly relishing his probing fingers. He laughed outright, bending to kiss her cold lips.

Arielle went under the water, sputtering as she surged to her feet. She shook the hair from her face, glaring at him. "Beast. Landlubbing shark bait."

Luc grinned. However exhausted Arielle may be, she filled his life with pleasure. "Husband. Lover. You know, it occurs to me that I've never seen your body in full daylight. Those freckles could have spread to other parts—mmm, intriguing." He tilted his head, scanning her thighs, and frowned. "I am very curious."

"Curious? I'll give you curious." Arielle's left hand curled into a fist.

"Mmm. I wonder, Mrs. D'Arcy, if the fiery color of your head matches those curls between your thighs."

She responded instantly and beautifully. First a stunned widening of her eyes, then a slow blush rising from her slender throat to stain the freckles high on her cheeks. He lifted an eyebrow, ogling her body beneath the wet clothing. He watched, amused and fascinated, as Arielle drew herself up to charge at him. Luc waited, anticipating Arielle's wet squirming body against his. He blew her a kiss and waited. . . .

Before either could move, Mrs. Parkinson cried out, and Luc quickly dressed, striding to the wagon.

The next day they pushed onward, nursing the family and demanding every drop of strength from the mules.

The first day of August, Smithson greeted Luc with a bear hug. They had just arrived at Fort Boise, a trading post of the Hudson's Bay Company. The burly wagon master scooped Arielle from the wagon's bench and whirled her around like a child caught against his bulk. "Thank God you are safe. The widows have been at me night and day to send a party to rescue you. Damnation, what . . . ?" he said just before the women swooped around them, hustling them to baths and a quickly prepared meal.

Lorenzo licked his paws, preening like a hero in Lydia's arms.

Arielle ate ravenously, then fell asleep, her head against Luc's shoulder, as she had for the past three days. "Ooh!" Anna cooed, clasping her hands. "Ain't they sweet?"

Luc fought sleep, easing Arielle gently into the women's waiting arms. Her fingers dug into his shoulder, though her eyes didn't open. "No. You aren't leaving me, Lucien. Not now," she whispered sleepily, locking her arms around his neck. "Don't you dare leave me, you beast."

Smithson's thick brows shot up. Siam grinned and Glynis wiped away a tear. "She's stuck to you tighter than a tick, boy," Smithson grumbled uncomfortably. He jerked his head to the tent the women had prepared. "Up at four, leave at seven. You better get some rest," he murmured.

The women moved aside as Luc carried Arielle to the tent. She snuggled into his arms as she had the last three nights. Too weary to protest, Luc allowed Lorenzo to curl at his feet. After all, Luc held an angel in his arms.

The Burnt River portion of the journey tested the experience of the emigrants, the strength of their wagons and stock. Rocky, steep grades slid into several crossings of the river, then rose and curved along the treacherous mountainside. Wagon wheels broke, tempers rose, and the women of the "widow train" proved their endurance. Their bond ran deep, tested in freezing rain and mud. No matter how exhausting the day, they shared tea in china cups and dreams at night, comforted each other at every trial. Every meal began with a prayer, manners carefully intact. Around their campfire each night they sang hymns and practiced gentle, quiet conversation. The "widows' " heads were high now, their shoulders straight. They were women moving toward their destinies, futures as honest wives.

Arielle's horses met every challenge, obeying her orders when the other stock panicked. She dug rocks from their hooves and sneaked them bits of dried apple for rewards. She groomed their mottled gray coats meticulously, crooning and hugging and petting each massive horse.

The "widows" decorated straw hats with flowers for the mares, cutting holes for their great ears. Zeus disdained the hat, but at times looked pleased with a rakish coronet of wild flowers, rather like his namesake.

Toughened men stopped their work to stare at the small woman riding the powerful stallion's broad back, her tattered straw hat bobbing at each carefully placed step. Arielle moved between the giant horses, under them, leaping from one back to another, and always crooning, coaxing, laughing outright with the challenge as the beasts whinnied and nickered.

The Parkinson episode marked a difference in Arielle and Luc's relationship. When he was away from camp, hunting or helping Wilson barter with the Indians, Arielle longed for the sight of him. When she saw him, her heart began pounding and she clasped her arms around herself to keep from running to him.

Once in the looming shadows of the mountain dusk, she could not restrain her joy when Luc returned from a short hunt. Dirty and tired, walking his horse with its burden of butchered elk, he stopped when he saw her. Siam took the horse's reins and continued walking to camp, while Luc stood, arrogantly defying her to come to him.

Evening mist clung to the valley, hovering about the river and mingled with the campfires. The scent of pines blended with Marie's wild berry sweetbread.

Suddenly shy of Luc, Arielle had clasped her hands behind her back, fighting her joy and the impulse to throw herself into his arms. When Zeus nudged Arielle's back, urging her toward Luc, she resisted. The stallion nudged again, and Luc's teeth gleamed in the shadows of dirt and his beard. "You're dirty," Arielle managed huskily as Zeus's last nudge brought her to stand near Luc. "And arrogant," she added for good measure.

His light eyes gleamed with amusement, laughter wrinkles crinkling at the corners. "Walk with me, *chère*?"

"Humph. I know where your walks can lead," she returned, looking shyly away at a herd of elk sliding into the rugged pines.

He leaned down to brush a soft kiss across her lips. "*Ma chère*, one look at your breasts unbound, at the delicate curve of belly into thigh, of rounded buttocks and dimpled knee, of slender enchanting ankle and tempting toes, would cure all my ills. I am famished for the sight of silken flesh and freckles and that red mane curling over it all."

"Lucien D'Arcy!" The words exploded softly into the cool mountain air, scented of pine and campfires. She realized she had been holding her breath.

"Fine. I will wither away, longing for one full sight of my bride. A kiss then, freely given, would do." He spread his legs, and settled his tall body into the timeless stance. "You may begin now, wench."

"Cocky landlubber. Beast," she railed, throwing out her left hand. "Jump, you say. Fetch. Kiss you when you want." She glanced at Zeus, who waited patiently, eyes alert. "There. Kiss him." Then taking flight, she began to run through the pines, only to have Luc pluck her from her feet. He continued running, bearing her weight easily and bearing her down into the first lush stand of mountain grass.

Lying over her, he captured her swatting hands easily with one of his and panted heavily against her throat. "You're damned fast. Must be your wanton blood."

"Oh! Wanton! And I was so glad to see you, too!" she exclaimed.

Luc raised his head, his fingers stroking her cheek, the silvery eyes warm and gentle. "There. You were glad to see me. You might even love me. Admit it."

"Never." She turned her head to watch Zeus and the mares graze around them, much like friends sharing a parlor rather than a mountain glade. A brook rippled nearby, and a child cried in the mountain shadows separating them from camp. Luc's thumb smoothed the rapid pulse beneath the skin of her wrist. "We should get back," she whispered huskily, aware of Luc studying her.

"I want children with you," he said quietly, slowly. "We could have a good marriage. I want you with me on my homestead . . . my parents' homestead. It would be a good place to raise horses and children."

Arielle listened to his racing heart, caught the vulnerability cloaking him. She saw him growing old, the aristocratic features still handsome. She waited, half praying that he would admit caring for her in the deepest, most treasured way. The sound of her heart rose to her ears, the heavy pulse in her veins waited—

Something dark and wary flickered in his eyes, stilling his expression.

Arielle closed her eyes and listened to the rapid beat of her heart. She stood too much to lose with this man. Too much to win to act rashly now. "Let me up, Lucien."

He eased to his feet, drawing her up. The horses grazed peacefully while Luc slowly raised her hand to his lips, kissing her palm and folding her fingers over it. Then he took her other hand, laced it with his and walked slowly back to camp.

Exhausted by the trials of every day, they spent hours each night sharing their pasts. Arielle learned that Luc had been married before his Chinook wife, Willow. He diverted questions about his late teens and the early marriage, his expression hard. She laughed at stories of his sisters' antics and how often he took their punishment. Whenever he spoke of his mother, it was with sadness; she had never been strong. A sheltered, well-bred aristocratic woman, she was ill prepared to protect herself or her children. Jason D'Arcy had been exacting, demanding of his family, especially his son.

Each day Arielle waited for Luc to ask her to walk with him. He did so with gallantry, and Arielle noted the dreamy glaze to the women's faces as he brought her small gifts of flowers, a bright feather, or a pretty rock. Once in the shadows of night, Luc swept her into his arms and bore her to the pallet he had waiting. He made love to her desperately, hungrily, taking and giving. She matched his need, snaring him close, her heart flying with his. Wrapped in each other's arms, they slept quickly, and Arielle awoke to a gentle, seeking kiss, a playing, tempting fingertip on her lips.

In the daylight, Arielle wanted to drag him to the ground and . . . She pushed the thought from her mind each time it entered. Ladies did not have their way with men simply to satisfy basic urges. The whole matter of lusty, flaming desire—though at times exotically sweet and leaving her cheeks stained with tears—was sinful.

She wanted more from Luc, demanded more. She wanted love. She wouldn't settle for less from him.

While she was not one to change her plans easily, Thaddeus's well-mannered children began to pale beside Luc's dark, lovable rapscallions. Arielle found herself studying the heavy antique ring.

The wagons rolled westward, to the Powder River Valley, filled with sage and plump game birds, then on to the beautiful timber-covered Blue Mountains. The middle of August the wagons eased into the Umatillo Valley. Wallawalla, Cayuse, and Nez Percé traded vegetables for clothing. Then in the distance two snow-covered peaks surged into sight, and the winding gray Columbia lifted the emigrants' hearts. Their energies rose, anxious to finish the trip. With the final stretch of the trip, Arielle mulled her quest to marry Thaddeus.

She lay nestled in Luc's arms, returning to the wagons before the four o'clock rising hour.

While she and Luc were bonded temporarily by fate, the practical matter of marriage did not suit Luc's passionate, sometimes arrogant nature. He could be frightening when challenged—deadly, ruthless with thieves or those cruel to animals—and just the opposite, gentle and charming with her ladies. Then there was that bit of him still locked away, challenging her, frightening her.

Glynis was lost in her Jean-Pierre, seeking any chance to flirt outrageously with him. He always appeared astonished, then delighted. Their blended laughter filled the days and nights. Siam arrived promptly each evening at the widows' dinner table, freshly washed and shaved, and always with a small present for Glynis's delight. She managed to serve

him the biggest biscuit, the juiciest wedge of dried apple
pie. Siam touched her at every possible opportunity, his expressive eyes obviously happy. When she returned from
their evening walks, Glynis beamed, her clothing rumpled.

Smithson declared a rest day amid the fields of grass and
wild sunflowers. The day was devoted to washing and trading, preparing to push on the next day. Arielle suspected
that Smithson wanted to spend time alone with his new
family. With Mary on his arm, he seemed much younger.
The Nez Percé, fascinated with "Big Horse Woman" and
her groomed Percherons, stayed near the camp.

Nelson Bancroft took Eliza to the Whitman mission to be
married. Though the women were happy for Eliza and her
new husband, they grieved over losing her.

News came of the Mexican War, the British retreat from
the Oregon Territory. Toughened westerners held their
"powwows," traded with Indians and the emigrants, and
passed on.

Each night Luc drew Arielle into his arms with more
sweet, cherishing kisses than the previous night. He touched
her carefully, lingeringly, as though he expected their happiness to slide away.

At a small cabin outside Fort Vancouver, Thaddeus
Northrup studied his well-polished boots resting on the
rough table. Thaddeus tossed coins on the table, not bother-
ing to shield his contempt of the man's high, flattened forehead. When the Chinook messenger left, Thaddeus turned
his attention to Margaret Davis, who was polishing another
pair of his boots. His pregnant mistress no longer interested
him. She had entertained him for a time, a fresh young
widow, eager for his advice and help. He'd thought about
marriage to her to gain her dry land with its rumor of gold.

Fort Vancouver, a vacated Hudson's Bay Company fort,
had provided little opportunity for a gentleman of good
breeding, though he'd had some success with gambling until
McLoughlin, the Great White Eagle, sent word to cease.
Since Thaddeus's quiet discharge at Fort Leavenworth, he'd
been mulling opportunities. The money and jewelry he'd

taken from unprotected women when possible had served his needs well. Now it was gone, along with all the money his parents had sent him to invest in the Willamette Valley.

The Chinook runner had received a Flathead's message that Arielle wanted to see him.

She'd always wanted to see him, Thaddeus decided smugly. Any woman would want his company, a handsome gentleman accomplished at turning female hearts.

"Big Horse Woman," he muttered, remembering Arielle's love of the huge beasts. "A wealthy woman spending her time in the stables."

According to the Chinook messenger, Arielle intended to start raising horses, farming and establishing business near Oregon City. A rich woman, Arielle's dowry would support Thaddeus for years. He could live like a country squire. She had always fancied him, stumbling a bit and acting nervous and shy when he was near her. An elfin bit of a woman when he preferred full lush females or tight-channeled virgin girls, Arielle possessed an evil temper to match her untamed red hair and wicked left hand.

As her husband, he would have the right to curb that high fine temper any way he wished with little interference. Much like beating a horse, breaking it. In his experience pregnancy and childbirth weakened women, curbed their spirits, and he intended to keep Arielle's belly filled with Northrup brats.

Marriage to Arielle would suit his needs perfectly. Since his choice to leave the army voluntarily at Fort Leavenworth, rather than a dishonorable discharge, he'd had difficulty surviving. The arrival of Arielle would change his luck. He would take Arielle as his wife and live a proper gentleman's life of ease in the Willamette. If she died, or when her spirit was properly chastened, they could return East to the expansive Browning coffers. With the time that had passed, he would apologize for his youthful misconduct to the upper-class society. The hot, fanciful adventures of young blood could be understood, once they saw his maturity and Arielle's strong presence at his side. No one doubted her reputation as a fine businesswoman, though her unusual tendencies to take charge of it astounded many. He

would take the heavy reins from Arielle's hands and run the
Browning enterprises as he wished. Selling off the empire in
bits and pieces would be a start.

Thaddeus smiled, his thoughts skimming along to his
army discharge papers. He had placed a small fortune in the
right hands to make his discharge quick and easy. The army
had unpleasant ways of dealing with troublemakers. Margaret caught his smile, shyly returning it to him. "Come trim
my hair, will you, darling?" Thaddeus asked. "Then I have
something important to tell you."

That night Margaret quietly took her life.

The wagons pushed slowly across the unrelenting dry
countryside to the Dalles. There they faced "gougers," who
would ferry the wagons down the river to Fort Vancouver.
Several wagons took the ferries, but Smithson chose the
Barlow Toll Road, tracing an old Indian trail crossing the
Cascade Mountains. Mt. Hood's snowy peak shot high
against the sky, an obstacle the emigrants would have to go
around. They crossed the Tygh Valley, river after river to
Barlow Pass. Each day tired hearts lifted looking toward
their future; a mixture of stock, horses, mules, and oxen
pulled the wagons. Arielle's Percherons grazed on rich grass
and regained their strength lost over the arid country. Siam
and Glynis spent long hours away from camp, and Lydia exclaimed she had found her Garden of Eden.

Tedious miles passed, jutting peaks and deep forests, the
wagons breaking down in this last segment of the hard journey. Emigrants harnessed cows and horses and mules with
oxen, their clothing and shoes worn thin.

The women in Arielle's "widow train" grew stronger,
anxious, taking more care with their skin and hair. Work-
worn hands smoothed cherished clothing, fashioned on the
journey to be worn for potential husbands.

Arielle concentrated on the task before her, a slight shift
in her plans. A tiny adjustment to her marriage plans.

*She decided to acquire Luc, not Thaddeus . . . and on her
terms.*

Eighteen

Luc threw his weight into the ax's blow against the tree. There were easier ways of gathering campfire wood, but to work out his frustrations, he had selected a stripling tree.

Arielle had sent for Northrup. That burning thought sent another hard blow into the tree, jarring Luc's shoulders. He chopped down, then swung an undercut methodically, working out his frustration.

Siam had translated her request to see Northrup to passing Flathead Indians. When Northrup arrived, he would die.

Luc gritted his teeth. He didn't like the idea of his wife, the woman who tempted and frustrated him, sending for another man. Nor did he like the idea that Arielle was his bait. Tenacious, determined, Arielle drew Northrup to his death.

The ax sank too deep to draw out easily, and Luc stared at the cut, wiping away the sweat on his forehead. A ground squirrel ran down a yellow pine tree, carrying a pinecone, and scurried into a stand of alder bushes. Time slid by too quickly each day. Luc shivered, a cold chill sliding over his sweaty body.

He had a woman whom Northrup would want very badly, and when he came, he would die.

Then Arielle and the future Luc had barely glimpsed with her would be swept away like an autumn leaf on the wind.

Sacha Eberhart sipped tea with Arielle and Glynis the night before they arrived in Oregon City. The rest of the immigrants continued to Oregon City, but despite the constant cold rain, the women had demanded two days of rest and "beautification makings." Several women immigrants demanded that their husbands take charge of the widows' stock. The widows needed time for pampering.

Smithson unexpectedly grabbed Arielle and smothered her in a deep hug. When he released her, he patted her shoulder clumsily. "You've done a good job. My compliments. Mary has told me of your women, and I approve of your venture, though not your methods. You can expect us, once you're settled in." His jowls moved beneath his busy sideburns. "My farm is close. You come to me if things don't go as you want. I'll help."

When Arielle thanked him, he took her hand and shook it. "You're a bit of a scamp, Mrs. D'Arcy. A challenge for any husband. Poor Luc—or Lucien, as you have been calling him—has his chore cut out for him." Then he winked, and Arielle found herself laughing. She raised to her toes and kissed his cheek. Flustered and blushing, Smithson backed away to be claimed by a laughing, teasing Mary.

The tents were set, then Omar, Siam, and Luc chopped wood for huge bonfires for washing and food. The women were delighted with Luc's idea of a steam bath. Seated within the steamy shelter of branches and wagon covers, they shared dreams and excitement and fears. A pact was drawn that no woman would tell of another's past. If she decided to share her secrets with her husband, she would not include the unsavory pasts of the rest. In steam scented of pine boughs and herbs, they cried and encouraged one another. Lydia, at her height, mixed huge batches of oils and muds for weathered complexions and hands.

She crooned over refined batches of salmon oil, flipping

through her notebook to compare results. Traded from the Clackamas Indians, the salmon oil was strained, systematically purified, and scented by Lydia's loving hands.

Delighted with the luxury of lounging and tending themselves for a day in the steam hut that Luc and Siam had constructed, the women "purified," then shampooed and tried different hairstyles. The pines sheltered the festive activities, while Luc and Siam fetched wood for the fires, then took the boys fishing. Aloof and proud, Omar settled near the horses and oxen.

Sacha, a small, wiry gray-haired man dressed in a cloth suit, nervously sipped tea and informed Arielle of Browning holdings and inventories, which she noted carefully. A widower for years, Sacha was a prize catch, a courtly, carefully groomed man. His eyes jerked to Anna each time she passed carrying water to the baths. "That is a handsome woman," he stated. "Is she one of your widows?"

"Anna is available for marriage," Arielle returned, smothering a smile as Sacha straightened his string tie and smoothed the part in his hair. "I'll need her passage fare and more."

"Done."

"You have to court her, Sacha. I am not selling my ladies like stock." Arielle checked off her notes. "Now, about sewing needles. They are light, durable, and in demand. They would be perfect for transport. Also threads and fabrics. From my experience, the Indians trade easily for clothing."

Sacha shot her a fierce glance beneath his heavy brows. "Of course, Arielle. Needles, threads, and fabrics transport easily. The Browning Company will profit."

Arielle debated about informing Sacha of her marriage. She had sent word to Thaddeus at Fort Vancouver, and she didn't want him deterred by the D'Arcy name.

He drew himself to his full height. "Business as usual, Arielle? I see you haven't changed despite your hardships. I'll just take the wagon of goods and another back to the store and inventory them. That will leave you two wagons for transporting the ladies comfortably. I'll see that comfortable lodgings are prepared, and when you are rested, there

are several land parcels that you may choose for your farm.
Dr. McLoughlin is aware of your arrival, as he is of everything. My compliments on the way you've managed these
fine Percherons in what must have been dire situations.
They're a bit lean now, but they'll fatten on the good grass
of the Willamette."

Sacha glanced over Arielle's shoulder and beamed. He
strode toward Luc, who had been cutting wood without his
shirt. His chest gleamed with sweat, glistening in the dark
whorls covering his chest. "D'Arcy! What a pleasure to see
your face again, man!" he exclaimed cheerfully, clapping
Luc's bare shoulder and shaking his hand. "Your homestead
is waiting, the house built as specified. I've been keeping a
close eye on your Arabian stock at my place. I took the liberty of staking out a good pasture and building a sizable
lean-to for the stock. Finest piece of fencing in the country.
A few Flathead Indians turned up to help. Those you helped
barter for a good price on their hides. You'll be settled in
comfortably in no time at all."

"Sacha." Luc returned the greeting quietly. He watched
Arielle's face intently. "You've met my wife."

The small man's eyes darted to Arielle, whose lips were
parted as she stared up at Luc. She snapped them closed.

"Arielle Browning D'Arcy?" Sacha tasted the words
slowly, staring blankly at Arielle, then down to the thick
gold ring encircling her finger. His eyes swung up to Luc's
grim face. "You got married? I thought there wasn't a
woman alive who could trap you, tame you to hand."

Luc lifted Arielle's cold limp hand to his lips and kissed
the back of it. "Afraid so. Though I haven't had time to really experience my marriage to the fullest. My bride saw fit
to keep our vows secret. Perhaps it is time to reveal them
now, Angel," he offered in a slightly accented tone that revealed deep emotions coursing within him.

She cleared her throat and blinked herself back into reality. She realized that Luc had offered her a chance to refuse
him. She chose to accept his name. "Ah . . . are you well
known in Oregon country, Lucien?"

"He damn well stopped an all-out massacre caused by a

bloody drunk. Rescued a family from their burning cabin by
himself and another immigrant family stuck in the snow on
the mountains. Never a care for his own well-being. Is Siam
with you, Luc?" Sacha asked anxiously. "Nothing has happened to that mountain of beast and man, has it?"

"An Englishwoman." Luc's cool, steel-colored eyes
scanned Arielle's face, probing into her mind and body intimately. Arielle shivered, aware that her hunger for Luc in
the past few weeks could easily produce a child. His gaze
followed her trembling left hand down to her stomach, flattening over it. Was it amusement shading his eyes to dark
pewter? Or was it terror? "Glynis is breeding now," he said.

"Damnation. Holy hellfire. That's bloody well fine
news." He blinked as though caught by a sudden thought,
his eyes skimming down Arielle's flat stomach beneath her
skirts. His frown jerked to Luc's grim expression.

Arielle blushed, following the silent march of Sacha's
thoughts. The thought of Luc's child nestled in her womb
caused her heart to flutter. "Breeding, indeed," she managed
huskily, smoothing her braid with her trembling left hand.

"You'd be the man to do it," Sacha stated with a grin.
"Did you bring your mother and the girls back with you?"

Pain jerked across Luc's tanned face. "They didn't make
it."

Sacha's cheery grin slid into sympathy. "Too bad. Anything I can do?"

"Nothing." Luc's grim expression caused Arielle to slide
her hand into his big one. His warm, rough fingers curled
around hers immediately, and his light eyes skimmed her
face, the tension in his easing slightly.

The smaller man nodded, turning to Arielle. "By the way,
Thaddeus Northrup is in the country. I see him now and
again as he squires politicians around in his fancy army out-
fit. Quite the dandy, that one. A ladies' man, just as he was
in New York."

He frowned, studying Arielle, who had suddenly gone
cold. "Strange. I always thought that you had your sights set
on that one. Oh, well. Now you've gone and trapped yourself a good man. One of the best. I reckon you'll be staying

at his place once the ladies are settled. Must get back, arrangements to make, you know. Good seeing you, Luc. Congratulations. You can count on me to keep quiet about the marriage until you straighten out the details."

He doffed his hat to Arielle. " 'Mornin' to you, Mrs. D'Arcy. Now, if you please, I'd like to introduce myself to that succulent, admirable Venus named Anna. With your permission, I'll just begin now."

A moment later Anna stared blankly down at the dapper little man who bowed and suavely took the bucket from her. When it was delivered, he bowed, kissed the back of her scarred hand gallantly, and strode away whistling. Anna's mouth remained agape, her gaze following Sacha blankly. He stepped into one wagon, signaled the hired man on the other wagon, and began toward Oregon City.

Slowly Anna began to blush, a curious thing to see. Her large, trembling hand rose to pat disheveled gray hair. When she walked into the "beautifying tent," her broad hips began to sway.

Arielle chafed her cold hands together, aware of Luc's scrutiny. "Blast. 'Keep quiet' indeed. Sacha hasn't kept quiet about a thing outside of business. Telling him to stop the flow of secrets from his lips would be like asking one to put out a forest fire with spit. So you are well known here. You own Arabians and have commissioned a house. You might have told me sooner."

"The house was to have been for my mother and sisters. This was to have been my father's land." Luc shrugged, dismissing a sharp reminder that he was alone. "Now it's mine. A simple cabin with good grazing and farming land. I would like to see the women stay there while they are selecting husbands. They will have my protection."

Arielle turned the idea over, probing out the reasons why her ladies should not go with Luc. "The matchmaking could be a lengthy process."

He nodded, that revealing taut muscle sliding beneath his dark, damp skin. She dabbed away a drop of sweat at his forehead with her handkerchief before she realized her betraying left hand was out of control. She loved touching Luc, tending him in small ways. He always responded so delightfully, his eyes darkening with messages that thrilled her heart. When he touched her, a fingertip easing back a wayward tendril, then drifting to her mouth, she melted. Arielle forced her mind back to the subject. "I expect a continuous flow of suitors for each woman. Your household would be in constant disruption."

Luc smiled wryly and nodded. "True."

"So here we are, bearing the same easily recognized name," Arielle thought aloud. "I have a scandal on my hands before beginning my life here. If I live apart from my husband—that's you, Lucien—the complications could be enormous."

Luc's dark head went back. "You are free to do as you wish now."

"My freedom? A divorce?" Arielle's brows darted together. "Blast. Where would that leave me now? Within minutes everyone will know about the marriage. They'll put two and two together and wonder what we've been doing every night—" Her eyes widened and her lips clamped shut as a flush rose up her throat to stain her freckles.

Nancy ran toward them, lifting her skirts, her eyes rounded. She stopped in front of them, her hand reaching out to be braced by Arielle's. "Anna said to tell you. Glynis is expecting and the father is Siam."

"I know," Arielle said too patiently with a grim smile. Sacha's ability to keep secrets had not improved. "We'll hold the weddings at Lucien's house. Mary wants a second wedding in a home, and she's entitled to one."

"Luc's house? He has a house here?" Nancy asked rapidly.

Taking her hand and kissing it gallantly, Luc smiled. "A farm. You are all invited to stay as long as you want. If my wife agrees."

Nancy stared blankly at Arielle. "Oh," she whispered in a small voice, "that was the other thing Anna said . . . that you were married. We all wondered how soon you would be, and here you already are. How exciting! Anna says she's going to marry that little man just as soon as she can. Everyone is so excited. Lydia is preparing new scents for our bathwater."

Later that afternoon Arielle sipped her tea while she worked in her journal. Concentrating on her task, she was startled when Luc's hand drew away her pen. His boot propped on the limb beside her.

Legs spread, his chest bare with gleaming rivulets of sweat, he was the picture of demanding male arrogance. His head tilted, his betraying jaw cleanly shaven, Luc tossed the pen to the stump serving as her table. "Well?" he asked, his deep voice trimmed with his accent. "Are you living with me as my wife or not?"

His demanding tone jerked at Arielle's pride. Luc could be a bully, and she wasn't ready to lay her terms at his feet. Luc still carried his demons, hoarding secrets from her. She intended to spread them to the winds and tame the beast ruling Luc's dark side. She planned to do that in good time— when Luc was no longer under the protection and pampering of the women. She wanted to stake out every secret he'd hoarded so well.

Then there was Thaddeus. She wanted to resolve the serious crimes placed at his feet. She also wanted to ask Thaddeus to retrace his indiscretions and help the women along the way. She hoped that his honor would agree. Luc was too dangerous and could interfere. The results could be disastrous. "I'll think about it."

He inclined his head, challenging her. "I'll give you until you're rested. Then I'm coming for my wife."

"Will you now?" Arielle stood slowly and shook out her skirts, smoothing them. Then she looked up at Luc's taut expression, gauging that tense muscle flowing along his jaw and down his throat. The medallion gleamed, nestled in the dark hair covering his chest. She touched his nipple with the tip of her finger. "Perhaps it is I who will be giving you a small respite, *ma belle*. There are matters that I wish to clear away in the meanwhile."

"I look forward to tutoring your French, *ma chère*. I am not a pretty woman."

Arielle's left hand waved away the small error. "You definitely are not. You're big as a bear, too damnably charming, and an immensely wonderful man to cuddle and kiss. You're spoiled, arrogant, and demanding, to boot. No doubt I will have my hands full of keeping you in line."

When Luc's black eyebrows lifted, inviting her to continue, Arielle lightly tugged a whorl of hair on his chest and smiled before she walked away.

She thoroughly enjoyed Luc's dark puzzled look and carried it with her into her dreams.

He came in the night, as she knew he would, carefully gathering her into his arms and slipping into the night. How wonderfully predictable Luc was, she thought drowsily, snuggling against him. He bore the clean scent of soap, his jaw freshly shaved, the hair on his chest still damp from his bath. In the glade of firs and huge ferns, Luc gently lowered her to the soft pallet. He touched her with trembling hands, his kiss desperately hungry until she soothed him by sweet, delicate nibbles, a stroke of her tongue. They made love slowly, storing each nuance, each caress carefully away. Every touch told her he loved her. She leapt into the sweet mist, tearing at him almost savagely, her teeth nipping at his shoulder when at last time soared, pulsed, and hovered in their passion.

When Luc's dark head lay on her breast, she stroked the coarse strands, the tense muscles at the nape of his neck. He shuddered in her arms, nuzzling her softness and gently kissing the tips of her breasts. She listened to the uneven beat of his heart slowing, blending with hers.

Passion and fear drove him, his arms tightening around her. Bending to kiss his damp temple, Arielle promised that one day Luc would be free of his shadows.

One week later Arielle lay soaking in her gloriously scented, soapy bathwater. A small fire burned in the huge bedroom fireplace, easing away the chill of the early October afternoon. Siam and Sacha had taken the women into town for shopping in the early afternoon and hadn't returned. No doubt several bachelors had intervened along the way. In three days Siam and Glynis would be married, and none too soon, because Glynis's stomach had begun to round. Siam strutted around with a wide grin when he wasn't working furiously with Luc to prepare a nearby homestead.

Several men wanted to marry the three girls, accepting their dark-skinned babies. With Siam and Glynis, Sacha would marry Anna, wanting to waste no time at his age. Marie and America attracted several bachelors and were eager to begin their new lives. Omar and Biddy had married on the trail, and now lived in a cabin a distance away from the main house. Omar, silent and regal, had blinked away tears when Luc asked if he would like to work and live on D'Arcy land until he could afford his own. Harriet and Sally had shyly accepted suitors. Lydia couldn't wait to start nurturing the five small children of a widower-farmer, who loved herbals. She'd married the morning after their arrival.

A towering man, Swede, couldn't speak when he stared into Nancy Fairhair's shining blue eyes. Arielle doubted that Swede could manage a "yes" to the minister, or look away from Nancy for one minute.

Lelia caught the eye of a young timber man who spoke little but clearly worshipped her.

Anticipating Arielle's arrival, Sacha had established a small, neat store in Oregon City. On the banks of the Willamette River the small town included six hundred residents, gristmills, sawmills to cut planks for immigrants, taverns, tailor shops, cabinet makers, silversmiths, a doctor, lawyers, and a brickyard. Carpenters and builders blended with loggers and farmers. Arielle's Percherons drew immediate attention and challenges from other draft horsemen, which she would enjoy meeting. Leaving the household arrangements to her "cargo," Arielle also left most of the business details to Sacha for the time. She wallowed in the luxury of a clean house, filled with the scents of soap, lemon, and delicious cooking. The Oregon country was grand, waiting for her to step into the future.

Sacha had recommended purchase of land near Luc's farm, and Arielle planned to view the acreage soon.

For the present, she wanted to bathe and bathe and sleep late in the mornings.

She also wanted to contemplate the acquisition of Lucien Navaronne D'Arcy, who was never more desirable. Arielle slowly ran the soft washcloth down her arm, studying the D'Arcy wedding band on her finger. Underlying Luc's easy manner with the women who shamelessly pampered him, he seemed tense and determined.

Arielle ran the cloth beneath her chin, tugging away a wet strand clinging to her throat. She would deal with Thaddeus and with Luc carefully, exactly . . . when she was ready. She would enter Luc's shadows with or without his permission. He was keeping something from her, some dark, swirling, dreaded secret, and she wouldn't allow him to lock away anything from her. Arielle smiled dreamily. She had experience ferreting out Luc's ticklish spot on his lean ribs. He'd looked surprised the first time she explored that exciting adventure. And the fond pat on his rear, much as she would pat Zeus's rump.

Luc would not be allowed to hover in his beloved shadows once she was rested, her plans set into motion.

Luc and Siam slept in the lean-to with the horses while the women settled into the house. The bustling household sewed, starched, washed, and by the end of the day, Arielle had dropped into the massive D'Arcy bed. In the mornings she remembered shadows and warmth, of a tender kiss warming her lips in the night. Of a large hand claiming her breast, sweeping slowly around her to draw her to Luc's hard length.

She would recognize his clean scent forever and snuggled to the pillow he vacated before dawn.

The huge, long bath stood on a pedestal near a window that overlooked Luc's fields. Zeus set immediately to breeding his mares, a sight that awed settlers and Indians alike. Until the Percherons finished breeding, Luc's fiery Arabian stallion, Assid, and mares remained with Sacha.

Arielle settled down in the fragrant bathwater, closing her eyes. She lifted the long clean strands of her hair over the top of the bath, savoring the luxury. With the door's heavy ornate lock turned, she intended to enjoy these precious moments.

The D'Arcy house was plain, built of chinked logs. Its large parlor, kitchen, and dining room, and three-bedroom design allowed for more rooms to be added, and heavy pieces of ornate Spanish furniture dominated the areas. With butchering time near, Luc had begun hauling logs for a smokehouse. Baskets of apples appeared, and Marie baked pies while she designed a shelved pantry off the kitchen.

Arielle glanced at the huge bed topped with a massive headboard and draped by soft woolen blankets. Freshly polished with Lydia's beeswax and lemon concoction, the four tall posts gleamed in the firelight. Clean linens drawn from massive carved chests covered the feather pillows and the soft feathertick. Lorenzo yawned, rolled on his back, and exposed a fat belly. An excellent "mouser," the tom had finally gained Luc's wary approval ... though he prayed daily that news of Simon would arrive.

In a flurry of housecleaning, the women polished, washed, cleaned, and scrubbed the house, preparing for their suitors. With good-natured obedience, Luc and Siam moved furniture to one spot and back again. They fetched water, chopped wood, and reassured the very nervous, future brides.

Since the "widow train" sashayed through busy Oregon City, onward to Luc's farm, single men hovered like bees around honey. They clustered around the wagons, trying to get the women's attentions. Each "widow" kept her eyes demurely sheltered by her bonnet, her hands neatly folded. Bachelors of all ages popped up when least expected, some shy, some very determined. Through Sacha, Arielle sent word that any man expecting serious consideration must be clean and a gentleman. He must produce a written listing of his assets and understand that each woman was to be courted gently. If he couldn't provide payment of his bride's passage, terms could be made. Of the women who were to be married, Arielle had settled payment for helping with the proper wedding, another requirement.

She discovered early that morning that Luc had carefully

drawn each man aside and had performed intense, slashing interviews. He demanded the best of treatment for the women and threatened to reclaim them at the first sign of misuse.

Each potential groom was lectured as to the proper way to treat his bride. According to reports, Luc had said, "One bruise, one rumor of drink or hardship to any of the women, and I will come calling, no matter where you have taken her. She and her children will live with me, under my protection, until the matter is resolved."

Lately Arielle had begun to dream of weddings. And children. And Luc cuddling her on the huge Spanish-style bed until the grandchildren squirmed between them. Anxious to leave New York before her aunt manipulated the gate closed, Arielle had left her family's furniture and now longed for it. She wanted to bring more of herself to his home.

The ornate, heavy dark furniture in the bedroom reminded her of Luc. Huge, intricate, and enchanting. Since the Dalles, he had grown more tense; but matters between them would soon be resolved ... with her help. The flurry of potential husbands and the women's nervousness required a firm hand and all her attention. She intended to give this last bit of her venture its due. Tending and building an exciting marriage with Luc would be more interesting than the one she had planned with Thaddeus in mind. Luc did not offer love, but she would sooner have him than any other man or the loneliness that faced her each night.

Arielle eased deeper into the water, allowing her smug smile to curl her lips. Everything was settling down nicely, her plans successful. Lorenzo hissed, but Arielle was determined to saturate herself in luxury. "Hush, you scamp."

She ignored the slight tickling at the end of her nose for a time. When she slid a wet hand out of the water to rub it away, strong fingers caught her wrist.

Frightened at once, Arielle sank into the milky, scented water, shielding her breasts with a cloth. "Lucien! How dare you!"

"It seems I dare anything where you are concerned," he

muttered. "By the way, a locked door won't keep me from you, *chère*." He sat on a stool nearby, drawing off his boot. It dropped to the floor, then the other. Luc frowned thoughtfully at her, then stood and unbuckled his belt. He stepped out of his trousers and drawers, then placed hands on the tub, studying the milky water covering Arielle from toes to chin. His gaze warmed hungrily on her gleaming shoulders. "It occurs to me, madame, that I have never seen my wife naked in daylight. Before you hack away at our marriage papers, I am determined to see every inch of your delectable body."

Arielle squeezed her eyes closed, taunted by sunlight skimming Luc's broad, darkly tanned shoulders, the black hair covering his chest and the exotic gleam of his medallion dangling before her. Damp with sweat, his hair clung to his powerful neck, and a strand jutted across his forehead, adding to his rakish, devastating male appeal. He was fully aroused, his eyes dark with desire and that betraying muscle contracting beneath his cheek. She cleared her throat, aware of her rising blush. When she opened her eyes, Luc's silvery eyes gleamed with amusement. His lips curved sensuously. "Well?"

Arielle lay back in the tub. While she knew Luc had explored every curve intimately, she was very shy of him now. "Never. What you're asking is sinful, outrageous. Leave the room."

"Not until I see my wife naked, *ma belle*." Luc grinned, his fingertip strolling around her mouth. He bent to kiss her gently, his lips brushing hers, his teeth taking her bottom lip while his hand cupped her breast, caressed it.

Arielle found her fingertip touching his bottom lip. "Lucien, how did you get that scar?"

His hand slid deeper in the milky water to skim along her inner thighs. His fingertips stroked the sensitive opening, despite her tightly closed knees. Her thighs quivered instantly. "Mmm. Kissed a horse when I was a boy," he answered. "He didn't like it, but I won the wager."

"Kissed a horse? Oh, Lucien, you are magnificent!"

Arielle exclaimed, unable to keep her arms from reaching around his neck.

"Of course," he returned instantly with the certain air of a man who had been pampered thoroughly by the women. "What's this?" he asked, leaning over and holding her close against his chest, the deep rich accent trimmed with surprise and pleasure.

Arielle grinned, suddenly shy of him, yet wanting to attempt her new ideas of cuddling and cherishing Luc. She wasn't certain how to proceed. Luc's tender, devastating kiss seemed to be a good starting point. She returned the kiss with her heart.

Their eyes met and emotions tangled around them, hovering in the moment like gold dust caught on a sunbeam. She smoothed his bare shoulders, slowly caressing the tense muscles and cords. At first they didn't hear the insistent, hard knock. When it repeated, Luc's darkened gaze swept down Arielle's body against his . . . her pale breasts nestled in the thatch of dark hair, the bend of smooth flowing into hard. His fluent curses caused her to smile at his dark scowl. When he glared at the door, Arielle slipped deeper into the water. "They're back. Angel, your brood knows just when to pick their moments. I am cursed."

"Darling . . ." Arielle tried the name that had danced on the tip of her tongue a heartbeat earlier. She was rewarded by Luc's face pivoting toward hers, his expression blank, then the uneven pounding of his heart beneath her palm. She touched his nipple, circling the dark nub slowly with her fingertip, and Luc's gaze dropped to her play. A flush rose beneath his dark skin as his eyes lifted, locking with hers.

Bewitching Luc yielded such exciting returns.

He looked demented and confused. An exotic and a thoroughly displaced male, uncertain of his next step. He reacted beautifully when she arched slightly, allowing one rosy nipple to ease clear of the milky water.

Luc inhaled sharply, his expression grim. She enjoyed the ripple of his hard flanks, the hollow of hard muscle on his buttocks, and the jutting evidence of his desire for her before he jerked on his trousers. He flung one last hungry glance at her over his tense shoulder, then stalked out the door, carefully closing and locking it behind him.

Arielle hummed while she dressed, quite pleased with her efforts at Luc's seduction. She tried to comb her unruly curls while Luc and another man talked quietly in the large parlor.

Thaddeus rose from the brocade-covered settee when Arielle entered the room. From D'Arcy's scowling appearance and Arielle's rosy glow, he had interrupted a lover's tryst. He smiled, walking toward Arielle and murmuring how glad he was to see her.

His brain raged furiously. He'd hoped the rumors weren't true. But D'Arcy, a dark Spanish breed with unusually light, icy eyes, had smiled coldly and waved the matter in Thaddeus's face. Luc D'Arcy had married the bitch and claimed her wealth.

But that wouldn't stand in his way. Thaddeus had lounged at Margaret's hovel after his discharge, waiting for such an opportunity to arise. Now he would snatch it. With Arielle Browning in tow, he could return to New York. No one would question his shadowy reputation.

"Thaddeus, I am so pleased you came." Clearly surprised, Arielle's wildly tumbling curls caught the late sunlight. Dressed in loose workman's clothing, her body seemed childlike. He abhorred the trousers and barely shielded his displeasure. Her bare feet were small, pale, and shocking next to Luc's larger feet as she slid her arm around him, an easy gesture. There was no question of their intimacy as Luc's hand rested possessively on Arielle's shoulder. She wore proof of his ownership, the large heathen ring encircling Arielle's pale finger. It matched the heavy, dark furniture beneath Arielle's silver tea service. Thaddeus noted china vases and the chest containing the Browning family silverware. Light, starched doilies quivered across the massive furniture, dotted by gilt-framed photographs of her family. Arielle's neat set of journals, pencils, and pens arranged on a makeshift desk of planks and small barrels.

When he commanded the Browning riches, he would have a proper desk, one with locked drawers and stocked with fine liquors.

Thaddeus locked the image of Arielle's small foot next to Luc's into his brain, hating it. Only minutes before he'd discovered that D'Arcy had had two sisters and a mother, who had died recently. Thaddeus allowed Arielle to chatter away about news of their families and glanced at Luc D'Arcy, something vaguely familiar in the aristocratic, dark features. A memory stirred, stilling the air in his lungs—

There were three women near St. Vrain. A mother and two daughters, one named Yvonne. He'd wanted their wealth, charmed them, all the while having the shy little Spanish girl. He'd used another name—Bliss—to cover his plans for marriage. When the D'Arcy women's jewels and wealth were his, he had intended to disappear.

Then the raiders caught them, wounding him. He'd lain still for hours while the band raped the women, finally killing the mother. Yvonne, stupidly believing he would rescue her, had cried out for him for a time.

D'Arcy smoothed Arielle's hair gently, his silvery eyes locking with Thaddeus's. A chill rose up Thaddeus's nape as he realized that only Arielle's small hand tethered this man. D'Arcy's quiet presence bristled with predatory menace, a hunter seeking out his prey. Thaddeus shifted slightly, uncomfortably.

". . . You can stay nearby for a few days, won't you, Thaddeus?" Arielle was asking anxiously. "I want to hear all about what you've been doing. Then I have a serious matter to discuss with you."

"Of course, sweetling," Thaddeus returned easily and wondered how best to kill D'Arcy. With Arielle's money, and the land that she would inherit as D'Arcy's widow, Thaddeus could live quite comfortably. "But first give me a hug, my girl. I've been dying for the sight of you."

D'Arcy barely controlled his savage emotions, Thaddeus noted with satisfaction as he swept Arielle into his arms. Testing D'Arcy again, Thaddeus bent to kiss Arielle's cheek. The slashing silvery eyes darkened as Thaddeus held her closer. With little pushing, D'Arcy would be frothing at the mouth for a duel. Thaddeus noted Arielle's foils, crossed above the mantel, and reckoned that the woodsman breed would have little experience with the gentleman's weapons. If D'Arcy survived Thaddeus's deathly plans, running him through could provide entertainment and additional, rich lands to Arielle's dowry.

Arielle stepped back, clearly confused. "My goodness, Thaddeus."

He gave her his most charming smile. "I've missed you, Arielle. Of course I'm dying to stay a while. My commission has ended, and I'm thinking of settling in this country. Perhaps I'll start breeding draft horses. There's a need for them, you know."

Arielle's green eyes lit as Thaddeus knew they would. "Then you'll have me for competition," she teased, instantly at ease with the familiar subject between them. "I brought Zeus and his mares. Zeus is out of Jove, that fine French stallion Aunt Louise imported."

"Ah, yes. Louise. She must be all of what—eighty-two? And she still holds the reins of the Browning empire? I suppose if anything would happen to her, you would inherit those responsibilities?" He traced Luc's gaze to the ruby ring Yvonne had placed on Thaddeus's little finger. When Luc's eyes lifted and met Thaddeus's, they bore the dark, promising aura of spilled blood.

Arielle eased into the settee, drawing Luc to her side. "My brother, Jonathan, is now at the helm. I would inherit in his demise. Sit, won't you?"

Thaddeus barely kept his rage concealed with an easy smile as he sat opposite Arielle and her husband. She was obviously very happy. If Jonathan must die, so be it. He'd never liked the gangling, tall boy, who showed all the signs of Arielle's impetuous, sometimes savage nature.

He continued the visit, probing, exploring D'Arcy and Arielle's relationship and finding it distasteful. Arielle seemed blithely unaware of the bristling challenge between the two tall men, and Thaddeus promised that once his ring replaced D'Arcy's ornate one, he would break Arielle of using her left hand.

As a proper Northrup wife, Arielle would shield her blemishes—the ugly freckles—from the sun.

That nightfall Thaddeus dropped coins onto a rough plank table. The owner of the unkept cabin, a bear of a man wearing dirty clothes, scooped them up. His small eyes gleamed when he bit the gold, testing it. Thaddeus brushed a speck of dust from his well-tailored jacket, detesting the man. Once the deed was done, the killer—McPherson—would die, too. "D'Arcy will be in his grave within the week. I want no D'Arcy brat in Arielle's belly, though clearly he's had the bitch. I want an accident. A fall beneath one of Arielle's damned giant beasts, or a fallen tree perhaps. If I finish him before you, I'll expect my money back."

Nineteen

At nine the next morning Luc caught the glinting arc of steel in the shadowy forest above him. On the other end of a two-man timber saw, Siam stopped, his gaze following Luc's up the incline. The second flash a second later cut into one of three strong hemp ropes mooring the logs. The thick rope unfurled, tons of harvested logs shifted, straining the two remaining ropes. . . . They snapped beneath the weight. Siam leapt aside as the logs began sliding, pouring like giant spikes toward them, breaking the living trees like sticks. Pounding down the steep grade, the logs crushed two mules on the drag sled, killing them instantly.

Luc and Siam raced for safety, scrambling over fallen logs. Lower on the hill, Sacha's team of loggers scattered. A dog yelped and died, crushed by the logs that stopped as suddenly as they began, blocked by a small rise of land.

Agile for big men, Luc and Siam silently slid into the forest. Their prey—three tough men—crashed through the brush, panting with fear. Prepared for the westerners' skills, the men circled the set traps they had placed earlier. They waited beyond the traps. Once D'Arcy and the mountain man suffered snapped bones, the men could take their time arranging a fatal accident.

They waited, glancing at one another. One wiped away the sweat of fear.

"Gentlemen," Luc said quietly—too quietly—behind them.

Circled and caught between the deadly men and the traps, McPherson's dark curses cut through the lofty fir trees and huge ferns. Then, "Today, you die, boy."

"Perhaps. I am waiting," Luc drawled as Siam moved a distance apart.

McPherson's pistol never freed his belt. Siam's thick blade hissed through the air to slide into the henchman's throat. Disbelief spread over his coarse features, then dulled as he crumpled, already dead. His hireling stepped backward, stumbled, and cried out as he pitched headfirst into the jowls of a waiting trap. The third man ran, soon caught, his revolver drawn to fire. In front of him Luc's hand darted by the gun. The man saw the stick jamming the barrel, but couldn't stop his finger from pulling the trigger. The revolver exploded, shooting steel into his throat. Though Siam and Luc worked to save him, the man's lifeblood slowly stained the cold forest floor.

At that moment, miles away, Arielle caught Thaddeus's quick look of distaste as he studied the calluses on her palm. "You should wear gloves, my dear," he murmured, turning to study the Willamette River. "And a hat to keep your complexion as pure as in New York."

The cold winds preceding winter swirled up to the bluff where they stood, Zeus and Thaddeus's strong gelding grazing near the forest. Walking with Thaddeus, reliving the fine moments of their childhood, settled the ache for home within Arielle. She watched men from the Clackamas tribe fishing nearby. A new land waited for her, filled with tomorrows and dreams. She studied her calluses intently, then smiled up into Thaddeus's clear blue eyes. "I've worked hard for every one of these unsightly little bumps, Thaddeus. I expect there will be more," she returned gently.

She fought the smile curling her lips. Luc had kissed each freckle across her nose and lamented that he couldn't see to find more, lower on her body. He had laughed outright when she ran through the long list of remedies she'd used to erase the freckles. The mask of cow manure had first shocked, then sent him into guffaws. Only a severe bout of tickling caused him to stop. Tending Luc became more enjoyable every day.

Until lately. Once more the shadows swirled around Luc, reminding her of his raging fever in St. Louis, of the demons driving him.

Thaddeus fitted into the mystery somehow. Both tall, arrogant males battled a deadly game she didn't understand. The taut set of their bodies, eyes locking over her head, and the grim expressions were clearly visible, the air between them simmering with dark undercurrents.

"It's a hard, vicious, uncivilized land," Thaddeus continued. "Savages at every turn, little or no class distinction from the rabble that fills the nooks and crannies . . ." Thaddeus tilted her chin up with his knuckle. "Tell me, Arielle, are you really happy? Don't you wonder one small bit if a liaison between the Brownings and the Northrups would benefit both our families? Come now, I want the truth," he urged gently.

Arielle eased away, tightening the bow of her bonnet. The aura of this Thaddeus was much different from the one she remembered. She sensed desperation and menace. She intended to deal with the women's accusations of Thaddeus's misconduct, but in her own time. When she approached him with the subject, she wanted a clear mind. "Thaddeus, surely you realize that your family is in desperate need. They sent more to finance your business endeavors than they could afford, I believe. Your mother, poor thing, only wants you back. While you must return home to care for her, I have other desires. . . . My new life here."

A sliver of hatred darkened Thaddeus's eyes, soon shielded. "You must know how hard it is for me to accept your marriage, Arielle. I understand that the matter was kept secret until your arrival. There must have been good reason."

"There was."

Thaddeus waited for an explanation, and when there wasn't one, he turned his back to her. He scanned the wide expanse of cleared fields. "I didn't want to tell you this. But for your safety, I must. I have reason to believe that Luc D'Arcy is an agent of the Mexican government, here to incite sympathy for his causes."

Alarmed by his accusation, she caught his arm. "Thaddeus! You are mistaken. Luc frets because of the war, the turmoil in California, the unease of the English concession on the Fifty-Four Forty or Fight issue. He is deeply concerned about the Mexican War and has thought of joining the army. He is too much in control to bow to my wishes, but I could not bear to lose him now."

Thaddeus caught her hand in his, lifting it to his mouth. "Dear one. His roots are Spanish. His allegiance is the same. I want you to promise to be careful with him. He is a dangerous, dangerous man."

"He is my husband."

"And your lover? Arielle, you blush beautifully. Just let me hold you, comfort your poor torn heart. There, there," he crooned, drawing her into his arms and rocking her just as he had done when she was a child. The familiar action soothed her instantly. Years ago Thaddeus had always understood. He was a part of home that she hungered for, and Arielle allowed him to hold her. "Arielle, I want you to promise that if for any reason you want to leave Luc, or say . . . perhaps his past catches up with him and you are widowed, that you will allow me to take care of you. To marry you and protect you. I've spent long hours missing you, dreaming of a wonderful marriage, a beautiful alliance with you. A practical marriage. I'm certain if fate hadn't pulled us apart, we would have already had beautiful children. Because of my love for you, I can overlook this indiscretion— the hazards of the journey no doubt drove you into his arms."

Arielle stilled in his arms, listening to his soft, hypnotic tone. A deadly tone. She wondered fleetingly how many he had seduced with it. Was it true? What had happened to the man she once wanted so desperately? Luc's tender, husky accented tones went sliding by on the wind, and Arielle listened to her heart. She loved him and deep within Luc burned a tenderness for her. Thaddeus continued softly, bolstered by his success with many women. "We could have a partnership. I would allow you to continue building the business you desire. But you must allow my decisions to prevail, my dear. In New York, and I suspect here, you were a trifle independent."

"I think," she returned carefully, easing away from him, "that perhaps we should return."

He smiled tenderly, continuing to hold her hand. "You'll consider what I've said, won't you, dear Arielle? A marriage between us would far exceed the sham D'Arcy has placed upon you. My sources say you keep separate bedrooms. That he sleeps apart in the stable."

When she looked away at the geese flying across the clear blue sky, Thaddeus smiled. "That should be enough proof that he does not want all of you. Remember, dear, you have the mark of the devil in that left hand, and then your red hair. Perhaps D'Arcy lusts for the Browning coffers alone? With your resources, my dear, the Mexican cause would profit."

While Arielle wanted her mind free from the hustle of weddings that kept the household awake during the night, she could defend herself. "My left hand has managed Brownings successfully for sixteen years, Thaddeus. It held the reins for wagons that crossed an entire nation. No small task. My unfortunate tendency to freckle is not noticed out here, nor is my red—as you call it—red hair. And Lucien has his own resources."

Thaddeus's eyes narrowed. "I understand he has no heirs, save you. You would probably inherit his holdings."

"There is no reason to enter that speculation, Thaddeus," Arielle stated pleasantly, fighting the slight pinch of anger. Thaddeus's greed had surfaced when they were children; he always took the best riding horse, the choicest piece of cake. She disliked his interest in Luc's holdings, or her ability to inherit them. "Shall we go?"

When Thaddeus and Arielle returned to the homestead, Luc lifted Arielle down from Zeus's back and kissed her cheek. The small gesture surprised her, until she saw his eyes, his taut expression. His easy smile did not reach his eyes, locked to Thaddeus's. "Did you have a nice ride, *chère*?"

"Marvelous. Thaddeus has been catching me up on his wanderings. He's had quite the adventures since leaving Fort Leavenworth and resigning his commission." Arielle smiled cheerfully, carefully weighing a recent identification of Thaddeus.

Mildred, one of the girls collected in the trade from the Indians, had clutched her baby closer, and whispered urgently about the big blond gentleman who had just left the house. "It's him, ma'am. Traded whiskey for the use of a poor girl. She screamed all night. I'll remember those sounds forever. Since you're friends with him, are you going to tell me to go away?"

"Of course not, Mildred," Arielle had answered, hugging her. "You're mine until some fine beau plucks you away. He'll have to fight me and Luc to pry you away from us. I will deal with this in time. Don't worry."

Now she looked up at Thaddeus, at the wary, flickering hatred in his blue eyes as he returned Luc's stare. Could this man, this playmate and friend from her past, be such a beast?

". . . An accident," Luc was saying, his accent sliding softly around the words.

"This is a rough country. Toughs and thieves, killers everywhere. Tell me, Luc, how is the Mexican War progressing? To your satisfaction? Then there's California and the Bear Flag Revolt. Nasty affair, Americans wanting annexation and those with Spanish ties fighting it."

Arielle placed a warning hand on Thaddeus's arm, and Luc's gaze jerked to the contact, then to her face. The sudden fury riding him frightened her, then it was gone. She stepped between the two tall men, certain that the dark currents running between them were deep and deadly. She would find out why. "An accident, Luc? What happened?"

Luc settled back in the chair and placed his boots on the cot, kicking aside dirty bedding. At night the shack caught the freezing temperatures on the mountain. The three dead men were easily traced and had lived here. Wind howled around the cabin, sweeping through the unkept chinking.

Arielle was clearly attached to Northrup, her eyes lighting when she looked at him.

Thaddeus Northrup . . . Edward Bliss. A childhood friend of his wife's. A murderer, rapist, and predator of women. Luc stared at a spiderweb fluttering in the draft, listening to the hoofbeats coming closer, slowing . . .

Northrup entered the cabin, blowing on his hands as he strode straight toward the small iron stove. He built a fire quickly, his profile lit by the flames. He stood slowly, staring into the fire for a moment. Then he struck a match, lighting the taper in a bowl of fat on the plank table. He held the match higher, staring past it into the shadows where Luc sat. "How nice to see you again, D'Arcy," he murmured. "Recovered from your accident?"

Luc tossed the bag of coins he had taken from the men to the table. "Are you looking for this?"

"I thought perhaps those ruffians were the ones who had stolen from me," Thaddeus answered, pouring the coins into his palm. The ruby ring on his finger gleamed as he shoved the coins back into the sack. Very carefully Thaddeus watched Luc's eyes and eased aside his heavy coat to place the coins in his trouser pocket. "Thank you for returning them."

Luc fought his rage and the desire to end Northrup's life quickly. He tossed Edward Bliss's ring onto the table. "Is this yours, too?"

The heavy ring rolled slowly, back and forth, gleaming in the firelight. Tense moments strained by as the fire crackled in the stove and the wind howled around the cabin.

Thaddeus smiled, slowly, coldly. He picked up the ring,

studied it in the flickering light, and placed it on his finger. "A perfect fit. Just as Arielle and I am suited to each other. We understand the life that each of us wants. She's a wealthy woman, D'Arcy. But I'm certain you wouldn't have married her without that knowledge."

"Tell me where you lost the ring, Edward," Luc said quietly.

The other man studied the ring on his finger carefully. "Edward?"

"Edward Bliss," Luc supplied, his stomach knotting. Yvonne had loved this man desperately, had borne him a dead child. Believing him dead, she had mourned him until she died.

"You won't kill me, D'Arcy," Thaddeus said, as though to himself. "Arielle would toss you out. All I have to do is mention that you're threatening me, and she will fly to my defense. She always has. She's really easily managed if you know her background. You don't. We go back a long way, she and I. . . ." He smiled at Luc. "Well . . . enough to say . . . we go back to our childhood."

Luc stood slowly. Both men, equally tall, faced each other across the shadowy room. "Yvonne had a child, Northrup. She and Colette left a journal before they killed themselves in Baton Rouge. If I show that journal to Arielle, or your ring, she won't believe your story."

The blond man's face turned into a mask of fury. "Damn you. What do you want?"

"You will leave my wife alone. You will tell her that you must leave the country . . . and I promise you . . . you will leave one way or another."

Thaddeus's eyes narrowed. "So you would protect her from the realities of life. How amusing. Then she doesn't know about my possible liaison with your sisters. Yes, you wouldn't tell her that, would you, to protect her? I could take her off your hands. You could keep her horses and the fat Browning purse that she would have hidden away somewhere. Arielle is not a woman to undertake this venture without a great deal of money. When she decides to go back to the East with me, she'll pay you well. She's like that,

paying well for ... services. You see, D'Arcy, you don't
have a choice. Arielle is mine. All I have to do is claim her.
Make it easy on yourself and go along."

Luc's knife sunk into the table, the handle quivering.
"You led my sisters and mother to their deaths. Now it is
time for you to die. Do it well."

"Are you calling me out? A duel in this godforsaken
place? How droll. Arielle would be furious. You really
shouldn't let her rule you, D'Arcy. She's a headstrong
woman and must be kept in line. I know her very well. Each
gesture of that awful left hand signals just what she is thinking. She wants me. If you kill me now—providing you
can—Arielle will mourn forever."

"Then she will," Luc agreed, watching the wary shadows
cross Thaddeus's handsome face. Luc's fist caught the other
man in the stomach, doubling him.

Thaddeus fought well, throwing his weight against Luc,
pinning him to the cabin wall.

The table tottered and fell, the lamp's oil spilling toward
the stove. A spark from the wood arced into the oil. Flames
raced along the oil, found papers and more trash, igniting
the cabin while the men fought.

Thaddeus drew a derringer, the shot grazing Luc's upper
arm. He chopped Thaddeus's wrist, and the small gun
landed in the fire, the second cartridge discharged immediately. It struck the boot of Siam, who was standing in the
open doorway.

Thaddeus collapsed beneath Luc's methodical blows. The
cabin's fire raged, while Siam hopped and cursed in the
doorway. He limped to where Luc stood over the unconscious Thaddeus. "So this is the man Yvonne loved. Do we
see how he burns, eh, my friend?" Siam asked, placing a
hand on Luc's shoulder. "Or do you let your woman
choose? If you do not let her, you will always wonder."

Luc took a deep breath, scanned the raging fire, and
dragged Thaddeus out into the snow.

He sucked at air, smoke filling his nostrils. His raging
emotions demanded that he kill the unconscious man. Luc
had killed before, protecting himself, and revenging his

family's deaths. It would so easy to finish Northrup ...
Bliss ... now. Arielle would never know—but he would.
He would wonder if she loved the man she'd traveled west
to find. As if understanding his thoughts, Siam touched
Luc's shoulder. "If you finish him now, it is no less than he
deserves. But his life is mixed with your woman's. Choose
carefully, my friend. . . ."

Luc straightened, forcing his fists to loosen. He had to
know if Arielle would choose him and their marriage. Then
Siam said quietly, "I would like to kill him, too." He studied
the handsome, bloodied face as the cabin walls caught fire.
"Hell is waiting for this one. But I cannot go to my woman
with his blood on my hands. Nor can you. There is jail. If
we expose him, we injure the women in your life ... your
mother, Yvonne, and Colette will be smeared, and your wife
will be very unhappy. Sometimes, it is better to let an animal find his own justice, eh?"

Taking a long, steadying breath, Luc bent to lift Thaddeus
to his feet. "Help me get him on his horse. We'll take him
back to town."

Siam nodded. He stripped the two rings from Thaddeus's
limp hand and tucked them in Luc's pocket. "This one will
die badly and soon. It is not a sight I want near my wedding
day. If he needs killing later, then it is I who will take pleasure in his dying. You have your woman to consider, also,
eh?"

The next day Sacha held the stool steady while Arielle
stood on tiptoe on a ladder. The new store was taking shape,
and in the early afternoon Arielle was exhausted. The
women weren't able to sleep, the household under a siege of
nervous giggles and crying bouts that could erupt at any
hour. Swede and Nancy just sat and stared at each other;
Swede's nostrils had started a suspicious flaring, and Nancy
couldn't seem to catch her breath. Arielle sensed that the
two big people couldn't wait to tear at each other, much as
her Percherons. She refused to mention to Sacha that she
had seen him tossing pebbles at Anna's window, then blowing kisses.

While the household bustled with wedding plans, Arielle had spent long hours turning Thaddeus's offer over, and hadn't liked the shape of it. Nor had she liked Luc's absence from her bed the previous night, though he had entered her room and stood over her for a moment. He kept something pocketed inside him. His dark, thoughtful look when he suspected she wasn't looking nettled her. The general hubbub at the house did not allow conversation. Or kisses. Or cuddling. Or sweet lovemaking. She wanted Luc near her, laughing, talking freely. Teasing. Instead, he'd locked his secrets away from her—but she would ferret them out.

Sacha glanced longingly at Anna, who was sweeping the board porch outside. "Anna is a beautiful woman, in her prime. I can't believe she will marry me tomorrow. I have promised to court her as my bride, every minute, every hour, for the rest of our lives."

He turned to Arielle. "You're in a bad mood, Mrs. D'Arcy. Lashing out at this poor little kitten, waiting for his master to claim him, will not salve what bothers you."

Arielle glanced down at Lorenzo, licking his paws after a good meal of fish. She patted the last tin of needles and held her skirts as she descended the short ladder. "That 'poor little kitten' has survived the worst conditions, Sacha. He hides, waiting for me to mount a horse, then he howls, frightens the livestock into a near stampede. Only when I pack him into town in his cage will he quiet. He knows when I'm returning, too. He's thoroughly, lushly spoiled by everyone. I declare he has set about populating the West."

When the culprit hissed and arched his back, Arielle did not turn around. "Luc."

She caught Sacha's wary expression and frowned. The little man murmured an excuse about preparing for his evening with Anna. He wanted to practice a new poem he had just finished in her honor. He nodded. "I'll be tending the inventory of traps in the storeroom, Arielle. Wedding is tomorrow, you know. Damn fine one, it will be, too. Brides aplenty. I expect I'll see you tonight at the evening meal, Luc."

Luc's finger strolled down the back of Arielle's neck,

causing the hairs to rise. "My home will miss all the nervous brides when they are gone. Though I welcome having my own bride to myself. Our dinner table will seem enormous without the women, children, and beaus."

Sacha winked. "Reckon there will be children of your own clustering around the table if Arielle would quit stalling—" He stopped, blinked, and strolled out of the room whistling when Arielle rounded on him.

She had decided to thoroughly seduce Luc. There was no reason she couldn't when she applied herself.

She turned slowly to Luc, prodding his chest with the tip of her finger. "You. You invite these ribald, disgusting—"

He caught her finger and lifted it to his lips, nibbling on it. The message in his darkened eyes caused the breath to stop in her throat. "Blast!" she whispered in a soft explosion.

"How charming," Thaddeus drawled from the doorway. "Arielle, I wonder if you might want to ride with me out to view some property I'm considering?"

Luc's head lifted. His expression slid from vulnerable, tender need and desire to chilling stillness. Was that fear darkening his eyes?

"Another time, perhaps, Thaddeus," she answered, realizing that she must settle the matter of the accusations against Thaddeus soon. "Oh, dear. What happened to your face?" she asked, walking closer to scan the bruises.

Thaddeus looked at Luc, then rested his hand on Arielle's waist as she peered up into his face. "A slight fall."

Arielle stepped back, frowning. "I see. You should be more careful, Thaddeus." She glanced at Luc, then back to him. "When the weddings are finished tomorrow, I want to talk with you."

She turned to Luc, whose silvery eyes had narrowed dangerously. "Glynis tells me that Siam is nursing a wounded toe and hoards his tale. She's babying him and he's devouring every second of her care. I think," she said very carefully, "there are many things to be settled."

Twenty

On a hillside overlooking the D'Arcy farm, Thaddeus crouched behind a stand of brush, watching the wedding wagons leave in the late afternoon. Every single woman had been married within two weeks of arrival. In the shadowy farmyard Luc stood next to Arielle, towering over her. Thaddeus narrowed his eyes, noting the protective stance of Luc's hard body. The man was a savage, accustomed to fights, Thaddeus decided. D'Arcy was the perfect mate to Arielle's fiery moods and her left-handed thinking. He apparently hadn't told Arielle of Thaddeus's association with his sisters. She would have sought Thaddeus out by this time.

It was only a matter of time before she discovered the D'Arcy girls' condemning last efforts. Arielle was skilled at ferreting out secrets, and from the way D'Arcy looked at her, Arielle could lead him into hell.

D'Arcy belonged in hell, Thaddeus thought darkly, testing his bruised lip with his finger. D'Arcy was too dangerous to live; his death would increase Arielle's holdings.

After a suitable wait, Thaddeus could claim her easily. He knew her weaknesses, and the wait would not be long.

He needed the D'Arcy sisters' last journal.

The Percherons grazed in the lush field near the house; the fine-blooded Arabian stock milled in a pasture at the other end of D'Arcy's expansive holdings. Thaddeus's lips thinned. A long open-sided shed served as a barn, storage for harnesses and saddles, and an amount of hay. The house was crude, though spacious, nothing like the mansions of the Brownings. It would do for a time, until he could build a bigger one.

Thaddeus watched Luc bend to kiss Arielle, and she lifted on tiptoe to curl her arms around his neck. D'Arcy's big hand covered her breast possessively, then he swung her up into his arms and strode toward the house.

Thaddeus closed his eyes, rage sweeping through him. His blue eyes jerked open. He would remember to give Arielle a tea that would abort any unpure blood of D'Arcy's spawn.

Over the mountaintops sunlight shafted into the sprawling fields, spreading through the late afternoon shadows.

Thaddeus studied the long shed. A fire at night would draw Arielle and D'Arcy from the house; collecting the stampeded Percherons and the Arabians would keep Arielle and D'Arcy busy all night. The stallions were certain to fight. The house would be empty, the perfect time for a search. With the diaries safely destroyed, D'Arcy would meet his death quickly. If Thaddeus could not locate the diaries, he would coax D'Arcy to cooperate before his death.

"Catherine was her name." Luc poured wine into two glasses, lifting one to study the ruby shadows in the candle-light. He savored the lingering taste of Arielle's sweet kiss, her tongue, the silken skin of her throat, then sipped the wine, a sharper taste. He ran the palm of his hand over the guitar Arielle had just given him. "Catherine," he said slowly, placing the glass aside and drawing the guitar against him. He cradled it like a lover who had just returned to his arms.

He ran his fingers slowly over the cords, testing them—testing himself and the memories that had lurked within him for years. The fire in the rock-hewn fireplace crackled, and Arielle eased her arms around Luc, leaning her head against his arm. The soft press of her breasts eased the pain scurrying inside him. The gentle nuzzle of her cheek against his arm reminded him that she was not a weak woman, but one who would cling through the worst of times. "Tell me," she whispered, her arms tightening around him.

The musical chords slid from the past, his fingers running up and down the taut strings. Soft ballads ran into dark passionate tones. He tested a ripple of intricate chords, then a sweeping ballad he had composed years ago that still danced through his fingers. He knew Arielle would wait—he smiled, nuzzling her fragrant curls. He bent slightly, meeting the kiss she offered. The future beckoned in her kiss, but he must clear the past away. He closed his eyes, letting the music slide through his fingers and soar through the shadows. How long ago had he sat on his father's knee to learn the chords?

"Catherine was my first wife," he began softly. Slowly the tale of a young man lusting, loving a heartless woman unfolded with each soft chord. "She had me play for visitors." Luc shrugged. "I was a boy and honored by her pride. Later, I learned that the men who listened were her lovers. I burned the songs I had written for her . . . burned my guitar. . . ."

Luc continued with his story—running before a mob, his father fearing for his only son, for the family line. . . . Though Luc was innocent of Catherine's murder, he buried his music with her.

He accepted another sweet kiss, tasting Arielle's tears. Or were they his?

"I have a brother," he said, aware of the bitterness curling around his words. "A half brother, the child of Catherine and my father. How he fought my marriage to her! He told me on his deathbed that she had given birth to his baby and sold it to a childless couple. The family went north into Oregon country, and she blackmailed my father for years."

Luc shrugged. "Catherine was inventive. She drugged my
father into sex. To ensure her blackmail threats, she branded
her baby with a small *D* on his shoulder. He was sent off
with a medallion that matches mine.... I hope to find my
half brother one day. Half of what I have will be his."

Arielle traced the crease between his eyebrows with her
fingertip. "Your mother and sisters never knew?"

When he shook his head, Arielle stroked his cheek.
"Have I told you I love you, my darling?"

Luc frowned at her teary eyes. Was he dreaming?

"My darling?" she whispered huskily.

Luc carefully placed the guitar aside, his hands trembling
before he turned to her. With a cry Arielle flung herself into
his arms. Luc lifted her chin with his fingertip, kissed her
soft, sweet mouth, afraid that any moment his dream would
shatter into the shadows....

The tender, loving kiss clung and warmed and soothed.
"Chère, ma belle ..." Luc gathered her closer, shaking with
emotion. He brought her hand to his lips, kissing the palm.
"You have my heart, Madame D'Arcy ... My angel ..."

Arielle eased slightly away, her lips curling into a secret
smile, her palms framing Luc's hard jaw. "I—"

Omar ran into the room, Biddy at his side. She placed her
hand over the slight mound of her stomach, breathing hard
from her running. "The horses are gone, ma'am. Your big
ones and those fine black ones of your husband's. The shed
is burning."

Thaddeus forced the lock open on the ornately carved
Spanish-style chest. He tossed aside pictures and papers,
tearing a carefully rolled, antique parchment map. He
scowled, pushing aside a heavy sword in a scabbard, to pry
at the satinette lining of the trunk. When he found nothing,
he jerked open drawers, tossing aside finely woven linens
and heavy silverware.

Behind him, Luc's quiet voice sent chills to raise the hair
on Thaddeus's body. "Can I help you find something?"

Thaddeus threw a heavy tooled chalice at Luc. "You
bastard—"

The revolver drawn from Thaddeus's belt never fired; a quick chop of Luc's hand sent it to the floor. His fist sent Thaddeus sprawling back against the wall. With a scream he flew at Luc.

Arielle walked into the room. Her hair spilled down her shoulders, and she pushed it back with one hand. "Thaddeus!"

"He's attacking me! He's demented!" Thaddeus yelled as the men crashed into another wall. Two rings fell from Luc's pocket, rolling toward the fireplace and catching the firelight.

Arielle plucked the rings from the floor, studying them while Luc held Thaddeus against the wall. "This is your ring, Thaddeus. And I saw this woman's ring on your little finger earlier. What are you doing with them, Luc?"

Her eyes swept around the ransacked room and back to Thaddeus, who was breathing hard, his eyes filled with panic. "You've come after the journal that Luc's sisters wrote before they died, haven't you?" she said slowly as though to herself. She turned the large man's ring in her palm. "She described this perfectly. . . . This is the ring that Yvonne managed to keep through all of her terrible hardships. . . ."

She glanced at Luc, who had moved away from Thaddeus as though his nearness was a temptation to kill. Arielle studied the smaller ring. "Yes, this would be the ring she gave to you after you seduced her with the promise of marriage. She carried your child, Thaddeus. Her hardships caused her to give birth prematurely, and the baby died."

"*Chère* . . ." Luc began softly.

"Oh, Lucien—how they must have suffered!" She frowned at Thaddeus. "How could you, Thaddeus? How could you? I read their poor stories. . . ." Arielle bent, lifted a small stool away, and eased open a board on the floor. She held the journal in her hand. "Is this what you're looking for, Thaddeus?"

Luc latched the door and leaned against it. "That is my sisters'."

Arielle turned slightly, green eyes locking with silver. "I

am very angry with you. You should have told me about Thaddeus—Edward Bliss—the moment you knew."

Thaddeus slid along the wall, stopped by Luc's dark scowl. "Our horses are trained to come at our whistles, Northrup. Omar and a passerby helped with the fire, and it was soon put out." He took a step toward Thaddeus, who covered, shielding his face. "When I'm done with you, they'll take what is left to Oregon City."

Arielle touched his arm. "Lucien, my dear. Please."

Luc's scowl shot down at her. "Still defending him? Perhaps we should let him go free."

She stroked his taut cheek, her frown turned to Thaddeus. "Not at all, Lucien. Thaddeus realizes he must be punished. But I rather think he needs a lesson in respecting women. Get the foils for me, please, dear?"

With Arielle nearby, Thaddeus found a little bravado, straightening and wiping away the blood from his mouth.

Luc frowned. "You're not fencing with him, Angel. I forbid it. This is not a game."

She leveled a stare at Thaddeus. "Forbid away. This man's poor dear mother is dying because of a broken heart that he gave her. His father is bankrupt and once tried to commit suicide. He's barely existing. In Thaddeus's wake there are girls, used and tossed aside. I think it seemly that a woman give him a measure of revenge, Lucien. What do you say?"

For the first time since Luc released him, Thaddeus spoke. "You're jesting, Arielle. You know that this man has made me look guilty. He's taken my jewelry and concocted a story. He's humbugging you."

Arielle's eyebrows lifted. "I believe him," she said quietly. "Lucien, the foils, please. I wish to teach Thaddeus a lesson about betraying women. . . ."

Luc scowled down at her, his expression menacing.

"There, there, Lucien. Don't be so grim," she whispered. "If you'll just entertain Thaddeus, I'll change into my trousers. Won't be a minute."

Thaddeus fought the urge to run when left in the room alone with D'Arcy. His silvery eyes never left Thaddeus's expression. Minutes later Arielle returned to the room, smoothing down her loose trousers.

"It's not too late. We could marry still, Arielle," Thaddeus began. "You know how our families wanted marriage—"

"She isn't going to stop, Northrup. You will wear protection, Angel," Luc ordered, tossing her a mask and fencing vest.

"I won't fight you, Arielle. You could get hurt. All I want to do is show you how much I care for you. I understand how you could have become involved with him—"

Arielle slid into the vest, turning to Luc to lace her into it. She eased the mask over her face. "I really don't want to do this, Thaddeus. But someone must. It should be a woman. If Luc kills you—he's been protecting me from the hardships you created, Thaddeus, you should thank him. He is known in some parts of the land as the Dark Avenger and with good reason. I have an idea that he needs protecting from more deaths, and I can oblige him this time."

Thaddeus laughed outright, nervous and amused by the thought of being bested by a female.

Over Arielle's tousled, firelit curls, Luc's expression was deadly. Thaddeus knew that one wrong move now could cost his life.

His only chance to survive was to get close enough to Arielle to use her as a hostage.

Then D'Arcy would die.

Thaddeus caught the foil Luc tossed him and waited until Arielle took her position. Smaller than himself and a female, she stood little chance against him. Thaddeus found himself smiling. He lifted his foil in a salute and placed it aside Arielle's.

The match began slowly, intricately, each testing the other's skill. Arielle lacked Thaddeus's height and power. He lacked her agility, her body presenting a very small target. He couldn't hurt her; D'Arcy lounged against the wall like Arielle's Dark Avenger. She drew blood from a slight nick in his arm, then one in his thigh. Once he came too close to her hand, and D'Arcy immediately straightened away from

the wall. "Your watchdog is restless," Thaddeus panted between his parries.

"I love him."

"Impossible ... a woman of your breeding, your social
class, bedding a killer ..."

"You have killed souls, dreams, hearts, Thaddeus. I wept
when I read the D'Arcy sisters' journal last night. And I
loved Lucien even more for protecting me from the savagery of men. Though I have to admit I thoroughly enjoy a
bit of his savagery, which we haven't quite explored to its
depths yet. He's been holding back because he's a gentleman and my lover. He will father my children and no doubt
be at my side during childbirth. Lucien is a very tender
man." She nicked his hand, then stepped back. "You're tiring, Thaddeus. How tired they must have been, forced to
endure all those months...."

"Mating with a savage, you've become one. What honest
woman would challenge a man to foils and wear trousers?"
Thaddeus threw back, suddenly startled that his arm began
to tire while Arielle tossed the handle of her foil into her
left hand. Fear shot through him. That left hand signaled a
fierce, unyielding temper.

"Savage? Yes, a bit, I suppose. Perhaps ..." Arielle circled him, stepped agilely up into a chair and began a series
of thrusts, forcing Thaddeus to lift his wounded arm. Blood
stained his shirt, seeped through his wounds on his thigh.
Then she leapt down, their foils clashing in a practiced se-
quence.

Suddenly Arielle leapt aside, the tip of her foil slashing
across Thaddeus's upper thigh, barely missing his manhood.
Rage and pain caused him to thrust wide, and Arielle nicked
his other thigh, the rent cloth exposing his drawers. Another
quick flip, and she slashed away the buttons to his waistband. His trousers fell to the floor.

Tangled in his clothing, Thaddeus stumbled and fell on
his stomach. Arielle's foil etched a large "X" across his buttocks, just deep enough to graze Thaddeus's white rump.
Luc guffawed, jerked Thaddeus's foil away, and snared a

triumphant Arielle into his arms. She tossed aside the mask and beamed at him.

"The vixen and the bastard," Thaddeus snarled, struggling to his feet. The deadly tip of a foil touched his heart, and beyond it, Luc D'Arcy's thunderous silvery eyes narrowed dangerously.

Three hours later Thaddeus stood against the house. His tied hands were lashed to a post. Arielle, Luc, Omar, and the stranger worked feverishly to salvage what they could of the hay that had been put away for winter. The stranger was a westerner, lean and seasoned. His wintery stare at Thaddeus caused him to shiver. Once the fire's danger was past, the stranger had agreed to take Thaddeus into town for justice.

Zeus, a mountain of dappled gray muscle, stood directly in front of Thaddeus, staring at him. At Thaddeus's slightest move the stallion's ears lifted and he whinnied warningly.

The stranger led the horse bearing Thaddeus toward Oregon City an hour later. The chilly night wind swept back the stranger's long hair, swirled it around his head, as he pulled the horse into a shadowy gully that led into the mountains away from Oregon City. Thaddeus's bound hands clasped the saddle horn. "I can pay well for my release," Thaddeus began as the man dismounted and helped him down from the saddle. "I have money here in my pocket. Probably more than you've seen before."

"Don't really care about money," the man said, rolling a cigarette and lighting it.

Thaddeus frowned. "What is your name?"

The stranger scanned the night and the soaring firs. The smoke from his cigarette drifted on the wind. "Boone. Boone Davis. Sound familiar?"

"No. Should it?"

The man shrugged a heavily muscled shoulder and spat a stream of tobacco into the shadows. "Doesn't matter. But maybe you should know before you die. Margaret Davis was my sister-in-law. I was coming to bring her home to Missouri before I left for Mexico-way. Ma wanted her. You reached Margaret before I did. Reckon that was your mistake, Mr. Fancy Man. Now, if you'll just move over there a little closer to your grave . . ."

"*Nika tenas man.*" Glynis's English accent curled around the Chinook words for "my sweetheart." She bent to kiss Siam's flat, pale expanse of forehead, then excused herself to visit with Arielle in the bedroom.

Siam blushed, then scowled at Luc. "I will be Jean-Pierre now," he said firmly. The men settled down in the living room with the other new husbands, whose wives had demanded they return upon the report of fire.

While the brides giggled until dawn, the husbands became more surly. Swede declared that he would go mad soon. Sacha tried to lure Anna from the house by a poem he slid under the bride's door. She returned a note, "Dear Heart. The Society of Widows for the Purpose of Matrimonial Bliss is dissolving now. Until tomorrow—Loving you, Anna."

Luc closed his eyes and settled back to wait for the dawn. Lorenzo walked across Luc's stomach and curled against his stomach, purring loudly. Lorenzo's warmth wasn't exactly what Luc had in mind. His wishes ran to sweeter fare and hungry feminine purrs.

Eager to be gone again, the men rose before dawn, cooked breakfast, and harnessed the stock.

After another teary adieu, the brides began their new lives, waving back to Arielle and Luc.

"If one of those women finds cause to return before a week is over, I'll have an unpleasant discussion with her husband," Luc said between his teeth before he picked up a laughing Arielle and carried her into the house.

Twenty-one

....

Arielle's left hand caught on the bedroom doorframe, then her right, effectively stopping Luc's path to the huge bed. His silvery eyes darkened. "Now what?"

"I refuse to be stampeded into a precious moment. I want a bath."

Luc eased her through the doorway, carried her to the bed, and dropped her. He began ripping away his shirt, and a button popped to the floor. His hand jerked open his belt—"Later. Much later."

Arielle frowned up at him. "Now."

He inhaled slowly, then ran his hand through his hair. "Do you have any idea how I've waited for this? One moment alone with my wife? We've been infested with people from the time we met."

He warily scanned her tight smile and recognized the set of her chin.

"I want my moment."

Luc's dark, fluent curses in several languages continued while he began heating water for the bath. Only the promise in Arielle's darkened green gaze stayed him from pressing her. When she firmly latched the doors and blocked them with chairs, Luc began to whistle.

Arielle set the terms, banishing him from her leisurely bath and shampoo. When he knocked and was allowed entry, Arielle wore one of his shirts that reached to her knees. While Luc took his bath, she savored tending him. At his doubtful gaze when she lathered his jaw for a shave, Arielle explained, "Who do you think taught Jonathan to shave? Certainly not Aunt Louise."

Their tempting sweet kisses led to hungrier ones. When Luc left his bath, he was fully aroused. Arielle tested his strength, stroking him gently and nuzzling the wet whorls of hair covering his chest. She licked a drop of water from his nipple, her eyes widening when he firmly cupped her femininity, slipping his finger inside. "Lucien!"

A short time later Arielle lay beneath Luc, warmly sated. His heart began to slow from its race, and he nuzzled her breasts sleepily. "I am a skilled lover, you know," he whispered huskily, kissing one soft mound. "I intend to take weeks ... *months* ... proving my skills now that we're alone."

She stroked his back, damp with perspiration, and accepted his long, sweet kiss before they slept wrapped in each other's arms.

She awoke to his prowling hungry kiss, his body already thrusting gently into hers. Luc chuckled, nibbling her mouth and down her throat. The heavy fullness, stretched, easing solidly, deeply within her. She tightened the cradle of her thighs to his hard hips, capturing him fully and tilting her essence higher. "Darling—"

Arielle closed her eyes against the bright, autumn day beyond their bedroom, then opened them to Luc braced over her.

His silvery eyes traced her face, a long finger wrapped in a russet curl. There would be many sunny mornings with Lucien Navaronne D'Arcy, each as special as this one. Though Lucien didn't know about the coming child just yet, she would savor that special moment, too. "I love you, Lucien," she whispered, stroking his tense shoulders, loving him for giving her the due she needed.

Lucien would always give her the very best of care, the whole of his heart. She had found her quest. . . .

His scarred eyebrow lifted mockingly. "Secrets, my love?"

"None." Her breath caught as his gaze drifted downward, the melding of dark, hair-roughened skin against her pale body. His dark hand slid along her shoulder to her waist and on to mold her hip and thigh.

His gaze returned to her face, cherishing. "I love you, *ma chère*." He kissed her lips, supping gently at the moist contours. "I had closed my heart. Only you could have dragged me from the shadows. I love you," he repeated huskily.

"And I you. Shall we begin?"

That night Arielle brushed her hair and listened to Luc testing his skills with his new guitar. The firelight spread across the tumbled bed to Luc's long, dark body. His back braced against the bed that had been his parents', a huge down pillow crushed beneath him. He concentrated on his music, the enchanting melodies surging into passionate chords, swirling around the firelit room and tangling in her heart. The music softened, swayed, circled, drawing her.

Luc looked up at her as she stood by the bed. He smiled gently, and she knew that he had found another part of his heart.

In a lightning move Luc placed aside the guitar and drew her down on top of him, stripping aside her abused shirt to forage for freckles.

When their slight skirmish finished, Arielle straddled him, pinning his hands to the bed. He allowed the capture with a devastating grin, then kissed her breasts above him. "Blast!" Arielle managed as he suckled gently, and she melted around him. "Blast!" she whispered as Luc's eyes darkened to pewter, and he began to demonstrate his love once more.

The next day a farmer drove his wagon to the D'Arcys'. A five-year-old boy scrambled to the ground as soon as the wheels stopped. He ran to Luc. Around missing front teeth he lisped, "Do you have Lorenzo, my kitty?"

Epilogue
······················

The D'Arcy Ranch, 1850

"Mama! Papa, down!" Angelique Yvonne D'Arcy patted Luc's cheeks, her green eyes wide and pleading. Her cap of fiery red curls caught the July sun as she smiled hopefully from the cradle of his arms. Luc kissed the small, chubby hand of his daughter. The two-year-old giggled and squirmed to be let down.

Dressed in practical trousers like her mother, Angel toddled toward her mother in the lush meadow. Surrounded by dappled gray Percherons, Arielle coached Jason, their three-year-old son, to command the massive horses.

Zeus, his colts, fillies, and mares backed away warily as the tiny red-haired toddler hurled across the meadow to her mother.

Jason's black eyebrows met in a fierce scowl that Arielle bent to kiss away.

In the distance her eyes met Luc's, and for the moment the sunlight warmed and tangled between them.

Love clung to the fresh air, and Luc returned the kiss Arielle blew him. Emotions caught him, the past's shadows pushed farther away each day. He smiled, warmed by sunlight and love, and wondered if his wife knew about the third child nestled in her.

Arielle grinned suddenly. She touched Jason's black hair, then Angel's, then placed her palm low on her belly.

Luc returned the grin, smothering his chuckles. Arielle's childbirthing was a fascinating process. When she neared time, the brides would swoop from all corners of the Territory. For a brief time the Society of Widows for the Purpose of Matrimonial Bliss updated happenings in each woman's life. While they hovered near in the final hours, she demanded Luc's hand, clinging to it fiercely. "Blast! What do you mean? We push. . . . We? I can't believe I started all this because of Fannie Orson's challenges. . . . You landlubbering—sing to me. I want my song."

Then he would sing the song he had created for the moment, the songs of his love. In French this time he would tell her of his love, the days of sunlight and nights of dreams . . . of happiness filling their lives. Arielle would demand a translation, concentrating on birthing their child. She wanted his voice wrapped around her and their baby; she said she wanted the loving words.

Luc eased a lace handkerchief from his pocket and opened it to reveal his mother's ornate emerald necklace. Reclaimed by a friend, it would look magnificent on Arielle's pale throat. One by one the pieces of his mother's and sisters' jewelry eased back into his hands, keeping a heritage that would be passed to their children. Jason was learning simple music chords now, and when it was time, the other children would also learn the songs that had circled the D'Arcy family for lifetimes. He hoped his children would also learn the new songs of the great, spreading nation.

Arielle learned the Chinook jargon quickly, using it in her trading business. Her French and Spanish delighted Luc, though the children were already picking up phrases.

Luc grinned. He would have to start watching those phrases and keep them behind their bedroom door.

He breathed in the clean fragrant air. He had won the wager and kept his angel.

The shadows were gone.